COUPLE GOALS

LOVE IS A GAME, AND IT'S KICKING OFF...

KIT WILLIAMS

Harper North

HarperNorth
Windmill Green
24 Mount Street
Manchester M2 3NX

A division of
HarperCollins*Publishers*
1 London Bridge Street
London SE1 9GF

www.harpercollins.co.uk

HarperCollins*Publishers*
Macken House,
39/40 Mayor Street Upper,
Dublin 1, D01 C9W8, Ireland

First published by HarperCollins*Publishers* Ltd 2025

1

Copyright © HarperCollins*Publishers* Ltd 2025

Kit Williams asserts the moral right to
be identified as the author of this work.

A catalogue record for this book is available from the British Library.

ISBN: 978-0-00-876299-5

This novel is entirely a work of fiction. The names, characters and incidents portrayed in it are the work of the author's imagination. Any resemblance to actual persons, living or dead, events or localities is entirely coincidental.

Set in Bembo Std by Amnet

Printed and bound in the UK using 100% Renewable Electricity by CPI Group (UK) Ltd

All rights reserved. No part of this publication may be reproduced, stored in a retrieval system, or transmitted, in any form or by any means, electronic, mechanical, photocopying, recording or otherwise, without the prior permission of the publishers.

Without limiting the author's and publisher's exclusive rights, any unauthorised use of this publication to train generative artificial intelligence (AI) technologies is expressly prohibited. HarperCollins also exercise their rights under Article 4(3) of the Digital Single Market Directive 2019/790 and expressly reserve this publication from the text and data mining exception.

MIX
Paper | Supporting
responsible forestry
FSC™ C007454

This book contains FSC™ certified paper and other controlled sources to ensure responsible forest management.

For more information visit: www.harpercollins.co.uk/green

For any queer lover of football – you make
the game beautiful

Prologue

Ten years ago

'Goal!'

The crowd roar wildly. The home team fans are cheering, proudly clad in their team's distinctive orange colours, while the away team groans into their hands, lowering their blue scarves.

None are more engrossed than two girls, stood side-by-side on their tip-toes so they can see all the action. Their names are Adriana Summers and Maeve Murphy, and they are thirteen years old although Adriana would insist that she's *actually* thirteen and five months and two days, whereas Maeve is *basically* fourteen. They are wearing their homemade orange kits and matching tiger face paint to support their team: the Manchester Tigresses. But apart from their identical outfits, the girls couldn't seem more different from each other.

Adriana is the shorter of the two, with a mane of bright red curly hair that she has attempted to tie some of it up into plaited cat ears on the top of her head. The effect – if rather messy – is adorable. She is football mad, whooping and dancing in delight at the goal, shouting praise to her beloved team on the pitch below, and highfiving the crowd around them. Victory is now secured with an unassailable 3-1 lead and only a few minutes of the game left.

Maeve, on the other hand, couldn't have neater hair with her slicked back blonde ponytail, presumably tied by her mother, who has her arms folded behind them. Maeve notes details of the goal carefully in her little bulging notebook. She has recorded the results from every game she's been to, as well as keeping the ticket stubs, and a few precious autographs of players she admires.

'*What* a goal!' Adriana squeals to Maeve. 'Dimdore is so cool! And that pass to Miles was crazy! It's like they are psychic or something. They must be *best* friends!'

Maeve nods with a grin.

Having met a few months ago at Manchester's competitive Youth Football Academy, Adriana and Maeve have, to everyone's surprise, become best friends themselves.

Despite their physical differences and contrasting personalities, they seem to be tuned to the same telepathic frequency somehow. They just *get* each other. Trust each other. Love each other. And that carries over onto the pitch. They have this almost magical, uncanny ability to know what each other is thinking. Adriana would lob the ball seemingly to nobody, only to be met by Maeve's waiting boot because she'd anticipated Adriana's pass and made the run to be on the end of it.

'The Swans shouldn't have let that through,' Maeve shakes her head. 'Their defense is sloppy today. Pitts should have tackled to clear the danger instead of letting Fry put that ball into the box.'

'Hey,' Adriana laughs, giving her a playful nudge, 'whose side are you on?'

Maeve's normally stoic demeanor loosens a little at her friend's teasing, and she giggles along with her.

Maeve has previously struggled to make friends, so this sisterhood feels overwhelmingly precious to her. After all, Adriana's undoubtedly the most popular girl in the Academy, with all the girls, who love her sunny good-humour and endless team-spirit, and with the boys, who keep getting their first crushes on her sparkling sky-blue eyes and freckled button nose. She flirts breezily right back to any of the cute ones, especially when it leads to them being distracted before then beating them resoundingly on the field.

In fact, there is a boy from the Under 14s in the stands behind them, who now tugs on Adriana's hair to try to get her attention.

'Nice ears,' he scoffs, turning to his friends, who seem amazed at his confidence.

'I know,' Adriana shrugs, unrattled. 'Are you literally pulling my pigtails, Jeffers? Can you not think of a better way to flirt than boys in primary school?'

He blushes.

'Try again when you have come up with better moves,' she winks. 'Maybe then I'll flirt back.'

She leaves him scarlet, and turns back to Maeve as if nothing happened, who is just in awe at her friend's unshakeable confidence.

None of the boys ever bother Maeve in this way. Maeve would say it is because she isn't as pretty or charming as her friend, but Adriana would say it's because they're a) all too intimidated by her, and b) they maybe somehow sense she's not interested in them, even if Adriana is the only person Maeve has explicitly come out to so far. Even that wasn't planned. It was only because when discussing which footballers they had crushes on one night, Adriana had noticed Maeve was particularly quiet, and then Adriana had guessed, 'Megan Rapinoe?' Maeve had blushed from her ears to her toes, and nodded. It was one of the couple of risks that Maeve has only been able to take because Adriana makes her feel so accepted and loved.

It isn't that Maeve is *ashamed* of being gay, if anybody had pressed her about it. Other people are out at school and it isn't a big deal – in fact, Maeve admires their openness – but she can't bear the thought of having that kind of conversation with her mum. Her mum has told her she isn't allowed to date while she's at school, claiming it would distract her from her exams and getting a sports scholarship to a top university. And the thought of talking at all about s-e-x with her mum, makes Maeve want to peel her own skin off. So she keeps it shoved deep down inside her, along with every other feeling that her mum would think was a distraction, like her anger, her sadness, and her joy.

'The Tigresses are the *best*,' sighs Adriana happily. 'Moo, we *have* to play for them, when we're older. Urgh, but maybe it'd be too much work. Maybe I'm not the right fit for the team. I'm not as good as you.'

'You absolutely are,' Maeve jumps in to reassure her. 'And I'm not just saying that because you're my best friend. You just need to keep training, and not get distracted. Work isn't always a bad thing, Sunny.'

That's the thing about their friendship. No one ever takes Adriana seriously, they only ever see her as a fun, good-time girl. But Maeve encourages Adriana to go after what she wants, and to keep trying. Maeve helps Adriana push herself, and Adriana helps Maeve loosen up which means that together, they're both flourishing.

'Lets do it,' Adriana vows. 'Promise.'

She holds out a little finger. Maeve studies it with utmost seriousness. 'You mean, pinky promise to get chosen at the end of the Academy to play for the Manchester Tigresses?'

'Uh huh.'

'We'll have to work really hard. We'll have to be the best.'

'We can do it, if we do it together,' Adriana tells her. 'Easy peasy.'

Maeve nudges her head towards where the boys were behind them.

'And we won't let any stupid boys get in our way?'

Adriana nudges Maeve's elbow, waggling her eyebrows. 'Or any *girls*.' She adds with a whisper.

Maeve's head twists quickly to look at her mum.

'Sorry, sorry,' Adriana mimes zipping her mouth, then wiggles her ceremonial pinky finger.

Maeve smiles a rare toothy grin at Adriana. Neither of them can think of anything better in the whole world than playing football with their best friend so they eagerly pinky swear.

And afterwards, when the Tigresses continued their winning streak and went on to lift the title that year, Maeve and Adriana always secretly believed that somehow, their promise helped.

Chapter 1

Adriana

Now

'Shit shit shit shit shit!'

Adriana groans.

Her phone is buzzing, adding a corresponding throb to her headache. Maeve is calling her. Even in the headshot that she uses for her caller ID, Maeve looks responsible and professional. Adriana can just picture her dutiful frown if she were to see her own smudged hungover face right now. It's 7.32, and morning training starts at 8 a.m. sharp, and Adriana is in some strange bed in— wait, where *is* she exactly?

She looks around her, blinking at the unfamiliar blue-grey walls.

It's a nice place, she'll give whoever-he-is that. Swanky. That would make sense, as it starts to come back to her that this guy had bought her *very* nice cocktails last night. No wonder she got drunker than she'd previously promised – she can never resist a negroni on someone else's money. His houseplants are actually alive and thriving (unlike in her own flat), and everything is neat and orderly (ditto), with no clothes strewn on the floor except her own. But the spot in the silky bed next to her is empty.

Maybe he's already done a runner. That'd be ironic because normally it's Adriana who runs out to go to training, without leaving her number to the guy she's brought home the night before.

But last night, Drunk-Adriana must have been having so much fun that she had forgotten to set herself an adequate alarm. It's only with Maeve calling her that she has any chance of making it to training this morning. Thank God for Maeve, she thinks before leaping up but her head kicks back in anger at her sudden jolt. Wow, today's training session is going to be a really painful one.

Hungover-Adriana sprints around the unfamiliar room, picking up her things from the floor like she's doing a fiendish warm-up exercise with squats and jumps. There's her bright blue lacey bra and pants among the bed sheets, her sparkly mini-dress in the corner, and one way-too-tall platform heel by the monstera…

None of these items of clothing will be at all appropriate for running around the pitch in twenty minutes time. They were barely appropriate on the dancefloor last night – which is what was so fun about wearing them. It had been a long week of training where their coach had seemed off with them, and then last night it was her teammate Elisa's birthday, so of course Adriana had rallied a group of them to go out to their local pub. One thing led to another (or one pub led to a bar… which led to a club…). But Adriana has no regrets. She loves to work hard, play harder.

She's just searching for her other shoe – distracted by the stacks of books overflowing from the bookshelves onto the floor, when in her periphery a shadow appears in the doorway.

Oh my God, there's a man! This shouldn't really surprise her, a man does kind of usually come with the territory of a one-night-stand's bedroom, and yet it still somehow always does give her a shock to see him in the cold light of day rather than the darkness of the club.

Adriana freezes, crouched, as she looks up at him.

Well damn, she can't fault Drunk-Adriana's taste.

This man is toweringly tall, probably at least six foot three, with broad shoulders and toned arms. His hair is a golden brown, and he's clean-shaven over his square jaw, with a hint of light stubble from the morning. He's carrying two ceramic mugs of steaming coffee. And he's also very, very naked.

Adriana gulps. Suddenly she's remembering more of what they did last night, and exactly how good it was.

'Good morning, Addy,' the man grins, his voice is low and assured, and it sounds like it belongs on adverts for luxury cars, cologne, watches. That voice could sell her anything. 'I know you can't stay, but I thought this might help you get up. You mentioned last night you like mochas so I've taken the liberty—'

'Oh!' she smiles and gets to her feet, reaching out for the coffee. 'Thank you, that's so sweet.'

As they toast their mugs, their eyes meet. He had glasses on last night, she remembers hazily, but without them now she clearly sees the detail of their hazel colours – the same chocolate brown as her mocha, mixed within a calming, earthy green. Despite his otherwise unsmiling expression, they have a twinkle of humour in them.

Adriana racks her brain to try to recall his name. James? No, that's not right but J-a seems right. They'd met when Adriana was saying goodnight to the others. While she'd debated whether to order her own taxi, her eyes had landed on his, already looking at her from across the bar. It was hardly the first time Adriana had fancied a stranger in a bar, but as she looks into his eyes now, she remembers the unfamiliar jolting feeling she'd had last night too – a strange sense that she'd met him before. She remembers suddenly that she had in fact said this to him last night, when she'd walked over to him. He had raised an eyebrow, asking if that was a pick-up line.

'I'd definitely remember if we'd met before,' he had said. 'But how about we make sure this isn't the last time?'

Adriana's phone buzzes angrily again, pulling her out of the moment.

'Oh God,' she groans. 'I gotta go, I'm sorry, Jake.'

'It's Jacob.' He mutters, folding his arms defensively across his bare torso.

She winces. 'Oh God, I'm sorry, that's embarrassing.'

There's an awkward silence between them for a second, Adriana wobbling on her one shoe, wondering how to say, in case she hadn't last night, that she won't be seeing him again.

'Well, look I had a lot of fun last night. Like, a *lot*.'

'But not enough to want to see me again?' He cuts in.

She glances up at him. His tone is neutral.

'It's not personal,' she shrugs. 'I just, you know, have my rules.'

'Oh, I know,' says Jacob. 'You made it *very* clear last night. You told me approximately twenty-five times that you are not looking for anything serious.'

'It's not just not anything serious.' Adriana explains defensively. 'It's one night only. No rematches.'

'Sure,' Jacob takes a sip of his coffee. 'Just seems like a bit of a stupid rule to me.'

'How dare you!' she says, hands on her hips. 'You don't even know me!'

'But I'm telling you I want to,' says Jacob calmly. 'How *could* I know you, if you insist on this ridiculous one-night only policy?'

She shakes her head.

'Listen Jacob, this was fun. Really fun. Like, best one-night stand of my life kind of fun. Let's not spoil it now, okay? You can just think of me fondly as a fun memory.'

She thought the sexual compliment – which happens to be true – would please Jacob enough that he'd let her go, but instead it seems to have made him even grumpier somehow. As the world's biggest people pleaser, Adriana *hates* leaving someone displeased with her, especially someone who seems, beneath that sarcastic exterior, to be a sweet guy. But she just needs to get out of here.

'Now, where the hell is my–'

'Looking for this, Cinderella?'

Adriana realises he's holding up her missing shoe.

He puts the shoe in front of her, and as she slips her foot in it, he kneels before her, helping tie the strap round her ankle.

'Thank you, Prince Charming.'

Their eyes meet again, and Adriana has another unfamiliar twist in her chest. For the first time, she has a pang of doubt about her no repeats rule.

But no, no, she tells herself, it's not that deep. It must just be the caffeine rush from the mocha, and her being swayed by how good he looks, naked, kneeling before her so attentively.

'Just remember that you do have my number,' he says softly. 'If you ever change your mind.'

Instead, she ruffles his hair, and then skips towards the door. 'See you round, Jake.' She winks, this time doing it on purpose.

As the door closes behind her, the last thing she hears is him muttering under his breath, 'It's *Jacob*.'

⚽

```
Traffic is terrible!!!
```

Adriana lies in the team group chat, hastily typing out a message and hoping they buy her excuse as to why she's running late.

```
I should be there in 5 though!!! So sorry!!!
```

She doesn't know why she bothers to maintain the ruse, really, especially as the drinks had started as a celebration for her teammate's birthday. But it's the principle of the thing. Maeve hadn't come out with them last night – she barely drinks, even when they're between seasons, and clubs aren't her thing. Despite Maeve sometimes suggesting her friend could take training more seriously, Adriana is used to playing hungover now, and convinced she's just as good as when she's following Coach's schedule to the letter.

But this morning, no one replies to her message, not even with a laughing emoji. Not even a knowing hungover emoji from Elisa and the others.

A twinge of hangxiety starts to kick in. Adriana hadn't meant to make it such a big night last night – she must have got unexpectedly caught up in Jacob, and that addictive swooping in her stomach when they look at each other. And, Adriana tries to justify to herself, she wouldn't drink if she thought it genuinely affected her ability to play well or, obviously, if the team had a match. But it's pre-season! And the weather is gloriously sunny! And she had been feeling so cute in her dress and a particularly handsome man wanted to buy her negronis! I mean, what's a girl to do?

Adriana opens up her private chat with Maeve – in her constantly busy WhatsApp, her chat with Maeve is the only contact she has pinned to the top.

```
Assuming you're there already, is everything
ok??? Did something happen?? Also, babe, I
will owe you 4ever, but I neeeed to borrow
your spare kit today PLEASE????
```

```
Waiting for you on the corner.
```
Maeve texts back almost immediately, much to Adriana's relief.

Adriana leans back in her seat grinning to herself, thanking any and all Gods yet again for her best friend who always comes to her rescue. And so, now, for five whole minutes, she can just chat to her taxi driver – one of her favourite pastimes – telling him *all* about her date last night.

The memories have all returned to her now, like leaving Jacob's flat has somehow released them for her. They'd had cocktails across three of Adriana's favourite bars where he was very generous insisting on paying for all their cocktails. They'd talked about everything and nothing – early on they'd decided not to talk about work, jokingly saying that they didn't want to have the old date chat where you feel like it isn't a weekend at all – concentrating more on Adriana recommending places in Manchester to him, as he mentioned he'd only just moved there, that very week in fact.

'I must say, I'm finding Manchester to be *very* welcoming so far,' he'd smiled, before smoothly leaning in to kiss her. Then they'd walked along the water under glowing streetlamps, and got indecently hot and heavy on a public bench, until he'd hastily called them a taxi back to his place, where it turned out he's just as generous with his tongue.

'So all in all,' Adriana smiles, 'a very, very good evening. So why am I feeling a bit... sad about it?'

Mohammed, the name of the taxi driver she's quickly befriended, catches her eye in the mirror.

'Because you liked him? Because you had a nice time and you want to do it again?'

'Oh sure, I want to do it again, and I'm sure I will – with someone else.' She sighs. 'I could do it again *tonight* if I really wanted to. And okay, sure, he was particularly goodlooking, and interesting, and yes, *particularly* good in bed. But... ooh, we're here! Thank you *so* much, Mohammed,' she says, tipping him and quickly leaving a five-star review. 'You literally saved my life.'

'Just give the man another chance!' Mohammed calls after her.

Adriana laughs and wishes him a good day, closing the door behind her. She teeters on her heels and pulls the dress barely over her thighs, and when she looks up, she sees an unimpressed Maeve waiting for her.

Maeve looks immaculately put-together and clear-headed as ever, her blonde hair in her high ponytail, her pale face free from make-up. She's holding out a gym bag of Adriana's spare kit, and a homemade breakfast smoothie in Adriana's keep-cup. Adriana got them matching tiger-print ones for Christmas last year, a gesture of thanks to this one of Maeve's consistent acts of service (and selfishly encouraging her to keep to it). She can always be relied on to bail her out.

'Oh my actual God,' Adriana sighs, almost fainting into Maeve's arms, kissing her cheeks repeatedly. 'You are literally an angel on earth and I love you so very much.'

'Get off me,' Maeve mutters, putting the bag between them. 'You reek of alcohol and I don't want Coach to think I was the one being irresponsible last night.'

'I somehow think that's unlikely, babe. Also wow, your hair looks good today, did you use a different gel or something? No flyways at *all*, how do you do it?' Adriana tries, desperate to get back in her friend's good books.

Maeve rolls her eyes, but the tips of her ears are a little pink – a sure sign that Maeve's secretly pleased with the compliment. Unabashed, Adriana puts on her training top and leggings, before slipping on her trainers. She will run to the changing rooms to speed-change properly – it's one of her great talents and something she's had a lot of practice of lately.

Adriana puts one hand on her heart and with her other gestures with her pinky.

'I one hundred per cent pinky promise that I will never ever drink before training ever again.'

Maeve just sighs and puts her arm around her best friend, steering her to the changing room. 'I would be more likely to believe you if you hadn't already said that three times in as many weeks.'

'Have I really been out so much lately?'

Adriana pauses for a moment, her eyes settling guiltily in the middle distance, questioning her life choices. Then she grins. 'God, I love my life.'

⚽

Five minutes later, Adriana bounds into the locker room, having masterfully changed to cover up last night's antics.

'Goooood morning!' she sings.

She is met with a resounding, tense silence.

Her stomach churns in horror. What did she do wrong? Why today, of all the days she's been cheekily hungover and late for training, do her teammates hate her for it?

She looks around at her beloved team, arms folded over in their distinctive orange and black kit which gives them their Tigresses team name. Adriana prides herself on her ability to read a room, and right now her eyes are skimming like she's taking in a whole novel at a time. As she follows everyone's eyeline, she realises they're staring at Kevin, the assistant coach?

'You just missed an announcement,' he sighs, finally breaking the quiet.

'I'd hardly call it an announcement,' mutters Milo, one of the Tigress's forwards. Milo has always had a complete disrespect for authority.

'Well, a pre-announcement, then,' Kevin backtracks. 'An announcement of an announcement.'

'Oh my God,' says Adriana, 'the transfer window literally just opened, do we already have news of a new player coming in? Or has an offer come in to tempt someone away?'

Adriana looks to Maeve, who, as club captain and their star player, she thinks is the most likely candidate for being poached by another team. Perhaps she would even be targeted by the Women's Super League, the tier above them in the Northern Division National League. Maeve shakes her head imperceptibly.

Kevin coughs, trying to regain some dignity among the frustrated team.

'The club has been sold!' he announces. 'We have a new owner! We have been bought by the Astor family!'

Kevin is really trying to sell it as if it's good news, but it isn't at all convincing.

'Astor? As in the owner of that tech company?'

'Mark Astor, yes, that's right. He's a huge football fan, apparently. He's bought the Manchester Tigers and Tigresses as an investment.'

'Oh...' Adriana doesn't like to concern herself with the money side of football – she only cares about the *people*, and the game itself. 'So what does that actually mean for *us*? Like, do we get more equipment? They're not changing the kit again are they? I love our tiger stripes…'

'The new owner is also bringing in a new manager.' Maeve tells her in a low tense voice.

All the alcohol from last night twists and spins in Adriana's stomach, like she's back writhing on the dance floor.

'A… a new manager? Now? But what about Pappi?' Adriana bites her lip. She can imagine Maeve's glare without needing to see it. 'I mean, what about Coach Fernandez?'

Behind his back, the Tigresses affectionately refer to their coach Pablo Fernandez as Pappi, due to an old in-joke of him bringing his three children to their first training session, as well as his kindly, paternal approach to training them. But Adriana would never normally say this in front of Kevin. She must be flustered, and she realises needs to take a breath before she speaks next time to censor herself.

'Alongside meeting your new manager, Coach Fernandez is going to come and talk to you this morning to announce his… retirement,' says Kevin.

Milo rolls their eyes and scoffs indignantly, 'He's been sacked.'

'Sacked? You can't sack Pappi!'

The players around Adriana snicker, then laugh at her outburst and Adriana can't help grinning at the sound. She definitely thinks it's worth the embarrassment to lighten the tension a bit in this room. Other people's tension messes way too much with her own nervous system and she doesn't like the idea of anyone being upset.

Sure, there is actually a part of Adriana which is excited about the thought of meeting this exciting new coach, and proving herself by charming them. But it feels like she only just got to know Pappi and his systems. He's been the coach of the Tigresses for five years now, which is a pretty long time for a coach in football, but she only joined the team two years ago, with Maeve here a little before her. The first year felt like such a steep learning curve for her, getting to know everyone, getting used to the rhythm and routine, but in the past year, she feels that both her and the team have really found their groove. This season they were hoping that this solid, secure base would finally pay off onto improvements on the pitch in the off-season to build ready for next year and a potential promotion push.

Frankly, their track record isn't brilliant right now. Adriana, of course, firmly believes they are all talented players, truly with the potential to move to the top of the league table. Of course, Adriana believes *all* of her friends have the potential to be the best in the entire world. But so far that hasn't exactly been, umm, translating into tangible results on the pitch. She feels sure that with just a bit more time, now that they're all a bit more *familiar* with each other and if they didn't have any big upheavals…

Her body is pumping out adrenalin. Adriana is fine with change in theory, especially if it's the fun kind of change — a new challenge in training, or new club night, or handsome stranger to seduce — but it will all depend on what the new coach is like.

However, not everyone on the team likes change.

Adriana glances up at her best friend, whose jaw is tightly clenched. Oh God, poor Maeve. Adriana remembers when she got stressed for weeks after they changed the football kit (and that was just from black stripes on light orange to black stripes on... dark orange). Hell, Maeve got stressed when Müller changed the recipe for their high-protein yoghurt. As Maeve is their captain, she'll be expected to work even more closely with the new manager than the rest of them, and set an example on the pitch, being a leader to her teammates.

Adriana longs to give her friend a huge supportive hug — even if Maeve would probably shrug her off because she thinks the dressing room is in their workplace, and therefore a place they need to be professional.

'Who is it?' Adriana asks, realising nobody has posed the question. 'Who is our new manager?'

'Kevin hasn't told us yet,' Nat, another midfield player replies, arms folded.

'Enjoying the suspense, are you, Kevin?' Milo goads him. 'Does it make you feel powerful?'

Kevin looks at the large stopwatch dangling around his neck.

'Well,' he mumbles, awkwardly adjusting his jacket. 'I can tell you that you are all scheduled to go and meet her in five minutes. Pitch one, chop chop.'

Milo throws their hands up. 'I bet the men's team don't have to put up with this kind of bullshit.'

Adriana nods in agreement, almost despite herself. Adriana isn't a huge fan of Kevin because he hit on her after training in her first week at the club. It's not that she isn't used to getting hit on, thank you very much, but *come on*! Time and place! It makes her feel like he sees the women's team as a group of potential dates, not as professionals, and she knows it's not how her male counterparts are treated. Besides, even if she fancied Kevin (which she doesn't, he's nearly ten years older than her and way too laddish) she wouldn't sleep with someone that she works with. Not only would that be a slippery slope nepotism wise, but it would be way harder to never see a man again if she works with him, and that could lead to sleeping together more, and that would be against her 'no repeats' policy, which is working so well for her. Free and easy, that's what Adriana wants. That's what Adriana is sure she needs.

The thought of 'no repeats' reminds her of last night. She wonders what her fond nickname will be for him, when she's laughing about it later with her friends, to show it meant nothing to her and she's proudly not caught any feelings. Jacob-not-Jake? Prince Charming? No, that makes it sound way too romantic. Maybe to make light of it, he should simply be 'Great Bum Guy'...

As the squad around her start trooping down to the training pitch, Adriana shakes her head unable to believe she's thinking about some random man she'll never see again when her precious team are going through a big change. She needs to snap out of it and get her head in the game to make a good impression on the new coach.

Adriana is worried about the way this tension is showing the cracks in the team. Milo, Nat and Liv are muttering mutinously together, and the birthday girl Elisa (their first-choice goalkeeper) is looking morose. And worst of all is Maeve, sweet Maeve, who is looking an odd shade of light green. Adriana has a chance to squeeze her friend's elbow to show her support as Maeve's face softens for a moment, glancing down at her, although they don't have a chance to have a proper pep talk. Adriana tries to put all her love and support and pride for her friend into her smile back at her, in an attempt to let her know that everything is going to be alright. But the truth is – as the doors open onto the pitch to meet their new coach – she doesn't know if it will be.

Chapter 2

Maeve

Maeve takes another quick sip from her water bottle. She's hoping no one can tell she's feeling sick.

It's not that she's *sad* about Coach Fernandez leaving, she tries to convince herself. No, she has a professional respect for him, as is only appropriate for someone who has led her team, and bestowed her the honour of club captain. But it would be weak of her to be *sad*. Captains can't wallow. What is important is what the change in management will mean for the prospects of the team going forwards.

Of course, Adriana won't be thinking about all this, she's probably just worried about how Pappi's going to spend his retirement with his kids, or thinking about whatever – or *whoever* – she was getting up to last night. But Adriana's always found meeting new people to be easy, and she had Coach Fernandez wrapped around her little finger – who else would have accepted her frequent lateness and hangovers? Maeve has always found it harder to get people on side. The only thing she can rely on is her skill, and right now, she's feeling like the biggest imposter to ever infiltrate a professional women's team.

The truth is that Maeve's scared. She has been ever since she joined the Tigresses. She's scared shitless of messing up, of being shown to be a failure, and being found out. But she can't let that on. The captain should be a fearless, brave leader, setting an example for the rest of the team. Fortunately, Maeve is well-practiced at pretending to be fine so nobody knows what's really going on.

She pulls her shoulders back.

'Come on team,' she says. Her voice is low and barely raised, but everyone shushes immediately anyway, even Milo. 'Only one chance to make a good first impression.'

God, she sounds like her mother. But there's no time to think about that now.

The door from the meeting rooms opens, and three people emerge from the corridor and stride onto the pitch before them.

It reminds Maeve of watching football games with her dad, when she was little. The thrill of watching the players jog into the stadium through the tunnel, the anticipation of kick-off building. And like how usually they would be flanked by mascots, Kevin is there, like the player escort between the two of them. Try-hard Kevin just highlights how the two people on his either side ooze confidence and authority.

There's Coach Fernandez, usually the most quietly confident man in any room, looking a little dimmed today. It's understandable, Maeve reminds herself. She wonders how recently Coach found out about his forced retirement if the club wanted to bring a new manager in. He's been hiding it well up to now, but now his head is dipped, and Meave notices for the first time that he's got a small patch of balding on the top of his head, like a too-sharply mown patch of grass in the centre of the field. Her heart pines with affection for him. In reaction, she impulsively punches her chest a little, as if she'd just had heartburn. She won't let herself pity her coach. She won't have that disrespect for him by looking down on him after what he's achieved.

And the truth is, it's hard to pay attention to her coach – or she supposes she should think of him as ex-coach now – next to the woman standing beside him.

Maeve recognises her, of course. She sees it as an important duty as a player to have a fastidious knowledge of all the important figures in the game, from managers and assistant managers to even those politicians gifted the most corporate hospitality from the club. Besides, Women's Football isn't that huge a network – if you've played as much as Maeve has over the years, who has been a consistently called-up player in all of the teams she's played in for the near-fifteen years she's been playing football. But even if Maeve hadn't done her homework, she would recognise their new coach. Everyone here does, hence why everyone around her is standing open-mouthed and more alertly than usual. Because their new coach is Serena Hoffman.

Serena Hoffman was one of the rising stars of her generation of women's footballers, before a nasty ACL injury during the Euros final ended her playing career when she was only just beginning to hit her peak. But she then directed her ambition and drive into being a coach – as far as Maeve was aware, she most recently had been at the Loughborough Vixens, where she got them promoted.

It's not merely that Serena is tall – she's perhaps around Maeve's own five foot nine – but she carries herself with the confidence of a giant. Maeve would guess she's in her late thirties, though the only signs of any aging at all are the lines on her tanned face. Her ash-brown hair has a handful of elegant streaks of grey, and is tied back into as tight a high bun to rival Maeve's own sleek hair. But the first thing that you notice about her is her eyes. Behind simple rimless glasses, they're sharp, piercing, and silver-grey. They remind Maeve of a sword glinting in the light.

As if feeling Maeve's gaze, the new coach turns to her. Her stare is as unwavering as a sword too, and Maeve stands immediately to more rigid attention. She feels like a soldier meeting her new commander.

'Good morning players,' she says immediately holding their attention. 'Thank you for joining me. Now, I'm aware that this news has come unexpectedly to you all. But there simply isn't much time for us to waste on introductions or hand-overs. This has come at a vital time for the future of your team. Of *our* team. Soon, under my leadership, you will truly be earning your name of the Tigresses.'

But maybe it won't really be all that much change, Maeve hopes. Maybe Coach Hoffman has the same priorities as Coach Fernandez, and will just continue to keep the players on the same routines that the team – and especially Maeve – have become accustomed to these past months to keep that steady trajectory to build.

'So the centre of my vision for the team moving forwards is… *change.*'

So much for that thought then. The knot in Maeve's stomach tightens painfully.

'I have of course been studying all your records in advance of meeting you,' Serena continues, pacing now up and down the line of players, with confident strides. 'It will be interesting to see how you compare in real life to the stats I know of you. I already have many ideas of which of you will need the most moulding. Let's see if any of you prove me wrong…'

She stops in front of Maeve.

'First things first. Let me meet the player who embodies all that's good about what you do. Captain, step forwards.'

Maeve steps forwards with her hand outstretched.

'That's me, Coach. I'm Maeve. Maeve Murphy. Centre-back. It's an honour to meet you.'

Maeve can't help the ring of pride of stepping forward as club captain. It's always been there, since her being bestowed the honour by Coach Fernandez at the beginning of last season, lighting her up from the inside like a coal in a hearth. It's one of her happiest memories. Adriana had organised surprise drinks at their local pub to celebrate and Maeve had allowed herself a rare glass of Champagne at achieving a step she'd always dreamed of, savouring with her eyes closed the way the golden bubbles had popped on her tongue.

'Not so fast,' Serena holds her hand up. 'I understand that you were the captain under Coach Fernandez. But as much as I respect his judgement—' she nods her head towards him in a sign of deference that Maeve can't tell if it's sincere – 'we need a shake up. It's important we have a fresh start of the new era, so I've not yet decided who will be club captain under me.'

Maeve feels the imaginary bubbles on her tongue evaporate. Can everything she's worked so hard for since she joined the team just be snatched away from her that instantly, cruelly, without warning?

Adriana's expressive eyebrows are downturned across the pitch to her. Adriana has always been like an emotional crutch for Maeve, feeling the things that she doesn't let herself. Ironically, seeing Adriana look so devastated, Maeve feels it all the more harshly. She can feel the heat in her neck start to prickle. Fortunately her cheeks don't flush in quite the same way, and she hopes that the jacket zipped all the way up to her collar will hide her shame from the others.

'You will remain club captain for now, on a temporary basis' Hoffman explains. 'It may well be that if you impress me, you get the job permanently. But this is also a note to the rest of you players. No slacking. Everything is up for grabs. You have a clean slate to impress me. If you've always wanted to be captain, here's your chance.'

Coach Hoffman shrugs her hands expressively, and Maeve feels something shift in the atmosphere of the players around her. Under Coach Fernandez, she had felt she was respected as captain, not resented or envied because of it. But now, every one of these players who just minutes ago were her teammates and, she would hope was true, her *friends* – her only friends… now, they are all rivals. Rather than encouraging the team to work together in a time of turbulent change, it feels like Coach Hoffman is deliberately pitting the team against each other.

Some old familiar tension in the heart of Maeve's chest stiffens into a rigid burden. She knows what she must do. She must prove herself. She must be harder on herself than ever to maintain the highest standards. She can hear her mum's voice clearly in her mind. She must be perfect. She must not let even a crack through her defenses, on the pitch or off it.

Maeve forces herself to meet those strict grey eyes and finds some fight within her.

'Yes Coach. I won't let you down.'

Chapter 3

Adriana

Coach Hoffman claps her hands in a single sharp shock that echoes round the pitch.

'Let's get to business,' she says. 'I need to see how you're all performing. I'm going to set you three simple drills – or at least, they *should* be simple, for players of your supposed calibre. Firstly, an exercise to test your most basic, necessary technique. Passing. Do we think we can do that?'

She sounds kinda… patronising? thinks Adriana. Certainly Milo seems to think so, because they currently look like a raging bull, nostrils flaring. Coach puts her hand down in a sweeping motion, splitting the squad into two groups.

'Two lines facing each other,' she barks. 'On my whistle, first player in the first line passes the ball to the first player in the opposite line, who must then pass it back to the second player in the first line. After passing, the player will sprint to the back of the opposite line. The passes are to be fast, precise and with two touches maximum – one to control the ball, the next to pass. Keep that ball moving like a homing missile. On my whistle.'

Without any further delay, the coach blows her whistle, a short, sharp, shrill sound that immediately kicks in some innate instinct in Adriana. All the partying and alcohol and nervous tension evaporates. Now she is just raw adrenaline, running into her position in the second line. She and Maeve end up opposite each other. It often happens, without either of them particularly trying. It's like their friendship magnetically puts them together, but today, Adriana does it deliberately. She wants to be able to support her nervous friend.

Seconds later, the whistle blows for the first pass, and Adriana watches her teammates kick across to each other, heart in her mouth. Zuri kicks a perfect first touch, setting up Charlie for a neat pass across to Elisa. With neat sprints, the two then run to their next positions, to Maeve and Adriana's left. The drill continues to Rebecca, to Milo to Nat to Liv. Their passes are weighted like Goldilocks, neither too soft nor too hard, the perfect touch to find their target. The whole thing works fluidly. As the ball gets closer and closer to Adriana, she feels mounting pressure, but also pride in her teammates. Sure, the coach can intimidate them as much as she wants, but they're all professionals. They're all brilliant. *Of course* they can do an exercise as basic as *passing a ball to each other*.

And then Rebecca passes to Adriana. Adriana effortlessly controls it with one touch and sends it towards Maeve. She doesn't have to think, it's all muscle memory, in-built since she was barely five years old. It's a neat pass, no surprises, and Adriana almost doesn't wait to see it meet its target with Maeve before running off to the other side of the line. But out of the corner of her eye, Adriana sees the impossible: Maeve fumbles it. The ball misses her waiting foot, and she has to reach out to make extra touches to control the ball. The coach's whistle, which had been a regular beat like a metronome, blows extra long and hard and angry. Maeve's foot quickly corrects it, but not fast enough. In a match, that fumble could have lost them possession. And boy, won't Maeve know that too.

They keep going for another two rounds, the pace increasing with the coach's whistle, and then kicking in the reverse order up the line. Each time it reaches Adriana and Maeve's pair, Adriana is scared Maeve might fluff it again – but thankfully she is now as pinpoint as a machine.

The coach blows her whistle twice to mark the end of the exercise, and they all gather to hear the next drill, panting lightly. Adriana surreptitiously reaches across to squeeze Maeve's arm. Maeve tenses and shrugs her immediately off. Adriana tries to swallow down her hurt. She understands Maeve doesn't want to draw any more attention to herself in front of the new coach, but still, would it kill her to be a bit reassuring back to her sometimes?

The next drill provides an immediate distraction though.

'Dribbling,' calls Coach. 'Again, one of the most *basic* techniques for any decent player. The five-year-olds in my daughter's team can do this exercise. Let's see if you're up to scratch...'

While they were doing the passing drill, Kevin has set up an obstacle course over the other side of the pitch: zig-zagged cones, a slalom, and a series of gates made by two cones placed a couple of metres apart.

'Simply make your way through the obstacle course as fast as you can while dribbling,' Coach explains. 'First time round you will use your dominant foot, second time your weak foot. At each of the pink cones, five burpees. You will go one at a time, while the others all watch.'

She holds up the sleek electronic timer around her neck.

'Each time through the obstacles, you will be timed and I'll make a note. At the end of the exercise, I will be calling out who were the two fastest in the team, and who were the two slowest.'

Adriana feels her teammates tense. Pappi never pitted the players against each other. Their times were recorded, sure. Sometimes he even told them, pulled to the side, if they were performing faster or slower than their previous records. But they were only pitted against their own personal record. With Pappi, there was so much camaraderie, that even in supposedly 'competitive' matches in training, they all knew they were serving a higher purpose, the improvement of the team as a whole. And sure, there's a competitive streak in Adriana, of course there is, she *is* a footballer after all, but she likes to channel her competitiveness against *opposing* teams, not in-fighting.

Lining up to begin the dribbling obstacle course, Adriana tries to smile at everyone and lighten the mood.

'I hope this obstacle course doesn't bring up last night's kebab,' she whispers surreptitiously to Elisa and Charlie. But they do not laugh the way they normally do when Adriana plays the fool.

'Slowest two players... I haven't learnt your names yet, so I'm just going to point at you. The slowest two players in that exercise were you... and you.'

Everyone stares at her pointing finger like cats fixated by a laser pointer. Coach points first at a devastated Nat, and then at a furious Milo.

'What are your names?'

'Nat Basevi, Coach.'

'Nat Basevi,' she repeats, tapping it into her iPad. Nat looks crestfallen.

'And you?'

'Milo George, Coach. I'm only just recovering from an ankle injury.'

'How long were you sidelined for?'

'It was a grade two sprain,' says Milo. 'I took six weeks off and missed the end of last season. This is my first week back so I need to build back up in pre-season.'

But if Milo was expecting sympathy from Coach Hoffman because of her own publicised career-ending ankle injury, they have sorely misfired.

'That should be perfectly sufficient for a grade two sprain,' says the coach with no emotion whatsoever. 'If you have an issue with the medical team's assessment of your injury levels, I will expect to hear that reported through them. If you're here on the pitch, then I won't accept any weak excuses. You simply were the slowest in this exercise, Milo. That is a fact. If you don't like it, be faster next time.'

Milo's nostrils are flaring again with barely repressed fury. Adriana wishes she could advise them to be a little more respectful to the new coach, but Milo's frustration at themself always comes out as anger towards others. It's something that they can harness as a good striker at their best, but might be an issue with a strict coach like Coach Hoffman.

'And now for the fastest two players,' says the coach, in the same neutral voice, seemingly unfazed by the tension she's sent skyrocketing among the team. 'I will point again. The second fastest was... you. Name?'

'Zuri Akinyi.'

'Good work Zuri. Particularly impressive weak foot. Your burpees could do with some additional height though.'

Zuri is a winger so it's no surprise this drill played to her strengths. Zuri strokes her knotless braids, her grin proud as she nods. Adriana feels a rare flame of jealousy, which she tries to tamp quickly down. These are her friends. They should all be working together. Still. She would be mad not to want that coach's finger to rest on her as the fastest time.

'And the fastest player for this exercise was...'

Coach Hoffman seems to savour the drama, drawing out the tension as her finger roams across each hopeful face in the team like she's on a gameshow. Everyone is silent. Then Coach points to Adriana's left.

'Maeve Murphy.'

Maeve doesn't smile, just swallows, like if anything, more of a burden has been put on her shoulders.

'As we would expect,' says the coach. Without lingering, she puts down her decisive arm again.

'Right. Last exercise for now,' she continues. 'Two teams. You'll be on this 20x20 yard grid. The cones mark a 12 by 6 penalty box in front of each goal. In pairs, we'll have two strikers aiming to score, and two defenders aiming to prevent them from doing so. Three minutes of play, then swap. I'll assign you defenders and strikers – your position is irrelevant for this exercise. We'll do more focused training as per your positions in due course. But I want players who are versatile and up for a challenge. To beat the competition, you all need to be better at every position than every one of the opponents.'

'First up, the two losers from the past exercises are going to be pitted against the two winners.'

Before this can sink in, the coach is blowing her whistle, and she's watching Maeve and Zuri go head-to-head with Nat and Milo. Maybe it's all a psychological game, because while she's watching, Adriana can see that Maeve and Zuri are far more confident, being the aggressors even when they're defending. Maybe Adriana is imagining it, but she thinks Maeve's passing to Zuri is particularly careful, as if she's trying to make up for the earlier fumble. Luckily, it seems to be working. Adriana watches her best friend rock-solidly defend, showing her class as their best centre-back, clinging to Nat like a relentlessly annoying shadow, allowing Zuri to score. Maeve and Zuri retain possession the whole time, and Milo and Nat don't manage to score against them.

Milo's flaring nostrils look like they might catch on fire.

When it's Adriana's turn, paired with Rebecca against Charlie and Elisa, it's neck and neck, but Adriana manages to score a goal. Her relief is short-lived though, as Charlie then scores against Rebecca. In the final few seconds, Adriana is faced with a lightning quick decision: with Elisa already lined up in the goal, she has a chance to score – a 50/50 chance.

It's a simple luck of the draw. Adriana follows her instincts. She pretends to go left, but double-bluffs. And Elisa falls for it. She leaps to the right to defend, but Adriana's already struck the ball hard to the left, and it hits the back of the net. The whistle blows, and Adriana punches the air in celebration.

'Yes! Woo-hoo!'

In the whole exercise, Adriana is the only one to score twice, showing her quality as the team's best creative midfielder. She can't help celebrating a little further in relief, and perhaps also aiming to lighten the mood a little. Not that she's really thinking about it – scoring a goal is one of life's great joys, and Adriana knows how to do that, savouring the moment.

'Pow pow pow!'

To Adriana's surprise, as she meets the coach's eye, her finger guns shooting the air, she is rewarded with a rare smile. It's even more elating than scoring two goals.

'And your name is?'

'Adriana Summers, Coach. Midfielder.'

'Adriana Summers,' she notes down on her iPad. 'Good.'

That one word is enough to banish Adriana's hangover.

⚽

'God, I am *parched*.'

Adriana slumps dramatically on the bench in the dressing room, downing a whole bottle of Lucozade Sport.

For the whole of the afternoon, the new coach had been relentless in testing them all. They had done further trickier drills, then played five-a-side, match after match, all with the added tension of her watchful eye and tapping of her iPad, constantly judging them. Completely unlike Pappi, who would always tell people to cool off if there were rivalries on the field, Coach Hoffman seemed, if anything, to be sussing out and encouraging the tensions and hierarchies between the players. Adriana isn't quite sure what her endgame is yet.

'Adriana!' snaps Milo. 'You just sprayed my shoes! They're brand new! That orange colouring isn't going to come out!'

'That makes them unique?' Adriana suggests, trying to joke. 'Make them suit the Tigresses? Here, let me help clean them.'

Adriana reaches for the shoe, but Milo holds it tight and scrubs it furiously under the water tap.

'God, the new coach is tough,' Nat mutters.

'Tough can be good,' says Zuri.

'Sure, but tough can also be... tough,' says Nat, limply.

'It'll be alright, guys!' says Adriana, offering another Lucozade to Nat, who takes it gratefully. 'I know it's all new, but we'll get used to it! Change can be a good thing!'

'Oh, *you'll* be alright, sure,' Milo tuts.

'What's that supposed to mean?' says Adriana.

Milo imitates Adriana's shooting gun celebration. 'Just like with Pappi. Favouritism even on a hangover. I mean, jeesh, it's–'

'Enough, Milo,' Maeve cuts in, commanding the room. 'Today has been a lot for all of us. Let's not take it out on each other.'

'Okay, "Captain",' says Milo, but even their sarcasm is mercifully half-hearted. Maeve still commands respect among her teammates, it seems. Adriana wonders if Milo would even have said that at all if Maeve hadn't fumbled that ball earlier.

One thing is clear. All the old ways and rules of their team are out the window. Now, everything is to play for.

⚽

After everyone else has left, Adriana and Maeve head out into the cool night air together. Maeve sighs deeply, from right in her core.

'Oh, Sunny,' Maeve. It's an old nickname, from when they were kids together in the Manchester United Girls Academy, over a decade ago now. The nickname was basic, sure – from Adriana's Summery surname – but it holds years of affection.

Adriana pats her friend's knotted back. 'Oh Moo, I know.'

That one's origin was harder to remember, and the two of them still tried to debate it sometimes, when exactly it began. Maybe it was from Maeve's alliterative name – MM had become M&Ms had become Moo Moo, had become Moo. Adriana would never dare to use it in front of anyone else, Maeve would probably kill her if she did, but between the two of them, it's affectionately received. Even now, Adriana can't resist buying Maeve cow-themed presents. Maeve's bedroom is absolutely overflowing with little cow trinkets, which Maeve always jokes would be an issue if she actually ever had a woman round to see her bedroom.

'I absolutely fucked it, didn't I?' Maeve groans.

'No!'

'You're a terrible liar.'

'It was good! It was *good*! You were the fastest in the obstacle course!'

'Sure, but that's bare minimum for the captain,' Maeve shakes her head. 'It doesn't correct missing a literal *pass*. A *pass*, Adriana! I can't believe I fumbled a *pass*!'

'And she remembered your name though,' says Adriana. 'That's a good sign, right?'

Maeve shakes her head. 'I'm even more under her scrutiny. Sure, it's obvious that she is watching me, for me to prove my worth as Captain. But being in the spotlight like that means I cannot get away with any mistake, none at all. Not a stupid basic mistake like today. God, it's so humiliating! I have been passing since I was a toddler! Our Academy coaches would be so ashamed! My mum would have disowned me…'

'Maeve, sweetie, you're spiralling. Come back to earth. You are being way too hard on yourself. You know that, right? I mean, sure it's not *ideal* that the first time you touched the ball in front of the new coach it was a dud.'

Maeve groans again.

'But she's played the game at the highest level!' says Adriana. 'She'll know that doesn't mean you fumble *every* pass. I mean, you're the captain for a reason!'

'For now,' says Maeve, her voice cracking. 'And if I keep playing as terribly as I did today, I won't be the captain for long.'

'What do you mean, "as terribly as today", come on! You fumbled the ball *once*! Out of a hundred times!'

'Once is already a hundred times too many,' Maeve says sternly. 'I need to practice more.'

'You need to relax,' Adriana urges her.

'Relax?' says Maeve in a high pitched squeak. 'Do you realise how insane you sound right now? I can't relax!'

'Do you realise how insane *you* sound right now? I *know* you can't relax, that's exactly the problem!' Adriana. 'You're getting in your head already, I can see it. Please remember Maeve, that I know you. I've seen you go through this before! Remember the end of league game at the Academy? Under 16s?'

Maeve puts her head in her hands.

'Oh my God, Addy. Reminding me of all my past failures is not helping me right now.'

'No, no, because you only failed then–'

Maeve winces further into her hands. All Adriana can see is her ponytail, waving from side to side as Maeve shakes her head repeatedly.

'– I mean, you only didn't succeed as perfectly as you wanted to–'

'Keep digging, that's right,' she mutters.

'Because you were so in your head! You were so worried that if you let them score a single goal, there was no way you'd make the team, that you got rigid! You need to be able to be dynamic and play without fear out there.'

Adriana looks at her friend, how devastated and tense she is, and fears that she knows the end destination to her spiralling. She feels her own chest getting tight in sympathy too. She can't let them both sink under. Her friend's feelings are her responsibility, and Maeve needs cheering up. Fast.

What would cheer anyone up?

'Look, I have an idea,' says Adriana. 'Let's go out tonight.'

Maeve's head springs up so fast Adriana's worried it might pop right off.

'You're joking. Please, for the love of God, tell me you're joking.'

She looks so utterly horrified that Adriana has to laugh. 'No, I don't mean *out* out. Seriously, I have learnt from yesterday, that was the last time. I'm not going to get drunk before training under a new coach, I do have some sense of self-preservation. I don't mean go *out* out. Just hang out. A soft drink, somewhere relaxing. The Old Pig! For old time's sake.'

The Old Pig is their local pub, a student bar with cheap pints and free-flowing gossip, and the place the team go to all the time when no one has made other plans. All of their best stories start, 'Remember that time at The Old Pig, when…'

'We can get two piglet mocktails and a vegan sausage roll,' coaxes Adriana. 'I want to tell you *all* about this man I met last night. Maeve, he was so cute, honestly. If I was ever going to break my no repeat rule, he'd be a contender. I told my taxi driver this morning – he was as generous with his bank card as he was with his tongue.'

'Addy!' Maeve laughs, and the sound is music to Addy's ears. But then Maeve puts a hand on Addy's shoulder. 'I do want to hear about it, you know I do. Just not tonight. I'm sorry, I know when you're stressed you just want a distraction and a good time, but I am not like you. I've had a big day, and what I need is some small sense of routine. I need a meal-prepped high-protein dinner, and to do a Peloton workout to get rid of this lactic in my legs, before an early night.'

Adriana's heart sinks. Not just because she made the wrong suggestion — which feels as terrible a mistake for a people pleaser as, say, a footballer missing a basic pass — but also because she really doesn't want to spend the evening alone.

The truth is, Adriana hasn't actually spent an evening alone in... weeks. It's part of why she's been going out so much. Recently, it's been feeling better to wake up in an unfamiliar bed with someone else than to wake up alone in her flat which feels too empty. She can't hear her own thoughts if she's grinding up against some stranger in a dark nightclub.

'Okay! Okay!' Adriana says quickly. 'That was completely the wrong suggestion. Come to mine! Or I'll come to yours! I'll cook us dinner! I can make high-protein meals!'

'Addy, I say this with love, but the last time you tried to cook for me you literally set my kitchen on fire.'

Adriana had been trying to make them smoked aubergine directly from the fire of the gas hobs, and had somehow set the aubergine on fire. One of Adriana's favourite memories in the whole world was of Maeve, throwing the flaming aubergine across the room perfectly into the cold metal sink.

'Okay, but that baba ganoush was *delicious* right?'

'Best goddamn thing I've ever eaten,' Maeve admits.

They smile at each other and Adriana's heart lightens.

'I'm sorry,' says Maeve, sighing. 'I love you, you know I do, but I really need to just be alone tonight. And if I'm honest? I think that would do you good too.'

Adriana's stomach twists again. Maeve suggesting she needs to change her habits hits way harder and deeper than criticism from some new coach could.

'If you want to hang out, meet me here at 7 a.m. tomorrow,' Maeve offers. 'I'm going to do extra drills before training. Clearly, I need it.'

They both know Adriana won't be there. Adriana and mornings to not mix. Maeve puts a hand on Adriana's shoulder and squeezes it firmly.

'Have a restful evening, okay, Sunny?'

'You too, Moo,' says Adriana, swallowing hard.

Chapter 4

Maeve

At dawn the next morning, Maeve arrives at the training ground, her resolve strong and her flawless ponytail swinging.

She's feeling a little better than she was after yesterday's disastrous first session with the new coach, or at least, she's feeling focused on exactly what she needs to do. She's entered a state of single-mindedness that she's used to and where she thrives. It's been a part of her life for so long, this anticipation of training for the next big challenge. There have rarely been times she's not been preparing as if the next war is just around the corner, her body almost feels more normal when it's tense and shot through with cortisol.

She is proud of herself for how she coped last night, relying on the routines she's honed over the years. She efficiently made one of her high-protein tofu and peanut rice bowls, cooking in her airfryer while she did a quick Peloton exercise. She watched some of Serena Hoffmann's latest television appearances as a pundit, analysing what she most regularly comments on and criticises in players. She could have guessed: their new coach is strict and ruthless, particularly harsh on players who don't correct their own weaknesses. She's a coach after Maeve's own heart, really. Maeve had gotten into her pyjamas (ones Adriana bought her years ago which are not only too small but covered in cartoon cows), brushed her teeth, did a few yoga stretches, then sprayed her lavender pillow spray, put on her eye mask, checked her three alarms were set, and then put on her whale sounds (she can't relax to anything else). Thankfully, altogether, it was enough to quieten her racing mind for her exhausted body to sleep and wake early.

Maeve is glad she didn't give in to Adriana's suggestions to go to the pub last night. I mean, honestly, what planet is her friend on sometimes? Maeve smiles to herself, and sends her a text while she waits for her of a picture of her personalised water bottle, toasting the early morning sunrise.

`Here we go again! x`

The message comes back with an 'undelivered' symbol, which she half-expected. She only hopes it's from sleeping well in do not disturb mode, and not that Adriana went out again last night. She's starting to worry about how much she's been going out, but doesn't want to seem like she's nagging her.

As Maeve tucks her phone away and heads through the corridors, it secretly makes her feel proud, to be clocking in while her teammates are still literally asleep. She swipes her pass to open the door onto the pitch thinking about how she loves having the pitch to herself. When it's quiet, and there's no distractions, and—

She hears a slam of a football hitting the back of a net, followed by a wild whoop.

Maeve freezes. Someone is already training.

Now? Before the sun has even risen? Before *her*?

Maeve hangs back so that she can watch the mystery player, unseen. She's not someone Maeve recognises. Who *is* she?

The new player is small and lithe, with light brown skin and dark hair cropped in a short back and sides, cut shorter than any of the other women in the team, with messy waves on top that dances chaotically as the woman runs. And God, she runs fast.

She's throwing herself around with a commitment and physical exertion which impresses Maeve, especially as she's only training. She keeps going in for huge, bold kicks, hitting goal after goal from further and further away from the net, sprinting to the next practice ball. Maeve's trained eye sees the pattern in how she's practicing, the way she aims for the hardest-to-defend edges of the goal in its top corners. Occasionally she misses, because she was taking bolder risks, striking from more acute angles. And then, she throws the ball up, jumps and goes for a header from the middle of the net, and it lands right in the centre of the goal.

The stranger pushes her hair back from her glistening face, wipes her neck, breathing heavier. As Maeve watches, her heart is racing as if she was doing the exercises herself. The stranger fans her t-shirt — a white and red kit for a team Maeve doesn't recognise — and Maeve squints to read the name printed on its back above the number 9: CHOKSI.

Choksi. Something clicks into place in Maeve's mind. She's heard of her because Choksi had scored a number of impressive goals for Hoffman's old team, the Loughborough Vixens, and there was quite a bit of publicity around her. She remembers hearing about how Choksi was Serena Hoffman's protegee, a star player who she scouted herself and has been training with for years.

Now seeing Choksi's bold and confident energy, her impeccable form, Maeve can see why Coach has brought her into the club with her. Still, Coach Hoffman has moved unusually fast to already bring a new player into the Tigresses, and Maeve worries it's a sign of more shaking up to come.

But what should Maeve say to her now? She needs to make a good first impression on her new teammate, and she wishes Adriana were here to help ease it with her charm. Should Maeve admit she's heard of her?

For some reason, Maeve's mind goes to trying to recall good chat-up lines. What was that one Adriana told her to use that one time she was trying to persuade her to hit on someone at the pub? 'You seem familiar', 'Don't I know you?' Something like that?

No! Maeve shakes her own head. What is wrong with her? Not chat-up lines! She just needs a nice normal things to say to a new teammate who she is seeing early on the pitch one morning. She should just introduce herself.

To Maeve's utter astonishment, Choksi twists her arms around herself and pulls her t-shirt off. She paces the middle of the empty pitch in just her black sports bra, loose-fitting sports shorts and trainers, showing her abs are just as impressive as her toned shoulder muscles. She starts stretching her thighs out, gently thrusting out her hips and rocking forwards and back and Maeve can't cope anymore.

It's one thing to be checking out the competition. It's quite another to be *checking out* the competition.

Then a voice calls loudly across the pitch.

'Hello? Is someone there?'

Maeve's worst nightmare is coming true. The striker is squinting at where Maeve is stood in the dark corridor, and now she is jogging over. Shit.

'Yo!' the new player calls out casually. The woman seems completely unfazed that she's just in her sports bra. She stops before her, and cocks her head to one side, openly eyeing Maeve up and down.

'Ooh… Hey, you seem really familiar.'

Maeve might faint. The stranger pushes the messy waves out of her eyes, and Maeve sees them properly for the first time. They're the same rich brown as her hair, but with a brightness and spark to them, seemingly lit from a fire within. They are the most beautiful eyes Maeve has ever seen.

'I'm Kira,' she says, offering out a hand. 'I play upfront.'

Maeve realises she has a light American accent, though Maeve can't place exactly where.

'M-Maeve,' she stumbles, reaching out to shake Kira's hand. 'Centre-back.'

Maeve hopes Kira can't feel how sweaty her palms are because of her being the one who was just exercising.

'Oh, that's right,' Kira grins. 'I know who you are.'

'I… You do?'

'Well, duh, obviously I've watched you play,' Kira replies. 'You're supposedly one of the best players in our league so…'

Maeve feels wrong-footed. *'Duh?'*… *'Supposedly?'* She feels like the woman is showing off her knowledge, which is normally Maeve's thing.

'Oh,' Maeve retracts her hand, which feels like it's burning from their touch. 'Well, of course I've watched you too – when you were playing for the Vixens, I mean, not, you know, just now.'

Kira frowns, then her mouth twitches, amused. 'Just now? Were you watching me train, this whole time?'

Kira still makes no effort to reach for her training hoodie that's on the ground next to them both.

'Er, I… I mean, I arrived, and… saw you… yes I did watch you for a bit, sorry if that was weird of me…' Maeve trails off, feeling her cheeks scorching again.

Kira holds Maeve's gaze, wets her lip. 'And? Did you like what you see?'

Kira grins cockily. It makes Maeve imagine what it would be like to be with Kira in a dark bedroom, and the fact her mind went there only makes her panic more. Her brain completely overheats and she doesn't answer for too long.

Maeve has never trusted her own gay dar, but even if Kira *is* queer, someone as gorgeous as her couldn't *possibly* be flirting with Maeve, could she? Besides, if they're going to be teammates, surely Kira would also assume they would keep things strictly professional between them?

Maybe, Maeve realises, Kira's just asking for feedback on her training prowess! What should Maeve say? *'You're the most amazing player I've ever seen? I'm intimidated by you?'* She doesn't want to be weird and suck up to her too much. Maeve's frazzled brain tries to say something minimal and neutral.

'You're– I– You're fine,' Maeve mumbles. 'I mean, you're not *fine* as in– I mean. Your form is okay.'

Kira folds her arms. Maeve can't help noticing the hard lines of the woman's biceps and forearms.

'Excuse me?' says Kira. 'Okay? My form is "okay?" Is this the kind of astute feedback that made you team captain?'

Okay, that's confirmed it. Her new gorgeous teammate hates her.

'I–I'm a good captain!' Maeve folds her arms defensively.

'Oh, really?' Kira raises an eyebrow. 'And what if someone else wants to be Captain instead?'

It's clear to Maeve that Kira is out to rattle her and this is a direct threat. She has to hold her ground.

'They'd have to fight me for it,' she says firmly.

Kira eyes Maeve up and down again in a way that makes her neck hot, then she grins wolfishly. 'Sounds fun.'

Maeve doesn't know what they would have done next – Brawl? Kiss? – if they hadn't then been interrupted by the arrival of Coach Hoffman.

'Ah, Maeve. Kira. So I see you have already become… acquainted.'

Maeve realises the two of them are stood very close, a little breathless, and that Kira is still half undressed.

'What were you two getting up to?' Coach asks, her eyes sharp.

Maeve can't tell if the coach is asking what drills they've been doing, or something else, but Maeve's brain goes into meltdown.

'I was just– er, I mean, she was already…'

Maeve tails off.

'We were just warming up, Coach,' says Kira, innocently. Maeve's cheeks flush even harder.

'Quite,' says Hoffman, then glances at her watch. 'Well, I think it's highly likely that as two of our highest value players, you will be working closely together. Your teammates will be arriving in ten minutes, why don't you two go together to tell them to come straight to meet me here on the pitch?'

'Yes Coach,' Maeve says eagerly.

'And Kira?' says Coach. 'Perhaps you'd like to meet your other teammates fully clothed, so go and get kitted out first.'

Kira grabs the old shirt Hoffman throws over and nods, then flashes Maeve a cocky wink.

'See you later then, Murphy.'

Chapter 5

Adriana

Adriana arrives at the training ground feeling terrible. Her crumpled kit is as skewiff and limp as she feels. Even though she was coming from her own flat, and had actually managed to do a proper skincare routine, she is so used to riding on adrenaline and endorphins of the night before that she barely recognises herself in the glass doors.

She looks paler and more withdrawn than when she was hungover.

Even though she'd gone to bed early, she'd lain there staring up at the ceiling fan, thoughts racing round, and then when she had finally fallen asleep, she'd had one of her recurring dreams.

In the dream, distorted faces of people from her life stare at her in a constant carousel. One face after another, like masks being lit from strange angles, glaring at her, their faces unreadable. Dream-Adriana had read their impassive expressions as angry and disappointed in her. All the members of the team had been in last night's carousel, Maeve, Coach Hoffman, their now ex-Coach Fernandez, and then her family, and even Jacob from the other night, as well as exes significant and insignificant, faces of people from her life who definitely weren't deserving of late night rumination. Everyone she had ever disappointed, everyone who had ever been angry at her, everyone she hadn't been able to successfully please, all in this endless parade, where she felt that she had to justify her actions over and over, apologising. Every time making herself smaller and smillier until they might finally smile back.

The parade of masks started off slowly, but then sped up, one face after another, so that Adriana, begging and pleading with them, felt herself running out of time, unable to make any headway with any of them. When she woke up, her chest was tight, and she was breathless like she'd been running in her sleep.

She didn't know when exactly these stress dreams had started – she had managed to avoid them for several months now, she supposed through a combination of feeling more settled in the team, and fun nights out to distract her. Because the thing was, she never got the stress dream after a night out. If she'd been out partying, or with a date or with a friend, she always fell into an exhausted, dreamless sleep, and woke feeling connected and rested. She was grateful she never got Jacob-not-Jake's number, because there had been a moment of weakness when, thinking about him last night and his soft bed and even softer eyes, she had been tempted to break her no repeats rule…

Adriana tries to gather herself before she heads into the dressing room. It was just a dream. It was just a dream. Why does she always make such a big deal of it? Now is not the time to be a drama queen over something that's only in her head. Not when the rest of the team need her to give them a morale boost more than ever and she needs to be on top of her game to impress Coach Hoffman.

She's about to push open the doors, when her ears prick up to the sound of her best friend down the corridor. She's talking to someone, an unfamiliar voice. She can't hear the words they're saying, but Maeve's tone sounds kinda unusual? If Adriana didn't know better, she'd think that Maeve could be... flirting?

Two people round the corner. Maeve appears stiff next to a boyish shorter player with artfully cropped black hair that's curly on top, clear brown skin, and a distinctly cocky smile on her face. There's something so unabashed and *alive* about the shorter player that makes Adriana's face broaden into a smile automatically too. Adriana decides immediately that she likes her. (This, to be fair, is a pretty common reaction for Adriana to have upon meeting a new person, especially another footballer, to whom she always feels a sense of protective camaraderie.)

As Adriana watches, the shorter player looks over to Maeve.

'So what if I was?' Kira asks her. 'What are you going to do about it?'

Oh my God, she is definitely flirting with Maeve! Adriana can barely suppress her *glee*. All her worries go out the window for now because witnessing her best friend being hit on by a certified *hottie* is a real delicacy.

Adriana and Maeve's eyes meet across the corridor. Maeve's ears flush pink, and she looks immediately away, which Adriana recognises to be a tell-tale sign of her embarrassment. Adriana's chest does a surprised, delighted little cartwheel. Maeve fancies the stranger too! Maeve's always been absolutely terrible at hiding when she's into someone from Adriana although it really doesn't happen very often. Adriana had been worried that dormant romantic part of her friend might have been killed off forever amidst her fanatical regime of becoming Captain of the Tigresses the first time round. But it seemed that no, this bud of romance could bloom in the most stressful of soil. Adriana has to cover her mouth to stop herself from squealing.

But wait, who *is* she? Her face does seem kind of familiar, but why? Adriana skips over to them.

'Well, hello!' Adriana says brightly.

Maeve swallows and quickly looks at the floor. Adriana coughs politely, in the universal language of, 'Maeve, why aren't you introducing us?'

'Hi, I'm Kira,' the player grins confidently.

'Oh, of *course!* Kira Choksi! The star goal-scorer for the Vixens, Coach's old team! And what are you doing here today?'

Kira tilts her head.

'I'm your new player. Coach wants me to join the Tigresses with her.'

Adriana looks from Kira to Maeve. So, this cutie that Maeve clearly has the hots for… is not only going to be a fellow teammate, but surely a rival for the captaincy.

'Oh shit!' says Adriana. She didn't mean to say it aloud. Maeve pinches the bridge of her nose.

'Er, sorry, I mean, I'm Adriana!' she offers her hand out. 'But you can call me Addy.'

Maeve frowns at her curiously. She knows that normally, Adriana likes people to earn the right to call her that.

Kira glances between Maeve and Adriana, clearly sensing that *something* is going on between the two of them, but not knowing what exactly.

'Addy, great to meet you.' Adriana notes Kira has a hint of an American accent, as if she's travelled around perhaps. 'Your hair is incredible. Like, wow. How do you get it to bounce like that? Are you doing the curly girl method?'

Adriana beams. She *knew* she liked her.

'I really don't think we have time to go into all that now,' Maeve says sharply. 'Coach is expecting us to all be on the pitch, and we're here to fetch them. Perhaps *Addy* can go into her hair regime with you after this morning's session.'

'Buzzkill,' Adriana teases affectionately, which elicits a laugh from Kira. Adriana tries to grin at her friend and telepathically say, 'We will be debriefing later!' but Maeve, to Adriana's surprise, tenses her jaw, and strides on ahead.

⚽

On the training pitch, the team cluster around Coach Hoffman and Kira. Adriana notices the other players eyeing up Kira warily. She stands there, stretching casually – if anything, it seems like she enjoys the attention, a peacock wanting to show off their feathers.

As Adriana goes to slot in next to Maeve, she walks away, ostensibly to put her water bottle down on the side, not returning to the same position, instead standing further back away from Adriana. What is up with her this morning? Adriana can't work out if she's being paranoid, or if her best friend is being off with her? But why?

Adriana doesn't have a chance to speak to Maeve or move across to be next to her, because Coach Hoffman claps her hands sharply together, commanding immediate silence and attention from everyone.

'Players, good morning. I have a couple of important announcements and introductions to make before we start our training this morning. Firstly, I'd like you to meet the new member of your team and our first summer signing. This is Kira Choksi.'

As Coach Hoffman gestures towards Kira, her eyes crinkle, and she gives Kira a proud smile. Adriana feels a tiny flicker of something like jealousy and admiration, all in one. It's obvious that Coach is very fond of her fiery protegee, and Adriana is amazed by anyone who has won her respect.

Kira stands tall, arms folded confidently, looking boldly out at the team, instinctively making eye contact with everyone.

'Hey y'all, it's good to be here,' she says. 'I look forward to us winning a lot of matches together.'

Kira grins as her eyes meet Adriana's, and she gives the air a little punch. 'Go Tigresses!'

On someone less confident the gesture might have seemed lame, but Adriana can't help smiling back at her, and punching the air back in return. A few other members of the team do so too, laughing a little.

Adriana glances over to the rest of her teammates, mentally clocking who is smiling back, and who isn't, as it shows maybe who is feeling on edge about more changes to come during the summer transfer window. Rival striker Milo has their arms folded competitively – which is no surprise because it's clear they'll be competing for the same position – and Maeve – Maeve is looking several feet above Kira's head rather than at her actual face. This is highly unlike Maeve, who would normally be doing anything she can to be a teacher's pet for the new coach and prove herself as a welcoming captain.

'Kira is the first player I wanted to bring in when I accepted the job,' Coach explains. 'She was our MVP at Loughborough Vixens, and scored the most goals in the league last year when we won promotion to this division. So it was pretty easy to convince the new owner of the Tigresses that she was worth every penny to secure her transfer.'

Adriana wonders how many years they've been training together, and thinks of her relationship with Maeve, how their friendship and coming up through the academy and then into the team has made them so close that it's hard for anyone else to break through. She knows from her own experience how deep those relationships go with shared history.

'And, talking of our new owner—' says Hoffman.

As she says this, she gestures towards the side behind where she and the other players are stood. Adriana is surprised to see someone in the technical area to the side of the pitch, a tall man she hadn't noticed before, next to Kevin. A strange man always arouses Adriana's curiosity, but especially one who is being let onto the pitch before training. Why is he staying on the sidelines if he's the new club owner? If she was a powerful billionaire *she* wouldn't be hiding in a technical area, that's for sure.

At Hoffman's signal, the man has started walking over.

'Our new club director is here and would like to introduce himself.'

Adriana watches as the man strides into the light and into focus, and her stomach flips.

Because she knows this man. She knows this man in the Biblical sense.

It's Jacob.

Next to short Kevin he looks even more towering. Jacob's wearing a sharply tailored light grey suit with a tie, his hair neater than when Adriana had been running her hands through it, and his glasses have thick black frames that feel strangely out of place on the football pitch. In this outfit and his geeky demeanor, Jacob might be out of his natural habitat, yet still has a commanding presence, his shoulders back and expression clear and professional.

'Good morning, Tigresses,' he says, his voice deep. 'My name is Jacob Astor. I am your new club director, acting on the interests of my father.'

Astor? No. This can't be happening. Prince Charming Jacob is really the son of the club's owner, Mark Astor? Adriana's heart is racing, her cheeks flushed, blinking furiously.

'I understand that this is a time of significant change for all of you. Thank you for your cooperation as we work to improve the successes of the Tigresses.'

Jacob looks around at the team, his presence calm and commanding at once. Adriana's struck by the smoothness of his voice, low and assured.

'You are in the best hands with the leadership of Coach Hoffman, but I also want you to know that if you have any questions or comments about the impact of the new ownership, my door is always–'

His eyes land on Adriana's, and widen. His face blanches. The two of them stare at each other, in shock. It's like time stands still as the two of them realise their situation. To meet your incredible one-night stand a few days later... and one of you owns the other's football team.

Adriana shakes her head a little, not really knowing what she means, but just to try to rouse them both from this horrible realisation before her teammates notice. Jacob's cheeks go pink, and he turns away from Adriana.

'Uh–' Jacob coughs, and he adjusts his tie. 'Yes. My door is... always open.'

Adriana overhears Charlie whisper to Elisa, 'He's hot, right?' and then descend into stifled giggles.

'Well,' Jacob adjusts his tie again, blinking rapidly, then gestures at Coach. 'Coach Hoffman, I'm sure you can explain the other updates better than I can.'

Coach Hoffman doesn't seem to bat an eyelid at any changes in Jacob's behaviour, continuing brusquely.

'Yes, thank you Jacob. We have some more relevant information for you all,' Hoffman continues. 'So please listen carefully.'

Adriana tries to listen to Coach, but she's still breathing rapidly, staring at Jacob's side profile, his sharp jawline, his broad shoulders, trying to work out his expression. He looks, if anything, even more handsome in the broad daylight. But she isn't allowed to fancy him anymore. Not only does she have her no repeats rule, now she knows this man is *completely* off-limits.

'It may be that some of you players have never experienced being part of a team as it undergoes new management,' Coach is saying. 'New management is always a time of a lot of change for teams. The Tigresses haven't had a shake up in a long time. Too long a time, some would argue. With new ownership, there are going to be a lot of eyes on us. On me, and on each of you.'

At this, Jacob's eyes glance back at Adriana, and she feels her whole body spark. She tries to smile at him, but he's already turned quickly back away, folding his arms and nodding at Hoffman. She wonders if he is struggling to concentrate on her words right now too.

'We need to prove that we are a good investment, as much as the men's team,' Hoffman continues. 'The better we play, the more money we'll have to strengthen our team, and we'll be driving excellence both on and off the pitch.'

Coach Hoffman's silver eyes flash, and Adriana pays proper attention. 'Change works both ways. As well as bringing fresh blood in as I shape my squad, some of you might be let go and sold to other clubs who might be interested.'

A ripple of consternation goes round the players. Maeve's face has turned a sickly green, and Charlie and Elisa whisper to each other. Adriana's stomach does somersaults.

Under their old coach, the Tigresses felt like such a safe club to be part of, such a united team, that Adriana had felt their friendships kept some players from looking to move elsewhere. But with new ownership changing the mood of training, and perhaps the fate of the players on the pitch, Adriana can feel the camaraderie of the team falling apart around her. And it feels like Coach Hoffman and the new owner are trying to deliberately shake things up as much as possible. Adriana just wants to stay being able to play football with her friends.

'This is for the best, for the team we're building. We're only as strong as our weakest player,' says Coach Hoffman, her voice strangely neutral for someone talking about moving players on. 'Every team is in danger of falling to the standards of the lowest common denominator. We can't have anyone holding us back. So please be aware, that the results of your performance over pre-season will be recorded, and taken into account when making decisions about our business during this transfer window.'

Adriana, who has always thought of things in terms of the overall performance of the team rather than her own individual competitiveness within it, feels suddenly destabilised too. She doesn't even know where she is within the rankings of the team. Is she someone who should be thinking about captaincy to try and assert her place at the club? She quickly scolds herself, she would never try to take that from her best friend and that's Maeve's dream. But should she be worried about being axed? What if word has got around to Coach Hoffman that she sometimes doesn't behave as professionally as she should, going out partying on training days? Like she did just a few days ago… with their new club director, Jacob Astor?

'It was good to meet you all,' says Jacob, nodding his head respectfully to the team. Before he turns to leave, he looks meaningfully at Adriana. Her heart thuds. 'Please remember, my door is always open.'

He leaves, Adriana feeling like she's out to sea, buffeted by far too many waves.

Chapter 6
Maeve

Maeve is panting heavily when Coach Hoffman finally blows her whistle to signal the end of the training drills.

'Take five,' Coach instructs. 'Kevin, collate this data with the players' ongoing record, please.'

Maeve wipes the sweat from her brow. If there's one thing intense exercise is good for, it's helping to distract her from everything whirling around in her mind.

Now she's stopped, she can't help noticing Kira nearby, taking long gulps from her water bottle. The two of them had been neck and neck in the drills. She had tried to just concentrate on herself, but it's hard when every sense in her body seems to be magnetically pulled to Kira. As if feeling Maeve staring at her, Kira looks over at her too, their eyes meeting as they both breathe heavily. Maeve turns away before Kira can see how tomato red she's going again.

Maybe it's natural, Maeve tries to convince herself, to be obsessed with her new teammate, her last team's MVP. Perhaps this overwhelming sensation, of being set alight every time she is anywhere near Kira, is just a warning, signalling she should be wary. She is her rival after all – and that's not just Maeve being defensive, even Kira herself said this morning that she would fight Maeve for the captaincy, and with her history with Coach Hoffman, she's well-placed to get it.

Maeve is determined to keep her head in the game of these drills, especially after that intense speech from Coach and Jacob Astor about how they're expecting a lot of moves in and out of the team. She *needs* to remain as Captain of the Tigresses.

Adriana has run up to her, her eyes wide and hair wild, like she has news. But Maeve knows it's just going to be her asking her about what happened with Kira earlier, and she can't be distracted like that right now.

'Maeve! Maeve!'

'Not now, Addy,' Maeve hisses, feeling terrified that nearby Kira will overhear Adriana grill her for gossip. 'We need to concentrate.'

'No, Maeve, you don't understand.' Adriana's voice is high-pitched. 'I need to talk to you. Urgently.'

'After training,' snaps Maeve, her muscles tense. 'Can you *please* try to be professional?'

Maeve is so tense from Coach's announcements, and the gruelling training, that it comes out way harsher than Maeve intends, and she regrets it immediately.

Adriana blinks, almost tearful, like Maeve's slapped her.

'Addy, I'm sorry–' Maeve starts, but Adriana just shakes her head rapidly and then Coach is blowing the whistle to begin again.

Maeve feels a ball of guilt and worry in her stomach, but then Coach is speaking.

'Okay players, I want to see you all in a friendly. Eleven v eleven.'

Even the word 'friendly' doesn't sound quite right in Coach Hoffman's mouth. Maeve stands up rigidly. Exercises and drills are never going to fully show a player in action. This is the real test. She needs to put all distractions from Kira and Adriana out of her mind.

'I want to see how you'll perform in a game,' says Coach. 'But just because it's a "friendly", doesn't mean I want to see players being passive on this pitch. You're Tigresses! Live up to your name and show me how fierce you are.'

Kira grins, giving Coach a salute. Maeve tries to catch Adriana's eye, but she's still looking off out at the technical box. God, her friend really needs to learn to focus, Maeve's worried about her.

She remembers Adriana's well-worn advice not to get too in her head about things, but she can feel that the pressure is getting to her.

Maeve is not an aggressive player. In fact, she prides herself on having never received a red card in her whole professional career, which is unusual for a centre-back. Her disciplinary record is good. Maeve's well-known for her analytical, rock-solid defending and showing the opposition just enough respect to stay calm in the heat of a match, and she has excellent timing in her tackling, so she's never seen a red card for a late or reckless challenge.

'I'm going to read out who I want on each side. First team, wear bibs.'

Maeve stands there overthinking who is being assigned to each side. It feels like in a talent show, when the auditionees who are going to be called up to the next round are asked to step forwards. Are the players she's calling out in the top or bottom half of the training skills warm-up? Or is the coach trying to get a more even split of ability to make it a tougher test? More mind games from Coach.

'Kira, centre forward of course.' She throws her the last fluorescent bib.

'Aye aye Captain,' says Kira, obviously the only person to have answered back playfully.

'Murphy,' Hoffman calls. 'Home team, centre-back.'

Kira and Maeve's eyes meet across the huddle. That means they'll be on opposing teams and Maeve will be marking Kira. Kira grins a slow, wolfish grin at her. Maeve shudders. She tries to convince herself it's just anticipation of the game.

The players quickly huddle in their teams, and Maeve tries to breathe. She instinctively notes the position of Adriana's bouncing red curls tied up in a generous bun on the top of her head, when they get into formation ready for the whistle. Adriana is on the bib team alongside Kira, slotting into her preferred central midfield position, meaning she's an enemy too. It feels rather too apt for how paranoid Maeve is feeling right now.

'It's just a game,' she thinks to herself, though this phrase has never worked for her. 'It's just a game, where my job and lifelong dreams are on the line.'

Rebecca and Zuri call the coin toss, and the bibs get to kick off.

Coach puts the whistle in her mouth ready to signal the start of the game.

Maeve tries to clear her mind. But Kira winks at her from the centre-circle. Maeve's blood starts to boil.

Then the whistle sounds, and there isn't time to think. Adriana pings a perfectly weighted pass, and Kira is off like a bullet charging towards the ball and Maeve. Her body takes over, reacting as it's been trained to do, mirroring and monitoring Kira's movements, staying stuck to her, trying to pre-empt and get in the way of every move she makes so she can't turn and get a shot away.

They're a match.

Maeve notes with satisfaction that Kira is surprised at being unable to escape her defenses, with Maeve's marking doing the trick and keeping Kira quiet so far. Kira calls for the ball, which flies over from Rebecca, but it's Maeve's foot which sends it flying back to Liv, getting to it first.

'Urgh!' shouts Kira in unabashed frustration.

'Better luck next time,' says Maeve.

Kira's body tightens like a spring, Maeve's success fuelling her to raise her game. But Maeve's clearance has resulted in her team on the counter attack towards their winger Zuri, who dribbles up, managing to get past Rebecca and shoots – but it sails over the crossbar.

Maeve watches Adriana whoop loudly too, clapping her teammates to get them going. It's amazing how quickly this friendly has become tribal – Maeve really does feel like the bibs are her enemies. Normally Maeve and Adriana catch eyes after a goal is scored or missed, out of habit, but today,

Adriana's eyes are going over in the opposite direction. To where? The technical area again? What is she playing at? And does she really have to let down her curls right now, in a move Maeve first noticed her doing in mixed matches when they were teenagers, Adriana knowing her flaming hair would attract the eyes of men in the stands?

Maeve doesn't have a chance to read into Adriana's behaviour for much longer though, because Elisa takes her goal kick, and the ball is flying up the pitch and played in towards Kira.

'What the—'

'Fu—'

Kira is relentless. Kira darts, feints, sprints and springs. But Maeve is keeping up, staying with her and marking her player. She's in her flow, rock-solid against Kira's constant attempts, their bodies jostling as she puts another well-timed tackle in to clear it this time.

But even a rock can get worn down if it's constantly chipped away at. The more frustrated Kira gets at Maeve's defense, the more aggressive she becomes to try and assert herself.

With the bibs on another attack, the ball is played in from Milo — Kira pauses, and then barges hard past her, her ankle kicking just a breath away from being a foul.

'Fuck!' shouts Maeve.

But it's too late. Kira has broken free and is through on goal. Kira's sent the ball flying towards Charlie in goal — and scored.

The bib team whoop with cheers, Milo, Rebecca and Adriana running over to clap her on the back. Kira and Adriana high five, Adriana shouting loudly. To Maeve's jealous eyes, Adriana really does seem particularly keen to be seen having a good time in this match. Is she really that obsessed with befriending Kira and could she really ditch her so soon after all these years of friendship?

Maeve kicks the air.

Kira strolls up to Maeve, her face inches away from hers. For a crazy moment, Maeve thinks Kira might kiss her.

'Ha! You really can't handle an aggressive player, can you, Murphy? You know, some might say you're too much of a good girl.'

Maeve's cheeks burn, and her breathing hitches.

Is Kira trying intentionally to distract her with… flirty trash talking? Or is Maeve completely misreading? Regardless, she needs to refocus. She faces up towards the pitch, but Kira just will not leave her alone.

'Is this your attempt at having sharp claws, Murphy? It's more like you're worried to break a nail.'

Despite having been sprinting about the pitch for a good twenty minutes now, Kira seems completely composed, as she gets right up in Maeve's face after the restart. Her body is pressed up against hers. Maeve glares furiously back, breathing heavily, her muscles rigid and primed for fight or flight. Maeve knows that Kira is goading her. But knowing something doesn't stop it from working.

'I thought you wanted to stay Captain of the *Tigresses*? It's going to be so easy to take it from you when you're playing like this.'

Maeve sees red. It's all too much. A deadly combination of the adrenaline of the game, their sweaty bodies so pressed against each other.

Maeve lashes out, shoving Kira.

It all happens so fast. One second, Kira is up in her face, and the next, Kira's falling backwards, having lost her balance from being caught off-guard. She reaches out for Maeve's shirt, determined to bring her down with her.

'Ouch, Jesu—'

'Fuck!'

They end up on the floor. Maeve lands hard, her wrists painfully crashing down to stop her, her shins getting jabbed by Kira's studs. And somehow, there they are – Maeve on top of Kira.

This turn of events seems to surprise even Kira, who blinks rapidly up at her, for once lost for words.

But then, as their panting ceases and they're still for a moment, Kira whispers, 'Huh, I wasn't imagining it this way round.'

Maeve's face flushes scarlet.

And she's trying to struggle up, she hears a sharp, furious double blow of the referee's whistle.

'Murphy!' comes the call from Coach. 'Tackling when game wasn't in play! Go and cool off!'

'But— But *Coach*—'

'You do *not* answer back to the referee, Murphy,' Hoffman says, her voice low and sharp. 'Off the pitch – now.'

Maeve's vision blurs. She can't believe it. The pain in her wrist from the way she landed combined with the humiliation, the shock, the anger, the shame, brings tears to her eyes and a heavy lump in her throat. She feels like she's going to cry, or scream, or faint. But none of those responses would be at all appropriate. She can't bear the thought of losing control again, not in front of Coach, the team, – or worse, in front of Kira.

Maeve manages to bring together all twenty-two years of controlling and repressing her emotions, to walk off the pitch.

She feels like a child sent to have their tantrum on the naughty step. A puppy kicked for not executing the correct trick. She feels like… a complete failure.

But Coach Hoffman just blows her whistle, and the game continues without her as she walks down the tunnel.

She is drawn with both hatred and something teetering on obsession to watch Kira. She's like a firework on the pitch, with seemingly endless energy despite all the runs she makes, ruthlessly going for that goal time and again, no matter how improbable it is to get a shot away. Maeve watches Charlie, who has taken her place marking Kira. She watches as Charlie tries to defend against Kira, Kira backing into her so that their bodies jostle together, shoulder to shoulder. Kira easily overpowers her and darts away, but each time Maeve watched Kira tackle someone else it was like she could feel her own body being touched, like some kind of phantom limb. Maeve is left feeling like she's on fire with jealousy. Some crazy part of her thinks, 'That should be *me*, it should be *me* defending against Kira, I'm the only one who can match her.' But she shouldn't be thinking like that, they're supposed to be on the same team.

She messed up. Maeve *never* messes up. So she isn't used to having to deal with her mistakes, and it feels way, way too big right now to think she could ever get over it. She's never going to be renamed Captain now, she feels like she's completely blown it. Her mum is going to be so disappointed.

The tears start to fall down Maeve's cheeks and she hurries back to the dressing room.

She tries desperately to stop it, but her body doesn't seem to be obeying her command right now, and this terrifies her. She can't be seen like this. Praying that no one is watching her, Maeve heads as fast as she can to the second-floor locker room that no one uses. Then she shuts the toilet door behind her, and breaks down.

Chapter 7

Adriana

Adriana needs to find Maeve. She has shaken off her hurt from Maeve snapping at her earlier, and now she wants to comfort her friend, because she knows she'll be beating herself up for getting told to cool off. But also because she needs to tell her the crazy news, that she had an incredible one-night stand with their new club manager, and ask what the hell she thinks she should do about it. Plus, she wants to ask what's really going on between her and Kira. After months of having no gossip at all to discuss, Adriana can't believe how much has happened in one day.

Adriana had tried many times in the past, with varying levels of success, to get her friend to score off the pitch, but after her last relationship with a fellow footballer had ended (when Maeve had got a transfer to the Tigresses, a higher league), Maeve hadn't dated anyone since. That was over two years ago now. Adriana is excited at the thought of Maeve finally loosening up with some good old-fashioned snogging.

Adriana assumes Maeve would be waiting in the dressing room, but she isn't there, which is surprising because it's where Coach Hoffman would have expected her to go. There's only one place she could be and Adriana runs into the fitness suite, thinking Maeve must be on her favoured Peloton bike to work off some of her anger. But she's not there either. Adriana remembers another spot she could be – the barely used showers on the secondfloor.

But as she races up the stairs and opens the door to the long corridor, Adriana almost runs right into—

'Jacob!' she gasps.

'Adriana.'

He's holding a stack of papers and a briefcase, presumably just leaving some kind of meeting up here. But he's alone. They stand awkwardly facing each other. Adriana catches a waft of that cedar cologne. The last time she'd smelt that, less than forty-eight hours ago, she had been smelling it on his naked chest as she kissed his neck. It must be expensive, she thinks, to make him smell so incredibly attractive.

'Well,' she grins, trying to recover herself. 'Fancy seeing you here.'

But Jacob doesn't smile. 'This isn't funny, Adriana.'

'Really? I think it is *kind* of funny. When the last time we met, you were practically begging me to see you again.'

'I was not *begging*–' He corrects her.

'You're a lot cockier now that you're wearing clothes.'

Jacob blinks rapidly. Adriana smiles broadly as she watches him. She loves discombobulating men, especially ones as serious and hot as Jacob. He swallows, then recomposes himself.

'I want to make something very clear,' his voice is firm. 'I would never have– if I'd known that you were a member of this team, of course I would never have–'

'Would never have what?' teases Adriana, wanting to make him blush. But his expression is stony, and he folds his arms.

'Well no, obviously not,' she relents, realising she needs to play this a different way. 'Neither would I, to be clear! But it's not our fault, neither of us knew. It was an innocent mistake.'

Jacob wipes his glasses on a neat cleaning cloth he magicked from somewhere. 'It is very unfortunate.'

'It didn't seem that unfortunate at the time,' she says under her breath. 'I've been thinking about it a lot ever since, actually.'

Adriana glances up at him. She thinks she sees his expression soften, just for a moment, and is reminded of that evening they spent together, the way he'd looked at her when she thought he wasn't looking, the way his whole face had lit up when he'd laughed in the bar. But now, the stern man before her looks incapable of that kind of delight.

He just puts his glasses back on, and takes a step back from her. Even his tailored suit can't handle his muscles as he rubs his arm awkwardly.

'I think it would be better for everyone if we kept what happened between us, as, well, exactly that,' he tells her. 'Just between us.'

'I don't know, Jacob. I'm not used to being anyone's dirty little secret. I'm not ashamed of having sex.'

Jacob's hazel eyes are unreadable as he speaks slowly, his voice low.

'It's not because of that, Adriana, believe me. Have you not considered that if your teammates found out, that they might think you were trying to sleep your way to the top?'

She scoffs. 'As if! I'd just tell them I didn't know who you were! That I thought you were just a random hot man in a bar! That it's just a crazy coincidence that you're also the son of the new owner.'

'And you think they'd believe you?' His question hangs in the air.

'I–'

Adriana falters. A few days ago, she would have been defiant. She would have said that she had absolute faith in her teammates, and they had absolute trust in her too. But now… Adriana remembers Maeve snapping at her, Milo accusing her of favouritism from Coach Fernandez, and all the micro conflicts and insecurities rising to the surface now that the players are being pitted against each other. The way Coach Hoffman's new regime is breaking the team apart, now that everyone is so scared about the changing squad. Of course they would all be more suspicious of her sleeping with Jacob.

Adriana hates keeping secrets, but she agrees with Jacob. It's better this way, for everyone.

'You're right,' she admits. 'This is a time of a lot of change for the team. Everyone is really on edge, and I just think that the fewer surprises my teammates face right now, the better. I don't want anyone to think there was anything at all, you know, below board, between us. And I'm sure *you* wouldn't want anyone to think that you're using your position of power as a rich man involved with a women's team.' She looks at him unwavering.

Jacob winces. 'That's true too.'

But the two of them still stand there together, the atmosphere still tense. Adriana hates it. She would hate it with anyone, but Jacob isn't just anyone. Even if she wouldn't admit it to him, or even to herself, Adriana had kind of, you know…

liked him. It wasn't like her to keep thinking about someone afterwards. He had just seemed so kind. And hot. And into her. But now…

'Well. If that's all,' he says abruptly, looking round, and walks towards the stairs.

Adriana is trying not to be offended by how quickly this man has done a 180 on their night together – she understands that they're both just trying to be practical and, after all, her no repeats rule would still be in operation even if they weren't in this unhappy proximity together. But does he have to be quite so standoffish? They'd seemed to have a real connection, didn't they?

Adriana reaches forwards and grabs his arm.

'Jacob, wait.'

He turns, looks down at her hand and shakes her off. This seems particularly outrageous given the other ways this hand had touched him the other night.

'Look, I really want to clear the air,' she forces a smile. 'I agree with you that we shouldn't tell anyone. But if we're going to keep this a secret then you need to be, you know, normal with me. Is there something else going on?'

He looks away from her.

'I–' he sighs. 'I just wish you'd at least told me that you're a footballer. We could have avoided this whole… mess if we'd known we would be working together.'

'Yeah, well, sorry, but men tend to freak out if they find out that I play football for a living! I didn't want to go through yet another evening of someone trying to mansplain the offside rule to me. Most guys can't stand the thought that

I'm way better at football than they will ever be. And besides, we'd already agreed that it was a one-night thing so it just didn't seem that hugely important to give you my life story!'

This is all perfectly reasonable to Adriana, but Jacob still looks sour, avoiding her eyes. She throws her hands up.

'I hardly think you can get mad at me for not telling you my real job when *you* didn't tell *me* that you're a football club director!'

'I told you that I am a business manager which is essentially what a club director is.'

Adriana scoffs. 'Football isn't a business.'

Jacob raises an eyebrow. How dare he raise his eyebrow! At her, the queen of raising eyebrows!

'Yes, football *is* a business. And this?' He waves his hand towards their football pitch. 'This is *my* business now.'

'Well,' Adriana can't resist a dig. 'It's your *dad's* business.'

Adriana sees something tighten in Jacob's jaw. It was the wrong thing to say. He doubles down on his poker face.

'It is technically my father's business, that's correct. However, I am on the board and a director. And since he won't even—' Jacob stops himself, his jaw clenching even harder. 'I am the owner in absentia when he's not here, overseeing everything to ensure the club is operating at maximum profitability.'

'Profitability?' Adriana tries to laugh, joshing his shoulder. 'For heaven's sake, this is *football* we're talking about! Football is a celebration of athletic mastery and camaraderie! Football is about unifying communities in the essential story of victory and defeat! Football is about being human, not always about the bottom line! Football has a soul to it.'

Jacob's face is unmoved. He adjusts his tie. 'You're just doing your job, and I'm just doing *my* job. It just so happens that my job is essentially being your boss.'

Up to this point, Adriana's natural cheeriness had been winning out. Sure, they were having a healthy sparring match, but while Jacob might be grumpy around her in the light of day, Adriana's glow from their night together had been giving him a halo in her mind.

'It doesn't matter to me how you describe your job role,' he continues. 'Call yourself a "foot artist" if you want. It doesn't matter to me whether you love your job or hate your job, it only matters to me whether you deliver good results on the pitch, worthy of a salaried place in the team.'

She shakes her hair furiously. 'How dare you! I am not some product!'

Jacob shrugs a broad shoulder. 'Well, you may not like it, but since my father bought this club, didn't he implicitly buy its players too? Coach Hoffmann is here to offer her expertise and for any players that aren't up to scratch, they'll swiftly be moved on.'

'Jesus Christ, Jacob, you sound so cold about it all.'

Jacob's jaw clenched.

'I think it would be better if you called me Mr Astor.'

'Oh, do you indeed? I remember you wanting me to call you some other things just a few nights ago.'

The heat in Jacob's cheeks rise. Adriana feels rather pleased with herself for this reaction. But it does mean that she senses the phantoms of their night together in the air between them again. As she looks up at his chiseled face – his jawline even sharper with his jaw clenched, his blue eyes even brighter as he's frowning at her — something comes over her. She remembers how they were in that bar, in his corridor, in his bedroom. She remembers wrapping her arms around those broad shoulders and pressing herself against him. She remembers how wonderful it is to make this man lose his composure.

He adjusts his tie, even though it was already perfectly straight, and then adjusts his belt. But then to her surprise instead of leaning in and kissing her like she wants, he steps back from her.

'I would like to remind you, Ms Summers, that we now work together,' he says. But his voice isn't angry, or stern. Just regretful. 'Like it or not — and believe me, I do not like it at all — but I agree with you that it would be best for all involved for us to be completely professional from now on. You don't want your teammates to think that you are receiving any… preferential treatment.'

She can't help it. Right now, there's a part of Adriana that would really, really like some 'preferential treatment' from Jacob. But then she remembers the difference between this Jacob and the Jacob she'd kissed the other night. This is exactly why she never gets attached to men. The more you like someone, the more they'll let you down.

So she bites her lip and holds a hand out.

'I agree,' she says. 'Purely business.'

Jacob's large hand covers hers, and his eyes have softened now.

'Purely business,' he agrees.

Adriana doesn't know if it's her or him, but she does know that their hands linger held together for a little too long.

Chapter 8

Maeve

Maeve showers in water so hot it scalds her.

The only person she has told about this locker room on the second floor is Adriana, which she slightly regretted at first, but thankfully her friend understood that it's important to Maeve to have her own space sometimes. Adriana hasn't shared it with anyone else, or even followed her here before. Maeve's safe, for a short time, alone with her thoughts.

She aims the boiling water at the aching muscles in her shoulders, her back, her neck. She still keeps replaying her humiliation, Coach Hoffman telling her to go and cool off. Kira smirking.

She pumps some of the provided shampoo through her hair, and remembers her mum, when she was only a child, young enough even that she hadn't started playing competitive football yet, washing her hair in the sink. The smell of the rose Herbal Essences bottle that seemed to last for years. It had been a rare moment of physical contact between them. Maeve couldn't relax properly, even then. Maeve remembered noticing her mother's fingers with their nails bitten down to the quick. It was the one thing her strict mother couldn't really tell Maeve off about, since biting her nails was a habit she had been unable to control in herself. Later, when Maeve's mum moved her whole legal practice with her to Manchester to be closer to Maeve's football academy, her mum started getting manicures again, long fake nails, covering the bitten scraggles underneath with a shiny perfect layer.

Maeve jumps at a sound. The cubicle is so steamy now that she wouldn't see someone unless they literally came into the shower with her. Her mind leaps wildly into the image of Kira doing just that. In her imagination, for some reason, Kira's still in her sports kit when she walks into the shower, like she won't even let herself picture her naked body, that would be too far. She remembers the way Kira had looked up at her when Maeve had landed on top of her on the pitch. The foul that had got her punished by Coach.

This brings Maeve suddenly back to reality. What is she *doing*? Fantasising about her rival, who goaded her, and who is likely going to steal her captaincy too.

Maeve's been in here for too long now, she's starting to feel faint. Maeve turns the shower suddenly off but stands in the quiet steam for a moment, avoiding the reality of having to leave the privacy of this room. She rests her head against the tiles of the shower. Should she go and apologise to Coach? She cringes. Coach probably wouldn't respect that. Should she speak to Adriana? The thought of admitting she was jealous over her quickly formed bond with Kira makes her feel pathetic. She even wonders if she should apologise to Kira? It would be an excuse to see her... but no, it was *her* fault she was in this mess in the first place!

Apologising to her would just make her smug, and, even though Maeve has only known Kira for one day, she can't imagine her accepting an apology gracefully. She'd just rub it in.

She sighs. One thing at a time. One foot in front of the other. First, just try to leave the shower.

She wraps a towel around her body, and turns the corner of the showers back into the changing room.

She nearly jumps out of her skin.

There, sat with her back to the shower room, is Kira.

Maeve considers stepping backwards back into the shower, but Kira turns round to face her.

'Hey,' Kira says casually, as if Maeve being in a towel in her presence is completely normal. 'I came to check if you're okay.'

For once, Kira isn't smug, she isn't cocky, she seems to be just genuinely concerned.

Maeve's whole body is hot and red from the shower, and now from this. This confusing, infuriating woman. She feels strangely aware of her wet hair, hanging loosely down to her shoulders, making her feel even more naked somehow.

All she can manage to stutter is, 'I... Why?'

'Well,' says Kira. 'You were holding your wrist when you left the pitch, and I suspected you might have grazed your arm, but I know you didn't go towards the medics so—' Kira holds up a first aid kit and a bag of ice. 'I brought you some stuff in case you wanted to do it yourself.'

Maeve is probably gaping like a fish, she can't help it. She can't compute. Why is Kira being... nice to her?

'You seemed like when Coach told you to cool off it really got to you so, I dunno, I just guessed you might be beating yourself up about it, or something else stupid.'

'I– are you calling me *stupid*?'

'Yeah. Stupid,' says Kira, neutrally. 'Because you were defending really well, and Serena was really impressed.'

Kira looks right back for a moment, her expression unreadable.

'Murphy, I…' Kira pauses. 'Do you want to put some clothes on?'

Maeve's body heats again, and she's not sure if it's in shame or in pleasure.

'Right. Right. Yes, absolutely–'

'I mean, only if you want to– I just thought you– I mean, if you *want* to stay in your towel that's fine by– , I just, it's not–'

Maeve gestures to the bench next to Kira, feeling like there's a force field that she couldn't go too close to her herself.

'My clothes are just–'

Kira hands her the neat pile of Maeve's folded fresh kit. With one hand Maeve clutches her towel closed as if her life depends on it, and with her other reaches over for the pile, her hand grazing Kira's.

Maeve feels supremely awkward, wishing she could unaffectedly strip and dry and put her clothes on like she does with the other players in her team. There was something about training daily with her team which had made it all so completely asexual, just practical unclothed bodies, a different thing entirely from a naked body in a bedroom. In Kira's presence, her unclothed body suddenly felt very, very much like a naked body in a bedroom.

It's like she's thirteen again, puberty hitting, and suddenly scared to change in front of her friends, doing elaborate tricks with hoodies and towels to avoid anyone seeing anything they might judge her for.

If she *did* see her body... would Kira like her body the way Maeve likes Kira's?

Kira has the sense to look tactfully away, to the back corner of the changing room.

'It's okay, you know, losing your head in the heat of a game,' Kira says, her back still turned to her. 'Even in a match. Getting a card isn't always a bad thing. I've racked up so many I could start my own gift shop.'

Maeve barks with laughter, completely caught off guard by this joke.

Maeve quickly pulls on her pants, her sports bra, her t-shirt, and then, feeling safer now, her trousers.

'Serena respected it, today,' Kira carries on. 'She liked seeing you have the ability to be aggressive. And it was just unfortunate. It wasn't in your control that we fell like... that.'

Maeve is pulling her hoodie on, lost in her own thoughts but she *thinks* she hears Kira say, 'Not that I was complaining.' But she must be wrong. She takes a deep breath, and faces Kira's back — her firm shoulders and the sharply cut short hairs at the nape of her neck. Maeve wonders what it would feel like to the touch, and her fingers tingle as she imagines running her fingers through that bristle.

'You can— You can turn around now,' Maeve mumbles awkwardly, feeling like a woman showing her prom dress to her date. She feels aware of her hair still loosely round her shoulders, making her hood a little damp round her neck.

Kira looks back, smiles ever so slightly. Then she seems to remember something.

'Ah,' she says, and picks up the first aid kit. She comes towards her, gesturing at her arm. Maeve's wound from earlier is already bleeding through again, slightly staining.

'Oh,' says Maeve. Since Kira's appearance, she had not been aware of the pain at all. She rolls up her sleeve to see that her graze has actually started bleeding, and has in fact stained her hoodie. As she looks at the blood, it starts stinging like hell. It's a surface-level wound, but one of those broad grazes which bleeds like a bitch. The side of her forearm has been scraped away, whether by the ground or Kira's boot.

'Ouch,' whistles Kira, in the knowing tone of someone used to getting their own cuts and grazes. And indeed, as Maeve looks now at Kira's knees and legs, bare under her shorts, she can see hers are covered in a patchwork of new and old cuts, scars, and bruises; the proof of someone unafraid to throw herself around for the good of the game.

Kira reaches towards Maeve's arm, and, in order to study the wound, unexpectedly lays her hand around Maeve's hand.

A jolt races up all through her. Maeve's cheeks flare. She twitches her arm away and reaches towards the first aid kit.

'Oh, I can— I can do it myself.'

'I know you can,' says Kira, her warm hand reaching gently again for Maeve's arm. 'But I think it'll be easier if I help you. Please can I?'

Maeve feels disarmed. She's so unused to someone trying to help her. Normally they take her independence at face value and if anything she's the one helping others as club captain. It's only usually Adriana who insists on helping her even when Maeve pretends she's fine.

Maeve feels incredibly vulnerable. But it's not a bad kind of vulnerable. In fact, it feels kind of... nice?

Quietly, Kira carefully applies disinfectant to her arm. Maeve tries to hide her flinches, and Kira keeps on, unwrapping the bandage from its packet, wrapping it smoothly round.

'Coach isn't going to hold it against you,' Kira reassures her. 'That's not the kind of thing she holds records about.'

'But *I'll* know. It's on my own record,' says Maeve quietly.

'Then maybe your own record-keeping is too strict,' says Kira. 'Maybe it's a good thing to surprise yourself every now and again anyway. That's where some of the best breakthroughs happen. From breaking your own rules.'

Maeve doesn't reply to that. She just watches as Kira presses ice onto her wrist.

'Thank you,' says Maeve, so quietly she's not sure if Kira will hear, but then Kira looks up at her, with a warm, genuine smile. She finds herself longing for the cocky, arrogant Kira from the pitch – at least Maeve knew how to fight back with that. This one's tactics are far harder to defend against.

They stand together for a moment. Kira clears her throat.

'Murphy, there's something I need to tell you.'

Maeve's heart races. Why is she wishing Kira is going to tell her something personal? That she's gay? That she's single?

'Serena really was impressed with your playing earlier,' says Kira. 'Well, and with— with *our* playing, specifically. She said we bring out something in each other, on the pitch.'

Kira rubs the back of her neck. Maeve can't tell if she's smug trying to hide it with modesty, or is actually feeling bashful.

'She says she wants the two of us to spend more time training together,' Kira explains. 'With me as striker and you as centre-back, she wants us to raise our game to improve the team's play at both ends of the pitch. She thinks one-on-one training could help us push each other to be better.'

Maeve flushes. Kira holds her hands up.

'She is going to set some additional practices for us around training, with one of the other coaches. Would you be down for that?'

It's a lot to take in. She only met Kira *today,* and suddenly it seems like their lives are going to be very bound up in each others. Maeve turns away from Kira to think, busying herself with putting her wet towel in the wash basket, and then finding her little wash bag. It's cow print, a gift from Adriana. Maeve feels embarrassed about it in front of cool Kira, so she opens it with her back to her, pulling out a comb and hair tie.

There's a part of Maeve that's thrilled at this idea. Coach mandating that she spend more time with the most exciting, surprising, talented player Maeve's been on a team with? It's an incredible opportunity to improve, to really challenge herself. Training with a firecracker of a forward like Kira is really going to help her when it comes to actual games against the best strikers in the league.

That is how she *should* feel. But Maeve's also terrified. Look at what happened with being 'challenged' in this way today – she lost control of her own emotions, and lashed out against a fellow teammate. Kira is her rival for the club captaincy, after all. What if the more they work together, the stranger that competition will feel.

Maeve hears Kira stand, walk quietly towards her, her studs clattering lightly on the shower room floor. Already the increased proximity makes the hairs on Maeve's arms stand.

And then, of course, there's the complication of how Maeve is crazily attracted to Kira. It's hard to ignore even now, and the closer she and Kira work together, will she be able to hide that from her forever?

'Maeve?' Kira asks. 'What are you thinking?'

Maeve ties her hair up into her slick, practical ponytail, giving herself the feeling of some protective armour. In it, she is Maeve Murphy, professional footballer, club captain of the Manchester Tigresses. She turns back to Kira, holding her shoulders back.

'If that's what Coach thinks is best, then of course that's what we'll do. But to be clear, Kira, I want to stay as Captain. This team is the most important thing in my life. No matter how closely you and I end up working, we are not in this together. I'm not going to just step aside and let you take what's mine.'

Kira's arms are folded, the lithe muscles of her arms tightening. Kira opens her mouth to reply, but at that moment there's a knock on the door.

They both freeze, as if caught in a compromising position and realising just how close their faces are to each other.

'Moo? Moo, are you in there? Can I come in?' Adriana's voice calls from the other side.

Maeve closes her eyes in humiliation and Kira smirks when she sees Maeve's worried expression.

Adriana slowly opens the door, her red curls bouncing as she pokes her head cautiously around.

'Moo?'

Adriana takes in the two of them, stood alone in the private shower room. Adriana's expression goes from knotted in worry to that of a cheshire cat who has just been given a lot of cream.

'Oh! I didn't realise you'd have company!' Adriana squeals. 'I can come back later.'

Maeve wishes the two of them would stop *smirking* all the time.

'It's fine,' Maeve snaps, 'we were just leaving too. Separately. We're done here. Right, Choksi?'

Kira's head tilts slightly, as she just takes her time studying Maeve before she replies. Unlike her, Kira seems unrushed and unfazed, even now that they've been interrupted.

'Sure,' Kira shrugs.

Kira takes back the ice pack and Maeve feels her resolve wobble as she remembers Kira's tenderness earlier. But this is just another test. She won't let Kira mess with her head.

'I guess I'll see you at our extra practice, then, Murphy.' Kira touches a couple of fingers to her forehead in a salute. 'Be careful with that wrist.'

Chapter 9

Adriana

Adriana leans coquettishly against the doorframe.

'"Careful with that wrist, Murphy,"' Adriana does her best impression of 'sexy Kira', even doing a performative wink. 'How about you rest it by lying down in my bed, and I'll–'

'Addy! Please!' Maeve groans, covering her scarlet ears. She rushes to the door, opens it to check that Kira has actually left. 'Don't make a big deal out of nothing!' She hisses.

'Didn't seem like nothing to me,' says Adriana. 'Didn't seem like nothing when the two of you were pressed up against each other on the pitch. And it didn't seem like nothing when the two of you were alone in here dramatically heaving your bosoms.'

'We are not lesbians in a period drama, Addy, we don't have heaving–'

Adriana sing-songs, 'Maeve and Kira, sitting in a tree, K-I-S-S-I–'

'*Stop it!*' Maeve snaps.

It comes out way more intense and serious than Maeve meant it to from the shocked look on her face but still, it's clear Adriana's jokes have struck a nerve in her stressed friend. Adriana falls quiet. Being told off makes her feel not only worried about her friendship with Maeve and that she's pushed it too far, but it brings back unwanted replays of her conversation with Jacob earlier where similarly it felt that she was too much. She feels her lip quiver.

'Oh, Addy,' Maeve says quickly. 'I'm sorry, I didn't mean to overreact, I'm just— you know, feeling so stressed, and I…' She opens up her arms. 'Come here.'

Adriana falls into her and they hug tightly. To both their surprise, Adriana starts weeping into Maeve's shoulder.

'Woah, woah! Sunny!' Maeve sighs, stroking her hair. 'I didn't realise I'd upset you so much, I'm sorry.'

'No, it's not—' Adriana sniffles. 'It's not you, I just, I didn't sleep well, and I'm hormonal, and— and—'

'And what?'

Maeve pulls back, wiping tears from Adriana's cheeks.

'It's nothing,' says Adriana, avoiding Maeve's eyes. 'Just some… business stuff.'

Maeve offers Adriana a tissue from her bag, and Adriana smiles to herself. Adriana is always in awe of how prepared Maeve is. 'Business? What do you mean, "business"?'

'No, no it's nothing,' Adriana dabs at her face. 'I think all the stress in the team is getting to me. People fighting for the captaincy, and all this talk of people moving in and out of the team… I just want us to be able to have fun again.'

'It is a really weird time,' Maeve mumbles in agreement, pulling Adriana back into their hug. 'But it's going to be okay. Things will settle down. Change always feels the most dramatic at the start. It's all just very fresh, and surprising, but we'll get to grips with it.'

It sounds like Maeve is trying to soothe herself as much as Adriana, but she appreciates it nonetheless. Adriana's breathing returns to normal.

'Come on, let's get out of here,' Maeve. 'You're always saying we spend too much time in this training complex.'

Adriana looks up hopefully.

'Are we going to go... out?'

'No! We are *not* going *out* out, Addy.'

'Really?' jokes Adriana. 'Not even to The Old Pig? Not even *one* little bottle of wine each?'

Maeve laughs and shakes her head.

'Okay, okay,' Adriana gives up. 'Want to come back to mine? I think we could both use a break from thinking about... all this. We can put pyjamas on immediately, and watch some noughties TV, and I'll– Ooh, I can make you baba ganoush?'

Maeve squeezes her friend's cheek affectionately, then studies her face more seriously. Adriana wonders if her own secrets are visible on her face.

'You're right,' says Maeve. 'Let's go back to mine, and *I'll* make baba ganoush. That way, we won't have to deal with the fire brigade.'

They head out, Adriana squeezing her friend's arm with happiness and an overwhelming sense of relief. She won't have to spend this evening alone. Hopefully, that also means she won't have her dreams haunted tonight by Jacob's angry face.

Later, when she and Maeve have eaten a delicious array of dips and tofu noodles, they're laughing together on Maeve's sofa, drinking camomile tea with old episodes of *New Girl* in the background.

They do a good job of avoiding talking about everything to do with the team for, ooh, about two hours – but then Maeve shifts on the sofa and winces as she catches her arm. She rolls up her cow-print pyjama sleeve to study if the plaster is holding. (Adriana is also wearing a pair, proving you should always gift someone things you like yourself.)

'Does it still hurt?' asks Adriana.

Maeve half laughs, half sighs, as she looks down at her neatly bandaged arm.

'It's… It's fine. At least it's not my ankle, right? It's just a scratch, it's the least of my worries. Kira…' She tails off and then groans. 'I still can't believe I lost my cool like that.'

'Honestly, it's okay, I think you think it was worse than it was,' Adriana says, glad to be able to give her the reassuring pep talk she knows Maeve needs. 'If anything, I think you proved to Coach that you *can* be aggressive if you need to be. Keep her guessing and show that you can follow her instructions.'

Worry lines appear on Maeve's forehead and she sips her camomile tea.

'Oh God, I just don't think that now should be the time to make Coach guess about my performance. I want to be reliable, a safe pair of hands, you know? Like I always have been. It's the only way I'm going to contrast favourably for the captaincy next to Kira…'

Maeve's voice cracks a little on Kira's name, and Adriana studies her friend's face. Maeve definitely likes Kira, it's clear from the way she blushes and her throat catches at the name. But Adriana wonders if her friend even knows herself.

'Coach wants us to do extra training together, me and Kira,' Maeve explains. 'So I can't let her get to me, can't let her rile me up. But I find her…'

Maeve puts her head in her hands. Adriana rubs her fluffy-socked feet soothingly. Adriana hates seeing Maeve worry like this and just wants to fix everything for both of them.

'And then there's the whole *Jacob Astor* thing,' Maeve carries on, oblivious. Adriana freezes.

'Surely he was there today to watch and report back on us,' Maeve continues, unaware of her friend's shift. 'Is he there to see who to let go in this transfer window? And I wonder if he has a say in who is captain too. Would it affect sponsorship or something? Optics? There's just so much we don't know.'

Adriana relaxes. Maeve clearly doesn't suspect a thing about her and Jacob. Understandably, she's preoccupied by her own dramatic day.

Maeve gnaws at her finger nails. 'He is just this random man who suddenly has power over our careers! We don't know what his metrics are. We don't even know what he prioritises in a football player.'

'He is just thinking about money,' says Adriana, without thinking. 'He doesn't even *like* football.'

'What?' Maeve pauses, looking up. 'How do you know?'

Adriana flushes and tries to cover up her slip.

'Well, he's just a— he's just some business guy, right? With a rich dad? If he cared about football, he'd be more involved, not just watching from the sidelines barely looking at the field.'

Maeve ponders this. 'I guess you're right. But he's an unknown quantity which I really don't like. If only we had some way of knowing what he was thinking. Then we'd know how they're deciding between me and Kira – or someone else – for captain, and which players they might want to move on before the season starts.'

Adriana has a great idea. She puts her tea down, excited. She's going to fix all Maeve's worries. It's what she is best at, she tells herself, dealing with any little mis-steers behind the scenes without anyone even needing to know.

She's going to use her unusual relationship with Jacob to find out who is in the chopping line, and save them from being on the list of outgoing players.

And if it also means getting to spend more time with Jacob – *in a purely professional manner*, of course! – she can reassure herself that he does like her as a person, that their night of romance wasn't completely wasted, and that she is charming and loveable even when she's not seducing a new man because it's not the only way to prove her worth. Maybe she and Jacob could become friends! Stranger things have happened, she tells herself.

Adriana snuggles into Maeve's familiar sofabed, hugging one of the many cow plushies Adriana has previously bought for her friend. She is proud of herself for not confessing all this to Maeve. She's better at secrets than she thought. The less Maeve knows the more Adriana is protecting her.

'Night night,' Maeve kisses her friend sweetly on the forehead. 'Thank you for being such a good friend.'

'Night night,' Adriana mumbles sleepily. 'Back at you.'

Adriana sleeps well that night.

⚽

Over the next week of intense pre-season training, Adriana keeps looking out for opportunities to catch Jacob alone, without drawing suspicions of anyone else in the team. But on Wednesday, Jacob isn't there. She takes her restless energy out by sprinting even faster during a drill, and earns a rare compliment from Coach.

On Thursday morning, Adriana thinks she sees him in the stands, a tall silhouette just *watching*, like a sexy phantom of the opera. On Friday, she sees him talking to Coach Hoffman. He's wearing a deep navy suit and his shirt is unbuttoned at the collar, just enough to see a glimpse of his toned chest. His head is bent listening and nodding seriously to what Coach is saying.

Jacob glances up, his eyes catching Adriana's from across the pitch. Even though he keeps talking to Coach, his eyes stay fixed on Adriana. She is transfixed, like time has stopped. When he looks away, he then doesn't look back, and leaves shortly afterwards. Adriana is left unmoored. Maybe he hadn't been able to see her at all, maybe this is all in her head. Either way, it hardens her resolve to somehow form a good working relationship with him, and one that helps her teammates.

By the end of the Friday session, Adriana is on edge to talk to him.

So when she catches sight of his luscious dark suit waiting by the exit of the training ground, typing on his phone waiting for his driver, she sprints down the stairs shouting after him.

'Jacob! Er, I mean, Mr Astor!'

Jacob turns, frowning, like she's a charity collector he's already turned away.

'Yes? Can I help you?' He asks, his voice cool and unruffled.

Adriana glances around, checking that none of the other team members are watching. In the same moment, Jacob glances up to see his driver isn't here yet, and frowns at his flashy watch. Adriana doesn't know if he's doing a performance of being a busy businessman or if this is happening naturally, but either way, she gets the idea.

'What happened to keeping a low profile?' Jacob asks her in a low voice.

'Oh, it's fine, I'm here with a business proposal,' says Adriana brightly.

Jacob folds his arms.

'Well?' he seems unimpressed.

'I think we should get coffee together! A professional coffee,' she adds. 'At a professional daytime hour. Sunday afternoon?'

'You... want to meet me at the weekend?'

Jacob blinks behind his stylish glasses. Adriana wonders if he's remembering, like she is, her explaining to him her rules of not meeting people for dates after sleeping together, and how she would never go on a date on a weekend – weekends are for friends and family only. Although Adriana has thought about this, it wouldn't be sensible for them to meet in an evening after training – then they'd meet in a bar, and even if they didn't drink, it would feel too much like a second date. Whereas this, a coffee on a Sunday... is as far from a date as you can get!

'Yes! For business. To tell you about the team. From the perspective of someone who knows all the players well. If you or Coach have any concerns, then I can provide context, information you might be missing from your records.'

'Like... an informant?'

She doesn't like how that sounds, but Jacob seems curious so she just nods.

Jacob raises an eyebrow. 'I didn't see you as someone who would want to play the traitor. You want to snitch on your teammates so that I don't move you on from the club?'

'Wh-What? No! No! I'm not going to *betray* my teammates. Never!'

Jacob still looks unconvinced.

'I don't understand what you actually want to meet for, Adriana.'

Adriana racks her brains for how she can persuade him.

'One week of monitoring player's performance in practice drills during training is simply not an accurate indicator of their overall applicability. I want to ensure that you have all the information available. New perspectives. Performance... indicator... business... reports?'

'Ah yes,' Jacob says deadpan. 'My performance indicator business reports.'

'Urgh,' Adriana, throws her hands about. 'You know what I mean!'

Jacob cocks his head.

'But I have every faith in Coach Hoffmann's ability to test the capabilities of the players. Why should I need any additional information from you? Over a Sunday coffee?'

Adriana tries not to shirk under his intense stare or the abruptness of his questioning. They are clearly misunderstanding each other, but she doesn't know what Jacob *thinks* she's asking him.

'What if a player was just acting a little oddly this particular week? Off their A-game in times of stress? It wouldn't be fair – I mean, it wouldn't *make good business sense* – for them to be released from the team, if they're usually the glue that holds the whole team together?'

'Are you referring to yourself?' He pauses, seeming wary.

'What?' Adriana is taken aback. 'No, no, I'm not talking about me!' She considers talking about the captaincy or even saying Maeve's name, but it's too risky, it can never get back to her best friend. 'I'm being hypothetical.'

'Really? Because from what I've seen so far, you *are* the glue holding the team together.'

Adriana blinks rapidly.

'I– What? No I'm...'

The thing is, that is exactly what Adriana aspires to be. She's just never thought about it that way before. She can't believe that Jacob has immediately and intuitively identified something about her that even she didn't know.

'Huh,' she muses. Then, saying aloud her train of thought, 'I bet you're really good at your job, aren't you.'

It's Jacob's turn to look surprised now. Arms folded, they just frown at each other for a moment.

'Fine,' he says abruptly. 'I agree to your proposal.'

'What?' Adriana pauses, somehow managing to forget what the point of this conversation had been.

'Coffee. Sunday. Midday. Did you have a location in mind?'

Adriana does a happy little celebration dance. Jacob's placid face twitches in barely contained amusement.

'Yes! Ooh absolutely I do, I know *all* the cutest little coffee shops around here. I know somewhere that does a *life-changing* brunch. Most incredible hash browns I've ever had in my life, they're almost like little fried tater tots!' She suddenly stops in her tracks and becomes serious again. 'Do you have any dietary requirements?'

'I do not have any dietary requirements,' says Jacob. He folds his arms, studying her, frowning, like he can't work something out. He chooses his words carefully.

'And you really expect me to believe you're inviting me for a life-changing tater tot hash brown brunch just for business? Is that really the right... place for a work meeting?'

'As far as I'm concerned, a life-changing tater tot hash brown brunch could never be wrong.'

Jacob's eyes twinkle, and Adriana loves so much seeing him look at her like that again.

'But if you'd prefer,' says Adriana, 'we can just have pastries? Surely even the most serious business people are allowed pastries.'

His lips twitch into a smile now, playing along.

'Business pastries,' he says. 'Croissants or, at a stretch, a pain au chocolat. No cronuts.'

Adriana grins properly at him now. She's never heard someone try to be stern when they say the word 'cronut'. They smile at each other with a sense of a shared joke, being in on something together, and Adriana feels relieved and excited. She's won him over.

'I know just the place.'

Chapter 10

Maeve

'Murphy.'
'Choksi.'

Maeve and Kira nod curtly at each other, and start jogging in silence, beginning their warm-up around the empty pitch.

This has become a ritual between them in their additional one-on-ones so far this week. No niceties, no chit-chat, just straight into it. They talk during the workout and are very vocal about any critiques either can find about the other's playing, but they haven't had any *actual* conversations since Kira came to check that Maeve's wrist was okay.

Maeve always arrives at their additional one-on-one training a little early, to prove her reliability and conscientiousness in case it gets back to Hoffman, but Kira is inevitably late.

Today was no different. Maeve had been waiting for nearly fifteen minutes when Kira finally rocked up. Her face looked recently splashed with water, and she was chewing an energy bar. Maeve is absolutely exhausted after an already intense week of training with Hoffman and the team, but she won't show any weakness now.

They've ended up unusually having another one-on-one on a Friday night, after they were discussing schedules and realised neither of them had Friday night plans. A part of Maeve felt pleased Kira wasn't going out either. It made her feel less of a loser.

'You're late,' Maeve snaps.

'Oh, get over it,' laughs Kira.

'You're so disrespectful.'

'You're so uptight.'

'You're so annoying.'

'You're so hangry.'

Kira, still chewing as she jogs, hands over the last bite of her protein bar. Maeve hates to admit it but she is pretty hungry, now she mentions it. Reluctantly she grabs it and, even more annoyingly, does feel better.

Then it's just the two of them and the pitch, naturally synchronising their thudding feet.

'Ah, what an exciting Friday night,' says Kira.

Maeve snorts, despite herself.

'The glamorous life of a footballer,' Maeve replies.

Kira looks over and grins. 'No where else I'd rather be.'

Maeve doesn't know if she's being sarcastic, but she doubts it. She wonders if Kira, like her, has no life really, outside of this. Football always comes first. She wonders if Kira also sometimes wishes she had other things going on – more time to see friends, or family, or, God forbid, have a hobby. Maeve tries to remember when was the last time she read a book, or went to the cinema, let alone had a proper holiday. But Maeve can't ask Kira, that would be too friendly.

Instead, Maeve just asks, 'We're doing weak foot exercises this evening, right?'

'Mmm, Serena did say that, but I'm not so sure,' says Kira. 'In the friendly earlier, I thought our left feet were fine. Pretty good actually. I mean, I've always found it easier than most players, I've always been practically ambidextrous.'

'Ambidextrous is hands,' Maeve mutters. 'For feet it's ambi-pedal. Or two-footed.'

She hates that Kira gets to be so confident in her abilities, but it is, frankly, true. Kira's left and right are both as strong as each other.

'Oh whatever,' Kira shrugs. 'Who cares about the word as long as we can do it?'

'Well, I think we should do what Coach says,' says Maeve.

'Of course you do, teacher's pet.'

'*You're* the one who is Coach's pet.'

Kira raises an eyebrow, grinning. 'Jealous much?'

Maeve doesn't reply. Obviously she *is* jealous, not just of Kira's preferential treatment from Coach Hoffman, which come with its fears of losing her captaincy, but also of Kira having such a strong mentor relationship with anyone at all. Maeve has never had someone in an authority figure consistently rooting for her like that. She thinks guiltily of her mum, but that's not the same thing at all.

The reason Maeve and Kira hadn't met for training earlier this afternoon, for example, had been because Kira was having a one-to-one with Hoffman. And that was just seen as normal and natural for them both.

Maeve and Coach Fernandez had occasionally had additional check-ins, because of her role as club captain, along with Kevin and the other key members of the coaching team, but Maeve had admitted to Adriana she'd often found them demoralising. They made it painfully obvious that the women's football team wasn't as much as a priority for the club. She had often felt like the women's team were collateral to the paired men's team. They were only given resources as an afterthought from the men's. This wasn't only happening in the Tigresses' team of course. When the Manchester United men's training ground was being refurbished, the women were ousted and put in a portacabin to make way for them, for heaven's sake! How could they all improve at the rate of their full potential when they weren't given the chance? Women's football was getting bigger and bigger, and the Lionnesses winning a major tournament had helped a lot, but it often felt like progress was slow and hard-won.

It hadn't been officially said as much, but Maeve suspected that Mark Astor didn't care about buying the Tigresses, they'd just come as an 'extra' with the men's Tigers team, which is what he really wanted because of their rich heritage. Maybe that was why Jacob was here with the Tigresses – maybe his father was only bothered to be involved in the meetings of the Tigers. She wishes she could prove them all wrong single-handedly so that the team wouldn't be seen as second best anymore.

Maeve realises her shoulders have tightened and her pace gone erratic. She's getting distracted, needs to bring herself back to this evening's training. They find Kevin, who is leading their one-on-one tonight, but looks tired and only half-focused, glancing at his phone. Maeve wonders if he resents missing out on his Friday night.

'You'll be doing weak foot training tonight,' says Kevin, gesturing vaguely to a drill set-up. 'Dribble in an out of those using your left.'

'But Kevin, it's our last training for the week, and it *is* a Friday evening…' says Kira, perhaps noticing Kevin's heart isn't really in it. 'I think we should treat ourselves to finishing.'

'But you finished earlier,' argues Maeve. 'You scored in all of the drills.'

'Oh, I am always happy to finish again,' winks Kira.

A smirk is playing on Kira's lips and Maeve wonders if it's about her pleasure at scoring goals earlier or, like a teenage boy, at the everyday euphemisms of football terminology. Maeve rolls her eyes.

'Fine,' says Maeve. 'Kevin, would it be alright if we split the session? Do some weak foot training and then some scoring?'

'Wow, great negotiation, Murphy. Is that what you do as Captain? Give way to everyone's requests?'

Maeve clenches her jaw. She can't win with her. She tries not to let Kira get to her but Kira can wind her up whenever she wants. *That's* really what Maeve should really be working on in training – finding a way to block her out.

They do a weak foot exercise, dribbling in and out a set of six cones only using their weaker foot. They take it in turns, watching the other, commenting on the use of the front instep area to the inside of the foot to the outside and sole of your foot to go around the cones, moving the cones gradually closer and picking up speed to increase the difficulty. Kira is right, they're both pretty strong with their weaker foot, and even with their critical eyes on each other, there isn't much to pick up on for improvement tonight. So to increase the pressure, they then repeat the exercise but this time with the other player putting pressure on them. Kira dribbles and Maeve marks her, striking in for the ball with her own weak foot, working on their control. At first they're methodical about it, matching each other clinically.

'Alright,' says Kevin, reading from his script before scrolling on his phone again. 'Now, Kira, you stay on your weaker foot, but Maeve, you can use your stronger.'

'Fine,' Maeve brushes a stray hair from her forehead. Maeve is now able to get the ball from Kira's speedy feet more regularly, trying not to block it too hard so that they're not having to keep fetching, instead the challenge being to keep stealing it back from each other to be able to continue the drill.

'Okay, now make it more game conditions,' says Kevin. 'No cones, no lines, just Maeve on weak foot dribbling, Kira trying to get the ball from you.'

Maeve will obviously be at a disadvantage, and knows this means she'll have to take more of an ego bruising, but it is good for her to improve her ball control.

'Fine,' she says, begrudgingly.

But Maeve's also exhausted, and in her tiredness and relentless challenge from Kira, she starts getting frustrated, and in her frustration, gets clumsier in her tackles, mis-timing them or not winning the ball cleanly. So when Kira makes a particularly annoying move nutmegging her and is clearly about to shoot even though that isn't even the exercise, Maeve makes an aggressive tackle to stop her.

She overreaches, successfully knocking the ball from Kira's possession, but in doing so, loses balance and slides hard to the ground, nearly taking Kira down with her. She lands nastily on her already sore wrist.

Maeve glowers up, angry and bruised, wanting to vent her frustration. What is Kira doing, just staring at her?

'Wow, thanks for helping me up,' grumbles Maeve. 'Great team player.'

Kira rolls her eyes and with a sarcastic flourish, holds a hand out. 'Please, m'lady, how may I be of further service.'

Maeve ignores it and gets herself up alone. She winces a little and rolls her wrist to check it's okay. Maeve thinks she hid her reaction, but as they're putting the cones away Kira looks at her sideways.

'You hurt that wrist again?'

'Oh, like you care.'

Kira snorts. 'Come on, Murphy, I don't *actually* want my new team to fall apart upon my arrival, do I? That would be no good for my reputation either, if I join a team that does terribly in the league.'

Maeve realises she's been so obsessed about their rivalry for the captaincy that she hadn't really thought about this.

'I'm fine,' says Maeve, grumpily.

'Good.'

'Thanks so much!' says Maeve sarcastically.

Kira sighs. 'You really think I hate you, don't you?'

Maeve startles. She isn't used to people being so upfront and is caught off-guard by it, yet another thing about Kira that disarms her.

'Well… yeah,' shrugs Maeve. 'I mean, there's good reason. And that is… the general vibe you give off.'

'Well, I don't hate you,' Kira says softly. 'I actually find you very impressive. I'm glad to have a worthy opponent to practice with.'

Maeve is flustered and doesn't know how to respond. The thing is, she finds it reassuring to be able to be enemies with Kira because that's easier to channel her confusing strong feelings into. It's an outlet for her real complex feelings. So she tries to be sarcastic. 'I'm not your *opponent*, Choksi, I'm on your team.'

'Right. Maybe you should act like it sometime.'

Goddamit, how does Kira still manage to twist her way into winning the smallest and pettiest of fights between them? Maeve is even more begrudging now to follow Kira's suggestion and do finishing exercises instead of Coach's orders for weaker foot training, but annoyingly, she does think Kira is right. Kevin shrugs in agreement.

So they do some practice of Kira approaching goal. Maeve tries to block and tackle, but Kira's simply too good. She is relentlessly fast, bold, and confident, managing to escape Maeve's attempted blocks.

Maeve finds it both incredibly inspiring and painfully annoying. One after another, the balls hits the back of the net as she struggles to defend the goal by herself; and Kira, over and over, doing her stupid celebration, punching the air above her head and then in front, like a boxer, whooping with delight as if it's the first goal she'd ever scored.

'Oh get over it,' Maeve exhales, after she can't prevent yet another goal.

'Ha!' says Kira. 'Never!'

Maeve kicks frustratedly.

'You giving up?' Kira asks, in a mocking voice. 'Does baby want to finish early?'

'Don't call me baby,' says Maeve, with gritted teeth.

'Well, I think we're done here, baby,' Kira stretches her arms smugly. 'Kevin, shall we call it there? I can't keep watching Maeve lose forever. We'll pack up, go have a nice Friday.'

Kevin seems taken in by Kira's utter confidence, and perhaps he's influenced by the way Kira seems an extension of Coach. He heads off, already calling someone on his phone.

Maeve wishes she had a Matilda-like power to shoot lasers with her eyes and explode Kira's smug face. Kira is up in her personal space now, post-goal elation making her even cockier.

Maeve grabs up their training equipment and throws them into the store herself, and heads off to shower in the privacy of her secondfloor locker room. But Kira just follows her, still goading.

'Go on, say what you're thinking,' Kira tests her.

'What I'm really thinking?'

'Yeah.'

'Well, what I'm really thinking is that I wish your smug face would explode. Now fuck *off* and stop following me.'

'Ha! But the thing is, Murphy, I can't fuck off, can I? We're in a team together, we train together, we're going for the same goal, together…'

Maeve's so riled up that it's only when the door closes behind her and Kira leans confidently back on it, that Maeve realises Kira's followed her to what she still thinks of as her private shower room.

They study each other in a moment of silence, the only sound a light dripping of the shower and the whirring of an extractor fan.

Kira drops her training bag from her shoulder, and takes a slow, confident step towards Maeve.

'I also trust my instincts,' she says slowly. 'And my gut tells me that you really don't hate me as much as you're trying to pretend so hard you do.'

Maeve turns sharply away, trying to open her locker, but she can't undo her padlock because her hands are shaking. Just like she's been dreading, Kira has seen through her.

Maeve turns when she hears Kira's step behind her. Maeve's breathing is shallow and fast. Kira's so close now, and Maeve automatically steps back to maintain their distance – but her back lands against the hard and cold lockers. She can't move away.

Kira leans a hand over Maeve's head, and Maeve feels dizzy.

'If you tell me to stop, I'll stop,' Kira says softly, her voice barely above a whisper.

Maeve swallows.

'But I don't think you want me to stop, do you, Murphy?'

In all Maeve's conflicted feelings about Kira, about their rivalry, about her jealousy and admiration, lust and frustration, she hadn't ever contemplated what she would actually do if Kira wanted her too. Maeve feels the same charged tension between them as when they're on the pitch competing against each other, electricity in the air.

Their faces are very close now. She should know that Kira won't back down from a dare.

'You talk a big talk, don't you,' Maeve tries to sound confident. 'But you're all bark, no bite.'

'Oh, don't you worry,' says Kira, her voice low. 'I can bite.'

Kira's staring at Maeve's mouth. She instinctively wets her lip. And then Maeve leans in and kisses her.

Kira responds instantly, pressing her body into Maeve's pulling her face in closer to hers. Her mouth is warm and hungry, her lips soft but intense, their movements immediately matching each others' wanting.

All the thoughts that have been racing around Maeve's mind suddenly still. It's like when she's in full flow on the pitch, her focus completely honed to the game, moving in synchrony with her teammates, testing the limits of what her muscles can do. All she is aware of is Kira's body, so close, but not close enough.

Kira's as good a kisser as she is a football player. It would almost be annoying if Maeve weren't enjoying it so much.

Their bodies press into each other's, a tangle of limbs. Maeve's hands pull Kira closer into her, one hand clutching at Kira's back, the other stroking the back of her shaved head.

Kira's good on her word. Kira bites down on Maeve's lower lip. Maeve gasps in pleasure and faux indignation.

'Hey!' she says. Kira pulls back, eyebrow raised.

'Well, you did dare me.'

Kira's eyes sparkle. 'Where's that fighting spirit? Go on, I know you want to try to win.'

She's lit up even more brightly than when she's on the pitch. Maeve thought that playing football was Kira's natural habitat but now, she feels privy to seeing that really, it's this.

Maeve goes to kiss her again, and this time pays Kira back, biting her lip until Kira makes a gutteral sound in the back of her throat. Maeve desperately wants to hear her do that again. She kisses down her neck, grasping at her shoulders, her waist, her chest, her bum, tugging at Kira's training top.

Kira doesn't need telling twice – she whips her shirt off with the unabashed speed Maeve had noticed that first time she saw Kira, but this time, she gets to act upon her desire to stare, and lift off Kira's sports bra too.

Maeve takes in the view. Kira topless, her lithe shoulders look more muscular now they're bare, contrasted as they were with the softness of her small chest, her nipples like dark hickies, the colour of Kira's well-bitten lips. Kira has washboard abs, the kind that don't come naturally from training, even intense as theirs, but must be deliberately worked for. Over her abs are the loose string of her black sports shorts that Maeve had been tugging on so relentlessly when they were kissing, revealing the white waistband of what seem to be tight boxer-style pants.

Kira looks right back, biting her lip and, as if in exchange, pulling down at Maeve's sports shorts. At Maeve's eager nod, she slips them off, and then runs her fingers brazenly up the inside of Maeve's thigh, to the edges of Maeve's pants. Maeve feels momentarily embarrassed at how wet she is, this evidence exposing how much she's enjoying Kira's touch, but for once, Kira's cocky smile as she looks up at Maeve just elicits a smile from Maeve too. She's too turned on to deny it, and from the way Kira closes her eyes in pleasure as she pulls Maeve's pants aside, she knows that they're in this together.

Then they're kissing again, heavy and hot, while Kira's fingers are still making their firm, confident strokes and Maeve's unable to stop herself from moaning at how good it feels. The sensation of it all happening at once is overwhelming, like every part of her is on fire. Kira knows exactly what she's doing, she's there with her, her thumb on her clit, her fingers slick as they move up and down. Maeve can't stop herself from grinding into her, pressing herself harder against her, wanting Kira to fuck her.

Kira senses what she wants but seems to be playing with her, denying it, until Maeve groans.

Kira's mouth is against her ear. 'If you want it you'll have to ask nicely.'

Maeve moans in frustration and pleasure.

'Choksi—'

'Say please.'

Maeve melts.

'Please,' she says urgently. '*Please.*'

'Fuck.'

It feels so good that unbidden, Maeve's head flops back and smacks against the locker. She barely notices.

'You okay?' Kira, pauses with her fingers in exactly the right place.

'*Don't* stop,' says Maeve urgently, almost angrily.

Kira laughs, and Maeve finds Kira's other hand has snaked up to grip the back of her hair, between Maeve's and the locker, cushioning the blows as Kira's other hand stays between Maeve's legs. Maeve feels completely contained by her, held and gripped, daring to let her body be completely at someone else's command. Kira's breath fast on her neck.

'You can go harder,' Maeve pants. 'I can take it.'

It's Kira who groans in pleasure at that and takes up the challenge, until they're both crying out. And all too soon, the sensation is overwhelming, with Maeve clutching Kira's shoulders, her whole body tensing and releasing as she sees stars. It feels incredible to completely let go, like she's floating in a hot bath, like her blood is liquid gold.

Maeve goes weak in Kira's arms, waves still pulsing through her. Kira kisses her neck and gently strokes her hair and her back in slow calming motions that still keep Maeve turned on, even now.

Kira seems to sense as Maeve comes back to earth. She pulls back from the hug gently to look at her. Maeve blinks almost in surprise, like someone just told her incredible news. Kira stretches her hands over her head and exhales like she's just realised what they did. Then they both laugh. Kira's back to her usual smug self. She grins at Maeve.

'Turns out it was a pretty big Friday night after all.'

Kira's whole toned body is gleaming with sweat, and Maeve feels overcome with longing all over again. Maeve finds it almost unbearably frustrating that she hasn't taken those boxers off yet.

Maeve starts doing so, but Kira gently moves her hands away, kissing the top of her head.

Maeve feels silly suddenly, tugging on Kira's shorts with such desperation. Has she done something wrong?

'But I want to—Don't you want…?'

'Oh, I do, believe me. But I also just want to enjoy the satisfaction of a job well done. Another time. Give me something to look forward to through the weekend.'

Maeve feels destabilised, and doesn't know what to do, going from feeling lusciously confident to doubt creeping back in. She wants to go back to when they were two bodies, clearly wanting each other, instinctively knowing what the other wanted. Now, she feels thrown by the sudden end to their encounter. She rummages in the pile of clothes on the floor for her own shorts, putting them on to match Kira's. She doesn't bother putting her pants on, they're completely unwearable now and just rolls them up. Maeve starts reaching for her t-shirt, wondering what on earth she's meant to say next, getting in her head about it. *'Thanks?' 'That was incredible?' 'That was a mistake?' 'That felt so right?'*

'Hey,' says Kira, from behind her. Maeve turns to her shyly. Kira's gesturing with an arm. 'Come here.'

Maeve goes to her. Kira takes Maeve in her arms, and squeezes her in a warm hug. Maeve breathes out, her whole body relaxing again.

Kira leans them both back gently, so that they're both lying down on the wooden slats of the changing room bench. It's not comfortable, not at all, with the wood pressing into their bodies in odd unmanageable places. But Maeve nestles into Kira, a little bashfully. Her head is on Kira's toned bicep — frankly, too hard to be a comfortable pillow — until Kira seems to sense this and shrugs a little, so that Maeve's head falls into a softer part, her head on Kira's chest.

'I can't believe we're cuddling in here,' says Maeve.

Kira laughs.

'You didn't strike me as the type who would cuddle after...'

'Are you kidding me?' says Kira, sounding genuinely offended. 'You really *have* misunderstood me. Do you think I'm some kind of psychopath?'

Kira pulls her in more tightly so Maeve's face rests in the nook; and she feels their bodies relax into each other. It's strange, how this person who makes her feel so wound up can also make her so at ease.

Maeve wonders whether they're going to talk about it, what each other wants next. She would feel like a pathetic teenager if she were to say 'what are we?' after one heated encounter, and she wants to seem cool. Plus, Maeve doesn't even really know what she wants, except that she wants the captaincy, *and* she wants Kira. Even more so, now that she knows how incredible it feels to hook up with her. Her body shudders again at the thought of what they've just done. At the training ground. Where anyone might walk in.

'Sooo...' says Kira. 'We should talk about it, huh?'

Maeve laughs lightly, nodding her blushing face into Kira's shoulder. Her ex-girlfriend Hannah had always just left things unsaid, and Maeve had felt too paranoid and scared of messing up to bring it up herself either. It had taken Maeve's transfer to the Tigresses for Hannah to finally say that she didn't think their changing lifestyles would suit them and voicing what they'd both secretly been thinking for a while – that they weren't happy together anymore.

'Well,' says Kira. 'I can go first. That was really fucking hot.'

'Mmhmm,' agrees Maeve fervently.

'*And,*' says Kira, 'we've also got our careers to think about. I sense that you're like me, and your career is kind of, well, everything to you?'

Maeve nods into Kira's chest, worried about what's coming next.

Without even realising she's doing it, she starts tracing her hand down Kira's soft side, running her fingers over where her torso becomes her hips, over the lines of her abs, over the beautiful lines of her chest.

'Maeve—' Kira's voice strains. 'If you keep doing that I'm not going to be able to keep this conversation going.'

'Oops, sorry,' Maeve apologises, giggling.

'No you're not,' says Kira. Maeve loves hearing the smile in her voice, even when she can't see it.

Oh shit, she thinks. It would be very easy to actually… like Kira. Properly like her. She needs to be careful.

'Because the thing is, we both want the same thing—' says Kira.

Maeve tenses. Does Kira mean that she wants to date her?

'– to be Captain?'

The words are an unwelcome bump back down to earth.

Maeve sits quickly up, putting her t-shirt on, the embarrassment building inside her.

'Maeve. Maeve?'

Maeve can't cope right now, with what it does to her to hear her name in Kira's voice, when she's still there, sitting up on the bench, topless and confused.

Kira reaches a hand out, grabs for her more roughly. 'Murphy, come on! Talk to me!'

'What do you want me to say! You're right! We both want the same thing, there can only be one captain! So,' she shrugs angrily.

'So? So what?'

Maeve shakes her head, putting on her hoodie, her trackies over her shorts, remembering again that she's commando, the reasons why, the memory of Kira touching her. She forces herself to look at her, trying to pretend she's fine with what's just happened between them and it doesn't have to mean anything deep.

'I'll see you on Monday, okay? One-on-one training. Let's just… concentrate on our jobs. Maybe this– this side of things will… die down.'

'Is that what you want?' Kira asks, folding her arms.

'No!' Maeve wants to scream. *'Obviously what I want is for us to do that again, preferably right now, but if not, then in my bed, as soon as possible, when we can really take our time, and I can compete with you to make you feel as good as you made me!'*

But instead, Maeve swallows all her desires down, as she's used to doing, and just nods.

'I'll– I'll see you on Monday. I'm… I'm sorry.'

'What are you apologising for?' Kira calls after her.

But Maeve's already leaving, so that Kira doesn't see the emotion on her face.

Chapter 11

Adriana

Adriana taps her heel against the elegant leg of the cafe's table. Every time the door opens, something in her jolts and she lifts her head to naturally give a broad winning smile to the man who just entered. But it's not Jacob, just some dude now trying to smile back at her. She sighs and tosses her carefully conditioned hair, readjusts herself on the chair to reset.

It's now two minutes to midday, so he could be here any second. Jacob strikes her as someone who would be a stickler for being on time, so she made a concerted effort to arrive early. She wonders if there's an etiquette to arriving on time for a date, whether it's better to look more casual by being late. She doesn't know – she hasn't been on a 'date' since she was sixteen with her ex Dylan, and he was so insistent that they were 'casual' that it was only to go and make-out at the cinema.

She reminds herself it doesn't matter, because this is *not* a date. It's a business meeting.

It's a shame, really. Only because this is a perfect date location. Honey is a recently opened cafe which turns into a bar in the evening, and it's a little off the beaten track in the city centre, so there's no tourists or freelancers with laptops, only a few similarly clued-in couples sat on their high bar stools or soft low armchairs, sipping expertly brewed coffee from artisan hand-thrown ceramics. It has an intimate and understated atmosphere, with exposed brick walls and warm lighting, an oasis of well-tended luscious plants, and a few chic design details which nod to the symbols of the city – artwork depicts anatomical illustrations of 'worker bees' and the tables each have little unique vases with single red roses, connected to the symbolic rose of Lancaster.

Adriana knows this all because she's actually friends with the owner. She went to school with the daughter of the head pastry chef, Emily d'Montford, and their families have stayed friends – as Adriana tends to do. She came to their opening night with Maeve a few months ago and it had been such a fun evening. She got to try a sample of all the different pastries and espresso martini, and she had even taken a hot chef home with her, who she'd insisted on calling The Bear even though he was nowhere as intense as Jeremy Allen White's character in the TV show. He'd had incredible forearms, she remembered. He had been an ideal one-night stand. Hot, but she hadn't felt anything romantic for him.

The door opens again, and this time, her stomach lurches for good reason. Jacob's here.

Jacob's wearing a light brown bomber jacket over a simple but box-fresh white t-shirt, straight-cut chinos, and a thin gold chain which makes her think of Connell from *Normal People*. Adriana realises she's not seen Jacob in casual clothes before. But even though he's not wearing his customary shirt or tie, his clothes are of the intentional design and expensive fabric which hardly makes it look 'casual' either.

He looks so good, Adriana forgets to do her cute smile and wave. Instead, he casts his eyes round the room looking for her, attracting the curious looks of other women in the room. Adriana feels just a little smug that it's her that he's meeting, and sits up straighter, tossing her hair. His eyes find hers, and he smiles back. Adriana feels like she's in a parallel universe, where the two of them are simply a new couple, meeting for a second date in a cafe, pleased to see each other.

He walks slowly over to their little corner table.

'Hey!' says Adriana, finding herself flustered. 'You found it okay! Cute, right?'

She stands, not knowing whether they'll go for a hug, kiss, or even handshake. Jacob doesn't seem to know either. He stays standing, and pushes his glasses up his nose, his intense hazel eyes on her.

'So, Adriana, what do you want?'

Adriana flushes and gawps at him.

'Umm... Well... We can get straight to business then—'

'I meant, to drink,' he corrects her.

Adriana is mortified. She isn't used to being flustered around a man.

'Oh, it's okay,' she says. 'I'll— I can get my own.'

Jacob raises an eyebrow. 'If you prefer.'

He turns on his heel towards the front.

'Oh, but it's actually table service,' she calls.

'Oh,' he says.

He sits on one of the bar stools, though he's so tall that it's more like he's just leaning against it. He fidgets, not looking at her but over towards the counter, perhaps trying to catch the tender's eye as soon as possible. Well, this is awkward.

She looks over too.

The counter is piled with plump, flaky pain au chocolats, chunky cookies, and elegantly iced cupcakes. They, too, have designs featuring the shapes and colours of bees and roses, and Adriana finds them to be a deadly combination of delicious and adorable. Her favourite at the launch had been the honeycomb brownies, but she wonders if Jacob would judge her an inferior 'product' for the team if he saw her breaking her nutritional diet quite that emphatically.

Under Pappi, Adriana would sometimes defiantly ignore the nutritionist's recommendations, probably consuming too much alcohol and cheese for someone whose body is her job. Yet she's blessed with a constitution and metabolism which, at least for now, in her early twenties, means she can enjoy her favourite treats without ever worrying it will affect her game. Her view is that she plays better when she's happy than if she were to start resenting her training for restricting her life outside of it. Far better to be happy and keep things in balance, than miss out on a whole world of pleasure when she already gives so much for the game.

'Well, well, well, if it isn't my favourite customer!'

Adriana beams up at a welcome familiar face, who has bustled over to their table. 'Emily, how *are* you? It's looking so good in here! The dangling bee lamps are new, right?'

But Emily doesn't seem to care about the elegant lighting in her own cafe-bar — she's too busy ogling Jacob.

'Well, and aren't you a sight for sore eyes? Who is this handsome young man?'

Adriana is expecting Jacob to be standoffish, even snobby about Emily, but she's surprised that he smiles at her — properly *smiles* — and introduces himself.

'I'm Jacob. It's a beautiful place you have here, I'm glad Adriana suggested meeting here.'

'Oh *my*!' says Emily, fanning herself with her rose-patterned apron. 'Well, aren't you a gorgeous couple!' Emily steps back from them, forming edges with her fingers like they're a frame she's watching them both through. 'You look like you should be on the front of Vogue! And what do *you* do for work, Jacob?'

Jacob coughs, about to reply, but Emily seems to then forget she's asked a question.

'Oh, but for heaven's sake, you haven't come to chat to little old me, have you? What can I get you both? Addy, I seem to remember you're...' Emily clicks her fingers. 'A coconut milk mocha?'

'Bingo,' Addy smiles at her.

'And at the opening I saw you sneak a second of the honeycomb brownies. Can I get you one of those too?'

'Emily, you're the best.' She grins.

Adriana feels Jacob's eyes on her, and she wonders if he's judging her, just as she expected, for having such a sweet tooth. Defiantly, she decides she definitely *will* have the brownie. The sugar might take the edge off their awkwardness.

'And what about you, handsome?'

'A cortado, please.'

'Uh *huh*,' says Emily, wiggling her eyebrows, as if Jacob's order of coffee had been deeply euphemistic. 'And are you too serious for a pastry?'

Jacob chuckles. Chuckles!

'It would be rude not to. A croissant, please. For me, their simplicity is the best way to appreciate the skill of the baker. I have no doubt yours will be wonderful.'

'Oooh, I can see why she likes you!' Emily playfully nudges him with her elbow. 'Well done. You have triumphed where hundreds of men have failed! I've been trying to set her up with my most eligible bachelor friends for *years* but she has this whole stupid 'policy' of not dating, which includes never seeing a man in the light of day, especially at a precious weekend.'

'No, Emily, we're not–' Adriana tries to cut in to correct her before it gets more awkward, but her friend is a real yapper, and she doesn't seem to hear the warning in Adriana's voice.

'I mean, if you ask me, it's all a defense mechanism,' Emily carries on oblivious. 'Tale as old as time. Someone gets their heart broken once at a formative age, of course they're going to be wary of letting themselves fall in love again.'

'*Emily–*' Adriana tries again, mortified.

'And then of course, she has her work,' Emily says to Jacob, ignoring Adriana. 'It takes up so much of her life, her priorities, and that's marvellous, I mean, I know *that* feeling!' Emily gestures around. 'I respect a – what is it the kids are calling it? A "girl boss"? But it seems a shame, someone so overflowing full of love, holding herself back from romance.'

Adriana now realises it was the worst idea in the *world* to bring Jacob here.

Thankfully, an oven alarm starts beeping behind the counter, and Emily's ears prick up.

'I'll bring that all right over,' she says, and bustles off.

Adriana and Jacob are left alone. There's a beat of silence between them, only the sounds of others talking and the speakers playing light jazz.

'Oh God,' Adriana mutters, hiding behind her hair.

'Well, she seems nice,' says Jacob, and there's a lightness to his voice again, just like when they first met.

Adriana looks up at him, and they both start laughing. For a golden moment, Adriana feels her plan having *worked*. Here they are, ice thawed, and back to the ease between them.

They take each other in, finally relaxed.

Jacob has hung his jacket on the hook under the table, next to Adriana's denim jacket. Adriana can't stop noticing how broad his chest is, how toned he looks under his simple white t-shirt.

'I like your shirt,' Adriana blurts out without thinking.

Jacob raises an eyebrow, laughter still in his eyes.

'I like your dress,' he says.

It's just a simple compliment, and probably just a polite reply to her own, but it makes Adriana blush. His voice is low and husky, and as he says it, his eyes cast down her body, just for a moment. Of course, she had spent a long time deciding what to wear – she doesn't have anything that says 'business' in her wardrobe, and wearing a buttoned shirt felt like sacrilege on a Sunday, so she'd tried to go for 'smart casual' in a pinstripe cotton dress, her legs bare underneath even though the weather wasn't *quite* warm enough for it, and her favourite chunky platform sandals. She hoped Jacob wouldn't be someone who would notice that the bright red paint of her pedicure was now a little chipped and uneven.

Fortunately, Adriana's lack of witty riposte is hidden by Emily's return, carrying a wooden tray with their coffees and sweet treats.

'On the house, of course.'

'Oh, Emily, no, I insist–'

'No, *I* insist. Just remember me as your caterer for your wedding cake, hmm?' Emily winks, and hurries away, humming to herself.

Adriana watches as Jacob cuts his croissant neatly in half, separates them, and scrutinises the pastry layers. He nods like an appreciative connoisseur, and bites into one.

'*Mmm.*'

The moan is too much for Adriana. It reminds her too much of their night together. She should not find a man simply eating a delicious pastry *this* attractive.

'Emily must be a witch,' he says.

He sips his cortado, and Adriana sips her drink. It's like a liquified bounty bar. Ambrosia.

'Look, Adriana,' says Jacob, a twinkle in his eye. 'I think we may have misunderstood each other the other day. I want to make it clear that I'm not expecting you to give me any kind of information about your teammates–'

'Oh, but I can!' says Adriana excitedly. She pulls out a notebook from her tote bag.

She is very proud of this, and hopes it will impress Jacob too. She spent hours last night, when she was anticipating this meeting, listing out the best qualities of her teammates. And of course, Adriana has a lot to say on that subject.

She cracks the spine on the notebook.

'Who would you like me to start with?'

'You made a... list?' He pauses.

'Uh huh!'

'Of all your teammates' best and worst qualities?'

'Well... kind of.'

She hadn't written any of their worst qualities. In her mind, this was completely justified because she herself found it very easy to ignore these parts of them and it's a great chance to sing their praises and get Jacob onside.

'And that's really why you wanted to meet me? To read out your judgement of your colleagues? That's it?'

Adriana grins over at him, but Jacob's face has changed. His arms are folded, and it's far more now like a judge on *Dragon's Den* than a relaxed man on a date. He's stopped eating his croissant, its lovely pockets of buttery pastry forgotten on the plate between them.

Adriana's resolve wobbles. But then she remembers Maeve, her face twisted with anxiety on her sofa, fearing losing the position she'd worked so hard for, and *is truly* such a good fit for.

Adriana decides not to start with Maeve, in case that makes it too obvious that she's biased in favour of her own lifelong best friend. So she starts instead with someone she fears is on the axe list.

'First up, I wanted to describe the skills of Milo George. They joined us a year ago and sadly towards the end of last season got a grade two sprain on their ankle. They had five weeks off, and then returned to pre-season training the same week that the club was bought by you. Considering their time off, their recovery has been truly impressive. So, even though they have been, umm, on *paper* lower down on the tables in our drills, and were on the bench during the friendlies, they have real potential.'

Jacob's arms are still folded, and his face is unreadable. Adriana has a flash of her dream where the masks judge her, where she can't persuade them to smile for her.

She doesn't know what she was expecting, exactly. Maybe for Jacob to write things down too? To nod encouragingly? To pat her on the back and say she'd successfully persuaded him not to let go of anyone on the team after all?

She coughs and flicks the pages of her notebook. Maybe trying to start with the players in danger of being on the transfer list was the wrong tactic.

'Well, okay, how about, actually, we start with the players who are in contention for the captaincy? I think it's useful for me to say what, as a player, I think are the most vital qualities for a club captain?'

Jacob just raises an eyebrow.

'Well, *definitely* the *strongest* contender is current club captain, Maeve Murphy.'

'Murphy? With the blonde ponytail?'

'That's her,' says Adriana proudly.

'Isn't she *your* Maeve? Your "best friend in the whole wide world"? Your "ride or die, platonic love of your life, soul sister from another mister"?'

Adriana flushes. She doesn't know what is causing her embarrassment more — that Jacob is implying she's biased, or that he is quoting, word for word, what she said on their first date as she'd happily told him all about her. She hadn't thought he would remember anything she said. She hadn't realised he listened so well to her, even when they were flirting and drinking.

'I— that may be the case,' she says, trying to recover, 'but she is a rock-solid centre-back, consistent and respected by all on and off the pitch for her conscientiousness. She is never emotional or ruffled, just a dependable leader.'

Jacob takes a final sip of his cortado.

'Isn't Maeve Murphy the one who was sent off the training pitch for losing her cool with Kira Choksi?'

Adriana flinches. Shit, maybe Maeve's fears had been founded after all.

'Coach wanted to see more aggression from Maeve. So it shows she's excellent at following her instructions. And she's now doing extra training with Kira.'

'I'm aware of the coach's training regime, Adriana. I don't know why you seem to think I need *you* to tell me.'

'I— I just thought...'

Adriana looks down at her only partially nibbled brownie. She can't bring herself to answer. It had seemed to all make so much sense to her, only a few minutes ago. But now, she just feels her heart pounding in her chest, feeling hot under Jacob's piercing gaze and realises what a bad idea this was.

'Did you really invite me here just to say all that? To convince me to make Maeve Murphy the captain?'

Adriana looks at his face and can barely think straight. Could it be that she had just wanted to... have an excuse to see him?

'No, of course not,' she swallows. 'I have pages on everyone else too!'

She turns her notebook to another page, and without looking back at Jacob, launches into her rehearsed speech.

'Nat Basevi. The *definition* of a super sub. Just because she's often on the bench, doesn't make her any less necessary than players that get more game time. We need that burst of fresh energy in the second half, or if a player goes off with injury or–'

There's a scraping of a chair and rustling of fabric. Jacob has stood abruptly.

'What? Are you–'

'I've heard everything I need to hear. I was a fool.'

'But– but–' Adriana gapes.

He throws down a twenty pound note on their table. Adriana stands too, confused and disorientated, trying to hand it back to him, mainly to try to get him to stay.

'But I don't– Jacob, it's on the house, and–'

'If you wanted this to just be a business meeting, then shouldn't the boss pay?' he says icily.

He swings his jacket over his broad arms.

'I really thought you asked me here to… I thought you were struggling with our agreement to stay professional. I thought you had changed your mind about your feelings towards me, and that this was… a real date.' He shakes his head, tutting to himself. 'My mistake. I apologise.'

He abruptly strides to the exit.

'Jacob? Jacob!'

He holds a hand up to her, stopping her in her tracks to follow him. She sits back down and watches him leave. Adriana holds back tears. She can't believe she doesn't even have the appetite to finish her brownie.

'Oh, honey-bun.' Emily bustles over and puts a protective hand on her shoulder, and eyeing up their half-finished pastries. 'Lover's tiff?'

Adriana swallows, shakes her head and sniffs, but knows that it simply looks like she's in denial. The worst thing is – maybe she is.

Chapter 12

Maeve

On Monday morning, Maeve is nauseous with nerves. Under Coach's suggestions, Kira and Maeve had agreed to do some additional one-on-one alone, before the others join them for training, and Maeve's been building anxiety about it all weekend. It's just going to be her and Kira this morning, no coach to lighten the tension between them or force professionalism.

She's arrived at the facilities early, constantly smoothing her pristine ponytail. She even wore make-up this morning, taking extra care with the mascara she barely ever uses, plucking her eyebrows and nicking her legs when she'd shaved. But it's stupid that she cares, when, of course, it's not like they're going to ever kiss again. It's not like Kira will even look at her, now that Maeve so thoroughly stated their rivalry after Kira had literally *just* hooked up with her.

'Oh God,' Maeve mumbles aloud to herself, her stomach twisting again at the thought of what a mess she's made, as she approaches the entrance doors of the training facilities.

The worst of it is that she hasn't even been able to speak to Adriana about it.

This past weekend was the first weekend Maeve and Adriana hadn't seen each other at least once in *ages*. Months, probably. Usually the only reason they don't is if one of them is visiting their family or is on holiday, but even then, they'd be texting constantly, Adriana sending photos and Maeve a constant source of listening and calming her ups and downs of emotions. Now it's Maeve who needs the soothing, but Maeve found herself unable to bring herself to tell Adriana about what happened with Kira.

She tried, several times over the weekend, drafting different texts in her notes app, or her thumb hovering over calling her, or suggesting that they meet up for dinner instead because she did really want to tell her. But then her stomach would twist at the thought of all Adriana's questions, and her inevitable excitement about the prospect of Maeve and Kira as a 'thing' when that felt very much far from the case. Maybe that was what was really stopping Maeve – not the thought of Adriana judging her for hooking up with her new teammate and rival on the pitch, but the liability of Adriana letting slip to the rest of the team in her giddy excitement at the thought of Maeve and Kira getting 'officially together'.

Despite Adriana professing to not want 'love' herself, and that casual is the best and only kind of relationship she ever wants to be in, she always obsesses with her friends' love lives. It's always been particularly feral with Maeve, perhaps because it happens so rarely. Look at how Adriana behaved when she had the faintest hint that Kira and Maeve had a flirty energy that day – if she found out she had been right she would probably explode. Adriana wouldn't be able to stop herself from trying to get the two of them into a relationship, no matter how Maeve might protest that it wasn't like that, and there would be no faster route to interminable awkwardness between Maeve and Kira.

And God, what if Hoffman found out? Not only would it feel awkward, like a parent discovering sex toys in your drawer, but she would presumably stop encouraging them from having one-on-one training together, and their unprofessionalism could result in not only the captaincy being permanently taken away from Maeve but maybe her being put on the transfer list. Would Coach want to discourage her protegee getting distracted, and think moving Maeve on would be the easy solution?

So Maeve had decided to keep it to herself, just until she had the opportunity to confirm things were settled down between her and Kira. Once things were back to normal (whatever that meant), she could reveal it to Adriana casually, safe in the knowledge it was already over.

But, even though Maeve does believe this is the most sensible thing to do, it still doesn't feel good to keep something from her best friend. And she doesn't have anyone else she can confide in.

So now Maeve paces the foyer, sipping and biting her nails to the quick, because Kira is late, and she worries she might not show.

Maybe Kira doesn't care about it at all. Maybe she's a player, used to hooking up with strangers and leaving chaos in her wake. Maybe she genuinely has no fear of catching feelings and just sees it as another satisfying thing to do with bodies, like playing football. Maeve wishes she could be like that, care less about these things.

But the doors slide open, and there's Kira. Her short hair's messier than ever on top, and as Kira's amber eyes meet hers she pushes it back from her forehead with a breeziness at odds with Maeve's tension.

'Murphy.' She says coolly.

'Choksi.'

Maeve and Kira give each other a curt nod, as per their ritual, like nothing else at all happened between them since the last time they were alone together.

'Good weekend?' asks Kira.

Despite her pounding heart, Maeve tries to seem nonchalant as she scans her ID card into the gates.

'Mmm,' Maeve nods, not wanting to admit that she just spent the two days wracked with worry and looping footage of Kira playing international matches, pausing the screen when Kira's face was shown. 'You?'

'Eh,' shrugs Kira. 'It started off promisingly, but the weekend was a bit of a let down after what I got up to on Friday night.'

Maeve's ears flush scarlet in surprise. As they stride down the corridor side-by-side, Maeve's heart is racing.

'Oh yeah?' Maeve swallows. 'What was that then?'

'Well, I don't mean to be unprofessional,' says Kira, still with a poker face. 'I don't know how much your team share with each other about, you know, life outside the pitch.'

'Try me.'

'Well,' Kira lowers her voice and leans into Maeve. 'Basically, I hooked up with this incredible woman, and it was so hot I spent the whole weekend thinking about what else I'd like to do to her.'

Maeve makes an odd squeaking sound. Her flush is quickly spreading over her body.

'Really?' she says finally, her voice high pitched.

'Yeah,' Kira continues. 'Very vivid. But sadly my imagination couldn't live up to the real thing.'

They have got now to the doors of the team's changing room. Kira opens the door politely for Maeve.

'Do you… Do you think you'll see her again?' asks Maeve.

'I don't know,' shrugs Kira. 'I'd definitely like to, but, I guess we'll see if she—'

The doors close behind them, Maeve takes in that the room is empty, and in the same second, pushes Kira against it and kisses her, hard. Kira moans her agreement into her mouth. Maeve can feel her smiling even as she kisses her back.

'Thank God,' Kira mutters, pulling her in closer. Kira's hands run over Maeve's hair, her neck, her waist, and Maeve feels herself melting into her. One brain cell remains, however, bringing Maeve back to reality. Their teammates will be arriving in an hour, and she questions whether they should really be getting turned on when they're meant to be practicing together.

'Shouldn't we be training?' Maeve asks, staring at Kira's mouth.

'Who says we're not?' says Kira, seriously. 'I think there are a lot of transferable skills.'

Kira's thumb runs under Maeve's top, tracing circles on the soft of Maeve's side, making her shudder, and the one brain cell of resistance loses resolve.

'That is true,' says Maeve, as Kira kisses her neck. 'What is it you're meant to be practicing this morning?'

'I believe I'm working on my touch,' Kira runs her hands down Maeve's back, squeezing her bum.

'Maybe later,' says Maeve, and grasps both of Kira's wrists, pinning them behind Kira's back. Kira grins in pleasure.

'You're right,' she says. 'It's good for me to remember to use my whole body.'

Kira's leg slides between Maeve's, and Maeve presses herself harder against her. She's so turned on, she would happily stay doing this all morning, but she has other priorities.

'I believe that *I'm* meant to be practicing defensive clearing with head.'

'I *have* been thinking a lot about what your head game might be like,' Kira teases her.

'Oh have you?' says Maeve. 'Thank you for caring so much about my performance.'

Though there's a playfulness between them, it's also charged with a burning desire. It makes Maeve's nervousness melt away, and she feels instead the confidence and elation that she normally only gets on the pitch. Focus, intent, her body alive.

Maintaining eye contact, Maeve slowly and gracefully kneels down before Kira. Kira swallows and a moan escapes her throat before Maeve has even touched her.

Maeve lingeringly unknots the tie on Kira's shorts, and pulls them down to the ground. She looks up at Kira in her boxers, her hands still dutifully held behind her back.

It finally feels like Kira's completely at Maeve's control, like she'd wish she would be in their competitions.

But then Maeve's teasing at the band of Kira's boxers, using her fingers, her tongue, and Kira's moaning. She pulls down Kira's pants, football is the last thing on her mind.

'*Please* can I use my hands now?' whispers Kira. 'I need to feel you.'

'You only get one touch,' Maeve says, still kneeling. 'Use it wisely.'

Kira's hand reaches down into Maeve's hair, grasping the band of her ponytail, and twists deliciously hard. All thoughts of plotting or competition evaporate. Maeve is just lost in eating Kira out, wanting to make her lose some of that cool, wanting to draw out the sighs of pleasure that Kira had pulled from her.

Kira is panting, gripping her hair, and Maeve can tell she's close, and Maeve's both desperate to bring that for her, but also for the moment not to stop — when they hear noises on the other side of the door.

The chatter of the earliest teammates arriving and heading down the corridor, straight towards them.

Maeve looks up at Kira, her mouth wet, and for a second they just freeze.

'Jesus Christ,' Kira groans, looking like she wants to punch every single one of these early arrivals. Then their self-preservation action muscles kick in. Kira pulls up her pants and her shorts, lunging away from the door to one of the lockers. Meanwhile, Maeve has sprinted towards the sinks, and splashes her face thoroughly with cold water.

She still feels dazed when the door opens and Milo, Nat, Liv, and Adriana walk in.

They notice Kira first, and all hesitate still unsure about their new teammate. Kira's reputation as arrogant has clearly ruffled feathers and much as the team admire or indeed fear her on the pitch, they haven't had the opportunity to click with her socially. What Maeve might see as Kira working hard through their extra training hours has just been seen as Kira deliberately not making an effort to get to know the rest of the players.

Adriana is the only one to give her an attempt at cheeriness. 'Hey Kira! Good weekend?'

Kira keeps her face in her locker, slamming it shut, and heads towards the showers to cool off. Maeve can tell that Kira is just so bamboozled and sexually frustrated by the unfortunately timed interruption that she can barely focus, but the others don't know that.

'Jeesh, what is her problem?' Milo tuts.

'Let's give her the benefit of the doubt, guys,' says Adriana, and Maeve feels a rush of affection for her kind friend. 'Maybe she just woke up on the wrong side of bed this morning.'

'God, maybe she needs to get a new bed,' grumbles Milo. 'Seems like every morning is the wrong side for her.'

Maeve's stomach twists. She hates hearing anyone being talked badly of, it reminds her too much of being bullied herself when she was in school. The cool girls thought she was weird for being football obsessed, and maybe they could somehow sense that she was awkwardly closetted. But hearing Kira specifically being criticised feels a different level of sordid and complicated. Should she stand up for her? But if she did, then surely everyone would question why she's suddenly defending her supposed rival for the captaincy? And, if they're going to keep hooking up secretly like this, then it's a good idea to maintain that she doesn't like Kira either?

She *could* join in, start criticising Kira too, because that would be a good cover to hide her real feelings. But she can't bring herself to do that.

'Like, I get that she's a good player,' Milo says, begrudgingly, still loudly enough for their voice to carry. 'But whatever, we're *all* good players. She acts like she's too good for us, just because she's Hoffman's special baby, and—'

Maeve can't stand it anymore. Not really planning what she's doing, she slams her locker shut loudly and heads into the changing room. The others all spin round noticing her for the first time, and all look guilty — even Adriana.

'Good morning, team,' Maeve interrupts, loudly.

'Morning, Cap,' Nat and Liv acknowledge her. Adriana avoids her eye, and Milo goes uncharacteristically quiet.

Maeve still feels tense and alert as she walks by them all to fill her water bottle, wondering if she should say something more, but then not knowing which side she should take. At least she stopped Milo from saying more, she thinks. It was a good defensive move.

They all go about changing into their training kit silently.

It's only then that Maeve hears the shower turn on. Kira must have been close enough to hear the rest of the conversation.

Fortunately the tension in the room is cut short by the arrival of the rest of the team, and all their general chatter about their weekends, and talking about the upcoming fixture that week – their first of the new season, and first under Coach Hoffman.

Maeve remains on edge, waiting for Kira to return from the shower, feeling the same uncertainty as to their relationship as she'd started the morning. Will she be annoyed at her for not speaking up more in front of their teammates, or understand that she was trying to be secretive about their... relations?

'Choksi,' Maeve calls out, trying to sound casual, as the others have all filed out ahead. 'You coming?'

'I was very close,' Kira calls back. 'But unfortunately I got interrupted.'

Maeve flushes and heads out, unable to face her. She only hopes they'll get a chance to carry on what they were doing another time very soon.

⚽

On the pitch, Coach is stern as ever in her smart navy tracksuit, authoritative next to Kevin and the other assistant coaches who have just arrived, looking at Serena with admiration and more than a little fear.

'Good of you to join us, Kira,' says Hoffman.

Maeve's head jerks back to see Kira's jogged up behind them, her hair wet and forehead still creased.

'Thanks boss,' says Kira. Maeve would have said 'sorry', if she'd been late, but that's Kira's unshakeable confidence for you.

Maeve studies her face for signs of whether she's angry, upset, or maybe still horny (which Maeve would secretly like this to be the case), but Kira's just a mask of indifference, listening half-heartedly to Hoffman as she stretches her hamstrings.

'So, Tigresses,' Hoffman claps them to attention. 'Of course you all know that this week is a big one. On Saturday, you'll be playing your first fixture of the new season. Your first since the team's new ownership.'

Maeve stands up a little straighter. She can't believe that in all the excitement with Kira, she'd not realised how quickly the first game had come around.

'Now, it should be a comfortable start for us,' says Hoffman, tapping on her tablet. 'Home match against the Bristol Robins. They're expected to be mid to bottom half of the table, and from what I've seen of everyone in training, we should have more than enough to beat them comfortably. I want to start the season by making a statement.'

Her gaze flashes around, and Maeve can feel the team's anticipation growing. 'All eyes are going to be on us. Announce your arrival as who the Tigresses really are, under your new management. You need to show them all you're here to go all the way. Non-stop winners in a serious promotion push.'

Maeve wonders if this is the club's ambition, if they're going to be freshening up the squad with more comings and goings before the transfer window closes. When will the issue of club captain be settled?

Maeve finds her eyes drifting over Kira's hands, her long, dextrous fingers. She doesn't know if Kira notices, but Kira starts fiddling, her right hand lazily circling her thumb against her finger in a hypnotic motion which makes Maeve zone out entirely.

'Murphy? Choksi?'

Maeve snaps back to attention, terrified she's been caught lusting too overtly.

'How were this morning's drills?'

Maeve's mind goes blank. She looks over at Kira, wondering who will manage to reply first.

'Yeah, it was very productive,' says Kira, with an impressively straight face. 'I think we'll need a bit more time, in the future, just to get really good at finishing.'

Maeve feels the heat flare in her face and can't believe how bold Kira is. Maeve finds it incredibly hot, and she only wishes she could be so daring.

'Yes, I'm learning a lot from working with Kira,' Maeve speaks up. 'But I agree, I think practice will make perfect. A lot of practice.'

Kira shifts a little. Maeve wishes they were alone so that they could keep practicing right now. Hoffman looks between them, her silver eyes flashing.

'Is that so,' she says. Maeve worries for a brief second that Hoffman knows exactly what is going on between the two of them. She has a sudden memory of being in Football Academy, lying to cover that Adriana had been sneaking contraband alcohol the night before, on a very rare occasion that Maeve hadn't done what an authority figure had wanted of her. But now, as then, there had been a slight twinkle in the eye, as if even if they did know, they were glad Maeve wasn't being a rat, was loosening up a little.

'Good,' Hoffman nods. 'Well, keep at it then. Keep pushing each other harder.'

Maeve's ears go pink.

Then Hoffman turns away from them to give feedback to Elisa about her goalkeeping.

Kira flashes a wink to her across the team, and Maeve can't help grinning back. Is this what it is, to be naughty? To not play by the rules all the time? Maeve can suddenly see why people do it. She's learning a lot from Kira indeed — like how to prioritise her own pleasure, her own wants, how to be a bit selfish and ruthless every once in a while. It might be no bad thing for her game.

But even as she's feeling the elation she notices a face turned towards hers in the group. Adriana is staring at her. Maeve quickly stops smiling as her face reddens further. She wishes it wasn't so easy for Adriana to read her every thought.

She tries to concentrate on Kevin explaining the next drill, but finds her eyes sliding back to Kira's back, her hands, her bum...

When they're finally given a five-minute break to stretch, Maeve feels a tap on her shoulder.

'Hey stranger,' says Adriana.

'Hey!' says Maeve, feeling like she's been caught red handed. She throws her arms round Adriana in a big hug, trying to cover her weirdness but definitely, obviously, overcompensating.

'Someone's in a good mood this morning,' says Adriana, suspiciously, pulling back. 'Did something happen?'

'Oh, nothing, nothing of note! Just, you know! Excited for the new season! Glad to be playing football with my favourite people! As in, you! You, my favourite person!'

Adriana tilts her head, her red curls like question marks round her face.

'How– how was *your* weekend?' Maeve asks. Now Adriana is the one to look away.

'Oh, yeah, it was… it was fine.' She mumbles.

'What did you get up to?'

'Oh you know… not much…'

That attracts Maeve's attention. She studies her friend's frowning face. She looks different than usual, her sunniness dimmed. She's hiding something. Or maybe Maeve's just being paranoid.

'You didn't go out did you?' asks Maeve.

'No, no,' says Adriana, looking a bit grumpy at being suspected of doing so. 'I just, you know, went for coffee…'

'Where?'

Adriana bites her lip. 'At Honey. Emily's doing well. The wildest thing I did all weekend was eat half of one of her brownies.'

'Only half of your favourite brownie?' Maeve frowns. 'What natural disaster got in the way of you having the rest of it?'

Adriana shrugs. 'Just wasn't hungry I guess. Anyway, what about you, did you do anything wild?'

Kira jogs past them, and wipes her face with her t-shirt, revealing the abs Maeve had licked minutes earlier. Maeve can't help staring as she replies to Adriana.

'Nope, I didn't get up to much either. Not much at all.'

'So neither of us have anything to report,' Adriana says flatly.

'Nope,' says Maeve. 'Just... just football, I guess.'

There's an uncomfortable silence between them.

Then Charlie and Elisa come over and hug Adriana in greeting, and Maeve peels off from her. She feels a little relieved. If they'd spent any longer together, she would have worried Adriana might see the trace of Kira's hickies on her neck.

And so Maeve takes a breath to steady herself, and jogs over to where Kira is waiting for her, the string of her shorts still wonky and half-undone.

Chapter 13

Adriana

Adriana loves nothing more than hearing the home crowd cheering. It fills her blood with excitement and she hops from foot to foot, eyes darting towards the door, longing to be out there already, singing along with the chants, bringing her A-game, earning the fans's adoration.

Her family will be in the stands as always, wearing their replica kit emblazoned with SUMMERS on the back, and holding up a sign in a glowing gold sun saying 'IT'S SUMMER TIME'. Her parents have been making signs like this one for years now, and just thinking about it gives her a boost.

She feels her spirits lift for the first time in days. Life is good again now the season has kicked off and everything will go back to normal. They're going to win this match in dominant fashion, she's going to make sure of it.

Always aware of the moods of those around her, Adriana notices how her own enthusiasm is helping infect the others too. Charlie and Elisa are like her, always more excited than nervous before a game, and their giddiness leads to them doing some pre-match jigging together, to get themselves hyped. Others in the team are harder to lift, but it doesn't stop Adriana from trying. She's brought a spare Lucozade for Milo, who takes it with rare gratitude, and she gives Nat's shoulders a massage knowing she sometimes tenses up.

'Don't worry about me,' sighs Nat. 'I'm sure I'm going to be on the sub bench the whole time.'

'Subs are as vital a part of the team as anyone else,' Adriana reminds her with a smile. 'They can make or break! When the shit hits the fan, you're who we need the most to come and save the day!'

Nat gratefully pats her hand.

Coach Hoffman gives the team a final pep talk, restating what the team already know of the tactics for the game.

'Right from the first whistle, be aggressive and press. Don't give them time on the ball or their defenders a chance to recover. Kira, let's see you get your first goal for the team and occupy the centre-backs. Midfielders, I want clean, quick passing to play through them. Defenders, remember what we said about keeping your shape and Elisa I don't even want to see you challenged today.'

Elisa punches her goalkeeper gloves together in agreement. 'Yes Coach.'

'Remember what I've been saying this week,' Coach reminds them, arms folded. 'All eyes are going to be on you today, so bring your own highest level and start the season with a home win in style in front of the new owners.'

Adriana's stomach flips. She wonders if that means Jacob might be in the director's box. She's been surprised not to see him around the training ground this week, although after how she messed up last weekend at Honey, it's been a relief. She feels so confused still about how things were left between them, and wishes she could clear it up. She's even considered texting him, very out of character for her, and found his name saved from when they'd met at the bar, as '*Jacob NOT JAKE!! HOT!!*'

Adriana's chest feels tight all of a sudden, and she is grateful for the chanting from the crowd in the stands rousing her. She can't go back into that spiral right now, she doesn't want it messing with her otherwise sunny mood, or worse, affecting her performance.

It would make sense, for him to be in the crowd today, for their first proper fixture, wouldn't it? She starts wondering if her hair looks good today and then gets annoyed at herself. Firstly, of *course* it does, her hair always looks incredible. And secondly, it shouldn't *matter* if Jacob is in the crowd, except perhaps to be thinking about the squad and who might not be figuring in the club's plans moving forward. Adriana is confident she's been doing well in training – really well, actually – as long as she's on her game today, she isn't worried about herself being moved on. Unless Jacob really did have a specific axe to grind with her. She suddenly has a vivid mental image of Jacob, in an lumberjack's open flannel shirt, sharpening an axe, and chopping wood, sweatily, before coming over to her and—

'Oh, and one last thing,' Hoffman announces, pulling Adriana from her reverie. 'Kira, you'll be Captain for today's game. See you all for half-time, Tigresses.'

Hoffman says it like an afterthought, so it takes a moment for Adriana to register what she's said.

The team all look to Maeve and Kira, who happen to be standing close, their arms almost touching. They look just as surprised as each other, and Adriana watches as something passes between them. To her eyes, it doesn't seem like the look between rivals competing to be named Captain.

All the colour drains from Maeve's face, but she manages to nod respectfully at Coach before looking at the floor. The recent strangeness between Maeve and Adriana suddenly seems unimportant, as Adriana longs to be able to pause time and comfort her friend. She can tell she's having to work hard to keep her face impassive.

Kira does her two-fingered half-salute to Coach, looking like a rock star thanking her fans.

'Yes Coach.'

Then Kira claps her hands together, unintentionally mirroring her coach, and says, 'Okay everyone, you heard her. Let's go and show them how sharp our claws are.'

The team's cheers of agreement are somewhat half-hearted and confused because none of them expected Maeve to be stripped of the captaincy just before the first game. God, thinks Adriana, this last-minute destabilising could impact their playing if they don't all rally fast. Could this have been another of Coach's tests to see what they're made of? And another fear runs through Adriana — could it be her fault in some way, with her conversation with Jacob drawing negative attention to Maeve?

The most Adriana can do, as they all run out to the pitch, is to jog fast up to Maeve, and squeeze her hand, just once, as hard as she can so Maeve knows she's there for her. Maeve's quiet smile back is pained.

Adriana usually feels she was born for this moment – running out onto the pitch to roars of the crowd but today Maeve's sudden demotion and Adriana's concerns about Jacob being there have taken some of her earlier sweetness out of it. As she arrives onto the pitch, she looks eagerly for that flashing sunny sign to steady herself.

Thank God, there it is, a golden sun, dancing happily in her direction. Even if it weren't for the huge flashing sign, Adriana would be able to spot her family immediately from, not only their matching kits, but also their matching ginger hair, the same bright shade as her own (except for her dad's, which is now greying a little).

Unsurprisingly, her parents and her older brother Felix are stood waving enthusiastically next to Maeve's mum, Helena. She is the spitting image of Maeve, except that she wears more carefully applied make-up, has finely plucked eyebrows which give her a permanently critical expression, and her smiles, when they rarely come, are more strained. The closeness between the two families has developed from carsharing since the Academy days though it still seems that Helena holds herself a bit apart, even after all these years. Adriana has a moment of hoping that this year might be the year things thaw, and Helena and Maeve might join them for Christmas or something – but then her heart sinks. She's worried that not telling Maeve about Jacob is the start of them beginning to drift apart.

No, she shakes her head. She runs to Maeve, deliberately smiling at her and pointing towards their parents. Maeve looks more than a little surprised, her usual colour still not returned to her face. It's only then that Adriana sees her parents have made another sign – this time, for her friend. Her mum is trying to hand Helena one with a painted tigress wearing a pirate hat on the front of a ship. It says 'Captain of our team, Captain of our heart!'

Adriana grimaces as Maeve jogs into position, not looking over towards her mum in the stands as the captains are called up to the centre for the coin toss. Adriana feels foolishly responsible, though of course there's no way she could have predicted this sequence of events.

Adriana knows Georgia, the Captain of the Bristol Robins, from previously playing together through the years through national age groups, and they've even been on a couple of nights out together. Georgia looks surprised not to shake hands with Maeve but smiles at Kira. Kira doesn't smile back, just grips her hand in what looks like a hard, intimidating shake. So it's going to be like that – Kira's the kind of captain who isn't here to make friends, but asserts dominance from the off. Again Adriana can't help but wonder if this is a tactic encouraged by Coach to intimidate opponents before the whistle blows.

Kira calls the toss. Adriana watches the ref flip it, and the coin glint for a second in the sun, then be revealed on the back of his palm.

'Tigresses to kickoff!'

Kira punches the air, and leads them into a huddle before she takes her position on the halfway line with Adriana ready to kick off. Kira's confident, aggressive energy is infectious, and as the referee blows his whistle, Adriana feels fire in her veins, wanting that win to get their campaign off to a good start.

Kira as Captain seems to be a lucky charm after all.

Within the first five minutes of the game, she has scored a brilliant goal, a rocket to the top left corner. The crowd whoop almost in surprise, but Kira takes it in her stride – quite literally. Before another ten minutes are up, she's made another two attempts, always a real threat in front of goal.

Her boldness and confidence sets the Tigresses up for an aggressive game, inspiring the rest of the team to maintain their lead and push for a second goal to kill off the game. The Robins are on the back foot, rattled by the Tigresses constant pressing.

Adriana and Kira link up well together, along with Rebecca and Zuri out on the wings. Maeve barely touches the ball in the first half, not having to make a tackle as the Robins are never out of their own half.

Not long into the second half, Zuri scores a goal and it's 2-0 to the Tigresses. The match feels very much in their control. The team all highfive and lift her up, as she celebrates by blowing kisses up to the sky.

By the time the final whistle blows, the home team fans roar in celebration, impressed by their team's dominant performance today. Adriana squeals wildly and leads all her teammates into a huddle hug.

'We won! We won!'

Even Kira is brought into the huddle, previous hesitancies set aside in the elation of winning.

Kira leads them in shaking hands with the opposing team – her vibe is definitely more cocky and gloating than how

Maeve would be doing it but she's doing what's expected of her as captain all the same. Adriana goes down the line shaking their opponent's hands and enjoying briefly catching up with a few of the opposing players who she knows, promising going for drinks soon, asking how their families are doing, complimenting their games.

Adriana turns to the stand to wave again at her still-cheering family. She notices Maeve's mum has already left. But there's something about the flashing of the sun sign that catches her eye towards the technical area. She had been so caught up in the game that she hadn't noticed that Jacob has been in the director's box all along.

Adriana's heart leaps to her mouth. He's wearing a petrol blue suit with the jacket off, his tie remaining firmly tight up to his neck but his sleeves rolled up to show off his toned arms. Despite the jubilation on the pitch, his team having just won, he's watching with his arms folded, with even more intensity than usual. As Adriana watches, he leans to say something to an older man, unfamiliar to her – a colleague perhaps, or could it even be his father? Both men's eyes turn to look, it seems to Adriana, right at her. The smile freezes on her face. They don't seem happy, and she worries they're talking about her. She doesn't know exactly what she did to piss Jacob off – did she mess up that much by asking him for coffee? Although she didn't get on the scoresheet today, she ran the midfield well, so she can only hope that Jacob couldn't justify her being transferred to another club.

Adriana feels a hand gripping her shoulder, and turns to see Maeve next to her.

'Great game, Addy,' says Maeve.

'You too!' says Adriana fervently, to try to reassure her. But Maeve's thinking the same thing.

'Ha, I mean, I barely had anything to do with it.' Maeve tries to smile but it's a little forced, and makes her look more like her mum. 'It was a great game. Really aggressive and dominating possession, just like Coach wanted.'

'Do you know why she…?'

Maeve shakes her head ruefully, again trying and failing to brighten her expression. 'We didn't talk about who would be captain today, so I guess I just assumed I would stay. It was silly of me.'

'Do you think this is a… permanent choice?' Adriana asks tentatively.

Maeve swallows and can't seem to bring herself to answer, just shrugs.

'Anyway,' Maeve tries to compose herself. 'It *was* a great game. Choksi did… I suppose she did a good job of leading with the aggression Coach wanted.'

'I heard that,' says a voice behind them. 'Careful, Murphy, I'll start thinking you don't hate me.'

Amongst the cheering and hugging between the players, Kira has been standing right behind them, and Adriana wonders how long she's been hovering. Is she going mad or does she always seem to be close to Maeve?

'Hey Kira, you smashed it!' Adriana gives her a warm hug. 'That was an incredible goal! Right in the first five minutes!'

Kira seems surprised, and Adriana quickly pulls away, worried that Kira's not a hugger – as she loves hugs so much herself, she always forgets that some other people don't and maybe sometimes they think she's too much.

'It happened so fast!' Adriana rambles instead. 'When I played you in, you did such a great job to control it with just one touch!'

'Well,' Kira, glances at Maeve. 'I've been practicing my touch a lot recently.'

Maeve looks quickly away and if Adriana didn't know better she would think Maeve is blushing. There's definitely *something* between them and she's not sure why her best friend can't talk to her about it, whatever it is.

'Thanks, Adriana,' Kira turns back to her. 'You did a great job setting it up for me, honestly. I wouldn't have been able to score without you. Great game. I couldn't believe Coach just dropped me into being Captain like that for today's game, it was so—'

Maeve clenches her jaw and walks off abruptly, making some excuse about talking to Georgia. Adriana's heart sinks. It must look like she's too busy being pally with Kira, when Maeve's still hurting from losing the captaincy.

The team all head jubilantly back to the dressing room where Hoffman gives them a rare, if not broad, smile of approval. Adriana feels suddenly nervous because there, too, beside her, is Jacob.

His expression is still neutral, even among the cheers, like he's about to have a board meeting or something, not that his new team has just made a super strong debut. Adriana tries to catch his eye to see if he smiles, but he doesn't look at her at all, facing towards the other end of the huddle.

'Congratulations Tigresses,' says Hoffman. 'You played the game I hoped you would, executing our plans well. Zuri, that was a brilliant goal, well done. Kira, watch out for your spin.'

God, she is never happy! But Kira simply nods, as if this is something they've talked about a lot in the past and she's eager with the constructive criticism.

'And great control in the midfield too,' Hoffman continues. 'I'd like in particular to bring everyone's attention to Adriana.'

Adriana, who had been staring at Jacob's forearms, starts in surprise.

'She has responded brilliantly to our training, and this is exactly what I was talking about with midfielders leading the press. Excellent game playing from you today, Adriana. You're working well with Kira. I can see that you two can become a duo that other teams will fear going up against. Well done.'

Everyone claps.

Kira does a half-joking, half-serious, bow, accepting the credit for the goal. Adriana instead finds herself trying to laugh off the compliment. She doesn't like being singled out in a team sport, and feels particularly embarrassed with Jacob watching her, knowing even he won't be able to avoid looking at her while she's the centre of attention.

'Oh!' mumbles Adriana. 'Umm, thank you, but really, it was, it was a joint effort. Everyone had a great game.'

She can't bring herself to look up, even as her teammates applaud her, and she just waves for them to stop.

'Now. You'll notice that I am not alone here and our club director watched today's game,' says Hoffman. 'I know Jacob wants to say a few words so over to him.'

She gestures to him, inviting him to speak.

'I'd like to take the opportunity to congratulate you on today's victory in such comprehensive style, Tigresses,' says Jacob. His voice has a practiced authority to it, but Adriana wonders if underneath that there's a sense of him not really wanting to be there, perhaps more used to being behind the scenes than communicating directly. 'I know this has been a time of a lot of upheaval, so I'm very pleased to see that the changes Coach Hoffman has been making in the team are already improving your performance on the pitch. If there aren't any questions for me—?'

He says it in something of a hypothetical way, but Adriana feels it's her chance that she has to seize. Show she has their backs. And if it means Jacob will *have* to finally look at her, well, that's just a bonus. She coughs loudly, and the team all stare at her.

'Uh, Ja-Jacob? I believe I speak for everyone when I say that the thing we're most concerned about is further changes to the squad. I hope today showed what a great team we already are.'

She looks around for reassurance, and everyone nods along with her which gives her the confidence to go on.

'We were told that with this new phase of the team, there are going to be significant changes – we want to know, how will you be deciding which players you might want to move on, *if any*–' she adds, to try to plant the seed of that not being necessary especially after the way they performed today. 'And, also, how you're making decisions about who will be selected as captain on a permanent basis?'

Adriana hopes speaking out like this proves that she doesn't want their one-night stand to cause any awkwardness between them, and she's also putting the team's best interests first.

'I– I'm sure we all care a lot about doing good *business* for this club, you know? We— we are not, you know, only here to put in our all to this team for *one night*, and then to just be thrown out tomorrow.'

Jacob's eyebrows raise with surprise at her mention of 'one night', and she can tell he has understood that she's trying to refer to their fling, but unfortunately, she doesn't think she's made much sense beyond that. Think, Adriana, *think*!

'I just mean,' she improvises quickly, feeling like she's digging herself a hole. 'I'm sure all of us want to be here with this team for the long haul. Not just for the sake of our individual careers but because we care about the cohesion of the group. Many of us are very loyal to the Tigresses.'

Jacob frowns and makes a gesture of being about to answer that immediately shuts Adriana up.

'Thank you, Ms Summers, I hope I can set you more at ease in this matter,' he says.

'As club director, it's only the commercial side which is my concern. As for the role of the captain, it's true that I will have *some* say in this, as a captain has additional responsibilities off the pitch, such as forging new relationships with sponsorships. But Coach Hoffman is making her decision based on the necessities of the captain *on* the pitch. And, as long as I have faith that her choice will also be suitable for any of these responsibilities *off* the pitch, then I will see no need to interfere. I believe that Coach will be making her recommendations to me by the end of this month after another few games, where she can gather more information to make her final decision.'

He looks to her to confirm, and Hoffman nods back.

'I will be informing Jacob of my decisions in two weeks. If he accepts them, then the last stage will just be a majority vote from the team to confirm that you all trust my choices.'

'So we'll all get a chance to vote?' Adriana checks.

Hoffman grimaces a little, as if it is a shame that this is given such a spotlight. 'It's not a popularity contest. It's a vote that you agree with my decisions. I may ask a few of you for your opinions, if I see fit, but I am not expecting any resistance to my expertise.'

'Are there any other questions?'

Jacob's blue eyes pierce Adriana for a moment, and then turn very deliberately away from her to show they're done here.

No one else has anything to add.

'In that case, I would like to congratulate you all again on your brilliant result today, and to thank you for your hard work over pre-season. I've ordered a selection of pizzas for you all, which have just arrived, if you'd like to follow Kevin. Thank you all.'

And then Jacob turns, and heads off alone, as the rest of the team chat excitedly about their food, and how fit Jacob Astor is.

Adriana's stomach does somersaults. Unfortunately, she agrees with them. Jacob seems to get hotter every time she sees him; every time he becomes more off-limits.

When Adriana's at home that night, the elation of their victory wearing off, she finds herself sliding open her messages from Jacob yet again, the empty conversation between them. Adriana types out an impulsive message and sends it before she can stop herself.

```
Are you mad at me? I feel like I shouldn't
have said that earlier but I just don't know
what's going on between us x
```

She throws her phone across the room, immediately regretting what she's done. Then she rushes to pick it up and read it again to see if it's as bad as she fears. She sounds so desperate and clingy! She sounds deranged! And *why did she put a kiss?*

She spends the next hour pacing and madly cleaning her flat – scrubbing parts of her kitchen floor she's never scrubbed before. She notices that horrible blue tick that shows he's read her message, but not replied. Later she lies in bed, scrolling to distract herself, praying a message from him will pop up. But it never does.

Chapter 14

Maeve

Maeve doesn't have pizza with the rest of the team to celebrate their win. Instead, she finds herself in Waitrose on the hunt for something to cook for dinner that her mother won't turn her nose up at.

It's a good thing, the right choice, she tells herself, studying the bags of pasta in too-fun shapes. What with Maeve's tiredness after the game, and having the captaincy taken away from her unexpectedly like that, she's too worried she wouldn't be able to hide her feelings if she had stayed around the team much longer and doesn't want to put a downer on their good start to the season. Perhaps now is exactly the time she should be a stoic captain figure, reminding the team of what she can be for them – but she's simply feeling too sore. She couldn't even prove her prowess on the pitch, seeing as she had barely anything to do today. Kira, Adriana, and the other forwards were playing a brilliant aggressive game, just as Coach wanted, which meant the Tigress's goal never came under any serious threat. She should be pleased, she knows. But in this atmosphere of competition between all of them, especially Kira and Maeve, she can hardly be pleased to have no chance to prove herself while Kira gets to be the hero who opened the scoring and set the tone of their win.

She wishes some of her teammates had pleaded with her to stay longer, but they're used to Maeve bowing out early and without Adriana's usual insistence that she join them, the others all just let her quietly slip away.

She had wondered if Kira would try to stop her at least, even if in a way that was coded between the two of them. Try to corner her in a dark room... But no, Kira was way too high on scoring and having the rest of the team include her for the first time. It was like their hookups a few days ago had never happened.

Maeve shakes her head, and, tries to make an executive decision about dinner. She fancies some comforting pasta, but the last time she made that for her mum she spent the entire night googling the calorific content and repeating her shock that the Tigress's nutritionists don't forbid carbs.

'I bet the *Lionesses* don't eat spaghetti,' she'd said.

Adriana had used to recommend that Maeve go with Helena to a restaurant instead of cooking for her. When they were teenagers training in the Academy they sometimes dined out together after matches with Adriana's family. It had been such a stark contrast, Adriana's family all as loud and boisterous as she is, and having all grown up in Manchester they are all something like local celebrities – her mum a popular councillor for the Green party, her dad an estate agent who keeps in contact with all his clients (and had helped get Adriana and Maeve cheap deals on their flats), while her brother Felix is an actor who has been on TV, so there was nowhere they could go without being 'spotted'. Helena would never have explicitly *said* so, but she barely hid her disdain for the whole thing, as if she found the Summers' popularity somehow tacky. Maeve had found it so hard to navigate their differences, she'd started to make excuses on their behalf to avoid these meetings. It was better to contain her to her own home.

Maeve ends up with the ingredients for a warm salad: fancy giant couscous, the plumpest chickpeas, a rainbow of vegetables, and a tahini and lemon dressing. Her mother only drinks cold Chardonnay – by the bottles. Maeve checks the list she's surreptitiously made of the bottles in her mother's house, so that she gets one she knows she likes. She feels pleased with herself.

She rushes home in time to have prepped and have the food in the oven when Helena arrives.

Helena doesn't say hello or hug her daughter. It's been drizzling a little this evening, and Helena makes a big show of being *drenched* – though she'd been in a taxi, and had an umbrella.

'Ohhf,' she shivers, drawing her cashmere cardigan closer around her boney shoulders. 'Do you not have any heating in this flat? You'd think with how extortionate the rent is that you're paying to these landlords that they'd at least provide working heating.'

Maeve hangs her mother's coat carefully above the radiator.

'Would you prefer a hot drink first, rather than wine, to warm up?' she asks her.

'Tea? With dinner? No, darling!' Helena laughs like it's the most bizarre thing Maeve could have said.

'Well, dinner should be ready in just a few minutes,' says Maeve, feeling she's doing everything wrong.

'Goodness, like a fast food diner! Trying to rush me out?'

Her mother looks round at the flat, wiping a finger over the top of a nearby bookcase, searching for dust. Maeve, having known her mother would do this, has pre-emptively dusted. When Helena can't find any dust there, Maeve looks away hiding a smug satisfaction that Kira herself would be proud of.

Maeve's chest aches suddenly at the thought of Kira, and a longing that she wishes she was here. What a stupid thing to think – to have yet another person Maeve finds difficult having dinner with her? Someone else to criticise everything Maeve does? But Kira is so different to her mother. Kira is so obnoxiously upfront, so open with what she wants, her confidence in herself not being threatened by others. However confused Maeve might be about her own complicated feelings to Kira, her certainty and chemistry make Maeve feel completely opposite to the doubt and coldness she feels around her mother.

'You didn't tell me that you're no longer captain,' Helena grumbles. Maeve closes her eyes by the fridge, having known this would come up. 'Well, you can't hide it anymore. How did you lose it? What did you do to mess it up?'

Maeve pours her mother's wine, taking the opportunity to keep her face hidden.

'It's the new coach, mum. It wasn't up to me. I didn't know until today. I don't know if it's a permanent decision or not.' She tries to keep her voice steady.

'Gosh, there's an awful lot you "don't know" considering it's *your* job. What *do* you know?'

Maeve hands her mother the wine, attempting to keep her face neutral. 'They're going to name the permanent captain by the end of the month,' she says. 'I'll tell you what happens.'

'Oh yes you will,' says Helena. 'You'll tell me when *you* are confirmed as Captain.'

Maeve nods. 'I'll do my best.'

While Maeve plates up their food, Helena talks about all Maeve's mistakes from the game, as if she is a professional coach. Helena has been involved in Maeve's football career enough to have picked up the basics, but she never really 'got' the game, so Maeve allows herself to ignore her mother's relentless attempts to backseat coach.

They sit down to eat at Maeve's small two-seater table.

'Well, that's quite enough work chat,' says Helena, as if it was Maeve who was going on about it.

Helena pointedly holds up their wine glasses to toast. It's one of the few times the two of them make eye contact. Maeve finds her mother's light grey eyes a little uncanny. They're so similar in colour to her own. It feels like one of the only things they share.

Helena asks after Adriana, and Maeve replies evasively. It's not that she thinks her mother would particularly care about her longest-standing friendship, unless it would impact Maeve's stats, but more that Maeve thinks she might cry if she were to start talking about her. The truth is that Maeve has been feeling more and more distant from her friend and the one good constant in her life, not understanding why this distance has crept in between them. The secret she's keeping about Kira must be poisoning their relationship far more than she'd ever want it to.

COUPLE GOALS

'Did you know couscous is pasta?' says Helena. She picks at the vegetables, carefully scraping the dots of couscous off. 'They market it like it's a health food, a grain or something, but no, it's just pasta in blobs.'

Maeve puts her fork down, sips her small glass of wine in silence.

Her mother has always been like this. Perfectionist, brittle, always needing to be right. It has clearly worked for her, in her career as a lawyer — though since Maeve moved to Manchester when she was a teenager, Helena became more of a freelance consultant, working with other legal firms to advise on how to cut costs and make redundancies. 'Everyone is replaceable,' was a common phrase Maeve would hear growing up. It had gained added bitterness when Maeve's father had left for another woman. Helena forbid Maeve from staying in touch with him, though young Maeve had experienced this as her father not wanting to stay in touch with her anymore. Replaceable. Now she tries not to think of him at all, as if even remembering him would be betraying her mum, and herself. It's hard though, especially as he was the person who introduced her to football.

It was her dad who first took her to a match. Sat on his shoulders, she had felt like she was flying on a cloud of cheers. She begged and begged to go back.

So then they used to watch the TV together when Helena was at work, Maeve cuddled up on her father's lap, loving the way they could roar raucously with approval when a goal was scored, or that she would see him cry or shout when they lost. You were allowed to be emotional about football.

They would have kickabouts in their garden, and Maeve took to it. Her mother couldn't understand why her daughter wanted to get dirty kicking a ball around like a boy.

When Maeve's father left, Helena would probably have succeeded in squashing the football out of her too, if it hadn't been for Maeve's PE teachers. She had been spotted practicing keepie-uppies at break-time, the ball like a magnet to her foot, drawing the attention and wonder of her classmates, who otherwise treated Maeve like she was invisible. There wasn't the option of football for girls at that school, but when it became obvious that Maeve was better than any of the boys her age, they'd made the team 'mixed' to help the school do better in local competitions. Helena had found it scandalous at first, but had been persuaded when she had been told that Maeve was the best in her year group, and could soon be playing competitively for the county. If she worked hard, she might be able to earn a sports scholarship to a top university. This captured Helena's imagination, and soon football, which had been Maeve's escape outlet, and way to remember her father, became her daily exam in which she constantly had to prove herself.

'You must work harder, Maeve,' Helena reminds her now, out of nowhere and Maeve tenses up. 'I didn't sacrifice everything in order for you to be half-hearted about your commitments. I hate to see you neglecting your potential.'

As if Maeve hadn't been trying! As if Maeve had asked to be stripped of the captaincy in such humiliating fashion in front of her teammates right before a game. Maeve pushes her own bowl away. She has no appetite.

Helena takes this as a sign to clear the table, taking their bowls somewhat passive aggressively, and then scraping Maeve's still-warm food into the bin.

Helena collects her coat and swings it round her shoulders. She clasps Maeve's shoulders and kisses her on the forehead.

'I have every faith in you, darling. You can do it. Make me proud.'

Chapter 15

Adriana

The day after a game the team don't usually have training, but Adriana wakes feeling blurry, flicking her phone screen, on and off, on and off again. No message from Jacob.

'Urgh,' she groans, burying her face under one of her many soft sofa cushions.

She sees that a few of the team have messaged and are going in to the ground today for some light recovery at the gym. Adriana normally wouldn't, preferring to balance work with rest, but today she wants a distraction. She heads there with less pep in her step than she'd normally have the day after a win. Before getting to the dressing room, she checks her phone yet again.

She knows that if someone had messaged her, the screen would light up, but maybe *this* time it will somehow refresh it to the answer she wants? What answer *does* she want?

Then, as she's putting her things down, her phone lights up. She sprints over to it.

But it's just an instagram notification. Elisa posting a picture of their gang celebrating after the game. Adriana hearts it, smiling genuinely back at their posing faces, Adriana with her tongue out in her classic photo face, Charlie caught comically off guard and Elisa doing a full blue steel — no wonder she was the one posting it, her jawline looks *sharp*.

Adriana looks back at the slice of pizza in her hand. It was nice of Jacob to order those in, right? Maybe she should have thanked him… Shit, she definitely should have thanked him. Is that a good reason to message again? *No*, she cannot double message, not when he's blue double-ticked her. *Urgh*.

After a bit of stretching and gentle cardio with Charlie and Elisa, Adriana checks her phone again, and when she still has no answer from him, she starts to think — what if he gave her the wrong number? She shakes her head, then opens up her chat with Maeve, which has been so much quieter than usual. She considers yet again whether to tell Maeve everything. She wishes she was here today — Maeve is usually up for any opportunity to be practicing more, but she is probably even now having extra training with Kira. Maeve probably can't stand the sight of Kira now she's got the armband instead of her. Adriana feels suddenly selfish, missing her friend. It's Maeve who had a more disappointing and surprising day yesterday, and, if she knows Helena at all, Maeve probably had to then deal with a drilling from her mum after the game.

In comparison, Adriana is getting on unexpectedly well under Coach Hoffman's firm hand, thriving under the pressure and attention rather than hardening or petrified with it, like Maeve seems to be. Coach even singled her out after the game yesterday — and she should be glowing with the memory, but instead it just makes her feel a bit disloyal. She feels the team breaking apart. She wants to do something about it, but that's what the whole Jacob message was about, and then here she is, back to the start of the spiral...

She sighs and rolls her ankles, tries to push everything out of her mind.

Her phone lights up again. She barely glances at it now, having exhausted herself with her spiralling.

It's a text from *Jacob NOT JAKE!! HOT!!'*

Her stomach backflips, and instinctively, like a cat with a cucumber, she throws her phone into her locker and slams the door behind it.

'Jesus Christ!' Milo startles next to her. 'What did that locker do to you?'

'Sorry, sorry,' says Adriana. 'Thought I... saw a spider.'

'I bet you amputated several of its legs with that.'

Adriana gingerly opens her locker back up, and, her heart pounding wildly, she opens the message from Jacob not even attempting to play it cool.

Adriana, you have made it very clear that nothing is, ever was, or ever will happen between us. It was always going to be limited to one night, even when we didn't know each other, and that is why, as we discussed, it does not seem necessary for anyone else to know. I assure you that it will not impact your job in any way, positive or negative. I would appreciate it if you could stop bringing it up as I don't enjoy being reminded of the situation.

Adriana reads it three times, her throat tightening up.

She had tried her best to reach out, and to smooth things over, and he clearly doesn't care *at all*. It's humiliating. It's patronising. It's... devastating.

It's an unfamiliar feeling rising up inside her but she feels on the verge of tears. The possibility of anything happening with Jacob is slipping – if it hasn't completely slipped already – through her fingers.

'*Stop bringing it up*', he says. He may as well be telling her never to speak to him again.

She knows he isn't going to be at the grounds today, an email from Kevin this morning happened to mention that Jacob Astor was going to be at sponsorship meetings in London next week so he's likely travelling down ready for those. Her chest feels sore. She rubs her sternum, thinking she maybe pulled a muscle or something. But no, it's only when she thinks about Jacob, and him not being there, that it aches. What is this? Does she... *miss* him?

But that would be crazy. She hardly knows him, and what she *does* know of him, is that he decidedly doesn't like her. She isn't meant to *miss* a man. Not a man who was meant to be a one-night stand and who has been very standoffish with her ever since.

'Hey,' says a quiet voice behind her. 'You alright?'

Adriana turns round to find Kira, studying her.

'Yeah, yeah, hundred per cent,' Adriana lies, faking a quick smile.

Kira doesn't look convinced, but also seems to know, whether out of not caring or out of consideration that Adriana doesn't want to talk about it, so doesn't push it.

'Just- just tired from yesterday, probably,' says Adriana, performing a self-deprecating eye roll. 'Maeve's probably going to remind me I should be more professional and eat better. Again.'

Kira just watches her, and Adriana feels like she can tell Adriana's lying, but leaves it. Kira seems to hesitate for a moment, then takes a breath and is back to her usual confident self. 'Well, that's a shame, 'cos I was gonna suggest we go out sometime. Next week, maybe. Between matches.'

Adriana perks up. She turns to face Kira properly, and tilts her head, her curls bouncing hopefully. 'Tell me more.'

Kira grins that wolfish smile, knowing her arrow has hit its target.

'I haven't seen much of Manchester's night life since moving here. You seem like someone who knows which places are decent.'

Adriana swells with pride. It's great to be seen, to be appreciated, for one's special skills.

'There's a night called like, Joust?' Kira ventures. 'At–'

'At The Basement! Yes!'

Adriana is impressed, it took her years of going out with her edgier friends to find out about Joust. Adriana is usually down for a night out, but right now? With the painful churning from Jacob's message, and Maeve's distance, and all the chaos going on in the team? It's *perfect*. It's necessary. It's life-changing.

'I am *so down*,' Adriana grins. 'I already know what I'll wear. We can do pre-drinks at mine, and then anyone who wants to can come *out* out with us afterwards.'

'Sick,' says Kira. 'Something to look forward to.'

But then Kira looks away from Adriana, coughs, a flicker of hesitation.

'I get if people don't really go out much on the team. It wouldn't have to be a wild one. But I guess I just thought, it'd be cool to try to, you know, hang out with everyone when there isn't a football between us… Do you think there's anyone else on the team who would wanna come too?'

Adriana realises what's happening here. Kira doesn't have the same fearlessness socially as she does on the pitch. She's come to Adriana as the expert in such matters.

'Oh, *absolutely*,' Adriana tells her. 'Everyone *thinks* they don't like going out, but then always has the best time. They just need a leader to follow! Leave it to me. We're going to get *everyone* there, whether we need to bribe or kidnap them first.'

Without waiting another second, she calls out loudly to the gym.

'Everyone! Tigresses social at Joust! After next weekend's match! Be there or be sad to have missed it forever!'

There's a cheer from the room, various levels of enthusiasm or groaning based on the player's usual willingness to dance to techno, but Adriana knows from experience that they'll be there, especially if they win next weekend's game as she hopes they will.

'Give me your number,' Adriana holds out her phone to Kira. 'Oh my God, are you on the Tigresses' group chat yet? I'm so sorry, that's my bad, I totally forgot.'

'No stress,' Kira shrugs, handing it over for Adriana to type her number in. Adriana is about to add Maeve when she remembers about Kira and Maeve's weird vibe and hesitates. Maybe she should talk to Maeve about it before she puts her on the group chat, in case Maeve doesn't want to be pressured into coming? But maybe things have changed between them? They need to get along better stat – it's the start of a long season and there's no space to have tension between teammates.

'How's Maeve this morning?' Adriana asks, trying to sound casual, as she types. 'Is she showering in her secret chamber or something?'

Kira blinks rapidly. 'I was going to ask you the same. I thought she'd have taken any chance to be training more.'

'Oh, I assumed she was training with you.'

'Nope… we haven't arranged our next one yet.'

Kira coughs and looks a bit shifty.

Adriana can't put her finger on it. Why would Kira be worried about Maeve? Maybe it's just that Kira feels awkward about how the captaincy was handled, especially if she also wants to be closer to the rest of the team.

'I guess she's mad with me about the captain thing,' Kira shrugs. 'Fair enough I guess. But I– It's not like it's up to me– not like I would, what, say at the beginning of the match, oh, no thanks Serena, I'm actually just going to let this other woman be Captain because she and I are–'

Kira clenches her jaw.

Adriana is about to ask more, when she sees across the room the door open and Maeve come through. She looks like… absolute hell. Her hair is wispily falling out of her usually pristine ponytail, and she's out of breath like she ran the whole way here, which is crazy, because often she *does* run the whole way from her nearby flat and doesn't skip a beat.

At the sight of Adriana and Kira stood so close and Adriana holding Kira's phone, Maeve puts her stuff in a locker as far away from the two of them as she can. Despite trying to make things better, yet again Adriana feels like she's made them worse.

Maeve throws her stuff into the locker, then slams it shut and heads out.

'Jesus Christ!' says Milo. 'Why does everyone have a vendetta against lockers this morning?'

Chapter 16

Maeve

After Maeve's mum had left last night, Maeve had stayed rigid and still on her kitchen chair staring into space, her mother's words echoing in her mind and feeling their heaviness sinking deep in her stomach.

Then she got to work, determined to prove herself. She'd made herself a coffee from her machine even though she knew it was a bad idea to have caffeine at that late hour.

Kira must have been plotting with Coach behind Maeve's back, she decided. She must have said or done something to prompt getting the captaincy yesterday before the game and Maeve needed to emulate that killer instinct to win it back.

She had sat at her small, dusty desk, the office chair squeaking from under-use with her double espresso and opened up a blank spreadsheet on her laptop. She needed some way to feel aware of and in control of how she is being ranked next to Kira. She knew Coach Hoffman was always recording their stats, so maybe Maeve should be doing the same. If she monitored her performance against Kira's, she could see where she needs to improve to get that captaincy.

She had inputted any data she could remember from hers and Kira's training, all the goals scored by Kira or saved by Maeve, times one of them was faster or slower in drills, and times they have acted as captain. She could remember it all fluently, like she'd been revising for this exam without realising it.

It didn't help that each time she added a column for the day of the training, she'd had vivid flashbacks to what she and Kira had done during their one-on-ones. She remembered Kira's hands, her legs, her neck, her sweat, her mouth, her tongue. She could have had a much better evening writing a chart of all the ways they had touched each other, the unexpected and terrifying moments of closeness she had felt, in those brief, hot hookups.

Maeve had felt herself getting distracted and annoyingly turned on, then rallied herself back to her task.

She didn't need to have any fancy formulas to see that, as far as the stats are concerned, Kira was in the lead. Way in the lead. If only she'd had more of a chance to prove herself in their first fixture, though she knew she should have been pleased that her opponents barely made it past the midfield and never really threatened goal.

Flashes of Kira celebrating on the pitch, and Kira kneeling before her, and Kira shaking hands with the other team's captain, and Kira taking Maeve's own hand in hers, Maeve's fingers in Kira's mouth raced through her mind.

Maeve had put her head in her hands. It felt like there wasn't a way out. Kira was going to win, and Maeve was going to fail, and everything Maeve had worked so hard for

for her whole career was going to fail. If she wasn't the best in the team, then she wouldn't be captain, let alone having a chance of getting promoted with the Tigresses, or a WSL club coming in for her. What if she has already peaked? What would her mum say then?

Then the speech that Jacob Astor had made floated back into Maeve's mind. Being a captain wasn't just about performance on the pitch. He'd said that he trusted Coach, so it was going to be more about who *she* recommended than anything else – that was going to be hard to undo when Kira was so obviously Hoffman's favourite, built up from years of Kira being her protegee and working with her at their previous club. But Jacob had also said the captain would have additional responsibilities. Well, she was proving she was more than willing to do anything, if only Coach seemed to care about her being more on time for training than Kira. And lastly, the team would have to vote on their agreement.

Maeve typed out three possible modes of attack:

```
1. Outplay Kira - unlikely
2. Convince Coach that Maeve is a better
   captain than Kira - unlikely
3. Convince the rest of the team that she
   is best for captain - ...?
```

Maeve had stared at the last one for a while. She *thought* she was liked and respected as Captain by the rest of her teammates, but it's not as if anyone had exactly given her a feedback form. She also worried that her approach of being a solid, safe pair of hands wasn't exactly the most rallying cry for support. She'd always worried she was most connected to the rest of the team through her friendship with Adriana – the friendship which Maeve knew had been disorientingly wobbly recently. Maeve blamed herself, that hiding her confusing relationship with Kira from Adriana was causing them to drift apart. But it wasn't that Maeve thinks the rest of the team *dislike* her without being Adriana's best friend. Maeve doesn't tend to rub people up the wrong way – unlike cocky, insensitive, stranger Kira.

It had been about 2 a.m. when Maeve had looked at the blinking cursor, and had a brain wave.

```
4. Convince the rest of the team that Kira
   is not suitable for captain - possible.
```

But when she arrives at training, Maeve's master plan doesn't get off to a good start.

She hears Adriana laughing at some joke Kira said under her breath, and fumes. Not content with taking her captaincy, was Kira trying to steal away Maeve's best friend too?

'Hey,' Kira claps too hard on Maeve's shoulder. 'Didn't hear from you all weekend. We haven't organised our next one-on-one session, Murphy. What happened to you being a teacher's pet?'

Maeve winces. She makes sure only Kira will hear.

'It's not like we'd have been training anyway,' she mutters. But Kira doesn't even fumble.

'So, you decided to give up?' Kira asks carelessly. 'Thanks for making my job even easier.'

Maeve snaps. She whirls around.

'Do you have to be such a dickhead?'

Kira blinks in surprise.

'Woah. I thought I was meant to be the fiery one.' She laughs.

Maeve grits her teeth. She's meant to be making Kira seem unlikeable to the team, not being awful herself. But when Maeve herself is always so terrified of not being good enough, Kira's relentless self-assurance rubs her up the wrong way.

'You know, I do know of a few good ways to relieve stress,' Kira stretches her lithe arms over her head, the muscles of her arms flexing.

Maeve catches her golden eyes, and for a moment, all she wants is to say yes. To hook up in their secret shower room. To be able to flirt lightly back, casual, unaffected. If only she could be like that. But Maeve must remember what's *more* important in life. She can't let a confusing crush sabotage her entire career.

Instead, Maeve shakes her head, and spends the rest of the recovery session trying to avoid her.

⚽

Coach Fernandez used to give them two days off after a match, but Coach Hoffman says they need to keep up the momentum, and brings them in on the Monday for a 'light' session which turns out to be a lot of particularly mind-numbing drills. The team mutter about it to themselves in the breaks, but Maeve tries to push herself, mentally keeping her tally on her pace compared to Kira's.

It doesn't help with Maeve's performance though. Maybe she's just too tired, or maybe her obsession with monitoring Kira is making her fall more behind. Other names are called out for praise from Coach, including Zuri and Elisa. But praised most of all, is Adriana.

Adriana is glowing on the pitch, her face only falling when it accidentally meets Maeve. Noticing this makes Maeve's chest ache. But she'll fix everything with Adriana once she's got the captaincy. One thing at a time.

It all seemed to make sense to Maeve when she was making that spreadsheet to try to make the team hate Kira, but in reality, she doesn't know how to make this happen.

Fortunately, fate intervenes. At break, Maeve overhears Milo complaining about how their calves ache from the drills they've been doing today.

'We should have had more recovery time after the match,' they grumble. 'I hate these kind of exercises anyway.'

'Yeah,' Maeve agrees. 'Apparently they're to help Kira.'

'Why do we all have to do stuff just for Kira?' says Milo.

'She's such a teacher's pet,' says Maeve, feeling guilty even as the words are coming out of her mouth.

Milo makes sounds of agreement, and Maeve feels like she's maybe succeeded. But then Nat glances over.

'You've been having extra training with Coach too though, right? You're kinda teacher's pet number two.'

Maeve can't tell if Nat is saying this jokily or sassily, but it doesn't feel great.

'Y-yeah well, it's not *with* Coach, it's just with Kira. So it means I only see more of *her*. Unfortunately! I've—I've really *tried* to like her, but she's just so – difficult! And irresponsible! And selfish!'

But at that moment, Adriana frolics in, tying her bouncing hair up, side-by-side, with Kira. They're laughing together, and Maeve feels like she's been slapped. She feels so jealous she has to look away. But she can still hear them, talking with Charlie and Elisa. Their conversation is loud and bubbly, even from Kira, almost as if she wants nearby Maeve to overhear.

'Guys! What do *you* think?' Adriana's asking. 'I think Kira should wear *this* one to Joust.'

'But I think *this* one—'

Charlie and Elisa gush over the pictures Kira shows them on her phone.

'Definitely the white! It's more eye-catching!'

'Definitely the black! It's sexier!'

Kira catches Maeve looking. She asks in her low voice, 'What do you think, Murphy?'

Unabashed, Kira turns her phone screen to Maeve, showing two mirror selfies of Kira in what appear to be identical slashed vests, hugging her torso and revealing flashes of bare skin in sharp angular lines. She looks androgynous, stylish, and incredibly hot. They're paired with different fashionable jeans, boots, and layers of chain necklaces. Maeve's face heats. She hates that Kira can be so casual in her tests of her like this, and it's always Maeve who comes out worse.

Maeve shrugs. 'Aren't they literally the same top?'

COUPLE GOALS

'No!' say Adriana, Charlie, Elisa, and Kira in playful joint unison, and then laugh together. Maeve's mouth feels bitter as she tries to swallow down her jealousy.

'Have you managed to get *Maeve* to come out?' Elisa, playfully nudges Maeve's arm. 'Well done Kira! Normally Adriana can only persuade her about once a year, after the end of the season.'

It stings. They make her sound like such a grump. Adriana usually talks with Maeve through all her possibilities of making a big event invitation even just to post on the Tigresses' group chat, wondering aloud about which emojis to use in the event description. Elisa is right that Maeve normally bows out well before the nights out, but she is always there at Adriana's pre-drinks, volunteering to stay behind to tidy up Adriana's flat while they're all out, and letting herself out with the key they each have to each other's flats. It's proof that she hasn't been imagining the cracks that have started to form in their friendship.

Maeve feels herself the centre of attention suddenly, all these expectant eyes. Adriana's bright blues, while she bites her lip. And then there's Kira's gold eyes, studying her reaction like it's a test, goading her as usual. Milo and Nat are also looking at Maeve curiously now, presumably remembering Maeve's insults about Kira just a few minutes earlier. Maeve feels ashamed and embarrassed, a school bully caught out by the teacher. Especially when, if she's honest, there's a part of her that longs for the thought of a sweaty dancefloor with Kira. To pretend they're just two strangers, pressing their bodies together in the dark. Maybe if things were different, they'd even be able to kiss in public.

But no, Maeve isn't going to have that kind of relationship with Kira — and maybe it's not just because they're fighting for the same thing. Maybe Kira wouldn't want anyone to know they were hooking up anyway because so far she's been very deliberate in cornering her when they've been alone. It's just like her first kiss, that was with a girl called Annabelle from the Academy, who had then asked Maeve not to tell anyone. Women are always ashamed if they fancy her.

Part of Maeve just wants to run away and hide. But if she's going to try to fight for this, she needs to throw herself into the fight.

'Yeah,' she shrugs, trying to sound casual and cool, and probably failing. 'Course. I'll be there.' Another challenge accepted.

Chapter 17

Adriana

The dancefloor flashes with strobe lights. They make Adriana feel even higher than she did earlier after their 1-0 home win to Coach Hoffman's old club, the Loughborough Vixens. Kira had scored, again, and seemed particularly cocky to have defeated her old teammates.

Now, Adriana is the perfect level of tipsy, and she feels like the main character in a film, shaking her sparkly sequin dress to catch the flashes of the red lights (and men's eyes) in the sweaty basement. She's happy to be cutting loose after another hard week of training, another win, and with two hard-earned days off from training ahead of her. Adriana loves being able to be out partying on a Saturday night like her non-athlete friends take for granted.

The DJ puts on a club remix of Chappell Roan, and Adriana screams with delight. She is euphoric, spotting her friends dancing around her in the crowd, like snapshots in a movie montage.

Strobe: Charlie and Elisa cut goofy shapes together, a cowboy lasso and the macarena. Nat, Milo, and Liv are starting a can-can, which no one else is joining in. Zuri and Rebecca are grinding up against two topless male twins. Kira is lifting her toned arms over her head, smiling lazily to herself, like she's remembering her win from earlier. And Maeve, looking so different with her hair out of her habitual ponytail, pushes the strands from her wide long-lashed eyes, staring at Kira, maybe to copy her effortlessly rhythmic movements.

For the timeless duration of the song, Adriana dances, feeling everything is right with the world.

Normally, Adriana would be looking round for if there are any hot men. It *is* a night out. And she knows that there are men looking at her. She would be indignant if there weren't. But tonight, no one is catching her eye. It's not that there aren't any finè specimens around. There's a ginger Scottish man called Scott she hooked up with a few months ago, who winked at her when she arrived, but seems to be respecting her clear one-night policy. As she eyes the possible strangers up, she finds herself comparing them to some kind of inner metric that she never had before. They aren't tall enough, or are too tall, or are somehow not quite the right kind of tall. They don't have the right shade of light brown hair, or their light brown hair doesn't look both neat and like she can run her hands through it. They aren't looking at her like they can see right into her soul, like he mysteriously knows deep parts of her, but still wants to know more…

In other words, they just aren't Jacob Astor.

Adriana closes her eyes on the dancefloor, feeling a rush of heightened emotion as she realises the truth of her feelings. Oh Christ, she really likes him. So much so that he has ruined other men for her. She knows it's completely crazy, especially as he seems to literally hate her, and doesn't want to see her anymore. But she wishes he were here.

The music is a bittersweet ballad now, and the feeling is a stab in her chest, a rush of emotion constricting her throat. She thinks she might start bawling her heart out.

She feels a firm body next to hers, dancing with her. She closes her eyes, and lets herself imagine he's Jacob, dancing with her gently and slowly, his hands a breath away from her hips…

But then Adriana sighs, and tosses her hair and faces him, only to see he's of course not Jacob. The stranger *is* gorgeous in a fashionably rugged way – just the right amount of stubble, a double nose ring and glowing bronze skin. She forces a smile, partly to stop herself from crying and tries to keep her emotions in check. He smiles back, and the sides of his eyes crinkle, and the thing is, from just this first impression, he seems like a lovely man. He just isn't Jacob.

He leans towards her, brushing her hair gently away from her ear, and says over the music.

'I hope my future wife looks like you.'

Adriana laughs, leaning into his shoulder. 'That's not a chat-up line I'm used to hearing.'

He smiles and leans in close again. 'I take Beyonce's advice! If I like it, I'll put a ring on it.'

Adriana hesitates, not knowing if he's a fuckboy who says this to everyone, or if he really is looking for something more serious with someone and is being upfront about that, even in a nightclub. But at the end of the day, it doesn't matter.

'I'm just a good-time girl,' Adriana shouts over the music. 'I'm not wife material.'

The stranger tilts his handsome face, frowning with disarming sincerity. 'Who told you that?'

Adriana blinks, taken aback.

'I– I have to find my friends. Have a good night.'

But she doesn't go to find her friends immediately. She goes to the toilet, sitting there quietly in the cold of the bathroom cubicle for a while as the buzz of her drinks starts to wear off. She puts her head in her hands, mind swimming with Jacob, yearning to text him, but still sober enough, thank God, to know that would be idiotic.

She wants to splash her face but her gorgeous sparkling blue cat-eyeliner took too long to perfect, so she settles for cold water on her wrists.

She takes a deep breath, eyeing herself in the mirror and gives herself a pep talk.

'You do *not* need him. He's just a man. A grumpy, grouchy, sexy man. There will be others.'

'*Yes* sister,' a stranger next to her, clicks her fingers emphatically. 'If he wanted to he would! He doesn't deserve you! Carpe Diem! YOLO! Shots!'

Adriana laughs and kisses the stranger on the cheek, feeling genuinely buoyed. Ah, the rollercoaster emotions of a night out.

Back on the dancefloor, she looks for Kira and Maeve. She feels most responsible for them– one the fresh blood, the other the least used to going out.

She decides she'll bring the two of them to the bar with her and down a tequila shot followed by a pint of water. It'll be good for them both, to have a bonding moment together to put the captaincy situation behind them.

The strange friction between the two of them was palpable even at the pre-drinks at Adriana's earlier after the game. Kira had been full of bravado even off the pitch, like leading the group in directions to the club, even when she's lived in the city for the least amount of time – but Adriana felt like it was coming more from a place of assumed independence than anything malicious. She could sense that Kira's bossing people around, encouraging drinking games, or having strong opinions about which of their outfit choices was the right choice, was her way of trying to fit in and find her place in a new team. Plus, she's really funny, and that comes across so much better when she was in group settings socially outside of the training ground. Adriana had been delighted when she'd seen Charlie and Elisa creasing up over Kira's anecdotes about a time she'd had terrible food poisoning but still tried to play competitive football, nearly ending in a Gary Lineker incident.

Maeve, on the other hand, had been distinctly off at the pre-drinks. It was difficult to put your finger on at first, because Maeve was trying so hard to be the image of a sociable person, laughing just a bit too loudly at everything, and drinking a bit too much, and it all just feeling like Maeve was trying to be someone she isn't. Adriana knows she isn't really used to drinking, or indeed nighttime socialising recently, so she is trying to give her the benefit of the doubt – but the issue was that the more Maeve drank, the more obvious it became that she was trying to ostracize Kira.

At first it was just little things that Adriana had overheard when she was herself being a social butterfly going round and topping up everyone's drinks – like Maeve rolling her eyes at everything Kira said in a group, or, behind her back, bringing up things Kira had said that she knew the other teammates had found abrasive. She noticed the two of them never spoke directly to each other, and if one of them moved circles, the other would go to another cluster. It was like they were repulsing magnets, pushing each other away around the room.

There had only been one moment she'd happened to walk in on the two of them alone in her kitchen, whispering something heatedly, but they'd pulled apart immediately when Adriana had walked in with her empty bottles. Adriana hadn't been able to get from either of them what the hell was going on between them, but that isn't the first time.

Now, Adriana spots all her other friends on the dance floor, doing a mental head count of the gang, and assuring herself that they're all paired up with each other and/or new friends. But she can't find either Kira or Maeve, even when she paces back and forth between different rooms including the smoking area, the toilets, and even pops her head out to the road outside.

She pulls out her phone to text them, despite knowing that the signal in the club will render this pointless, when she finally spots the long blonde hair, cropped white t-shirt and understated black jeans of her best friend.

She almost doesn't recognise her because Maeve is doing something so unexpected. It takes Adriana a moment to realise what she's seeing. Amidst the crowds of the other partygoers and dancers, in the flashing lights and pounding music, Maeve is making out with someone. Their hands are in each other's hair, Maeve pulling the other woman's waist closer to hers, pushing her a little up against the wall.

Then they pull apart, and Adriana sees the other woman's face.

She's a pretty woman with bambi long eyelashes, pink lipstick, blusher on her olive cheeks, and dangling earrings. Adriana's first thought is 'she's not even Maeve's type'. But her second reaction is to squeal with excitement for her friend. Surely it would be good for Maeve's stress levels if she finally got laid.

Then Adriana sees Kira who folds her arms. Adriana wonders if she's jealous that Maeve has paired up, maybe Kira wants a snog herself this evening to celebrate scoring another goal in their game today. Adriana still doesn't know for sure if Kira is queer, and scolds herself for having assumed so definitely just from her vibe.

Maeve and the woman part, their fingers lingering flirtatiously in each other's, as the stranger goes with her friends to smoke. As soon as they stop kissing, Maeve immediately seems to be meerkating around for someone else. Adriana herself, maybe? Maeve doesn't even notice that the woman she'd just been making out so passionately with had looked back smiling at her.

'Woohoo!' Adriana strides over, clapping her friend on the back. 'Maeve! Kissing a stranger in a club! This is huge!'

She skips delightedly. But her friend is barely looking at her, only at Kira.

'Yeah, she's hot. Isn't she so hot? She's my type, for sure,' Maeve slurs loudly.

'Maeve, what are you talking about,' Adriana laughs. 'You don't have a type. And if you did, it wouldn't be pretty femmes like her, I mean don't get me wrong, she's *gorgeous* and I'm all for it, but like,' Adriana counts on her fingers. 'Megan Rapinoe? Quinn? Your ex Hannah? Your biggest crushes have always been androgynous sporty types.'

'Is that so,' smirks Kira.

'No they're not,' says Maeve, blushing beneath her make-up.

'Where has your girlfriend gone now?' asks Kira, her voice low to Maeve. 'If you like her so much, don't you want to be back kissing her?'

'Yeah, I *do*,' Maeve, faces up to Kira. 'See? People want to kiss me. In public. Strangers fancy me. They're not hiding me away.'

'Lucky for some,' says Kira.

'Yeah,' Maeve sways. 'It is lucky for some. Lucky lucky lucky me.'

It's like she's gloating, but it's not ringing true. Kira looks visibly uncomfortable, and Adriana thinks this is perfectly reasonable. It feels like Maeve's gloating is personal, though she doesn't understand why.

Adriana follows Maeve's hair as she drunkenly strides off through the dancefloor. Adriana grabs her friend's hand and pulls her to the side, shouting over the music.

'Maeve, what the hell is going on with you this evening?'

'Nothing!' Maeve yells back. 'Why would anything be going on! I'm just dancing and flirting, like I thought I was meant to be!'

'Maeve, I'm serious,' says Adriana, concerned.

'Urgh, fine then, if none of *you* want to hang out with me then I guess I'll find that woman again—'

'Nope!' Adriana steps in. 'You're drunk. I'm putting you in a taxi.'

Maeve seems not to hear her. With the slipperiness of an eel, Maeve pulls her arm away and heads off towards the bar. But Adriana keeps following her, until she manages, like a sheepdog, to guide her towards the entrance, and out into the fresh air of the smoking area at the front of the club.

'Maeve, I'm serious. You've been off all night. You were being mean to Kira at the pre-drinks, and then what was that? It's not like you.'

Maeve slumps dramatically down right on the pavement. Adriana is taken aback at this role reversal. She's not used to being the sober one trying to make other people act more sensibly. Still, Maeve doesn't answer, just pouts like an angry toddler.

'What is going on with you full stop?' Adriana asks. 'You've been so *off*! For weeks now! It's like I don't even know who you are anymore!'

Maeve's face contorts. Adriana can't tell if it's from the discomfort of not being able to think clearly in her state of drunkenness or if it's finally all these crushing feelings coming through at once. Then she covers her face like a baby doing peekaboo, like she can't bear to have her expression seen. Maeve sniffles but doesn't answer.

Adriana crouches down to be at her level. 'Is this really all just about being Captain?'

'It isn't *just*! It isn't *just*! It's – that's my whole career! If I'm not good enough… I'm never good enough… She doesn't… She doesn't even like me. I'm such an idiot.'

Maeve is sobbing so heavily it's like she's struggling to breathe.

'Maeve, I'm calling you a cab, okay? You need to go home.'

'No! Shan't!'

'Who's done this to you? Why haven't you told me? I'm your best friend, aren't I? You're supposed to be able to tell me anything?'

Maeve mumbles something, and Adriana doesn't quite catch it.

'What?'

Maeve suddenly shouts it at her. 'Kira!'

'What about Kira?' Adriana looks at her blankly.

Maeve opens her mouth to answer, then shakes her head ferociously, drunkenly mimes pulling a zip across her mouth.

'You want to speak to Kira to apologise? I think that would be a good idea but you need to maybe do it when you're less drunk, and when she's less hurt.'

Maeve rolls her eyes and huffs. 'She doesn't *care*.'

'Umm, yeah, I think she does,' says Adriana. 'We all care! It's our team! And you were being a real dick to her!'

Maeve lashes out at the air, in a display of drunken frustration at herself, her inability to understand or communicate.

'Not like that. Kira... She... She doesn't care... about any of it. Not job. Not me. Not us. Not like I do.'

Maeve sighs dramatically, then suddenly picks up a half empty bottle of vodka that's been left on the pavement of the smoking area, and lifts it to her lips.

'Maeve! No!' Adriana snatches it from her before she drinks any. She's never seen her friend like this, and she's really worried about her. She's also, frankly, still disappointed in her. But she takes a deep breath. She knows that Kira rubs people up the wrong way, especially at first impression, with her brashness and her brazen confidence. But the more Adriana has seen of her, the more she thinks Kira really does have a kind heart – being confident in your own skill doesn't make you think other people are less worthy of respect and it must be hard trying to fit into the team as the only summer signing so far.

'Look, you're not used to alcohol. You're not used to going out. I'm trying to give you the benefit of the doubt here, Maeve, because I love you, but I *know* there's something you're not telling me—'

'There's something *you're* not telling *me!*' Maeve bursts out. 'What's going on with *you*, huh? I know you're hiding something.'

Adriana's taken aback by Maeve's sudden clarity when she's been so out of it and this being turned around on her. 'W-what? Maeve, remember you're drunk.'

Adriana feels bad for deflecting this truth, but she knows Maeve isn't really in a state to talk seriously right now, and Adriana doesn't want to pour her heart out only for her friend to not remember a word of it tomorrow.

'I *know* you, Addy,' Maeve mumbles. 'I have known you for a decade. I know I haven't been doing my side of our friendship recently, but neither have you. It's not just me. Neither have you. It's one thing to lie to me but don't lie to yourself. I'm going back to find the others.'

Before Adriana can protest, Maeve storms off suddenly back into the club. Adriana intends to go after her, but she suddenly feels so drained of trying to keep holding everyone else up instead of just herself. Maybe she should call that taxi for herself, but her heart feels so heavy. She just wants someone to comfort her. To look after *her* for a change, instead of her looking after everyone else.

She sits down on the side of the road where Maeve had been, and sighs deeply. She closes her eyes to try to compose herself.

'Addy?'

Her eyes open at the sound of that familiar voice. Adriana must be more drunk than she thought. Because there, like she'd just been fantasising about, walking past the club with his blazer over his arm and his phone in his hand, is Jacob Astor.

Chapter 18

Maeve

Maeve must be in Hell.

She wakes up on Sunday morning with a start in a sweaty furnace of her quilt, her stomach twisted, and stumbles to the bathroom. She flicks on the light, but then groans when it's way too bright, and immediately turns it off again. She sits on the floor before the porcelain throne, clutching at it.

Adriana's words from last night echo in her mind. 'This isn't the Maeve I know. This isn't like you.'

What is happening to her? Her throat feels dry and rancid, her head feels like someone forcibly removed her brain with a spork from how hard it's pounding and how unable she is to think clearly. And her t-shirt smells like… tequila?

As Maeve sits on the cold bathroom tiles, still wearing her t-shirt and pants from the previous night – she had the sense to take her jeans off to sleep at least – memories from last night start to surface in hazy bursts.

Kira cornering her in Adriana's cottagecore kitchen about how she needed to cool down. Adriana fighting with her on the side of the street, telling her off for how she'd been mean to Kira. And, worst of all, Kira dancing in the club, looking like an archangel fallen to earth. All Maeve had wanted to do was kiss her, right there, in front of everyone, and forget everything else. But Kira had made a point of ignoring her whenever they were in front of anyone.

It's fair enough, Maeve supposes, but it doesn't mean it doesn't sting. To have Kira's golden eyes looking down at her, not up at her from the locker room floor. To have Kira laughing with the other members of the team, people who were meant to be *Maeve's* friends and seemingly not care that Kira has just swooped in and taken her place. Kira just staring at her as if proving over and over, again and again, that Kira could do everything Maeve wanted to do and be better at it than her too. The truth was that although they appeared to fight on the surface, Maeve had felt drawn to Kira in a way she'd never experienced before, a way that felt even riskier than their secrecy and terrified her.

Maeve dry heaves.

Afterwards she slowly gets up from the floor and thinks what she would do if she was looking after Adriana in a similar hungover state. She makes herself a berocca and drinks it, wincing at the frothiness. She fills her personalised water bottle and sips from it. She makes dry toast and nibbles at it delicately. She showers, and puts on her softest pyjama-like clothes, her hair up in an old cow-patterned towel, another gift from Adriana. Adriana is everywhere in her flat, ghosts of their closeness.

Maeve picks up her phone to check if she has messages from Adriana, hoping she has checked she got home okay even if they did have a falling out. She finds nothing from

Adriana, but Maeve has six missed calls and a string of messages from an unknown number. She clicks on it first, trying to work out what the emergency is.

```
Hey May, it's Jess ;) x
I'm at the bar what would u like?
Hey?
Where did u go?
U still here?
Hey again we r just leaving the bar u
still up? ;) x
```

And then this morning:

```
Missed saying goodbye to you last night,
text me if u wanna get hungover coffee xx
```

Maeve groans and puts her phone back down to have some more toast before replying. She feels bad, but honestly, it's the kind of bad she'd feel about letting any admin task slip, like forgetting to reply to a time sensitive email.

Maeve's not used to kissing strangers and she doesn't know the etiquette of how much or little to say to someone she doesn't want to see again. There's nothing wrong with Jess, she seemed like a very lovely person, but then, what does Maeve know? It's not like they chatted much. Maeve saw someone making eyes at her when she was near Kira, and seized her chance. Kira should have been proud of her, for making a bold tactical move in the heat of the moment. Maeve knows now in the cold light of day it was a pathetic attempt to try and make Kira jealous, which just makes her feel stupider than she already did.

The perfect person to ask would of course be Adriana. But, even though Maeve, for the life of her, can't remember exactly what they fought about, she knows that they did have cross words.

She picks up her phone and sees with a jolt that she has had another message too – from the contact she has saved as just CHOKSI.

```
i don't want to hook up any more
```

Maeve reads it, and feels her face go immediately scarlet. She feels the punch of rejection, shame, and loss, right in the pit of her stomach. She reads it and re-reads it, feeling the panic bubble up inside her before realising she's actually going to be sick again. She runs back to the bathroom, and throws up.

Flushing the toilet and feeling worse than when she'd first woken up, Maeve brings her phone with her to the sofa, where, despite the summer heat winning the fight with her air con, she hides under her own blanket to read the message again.

In the time between her reading that message and going to the bathroom, Kira has already sent another one.

```
i don't want there to be any confusion over what we are doing or who we are to each other you have made it clear that you only care about being captain no matter what so fine, have it your way
```

Under the blanket, Maeve reads the message over and over, each time feeling like another wrench on her heart.

In the heat of the moment, angry and ashamed, Maeve types back with loud taps,

```
Fine.
```

And before she can stop herself, sends it with a swoosh.

She goes back to bed and buries herself into a cow-shaped pillow.

When Maeve wakes up, unsure how much later it is, her throat like sandpaper and her eyes like lab rats being tested with toxic eye drops. She manages to compose herself enough to put Mr Milkalot aside (he's now damp from her tears) and makes herself another piece of plain toast.

Maeve should be *happy* about Kira's message! She can be more ruthless if there isn't any – as Kira put it – 'confusion' about what they're doing. Maybe this is a sign that Maeve is on the right track, that she's successfully getting to Kira. So why doesn't this feel anything like a win?

Adriana is the only person who could understand right now. Or maybe Maeve could pretend she's heartbroken about someone else – this Jess person from last night?

Maeve, still sniffing, goes to check Adriana on Find My Friends to make sure she got home okay. That's when Maeve sees Adriana isn't at her flat.

She isn't at her family's, or anyone else in the team's. Maeve's pulse quickens, but it isn't like this is completely unusual – Adriana must have gone home with a man last night. And now Adriana is at – Maeve zooms in as much as she can – what might be one of the new luxury studio complexes by the waterfront?

Maeve sends a quick message to check in on her. It doesn't matter if they left things in a weird place, she just cares about whether her friend is okay.

Sat nursing her hangover alone, embarrassed, and rejected, Maeve can't help thinking her friend is likely having a much better time than she is…

Chapter 19

Adriana

Adriana wakes to the smell of freshly made coffee.

She opens one eye. Someone places a mug carefully on a marble coaster on the bedside table beside her. Then they get back into bed next to her, slowly and gently, leaning against the luscious pillows.

Adriana lets herself linger in the halfland between dreaming and waking for just a moment.

Did she dream it? Did she really break her one-night-stand rule last night, and end back here with Jacob again? And was the sex as unbelievably brilliant as she dreamt it was?

She'd thrown her arms around him when he'd found her last night, like he was her real-life knight in shining armour – well, a surprised businessman in an expensive suit. And he hadn't pushed her away, he'd just dropped his things to hold her, and sighed, not in displeasure but in something closer to relief. After they'd laughed together about the strangeness of their paths overlapping, it had felt like the coincidence threw all their previous conversations about maintaining distance out the window.

'I'm just finding it so hard,' Adriana had said, tearfully on the street. 'I hate being distant with you.'

'Well, I hate it too,' he'd said.

'Really?'

'Of course I do! I was always clear with you Adriana, when we met I told you I wanted to see you again, but you were the one who said it could never be something serious, and then with the whole complication of my role at the club, I just thought, I didn't want to make anything difficult for you, even if I hated it. And then I arrived at Honey thinking it was a date, when you kept insisting it was some business meeting. Isn't this what you wanted, for us to avoid each other?'

'No,' she had said, boldly. 'What I want is this—'

And she had kissed him. After that, they had just been unable to stop smiling at each other in disbelief.

'My teammates are all—' Adriana had gestured back to the club. 'Can we go somewhere... else?'

Her eyes had of course been wide and suggestive in the dark night. He'd called them a taxi with one confident gesture of his arm in the road, seeming to magic one out of thin air. And then they'd kissed the whole journey back to his, hands grasping at each other's bodies eager to make up for what they'd denied themselves over the past few weeks.

When he'd let her back into his apartment it had been like déjà vu, like reliving the memory Adriana had played so many times in her head since their first encounter.

They had been kissing against his front door, and she'd been pulling his shirt off there in the hallway, undressing him fast at first, and then, when it got to his belt, very, very slow, until he'd groaned with the delay. They had made it to the bed eventually, but had avoided sleep all night, prioritising instead the positions that Adriana had wished they'd got round to the first time. There were still so many more she wanted to see him in, to feel him in, to taste him in…

She closes her eyes tightly, making a wish before turning round to face the man beside her hoping that this morning will be different and she won't mess up this second chance.

'Good morning, Addy,' Jacob smiles. 'Are you any good at crosswords?'

Adriana buries her face in the plump linen pillowcase, trying to hide the outrageous size of her huge grin.

'Woah, woah, it's okay, you don't have to, but I'm afraid I do *have* to do the daily quick crossword, it's a sacred part of my morning routine…'

Adriana brings her face back up, but still can't quite look at him. She still can't quite believe what she's seeing.

'It's not– I love crosswords! I'm absolutely *terrible* at them, mind you, but…'

Adriana peeks back up. Jacob is sat upright, leaning against his pillows, with a paper newspaper open before him, open to the puzzles section. His hair is – in a way she could never have previously guessed it could ever be – *messy*, sticking out in all directions, from what, she realises proudly, was her own hands mussing through it so much last night. He's wearing a pair of glasses she hasn't seen him in before which she guesses must be his 'home' pair, their frames tortoiseshell and rounder than his usual slick rectangular frameless ones, and a blue checked pyjama shirt. She looks under the duvet to see – yes – it's a matching set.

'W-what are you looking at down there?' Jacob laughs.

'You are wearing a pyjama set.'

Adriana didn't know guys could wear elegant pyjama sets, she thought that was something only old men in Victorian times could do. Normally when she hooks up with men, the next morning they stay naked or in their faded boxers with holes, which often look like they're about a hundred years old themselves.

'Of course,' Jacob frowns. 'It's Sunday morning. We're relaxing in bed. What else could I be wearing?'

Adriana buries her face in her pillow again and screams.

'What?' Jacob asks, sounding worried. 'What's wrong!'

'You're just so… so… cute! I can't deal with it! You're not meant to be able to be this adorable!'

When Adriana resurfaces again, the tips of Jacob's ears have gone pink.

'Ah, well, if that's all, I can only apologise for surprising you,' he says. 'Don't forget your coffee, by the way. Coconut milk mocha right?'

This time Adriana is rendered speechless.

Jacob bites his lip, holding back a smile. 'You converted me at Honey. I've been drinking it myself. It's like drinking a bounty.' Then he clicks the end of his pen. 'Now, what do you think might be 2 down, five letters, with the clue–'

Adriana leaps up onto him, straddling him in a hug, ducking through his arms to be buried next to his chest, under the newspaper.

'Hey!' he says, though he doesn't sound cross at all, 'I was about to crack that one.'

'You can keep doing it,' Adriana, nuzzles into his neck, 'I'll just stay here. I'm helping.'

'Oh sure, I'm sure that will be very elucidating,' Jacob teases.

'Read me the clue again,' Adriana whispers in his ear.

Jacob coughs, his voice breaking a little as he gamely reads another crossword clue.

'Five letters, hopefully beginning with C, "how to drink fruit; avoid falling in one".'

Adriana repeats it, in between kissing his neck. Through her lips, she feels him laugh low in his throat, and feels him get hard between her legs.

'Oh, hello,' she teases him. 'But I thought this pyjama set was only to be worn for "relaxing in bed?"'

Jacob sets his crossword aside and takes his glasses off. 'I personally can think of some *very* relaxing things we could do…'

And strangely, it is. They kiss playfully at first, but then there's a softness and tenderness that she doesn't remember being there last night. Adriana sighs contentedly, her body relaxing into his, and Jacob responds by holding her even closer to him, pulling their bodies so that they are entwined. They lie on their sides facing each other, her body tucked into his, so that she feels like she can feel him all around her. She feels turned on, sure, but she also feels… something else, something she didn't even realise she could feel with someone in this way. She feels safe. She feels cared for. She feels at peace.

Jacob moves her gently into position, her back against the pillows. 'Are you comfortable?'

'Mmhmm,' she nods, her face flushed with warmth and desire.

'Good,' he says. 'Because I want to stay here for a very, very long time.'

Adriana leans her head back into the pillows as Jacob slips down under the covers between her legs, his hands stroking her thighs, pulling down her underwear and bending his head to reverently kiss her.

He licks slowly, so slowly, like he's savouring every trace of her. Adriana's toes curl in pleasure, and her back arches into blissful relaxation. Jacob makes the same motion again, like repeating a favourite line of a poem. Then he circles her clit, tracing mysterious patterns that unlock something in Adriana, taking her to another realm entirely.

He teases her, alternating his fingers and his tongue on the surface of her, when she's begging for him to be inside her now.

'Please,' she gasps, 'Please.'

He teases another finger, just the tip of it, and Adriana feels herself burning with desire. He doesn't keep her waiting for long. He kisses her clit again, as he pushes two strong fingers smoothly inside her. Adriana cries out. It feels even better the second time, and the third, and the fourth, and as he keeps fucking her with his fingers, Adriana can just let the sensation build and build in her, losing herself in how good it feels.

When she comes, she comes in his mouth, long and hard and slow. Jacob keeps his mouth pressed close to her, like he wants to taste her every pulse.

Adriana blacks out a little, seeing constellations of stars swirling, and as she's coming back to earth, she rouses to find Jacob has moved back up the bed to wrap his arms around her. She flops onto his firm chest, and lets herself be held. He strokes her hair, and runs his thumb along her bare shoulder, tracing the edges of her collar bone, her shoulder blade, her neck. Every nerve in her body is tingling.

When she's recovered, she feels light, bubbling, amazed, and starts giggling. Jacob, instead of being surprised, laughs along with her. They remain like that for a while, just holding each other, laughing, like they're high.

Adriana is just enjoying the feeling of their warm bodies this close to one another, and is just on the edge of having a thought, of wondering if she should talk to him about… well, *this — them — what are they doing*, but also not wanting to say anything that could burst this bubble when Jacob speaks.

'I'm so sorry, Addy,' he says, his voice low and Adriana feels a swell of panic at what he's going to say next. 'I think your mocha will have gone cold.'

Adriana throws her head back into his chest and laughs. She feels like she's floating.

'I'll make you another one,' Jacob offers, getting up and stretching, topless but still in his pyjama trousers, which Adriana has to admit, she finds strangely sexy for something so dweeby.

'I'll help,' Adriana stretches too.

'Like how you "helped" with the crossword?' Jacob raises an eyebrow, but then he surprises her by holding out a hand to help her out of bed — scooping her up before putting her feet on the floor.

Adriana giggles and puts on Jacob's pyjama shirt, buttoning it half up. It's like a shirt dress on her and she hopes she looks as cute as she feels in it.

'Do you have any boxers I could borrow?' she asks, not because she needs them, but because she wants them, and she suspects Jacob will find it hot too. Jacob rolls his eyes and opens a draw in his walk-in wardrobe, throwing her a pair of blue cotton boxers that probably cost as much as her fanciest lingerie. He takes her in.

'You look insanely good like that,' he says, and kisses her again. Then he gestures for her to lead the way to the kitchen so that he can watch her walk ahead and admire how good she looks.

Adriana remembers Jacob's open plan kitchen from her first visit, but this time, it strikes her differently. Amidst the tall shining surfaces of the sleek kitchen, she searches for the traces of *him* amidst the reproduced luxury. The choices of fresh fruit in the bowl – pineapple, kiwis, passionfruit, pomegranate – and the bold red coffee machine. An eye-catching oddity in the kitchen is a teapot in a bobbly knitted cosy in clashing colours which looks like it would be more in keeping at Adriana's own flat than Jacob's.

'My grandma knitted it,' explains Jacob, seeing what's caught her attention. 'She's been knitting for five decades, I didn't have the heart to tell her it's hideous.'

They both smile. Then Adriana looks through into the living room. The most noticeable thing about the room is the tall glass windows looking out onto the water, so that you barely notice the room is practically empty. With its brown leather sofa and low glass coffee table, it's tasteful and sophisticated – but characterless. It feels like a house not a home, the place of someone who only moved a few weeks ago and hasn't spent much time in it. Piles of unpacked boxes, neatly stacked in the corner so that they're out of the way, until they're ready to be opened. In fact, the only source of colour is bookshelves, which Adriana notices have been filled before anything else in the room, its chunky hardbacks and paperbacks neatly arranged. Heading over to it she chuckles to herself.

'What's so funny?' Jacob calls out from the kitchen, like his hearing is perfectly tuned to her every sound.

'Was the first thing you unpacked when you arrived your books? And… they're arranged alphabetically?'

'Of course,' he says. 'How else would you recommend?'

She shakes her head, smiling as she traces her finger along their spines. She hasn't read a book in years, preferring to hear stories from the lively mouths of her friends in pubs and clubs, not written down in quiet black and white. There's a lot of intense business and economics non-fiction. These look denser than she would ever want herself, and frankly she can barely make her way through some of their *titles* because they're so long. But there's fiction there too, ones she recognises from some of her nerdy friend's shelves – Bernadine Evaristo, Andrea Levy, Anne Enright. Why is it that she, as someone who doesn't like reading herself, finds it so attractive that he does?

'Anything you want to borrow?' he offers. 'You're welcome to, but I must warn you, anyone who borrows my books is not allowed to dog-ear any corners.'

'Yeah, I have always wanted to read... *Mathematics for Economics and Business Fifth Edition.*'

'Ah yeah, that's a good beach read that one,' Jacob laughs. 'Incredible plot twists. Turns out trickle down economics doesn't work at all! Didn't see *that* coming.'

Adriana skips back into the kitchen to find Jacob frothing milk for her mocha, the tendons in his bare arms flexing as he stirs it at a clearly practiced angle. How is she getting horny for someone because of the way he froths milk?

Adriana lifts herself up to sit on the corner of his kitchen island, kicking her feet.

'So what do you have on today?' Adriana asks him.

Jacob shrugs one shoulder, maintaining a firm look at the drink. He opens his mouth, then seems to change his mind.

'Well...' he goes quiet and looks away from her. 'Honestly? Nothing. I'm free as a bird. But that– you don't have to– I'm not expecting you to spend more time with me.'

'Oh,' Adriana pauses, feeling her heart drop. She had just assumed they would spend more time together, that seemed to be the flow of the morning, but that was foolish of her. He wants her to go, of course he does, maybe that's why he's been making her this coffee so that he feels less bad about throwing her out.

'Unless,' he says, his eyes still trained on the milk he's pouring into her mug so he doesn't have to face her. 'Unless you wanted to? You have a couple of days off from training after your big win, right?'

He puts the mug in front of her, still trying to avoiding meeting her eye. He has made a dextrous floral shape on the top of her drink. A man of surprising talents. He finally glances at her.

Adriana feels flustered. It still feels like a dream, being here with Jacob, when she was so convinced just hours ago that he never wanted to speak to her again. It feels like their relationship is still so delicate, hanging in the balance. But she is starting to suspect they're both playing a game of chicken, trying not to reveal how invested they are in the other. Since their tipsy conversation last night, and all the ways Jacob is showing tenderness for her now, she realises his distant behaviour had just been self-preservation, and because it's what he thought *she* wanted. And that was fair enough – she *had* literally told him she would never see him again.

Adriana takes a sip, and moans in appreciation.

'I would love to spend more time with you today, Jacob,' she says. 'I just have one rule.'

She can see it more clearly now, through his poker face. The way even his seemingly impassive face can fall.

'Oh goodie,' he sighs. 'I do so love your rules.'

He tamps down the coffee granules on another coffee before pulling it hard back into his machine. Adriana keeps looking at him until he, almost as if against his better judgment, looks back at her.

'My one rule is,' she says, 'please can we not talk about work?'

Jacob releases a breath, and snorts, shaking his head. He presses the button for the coffee. 'Well, that depends. Please can you clarify what counts as work?'

Adriana counts it off on her fingers, hope rising in her chest. 'No talking about football.'

'Damn, I really wanted to mansplain the offside rule to you.' He teases.

Adriana grins through continuing – 'No talking about training, or our "business agreement"'.

Their smiles have become more serious now. Jacob steps towards Adriana, still sat on the kitchen counter, stepping inside her dangling legs so that she automatically wraps herself around him again. He touches the side of Adriana's face softly. There's a tenderness in his frown which makes Adriana's chest ache.

'I just… It's so…' She takes a deep breath. 'I feel so good right now, Jacob.'

He kisses her and runs his fingers through her hair and Adriana feels herself falling more.

'Wait.' She pulls back, eager to put her cards on the table so there are no more misunderstandings between them. 'It feels like things have felt really awful between us the last few weeks,' she continues in a rush, 'and it was so, so nice last night, and so lovely to be able to just… hang out. Like two normal people, getting to know each other? Right? So I'm not saying let's *never* talk about it again, but just please, not right now? Not today?'

'But don't you want to talk about–'

Adriana groans and feels her face fall into a pout.

Unexpectedly, Jacob barks laughing. Adriana blinks up at him, and he pinches her cheek, shaking his head.

'Okay,' he says. 'I can't say no to that face, it's like kicking a puppy.'

Adriana feels the high of getting her way, like getting given seconds of a delicious meal when she thought the food was all already eaten.

'I thought you'd love kicking puppies,' she jokes.

'I'll leave the kicking expertise to you.'

'Hey! No talking about work!'

He grins, mimes zipping his mouth. Adriana, playing along, mimes unzipping his lips with her own fingers. His lips are surprisingly soft, and at her touch, he stops breathing. Adriana lets the trace of her fingers slow, and then doubles back, at his lips parting at her touch so she puts her fingers in his mouth. He sucks and pulls her close towards him. Their kiss becomes more urgent, the heat between them rising again.

'No, no,' he says, pulling away, holding her hand to keep a distance between them. 'We can't have sex again, Adriana, not until we've both had some food. It's not good for our blood sugar levels. You're an athlete, we need to be looking after your body.'

Adriana feels as high as if she'd been having constant sugar all morning.

'How would you like to top up your blood sugar then, Mr Astor?'

'Well, you know, I am kind of craving honeycomb brownies…'

Adriana stares up at him.

'Really? You wanna go back to Honey?'

Jacob looks nonchalant, shrugs. 'If you want. I feel like we deserve a do-over after last time.'

Adriana squints at him. No, she realises, he's just *trying* to look nonchalant.

'You're practically drooling!' she squeals with delight. 'I *knew* you were eyeing up my brownie before.' She kisses him. 'Let's go. Oh, but… I only have my going out dress with me.'

Adriana looks at the really wonderfully skimpy dress scattered on the floor by the front door from where he unzipped it last night.

'Well,' he says, pointing at his own shirt on her. 'You've already raided my wardrobe. Want to see if I have anything else you can wear outside the house?'

Adriana squeals with delight, and lets him lift her down from the counter and guide her to his bedroom, where she looks with a practiced eye over the rails of his wardrobe. Jacob doesn't have many clothes, clearly prioritising quality over quantity.

'I mean, do you think I can get away with wearing your boxers as shorts? It *is* the summer.' She asks, after only finding suits. Then she pulls on a plain white cotton t-shirt of his, the simple style she remembers him wearing so gorgeously at their last visit to Honey.

She steps out and poses for Jacob, who is dutifully waiting by the door. He's wearing belted caramel shorts and a white linen shirt with a navy baseball cap and sunglasses in his hand. Jacob seems unable to do anything less informal than 'smart casual', but he does look incredibly handsome.

'Do you think this is indecent?' she asks, of her own outfit.

Jacob's eyes fly up, taking her in in his t-shirt and boxers.

'Honestly, I *do* think it's indecent,' he says. 'But only because it is… Well, you look very, very hot in my clothes. I don't think anyone will complain, especially not me.'

She slips on her shoes. Thankfully, she made the decision to wear trainers to the club – better for dancing.

'And it's such a shame I don't have any spare underwear with me,' she says coquettishly. 'I guess I'll just have to go without any.'

Still not believing the turn her weekend has taken, Adriana skips off out of his front door. Jacob groans happily, and follows her.

Chapter 20

Maeve

Maeve only makes it out of her house in the late afternoon on Sunday, wearing sunglasses to hide her puffy eyes with dark circles underneath them. She decides that given her body feels like it's been through a meat grinder, she will just have a *light* jog today.

She heads down towards the park, thinking it will be quieter than town but immediately regrets it when she sees that the park is full of couples and groups of friends spread out on picnic blankets, blasting reggae music and laughing with each other enjoying the late September sun. Maeve is ashamed at how lonely she feels. Without Adriana, and without the rest of the team, who she felt were all increasingly off with her on the night out, who does she have? She can hardly ring her mother – that would be even more punishment, because she'd just ask if she's won the captaincy back yet. It's tempting even to message that pretty woman from last night, Jess, just to have some company and take her up on that offer of a hungover coffee. But she thinks it would be cruel, to meet someone only as a distraction. Maeve still has some moral compass, even if it feels like she's been confused by its swings recently.

She sees a short-haired woman sunbathing on her front, bikini nonchalantly open to show her glistening brown shoulders, and for a moment Maeve thinks it's Kira and stumbles. But of course it's not her.

The memory of Kira's message ignites a fire inside Maeve, the hurt and embarrassment fueling her to make her jog into a run now. She strides past groups with adorable toddlers or playful puppies, full families with proud parents and happy children, couples holding hands and kissing, rubbing suncream into each other's backs. She pushes herself harder and harder, through her hangover, through the pain, through the regret and doubt and worry, until it's just physical exertion. Maeve's favourite way to cope.

She reaches the wall but pushes through it. She has nearly lapped the park now and with every stride, her body aches but her mood improves.

Then she sees a familiar mass of bright red hair. She's not imagining it this time — it really is Adriana, just further down the path with her back to Maeve. She's with a tall man wearing a navy cap and sunglasses. Maeve, breathing heavily, slows her run to a slow jog as she squints to make out who he is. It's against Adriana's self-dictated dating rules to be with a man on a weekend daytime — it breaks her 'casual' boundaries. She spends one night with a man but doesn't stick around for breakfast. It's definitely not her brother but could he be some distant family member or friend Maeve hasn't met? Adriana does have a lot of friends…

The two of them buy ice-creams from a parked-up van, and it *looks* like Adriana is on a date. The way she's hanging off his arm, and he's looking nowhere but at her, like she's the true sun lighting up the summer's day. She has a comically tall triple stacked cone with strawberry, chocolate, and mint-choc chip; he has one ball of vanilla in a tub. As Maeve continues to watch, she sees Adriana playfully offer the man a lick of the ice-cream, which he does slowly, in a way that seems to be very suggestive to Maeve – she thinks she should look away, feels she's intruding on an intimate moment – but then he gets some on his nose. Adriana laughs, and he leans down to bring his face close to hers so that she can kiss the ice-cream away. This leads to them kissing on the mouth, Adriana's ice-cream starting to drip to the ground, forgotten.

Maeve adjusts her baseball cap lower on her face and steps back into the shade of a tree to keep watching without being seen, wanting a better glimpse of this mystery man. Adriana is clearly into him enough to throw all her dating rules out the window, yet she hasn't mentioned him at all to Maeve.

Could this be someone she's slept with before? Maeve just thought last night that Adriana was trying to have fun with the team, but maybe the real reason that she wasn't interested in any of the men that approached her was because she already has someone in her life. As Maeve watches he does seem to be a bit familiar somehow but she can't quite work out why. Does he match up to the descriptions of any of the men Adriana used to show her on dating apps, or as friends of friends met at one party or another? Could Maeve recognise him from any of Adriana's one-word descriptions of them? 'Marvel-lous Mike' (who was very into comic books) or 'Too Much Tongue Tom' (does what it says on the tin)?

Maeve watches, feeling like a spy (or just a bit of a pervert).

Adriana and the man have remembered their ice-creams and started walking again, towards the duck pond happily strolling hand-in-hand. Oh God, are they going to go on the swan-shaped pedalos? Maeve can't bear it.

The man seems to be serious, rarely smiling as he speaks, and yet Adriana looks adoring at him, laughing in a way Maeve can tell is completely genuine. Maeve hates to admit it but it makes her stomach ache with jealousy, not just for having someone to flirt with, but because it used to be Maeve making Adriana laugh like that. She feels replaced in yet another area of her life. She has missed seeing Adriana's eyes teary with laughter, her golden mane dancing with each new delight. Adriana's always so quick to find joy in things, and she casts a glow over the people she's with too – Maeve feels desperately sad that she hasn't been part of that world for what feels so long. In fact, the last few times they have talked it's mainly been Maeve chiding Adriana for not being professional enough, and even though she really believed it was coming from a supportive place, she regrets it now.

She wants to reach out, but feels insecure that Adriana doesn't want her anymore – after all, she didn't reply to her message checking in about her being okay this morning. Clearly too busy.

And then Adriana playfully swipes at the man's cap, and puts it on her own mass of curls. He takes his sunglasses off to put on her face too. Maeve sees his face clearly, and a jolt of recognition goes through her.

No, it can't be. She looks again and really tries to focus which is when she realises her suspicions are right. *Jacob Astor?* The son of the new owner. The man responsible for all this mess in the team.

What the hell is Adriana playing at?

What would her other teammates think, if they knew? Adriana's been getting praised by Coach Hoffman recently – Maeve had thought it was all well-deserved, but has that been Jacob's influence? Surely Adriana isn't trying to sleep her way to the top? But then Maeve checks herself, hating that she's even entertaining this idea for the briefest of seconds. It's like all the worst *Daily Mail* articles ever written that if a woman achieves something, it's because of who she was sleeping with rather than her talents. Still, it doesn't look great for her professionalism.

Maeve shakes her head. She is so utterly confused. She should give Adriana the benefit of the doubt. But she realises the only way she can get the truth about this is to actually talk to her friend. It's clearly overdue. She will confess her own secret about Kira, now that whatever they were doing is so painfully and permanently over between the two of them. And hopefully that will make Adriana feel comfortable enough to tell her whatever is going on here. Maybe Maeve can advise her to leave this man alone, before it's too late and things get even messier than they probably already are. There are way too many complications going on, and Maeve just thinks everything would be better if things went back to how they were before.

Maeve texts her friend, it still stinging she hasn't already replied to Maeve's earlier message checking she's okay.

> Hey Sunny, I want to apologise for how I
> was last night. I can't hold my drink, but
> that isn't a good enough excuse. You were
> right, there is a lot going on with me, and
> I wish I could talk to you more about it.
> I feel like we haven't caught up in too
> long. Come round for dinner? x

She sends it and watches Adriana anxiously across the park. She watches, waiting for the moment Adriana will look at her phone, nervous to see how she'll react to Maeve's message – if Adriana will open the message and look pleased at Maeve's name, or, worse, if she doesn't and then puts her phone back away.

But as Maeve watches Adriana doesn't check her phone at all. She just pulls Jacob Astor into the queue for the swan pedalos.

Maeve walks home feeling more alone than she can remember.

⚽

Adriana finally replies later that night, saying she's busy that evening and the following, but yes to dinner after training on Tuesday. Maeve felt upset by the way the message was not in their usual tone, rushed, without even any of Adriana's baffling but cute emojis.

Maeve tries to remind herself of her plan to make Kira seem un-captainlike to the rest of the team to have something to focus on, but it already isn't sitting right with her. She tries to channel Kira's confident, aggressive attitude, but the truth is that she's actually feeling vulnerable, twitchy and paranoid.

She and Kira had previously organised meeting for one-on-one training on Monday, but Maeve isn't sure whether Kira's text to her over the weekend — 'I don't want to see you alone anymore' — includes the one-on-one trainings? It isn't in Maeve's nature to go against Coach's orders, but she feels so ill at the thought of seeing Kira, and while being watched by Kevin too, that for the first time in her life she feigns sickness. It doesn't even feel that much like she's feigning.

To make up, Maeve instead spends her 'day off' on Monday training alone in her room, crunching sit-ups and push-ups until her muscles spasm.

⚽

Walking into the dressing room on Tuesday, it's like she's being punished for lying, because she comes face to face with the last person she feels like seeing right now: Kira.

The two of them stand facing each other silently. Maeve feels like they're the only people in the world. Maeve doesn't think of herself as someone who believes in auras or anything like that, but she has this sense of Kira surrounded by red waves of loathing. Even as she looks so disgusted with her, she's still the most beautiful woman Maeve's ever seen.

'Recovered from your 'illness' have you, Murphy?' says Kira.

Maeve flushes. Maeve tries to match her energy, but it barely lasts a second before she fails and she has to look away. She feels ashamed and upset, terrified she might start crying. Did Kira always hate Maeve, even when she was hooking up with her? Was it always part of a plan to distract Maeve and then end things when Kira had got what she wanted? Maeve feels like she's doubting everything.

Kira turns without saying anything to Maeve, picks up her stuff.

'I'm going to change somewhere else,' Kira tells the others. 'See you guys on the pitch.'

Maeve feels the humiliation of past experiences course through her body. Girls refusing to change with her, calling her a dirty lesbian, as if she wouldn't be able to keep her hands off them.

Maeve glances at Nat, Milo and Liv, who have been in the locker room the whole time and watched this exchange.

'Hey,' Maeve mutters, embarrassed.

'Hey,' they reply, looking awkwardly from her to the door slamming closed behind Kira.

'Bet you had a bad hangover after Joust,' says Milo, after a moment.

'Yeah, it was... a bit of a struggle!' Maeve, tries to joke but it feels feeble. No one laughs, and no one continues the conversation. Maeve feels her stomach clench. She wishes she had the skill for this, like Adriana.

She used to be better, didn't she? Before Kira came along and knocked her confidence like this.

On the plus side, in training, Maeve's shame and humiliation seems to be good for her performance. She feels like a race horse with blinkers on, using it to fuel her focus. Coach doesn't praise her, but she can't find fault either.

However, there *is* someone playing noticeably badly today.

'Kira! Again! That was an open goal!' Coach is exasperated. 'Focus! What the hell is happening with you today? Did you catch an illness from Maeve?'

Kira doesn't reply with her usual brashness. She doesn't even lash out. Just winces.

'Kira, if you play like this I'll have no choice but to sub you out for this week's game.' Hoffman sighs. 'Alright. Nat, get up here please. Let's try that set piece with you taking Kira's place.'

That brings some energy into Kira, a cynical eyebrow raised towards where the other strikers are stood. It's very abrupt, Maeve can understand that, and she too can't help feeling that Coach is being unusually harsh on her – but that's the other side of being Coach's protegee, she supposes. She'll always expect you to be the best, and be brutal if you drop from that standard, even for a moment.

Kira doesn't acknowledge Nat as she jogs past her, which seems rude as they normally fist bump or high five to keep up the team spirit and energy in training.

Maeve feels as if her mother is stood behind her own shoulder, whispering to her to seize the moment. Maeve tries to do so. She points out Kira's faux pas out to the defenders near her, stage-whispering her commentary quickly.

'Ouch,' she says to Milo and Nat. 'It's not Nat's fault! That's not great leadership, is it? Kira's not exactly a team player, is she?'

The others nod, if a little warily. Then Coach blows her whistle for them to continue working on this set piece for the weekend's game.

Maeve should see this as a win, shouldn't she? Even if it was a bit of an own goal from Kira. That's two modes of Maeve's attack plan against Kira successfully carried out with Coach also seeming to be unimpressed. So why does she feel so hideous?

Watching Kira sat on the bench, her head down, her hair carelessly mussed to the side, and expression subdued, Maeve's chest aches. She remembers their first meetings, when she and Kira had wrestled on the pitch and Maeve had ended up being sent off – how Kira had encouraged her afterwards.

As if she can somehow sense Maeve's eyes on her, Kira then looks up, and their eyes meet. Kira doesn't even look angry with her anymore. Just very, very sad.

Maeve swallows painfully, feeling so lost and confused. Maeve really had thought she was just playing a game Kira had started – that Kira's ruthlessness on the field was something she should be trying to channel off the pitch in their rivalry – but now she can see that it isn't a game at all. She's really hurt her. And in this situation, both of them have been so obsessed with winning that they've lost.

The rest of the training session passes in a blur. Nat doesn't score from any of the set pieces and during the drills, it's much easier to stop Nat from scoring after being used to going up against Kira's more aggressive style of play.

Coach calls Kira and the rest of the extended team back over, talking through the recap of their session, concentrating particularly on the attackers, and complimenting Adriana's performance as a support midfielder, being a continuous playmaker. Maeve watches her old friend's face as she receives the praise, as ever unable to just take a compliment, handing the praise to her other midfielders. Maeve is really looking forward to catching up over dinner realising how much she's missed her when she hears Coach Hoffman calling her name.

'Murphy?' Coach tries again. 'Are you listening? Could you stay behind for a moment please?'

Maeve's stomach flips, but of course she nods and lingers behind. Could this be it? Could Coach be about to tell her she's Captain? Her heart pounds with confused hope at how quickly this might be happening.

Kira goes past, head held high, and doesn't even look at Maeve. Maybe she knows? Maybe that's the real reason she was being off today? Maeve had thought it was about them, but maybe this is confirmation Kira didn't care about her like that.

Then Maeve is alone with Coach Hoffman, until she turns and gestures towards the stands, calling over… Jacob Astor.

Maeve's heart pounds harder. If it's the two of them, surely this *is* a conversation inviting her to be Captain? She tries to hold back a smile, starts practicing how she'll gratefully receive the invitation.

And yet, as Jacob strides over, Maeve just keeps seeing the ghost of him holding hands with Adriana in the park, him leaning down to tenderly kiss Adriana's forehead. Maeve tries not to meet Jacob's eye, as if he'll somehow be able to tell she knows his secret, feeling incredibly awkward around him. It's hard to look at him without trying to see what Adriana sees – even if she isn't attracted to him herself, she can tell that Jacob is a handsome man, in a classic sort of way, with chiselled cheekbones, a strong angular jawline, and stern forehead, like a Greek statue in a museum. Adriana might end up with the bold extroverted type more often from the way she tends to meet them, on dancefloors, at parties or bars, but she's often felt her friend would be better with someone the more quietly geeky type, like Adriana's favourite characters in the romcoms they used to watch. Maybe that's what this man is for her.

She only wishes that Adriana could have found that in someone who wasn't a colleague so it wasn't going to be such a complicated situation. Then Maeve remembers her own fling with Kira, and reminds herself she's really not one to judge.

Coach Hoffman and Jacob nod at each other, and Maeve knows that they've discussed this beforehand.

'Murphy,' Coach begins. 'I'm afraid this isn't going to be a fun conversation.'

Maeve is so stunned that she feels numb.

Coach Hoffman and Jacob are equally stern as they contemplate Maeve.

'Tell me. What does a captain do, Murphy?' Coach asks her.

Maeve swallows, her throat dry. She's still frozen.

'Well?'

Maeve coughs, feeling like she's being tested and desperately tries to remember the exact words Jacob had used.

'They set an example?' she ventures.

'Exactly,' says Hoffman. 'They set an example, not just of the standard of play, but also the standard of behaviour. They represent the *team*. I don't know what kind of captain you were under Coach Fernandez, and I don't really care. All I know is that under me, you have not been doing that. I may not be in the dressing rooms or "nightclubs" with you all, but I have eyes, Murphy.'

Maeve feels the blood drain from her face, wondering if Coach Hoffman is about to say that she has sensed the chaotic sexual rollercoasters going on between Maeve and Kira.

'Your evident animosity towards Kira Choksi is unprofessional, and distracting for the team.'

Maeve's heart is hammering. She doesn't know if it's better or worse that Coach seems not to have any idea of any romantic complications between them – she has hidden her true feelings better than she thought but to hear it's distracting for the team comes as a curveball.

'People feel they have to pick sides between you. They don't want to. It distracts your fellow teammates from the game.'

Coach Hoffman removes her glasses, pinching the bridge of her nose.

'I understand that you may be "upset" with the decision made for Kira to be Captain at the fixture last week. However, your reaction to that is, in itself, an indication to me that you are not a good fit for the role of the captain. I should not have to justify myself to my players because you should respect my leadership and vision for the team.'

Maeve swallows, the tips of her ears red.

'Murphy, you're a talented footballer. I can see that you're pushing yourself to play well. But playing well takes place off the pitch too. I hold my players to the highest of standards, and you're falling short of what I would expect from someone who is trying for the captain position.'

For this whole time, Jacob Astor just stands there, his expression, seemingly, unmoved. It feels particularly humiliating to be accused of being unprofessional when he is right there, secretly dating a player in his own team.

'I expect you to change your attitude and be there at all future scheduled additional training with Kira,' says Hoffman. 'I hope I do not have to talk about this with you or with her again. Off you go now.'

Maeve walks away like she's forgotten how to, surprised her legs can keep holding her without her instruction. It's like having a dead leg, but all over, she can't feel any of her limbs, can't feel anything.

Chapter 21

Adriana

Even though Adriana spent the past two nights with Jacob, she's still excited to see him today. Not only has she completely broken her 'no repeats' rule with Jacob, here she is breaking it again, in new ways.

Five minutes ago, Adriana was in the training centre, grabbing her bag, texting Maeve on the way out wishing her good luck with Coach, saying that she'd meet her at Maeve's place for a late dinner, and that she'd bring their favourite chocolate pudding.

Now, she's waiting in a booth in a members only bar. She had messaged him during today's break, asking if they could meet before she went for dinner with Maeve, so that she could ask his opinion about what she should share with her friend about their relationship. It was strange, seeing as they'd spent all weekend together, but they'd stuck to Adriana's request to not talk about work or their situation. Jacob had texted her, saying he'd meet her there as soon as he could. It feels particularly murky for him to be talking to Maeve with

Coach right now, and then coming to see her to discuss what Adriana can share with her friend…

Adriana feels something twinge in her chest, like asthma. She tries to remember the advice Maeve had given her years ago — taking deep breaths, breathing in for four seconds, holding for seven, exhaling slowly for eight. She tries to focus on the room around her, counting things she can see, smell, hear, in the bar.

The room is all shades of rich brown. Round leather chairs, facing each other over bronze-edged wood tables. The light is low and amber, and the focus in the room is drawn to the bar, with suit-clad bartenders and cushioned bar seats. It's swanky, but in a way that lacks any real soul. She feels like she could be anywhere in the world. Perhaps the 'international hotel' feel is part of the appeal for the other patrons — most of whom are older gentlemen in suits, or a couple of city-slicker women in nicely tailored business wear. Adriana feels self-conscious in the hoodie and sports trousers she slipped on for dinner at Maeve's tonight and tries to hide her trainers under her booth seat.

Adriana sighs and leans back, remembering the past days — how after they'd left the park he'd asked, so tentatively, if she was hungry, did she want to have dinner together? One thing led to another and then… she'd woken up in his soft sheets again, to another hot mocha brought to her, and Jacob in his glasses with a new crossword.

Adriana knows what she *should* say to him. She should say this has been wonderful but they can't keep doing this. Even if she was willing to break her lifelong casual policy for him, they both know it's far too complicated with their work being too wrapped up. She can't go to training and pretend not to notice he's there watching her, then go back to his house afterwards? She can't sit in a members' bar while he's talking to her teammate... and yet...

There's Jacob, striding over to her booth and smiling at her. Suddenly, the bar doesn't seem boring at all. Adriana is struck as ever by how her whole body lights up when she sees him.

'Addy,' he sighs. He leans as if to kiss her, automatically, then stops himself. He stands over her, hesitating over how to greet her, what to say.

'Don't tell me what you said to Maeve,' Adriana holds up a hand. 'I want to hear it from her, not from you.'

Jacob holds her eye. 'You sure that's what you want?'

'I don't want to put you in a weird position,' Adriana explains. 'And I also don't want to have to feign surprise when she tells me. I'm terrible at lying.'

'Well... that could be a problem for us.'

'Urgh, not that you need to worry about me keeping *our* secret... I *thought* I was bad at lying, but I swear I haven't told anyone about us, and I don't think they'd guess... Maybe I just haven't ever *wanted* to lie about something before.'

Jacob nods seriously, and slides next to her in the booth, gently touching her hand, as if he can't help himself and keep up the pretense. Adriana smiles at him a little distractedly, biting her nail, looking out the tall window of the bar. She can literally see the corner of the training pitch.

Jacob reads her mind. 'Are you nervous someone could see us together? Because I assure you it's a members only bar, and I checked that there is no overlap with your teammates.'

Adriana laughs. 'Thank you, that was thoughtful but no, I'm sure no one I know would ever come here, trust me. It's not exactly my usual…'

She waves around at the clothes of the people around them, all in suits like Jacob's, or equally formal dresses and topknots.

'Unfortunately, it *is* my usual vibe,' Jacob laughs. 'The only upside is that the cocktails are very fancy too.'

He slides the cocktail list towards her. 'Hair of the dog?' he asks her. They'd drunk negronis at the small plates restaurant he'd taken her to last night.

Adriana catches his eye and the two of them laugh together. Other business people in suits turn on their bar seats and booths to frown at them.

'Shh,' Adriana puts a mischievous finger to her lips, teasing him. 'This isn't a bar, it's a library.'

Jacob sniggers. He effortlessly nods to get a server's attention, orders two negronis, before his full attention returns to Adriana. She can't help it, she loves that when she's with him in these kind of settings, she can just relax, not having to always feel like it's her responsibility for everyone to be having a nice time. Adriana loves talking to people, it's true, but sometimes it gets exhausting feeling like every time she meets anyone, even a member of staff in a bar like this, to feel the need to befriend them. She loves that Jacob just always knows how to handle the situation in a calm and assured way.

'So,' he says. He raises an eyebrow to check it's okay for him to take her hand.

'So,' she repeats, worrying about what he's going to say.

Jacob swirls his thumb over Adriana's knuckles. She finds it incredibly soothing.

He looks at her intently. His eyes are the sky of a spring morning. 'Addy, can I say something first?'

Adriana feels the panic rise in her chest, but tries to concentrate on Jacob's hand in hers, as she nods.

'I had such an amazing time with you this weekend.' His eyes don't leave hers. 'And... I'm just so scared.'

Adriana feels tears welling in her throat, expecting the next words to be what she's thought herself that they can't keep doing this.

'The stakes feel so high,' he explains. 'And not just about... what is happening between the two of us – though frankly, that would be scary enough.'

Adriana smiles a little at that. It's a relief to hear him say it's a lot for him too.

'But it's the things outside of us,' he says. 'For us, for you, for me. This is your *career*. Here I am, having... professional conversations about the lives of your closest friends.'

He closes his eyes and exhales.

'You said you only want something casual. This? This isn't casual. It's not casual to be playing with our careers in this way, and those of people close to us – your teammates, and my family. And...' he coughs. Takes a deep breath. 'Addy, I don't– I don't feel casually about you. The fact that we have been on, what, two dates? And I am already feeling...'

He shakes his head, smiling at her ruefully. Adriana's heart swells.

'I know I'm not a 'casual' man in general, arguably I take everything I do too seriously – someone very wise and hot told me that not too long ago –' Adriana smiles at him, tears forming in her eyes. 'But even *I* am not usually fantasising about the future when I've been on two dates with someone. I don't get excited about people like this. Because I do— I feel so… unbelievably happy around you. I know you must be used to making people feel like that, you're like a permanent beam of sunshine. But do you understand how rare that is for me? How unexpected? I don't take it for granted.'

Gently, so gently, he reaches over and traces a finger along Adriana's thumb.

'Jacob, I don't feel casually about you either,' she admits, her voice breaking a little because she can't believe she's doing this. 'My rules are already out the window with you, and I– I would break them all, for you.'

Jacob tilts her chin gently towards him like she's the most precious thing he's ever touched and kisses her. Adriana's body relaxes into his, and for a moment, it all feels so simple. They feel the same way! Maybe all along, she secretly *did* want to meet someone, someone who would make her feel safe in trusting him with her feelings.

But then, the server delivers their drinks to their booth, and she is jolted back to reality. The very fact that they're here, sneaking around, within metres of their workplace. She pulls back, biting her lip where she can still feel Jacob's touch.

He seems to know exactly what she's thinking.

'I don't want to be hiding,' he says, his voice low. 'When we should be just able to enjoy this rare thing happening between us, let it grow in its own way. I wish it wasn't like this.' He says with a heavy sigh.

'But it *is* like this,' Adriana reminds him. 'This is the reality of our situation.'

She is surprising herself by being the one to be the reality check. As incredible as she finds Jacob's confession — and she really does, it's incredible when the person you have feelings for feels the same. But being with Jacob also allows her to feel safe in bringing out this more serious side of herself. It reminds her of being with Maeve, all those years ago at Football Academy — how it felt like she was the only person who didn't just *like* her or feel charmed by her, but also really *respected* her, and so it had given Adriana permission to start respecting herself. Jacob brings that out in her too.

He nods, never taking his hand from hers.

'We both want to be with each other,' she says. 'But we also both want our careers here with the Tigresses.'

Jacob's face crumples suddenly, when he realises what she's getting at. He takes his glasses off, pinching the bridge of his nose, pulling his hand through his hair.

'It just feels so ironic,' Jacob mutters. 'I never even wanted this job. My father…'

His jaw clenches again, as if he's gone somewhere else. Then his eyes focus on her again, and he sighs.

'Sorry,' he says. He reaches for their ignored drinks, toasts a little wryly to the edge of her negroni, then takes a long gulp. He winces again, but his shoulders do seem to loosen a little.

'You can tell me, if you want to,' says Adriana softly. 'I'll listen. But you don't have to tell me anything you don't want to share.'

He nods, swallows. 'You're right. Thank you. I'm just not used to... talking about this kind of thing.'

He takes another mouthful, then a deep breath.

'My father is not a nice man. In fact, he's a bully. That feels like an important thing to say upfront. He is powerful, and successful, and rich, and he is used to getting his way. He surrounds himself with yes men, people who are only looking for money and power too. He wanted me to always work for him, which is why I've been thrust into this when I never wanted to be involved in running a football club.'

His whole body is tense now and his hand has slipped from Adriana's.

'But that's my biggest fear. That I'll follow in his footsteps and become a heartless bully like him because he never listens to anyone else, or cares about their feelings. When you and I saw each other again at the training grounds, and realised who each other were, I was wary, I was defensive. But then it seemed like you were not only confused about how to be with me, but also...'

Jacob's eyes search hers, then look down, swirling the block of melting ice round his empty glass.

'It seemed like you were almost scared of me? The fact that you thought I would do something so... so immoral as to punish you for our one-night stand? I think that just freaked me out.'

Jacob's head is bowed as he speaks, his habitual poker face slipping to show the cracks of vulnerability and pain beneath. He covers his face with his hand, as if trying to hide himself from her. Adriana reaches over and gently takes his cold hand in hers, warming the fingers beneath her own.

'Jacob, I don't know your father, but I know you're nothing like him.'

Jacob peers at her over the edge of his glasses, his eyebrow raised self-deprecatingly.

'Am I not? I think if any of your teammates saw me here, holding hands with you… Wouldn't they think that I was abusing my power? Wouldn't they think that I was just as bad as him?'

Adriana bites her lip and sighs deeply, then takes a sip of her negroni. She wishes she could say something to make it all better, of course she does, both for him and for herself. But that's exactly why they're still here. There isn't a solution.

'What would you rather be doing?' she asks him instead.

Jacob smiles in surprise. 'Oh, what everyone wants to do, I suppose. Sit around reading all day. Adopt a cat. Go on sunny walks in the park at the weekend with a gorgeous red-haired footballer.'

Adriana grins back at him, kissing his cheek quickly, because she can't resist. Something feels a little lighter between them.

'I do enjoy some aspects of my work right now,' he says. 'I enjoy being good at it. I enjoy feeling useful. The only ways I've been able to be useful in my life have been during business meetings, securing a deal. So, I guess… I wouldn't mind doing that, but for a business I believed in? Or a charity? Though, ha, my dad would have a fit if I used his expensive education to help other people…' He sighs, shaking his head.

'I like finding out more about you,' Adriana reassures him. 'And the more I do, it's yet another reason I find myself liking you.'

He squeezes her hand, and sighs. 'I may not have asked for this job, but now I'm here, I want to do it well.'

Adriana can understand that all too well. In fact, she admires it about him.

'So as far as I can see, there are two options,' says Adriana, after a while. 'Either, we actually end things between the two of us, and keep seeing each other only across the pitch in a purely professional capacity.'

She looks at him cheekily, gesturing with their still-clasped hands. 'That didn't go so well when we tried it last time, did it? So the alternative is that we have to keep doing… this. To keep both, we need to keep it a secret. From everyone. Our friends, colleagues, family…'

She hates the murkiness of it, but she can't bear the thought of losing him, or her job. So what alternative does she have? The two of them nod in mutual agreement. It feels bittersweet.

'I'm sorry,' he says quietly. 'I'm sorry that it isn't different.'

He reaches out to hold her in the booth, cupping her cheek, his other hand stroking her hair. And then his face breaks into one of his rare, wonderful smiles.

'But I have to admit, even when it's difficult, I find it very hard not to be happy, when I'm with you.'

Adriana thinks her heart might burst. She feels light and giddy and like she might say something very silly.

'I'm willing to do anything to mean we can keep seeing each other,' says Jacob. 'And if that means keeping it a secret, then fine.'

Adriana kisses him in agreement. Even though she wishes it were different in so many ways, the truth is that she also feels closer to him than ever. She wishes they could spend the rest of the night together, again. But she has to go and see Maeve, and lie to her...

The server is back, subtly taking their empty glasses and asking if he can get them anything else.

'Would you like another drink?' Jacob asks her. 'Or no time before seeing Maeve?'

Adriana sighs guiltily, checking her phone. It's time for her to go, really. She doesn't want to be late for her friend, and yet the thought of leaving Jacob right now, when they've been vulnerable with each other and when they've agreed to see each other more, fills her with regret. Plus, she's definitely putting off seeing Maeve.

'Urgh, it's so weird, I'm not used to avoiding her!' Adriana sighs. 'I feel like the two of us haven't caught up in so long, and things have been so weird. She's hiding something, I know, and obviously I'm hiding –' she gestures between them. 'A *lot* too. And we know each other so well, we can tell. I want to be back to normal with her, but I just don't know how that's going to be possible so I...'

She flops her head onto the table and groans dramatically, her frustration getting the better of her. Then she remembers where she is and quickly lifts her head back up, trying to pretend to be professional. A server is stood there, watching her with wide eyes.

She picks up the cocktail menu, all of the drinks looking incredibly delicious, and none with a price next to them. 'Maybe I could have… a half?' she says.

'A half cocktail?' teases Jacob.

'Urgh,' Adriana blushes. 'I don't know what I'm saying.'

Jacob nods, puts his hand on her forearm, and says quietly to the server, 'One negroni please, and some water.' He smiles at her. 'We can share.'

Adriana feels so grateful for him taking the initiative while she's spiralling that when the server disappears, she leans over to kiss him. She doesn't have to think, it just happens. Jacob blinks at her in surprise, then pulls her face back into his, to kiss her deeply. Adriana feels dizzy. She isn't used to kissing in public full stop, but she would never have allowed herself to hope that Jacob, specifically, would be okay with kissing her in a place like this. She wants to make the most of it while there isn't a fear of bumping into a teammate.

Their one cocktail arrives, and they playfully toast each other with it against the other's water glass, each taking one sip, then swapping over. They talk a little more, Adriana asking more about his knitting grandma, who it turns out also inspired his love of crosswords, and reading. But she knows she should be making a move to get to Maeve's.

'I really do have to go,' Adriana says, feeling disappointed to have to cut this short.

'Good luck,' says Jacob. 'Remember, even if it's feeling a bit strange right now, she's your oldest friend. I'm sure she absolutely adores you. It's going to be okay.'

Adriana looks up at him. How could she ever have thought that face was anything other than kind?

'So… Can I see you… soon? You can tell me how it goes?'

She nods up at him. She loves watching his poker face spread into a smile.

'As soon as soon can be,' she says. 'I'll text you right after dinner.'

Then Adriana gives him one last kiss before she leaves.

Chapter 22

Maeve

Maeve wants to cook something special for Adriana tonight. Using food to show how sorry she is, her gratitude for her friend, and hopefully put them both in a good mood to talk. So Maeve has spent hours choosing and painstakingly making a new recipe from scratch – a galette with a handmade pistachio paste. She had made the pastry herself the night before, grateful for the distraction from her heartbreak. The photograph accompanying the recipe had a galette with intricate pastry flowers as decoration so, despite having never worked with pastry before, Maeve had tried to make those too, snapping at herself when she messed some up.

Now, she opens the oven to check in on the pastry and sees the flowers have all lost the shape she'd worked so hard to painstakingly create. She starts tearing up at the sight of the burnt blobs.

She knows it's ridiculous to cry over pastry, but Maeve feels like she can't do anything right at the moment. She had just wanted to do something nice for her friend, but this feels like a bad omen for the evening.

On the table is a little bowl of homemade hummus with a platter of vegetables and breadsticks to dip. Maeve's stomach has been rumbling, but she has left it perfectly untouched for Adriana's arrival. She checks her phone again. Adriana is fifteen minutes late, now, which isn't that unusual because time-keeping isn't one of her strengths, but she'd normally at least message.

She checks Adriana on Find My Friends. She seems to be... at a bar round the corner from their training grounds. And unless the dot hasn't updated, it seems like she's still there and hasn't even left.

Maeve feels her face flush and the tears welling again. She removes the pastry blobs entirely, throwing them in the bin.

By the time the doorbell goes, Maeve has tried to waft away the smell of charred pastry blobs. Maeve tries not to be upset that her friend is thirty minutes late for the dinner she put a lot of effort into preparing for them, that she didn't bring the pudding she promised, or that she smells of alcohol. But it certainly doesn't make her feel any better.

Maeve tries her best to act like everything is normal, but the two of them hover awkwardly in Maeve's doorway.

'Let me take your jacket,' she offers. She would never normally formally request her friend's jacket, for heaven's sake. Normally Adriana strides in and flops straight on the sofa, or helps herself to anything from Maeve's fridge, or strips her bra off to be more comfortable. Now Maeve feels like a butler, or a stranger, meeting a version of her oldest friend she doesn't recognise.

'Did you go somewhere for drinks after training?' Maeve asks.

Maeve intends the question to sound casual, but then Adriana looks shifty and, clearly lying, snaps, 'No?'

'Oh,' Maeve pauses, trying to give her friend the benefit of the doubt. 'So what did you get up to after training today?'

Adriana looks round the room. 'I just… went for… a walk.'

'Okay,' Maeve nods.

She wonders if she should be worried about Adriana lying about drinking – for a second her mind flashes with worries of her friend having an alcohol dependency, that *that's* the big secret she hasn't been telling her – knowing too that Adriana's brother had struggled with drinking a few years ago, and Adriana had helped encourage him to attend his first AA meetings. But, she thinks, with a sinking feeling, perhaps it's more likely at the moment that her friend is lying to her about going for drinks with other members of the team because she knows Maeve wasn't invited and she doesn't want to make things more awkward than they already are.

She turns to the oven to hide her face. She feels like she's back at secondary school, the girls bullying her by avoiding her, pretending she didn't exist and they couldn't hear her, not inviting her to any social events. They would say loudly to each other in her earshot that they didn't want a 'dirty lesbian' at their parties, even though now several of those girls are openly queer themselves.

She's been carefully trying to keep the galette warm on a low heat in the oven. It's now dried out, but she tries to zhuzh it a little with some more olive oil to make it edible. Maeve gestures to her to sit down and eat the hummus platter. Adriana sits but then, just gnaws at her thumb.

'Did you want a drink?' Maeve offers. 'I have that rosé you like. Or white? Or–'

'I'm actually all good, thanks,' says Adriana. Well, at least it's reassuring for Maeve's 'is Adriana a secret alcoholic' theory, but it doesn't help with the terrible atmosphere in the room, the strange silence between them hanging heavy in the air.

'Music!' Maeve suggests. 'I'll put some music on! Would you like to DJ?'

Adriana shakes her head. Maeve feels her disappointment start to overwhelm her. It's bad enough to turn up late and lie about where she's been but now can her friend not at least try to make some effort with her?

Maeve puts on a playlist Spotify suggests for her, 'Dinner Party With Friends', feeling silly when the jaunty pop starts playing. Maeve says their food will be warm again in a minute, and Adriana thanks her politely, like she's just her waiter. They sit in silence, Adriana avoiding eye contact, drinking some water, checking her phone.

Normally Adriana is so good at setting people at ease, even strangers. Is Maeve really *so* awful that she's being punished like this? By her oldest friend too? She thought she'd already apologised and they would be able to move on from her behaviour at the club the other night. This feels horrible.

Maeve makes an excuse for needing the loo, then looks at her reflection to give herself a pep talk.

Because it isn't just Adriana, is it? It's her too. She feels like a wounded animal, hurt by Kira seducing her so intensely and then dropping her, hurt by seeing Adriana with Jacob, hurt by Coach Hoffman and Jacob telling her that she's not meeting the standards they expect..

She feels so overwhelmingly sure that she isn't good enough. Not good enough for her friend, for Kira, for the team, for her mother, for anyone. She slaps her own cheek, trying to wake herself up from this pity party.

She goes back to the kitchen to serve up their food, cutting a careful triangle of galette each, with a fresh salad on the side, and brings it through to Adriana. The plates and crockery are all from a set which Adriana bought her years ago from a charity shop – all with pink cartoon cows on.

Adriana picks up a pink cow pattern fork, and spins it, gnawing her lip. Maeve wonders if she should have, what, bought different crockery?

Then the song changes, and 'Murder on The Dance Floor' starts playing.

The two of them glance up, unable to help catching each other's eye. The song was always played as the final song at the Football Academy end of season 'discos', where they had all screamed over the chorus making it 'Murder on "Zidane's" Floor' in homage to Zinedine.

It gets to the chorus now, and, unprompted, when it gets to that line, they both sing along, saying Zidane.

They laugh quietly with each other. The tension in the room dissipating enough to finally be with each other.

'Hey,' says Maeve quietly.

'Hey,' says Adriana. And Maeve realises that her friend looks as terrified as she is.

'I'm so sorry,' Maeve blurts out. 'I don't know exactly what I've done to upset you but I do know I have been a terrible friend recently. I'm— I haven't been… I haven't been doing so well.'

Adriana swallows, her eyes softening as she reaches over to take Maeve's hand, but now Maeve is finally saying what she's been holding back she can't stop herself.

'And I think I find it really hard to admit that, so I just sort of, withdrew. From you, from all of it. I have been so focused on this—' she shakes her head again. 'This captaincy obsession, and… tonight, you know Coach wanted to speak to me? With… With Jacob Astor?'

Maeve studies her friend's face as she says Jacob's name. Adriana's face flushes red, and she looks down at the galette she's poking around her plate. Maeve leaves a gap to see if Adriana wants to take the opportunity to talk about the nature of her relationship with Jacob, but she doesn't. Adriana just sucks on her empty fork. Maeve sighs, a little hurt she didn't take the chance, but continues.

'They… They said that I'm not meeting their standards. Said if I want any chance of being renamed captain, I need to improve immediately.'

Adriana's head jolts up to her in surprise. Maeve knows her friend, she's not that good an actor. Even though something is going on between her and Jacob, he's clearly not told her about this.

'But *why*?' Adriana gasps. 'You're one of our top players?'

Maeve sighs, bowing her head. 'Because of Kira. Because of the way that she and I… Because I'm…'

Maeve's throat feels so dry and like it's tightening. Being punished by the team mingles with her heartbreak at Kira not wanting to see her anymore. 'Kira hates me now, maybe she always did, and I'm meant to be okay with her but *she* is the one who...'

Maeve swallows down her tears, covering her face in her cow-print napkin.

Adriana goes and hugs her at last, and Maeve can't stop a few tears spilling onto her friend's shoulder. But she pulls herself back together, hardly, not letting herself fully give way to the emotion. While she's trying to stem her tears, Adriana goes back to her seat and takes a long sip of water, watching her. She seems to be choosing her words carefully.

'Kira isn't as untouchable as you think, you know,' says Adriana. 'I don't know what was going on with you two. But whatever you said to her on that night out, or whatever it is you've been saying to her in your one-on-ones... She was really upset, Maeve. Really genuinely upset.'

'How do you know?' Maeve hesitates.

'We've been...' Adriana nervously curls a loop of her hair behind her ear. 'Well, we've been hanging out a bit.'

Maeve's chest swells with a fiery jealousy.

'*Hanging out*? What does that mean?'

'You know, she doesn't have many other friends here,' Adriana speaks quickly. 'It's important for the team to feel like a unit, right? It affects our play so much if we have a weak link in the bonds between us – it's like Coach said to you right?'

Maeve feels like Adriana has slapped her now.

'–And when Kira first joined I think she struggled to make friends, because everyone just thought she was this arrogant, I don't know, lone wolf – but really we were probably all a bit jealous right? Because she's so fucking brilliant on the pitch, and we were just scared of change, and her being Coach's favourite. But then Kira was telling me that in her old team, everyone was kind of nasty to her because she was Coach's favourite, but that's basically because Coach is like Kira's most consistent family now, seeing as she's followed her across different countries and teams…'

Adriana trails off.

Maeve wants to throw her plate across the room. Wants to tip up the table, and scream. She knows it isn't rational to be jealous of her straight best friend and her former – well, whatever Kira was. But she wishes it was *her* that Kira was talking to. The thought that while she's been alone, crying, feeling like no one in the world cares about her, Kira and Adriana have been sitting around bonding. While Maeve's been hurting about the captaincy, her friend has been chumming up to the player who took it away from her.

'Look. I know you might not want to hear this, Maeve, but I say this as your friend. As your oldest friend. Your *best* friend.'

Maeve's whole body tenses. 'Best friend' suddenly rings a bit false, which terrifies her.

'If you want to win Coach Hoffman over, and get back in her good books,' Adriana's blue eyes are wide and earnest, speaking slowly and surely. 'You have to mend your relationship with Kira. Whatever it is you don't like about her, you have to learn to put it aside. For the good of the team, Maeve. For your own good too. At the end of the day, it has to be about the team, right? That's what football is about?'

'Oh yeah?' says Maeve. Her hands are shaking. 'Did Jacob Astor tell you that?'

Adriana freezes. 'What— What do you mean?'

'I saw the two of you yesterday,' says Maeve. Her voice is harsh. 'In the park.'

It's Adriana who is the trapped animal now, her eyes searching Maeve's. Maeve waits, to see what Adriana says in response. To give her friend this chance to be honest with her on her own terms, not just because she has been caught. Adriana grabs a handful of her hair in her hand, twisting it.

'We… We just bumped into each other. And talked about… business.'

Maeve's eyebrow shoots up. 'Business?'

'Jacob has nothing to do with decision making about who should be club captain,' says Adriana hurriedly. 'Remember, he said? After the first game, he said it's just his responsibility to ensure the team is making a profit for his bully of a father.'

Maeve's eyebrow arches. Bully of a father? She is pretty certain that wasn't something Jacob said in front of the team.

'He said he respects Coach's expertise,' Adriana continues, 'and doesn't plan to influence her decisions. It's not him you need to worry about, okay? He has nothing to do with it.'

Maeve knows it's hypocritical of her, when she hasn't told Adriana about the true nature of her relationship with Kira, but she feels so hurt, so disappointed and confused by Adriana blatantly lying to her. Not only lying to her about her relationship with Jacob, but using it as a chance to tell Maeve off about her own behaviour. To act like she's so high and mighty when really she's what? Sleeping with the boss? Of course Adriana doesn't have to feel scared or worried about her future, when *she* has this insider information into the workings of the team, and his good favour to guarantee her place in the squad.

'It's Kira you need to concentrate on,' Adriana urges. 'She's your way back into Coach's good books. Not Jacob. Trust me.'

Maeve can't stop herself from laughing cynically at that. That word that was always a given between them now feels broken.

'Trust you? You want me to trust *you*? Right now?' She is so angry she stands up, collecting up their untouched plates, and pacing to the kitchen. 'Why should I? You haven't given me reason to trust you. You haven't been there for me when I've been going through all this change, you haven't been there for me when my mum— You've been avoiding me for weeks, lying to me, patronising and insulting me, going behind my back to talk to *Kira* about me—'

Maeve's shame and loneliness come out in one big wave of humiliation and anger.

'You couldn't even show up on time to eat a fucking *galette*?'

Maeve opens the bin lid, and throws all their food in.

Maeve stares, shaking, as Adriana just sits there, in her chair where the two of them have had so many deep conversations over the years. Adriana's eyes are closed, and she seems to be doing some kind of deep breathing. Is she seriously just meditating right now, as Maeve is going through all this? As Maeve dared to try to share her feelings with her, finally, and Adriana doesn't give a single shit enough to even listen and have a proper conversation with her.

Adriana slowly gets up, picks up her jacket, and walks out the door without saying a word.

Chapter 23
Adriana

Adriana avoids talking to Maeve for the rest of the week at training, still in shock and upset at their inability to understand each other or reconcile. She feels so guilty that her keeping the secret of Jacob continues to create distance between them, but after her conversation with Jacob in the bar, she doesn't feel she has a choice. And it shouldn't change that she thinks her advice to her friend about being nicer to Kira is still true – yet her friend lashed out, and now there's clearly no trust between them. She doesn't think it's only her fault or Maeve's, but what she does hate is that she can't see a way out of them becoming closer again unless something changes. It never stops feeling awful. In fact, her chest has started hurting badly when she thinks about Maeve, as if her heart is literally breaking. When Adriana thinks about it too much, she struggles to breathe.

But she has the best distraction. She has spent every night staying with Jacob. When it's just the two of them, everything is okay in the world. Lying in his soft bed, head on his broad chest, Adriana feels her whole body, mind, soul, completely relax. Adriana can't believe how much she has loved doing 'normal' domestic things with Jacob. One night they made dinner together — Jacob is a much better chef than Adriana, thank goodness, but she helped go to the shops and prepare the fresh ingredients, and he makes a simple tomato pasta feel like luxury. Another night they ordered in a huge takeaway to watch a romcom together — Jacob had teared up when the lovers finally got together, and Adriana had laughed, kissing his adorable wet cheeks. But then, the morning would come, and they would leave the cocoon of his home, and she would become Adriana the footballer and he would be Jacob the club director, and her chest would start hurting again.

Now, Adriana's going to have to face the challenge of being 'Adriana the footballer' all weekend, because the team have an away match in Liverpool.

The team get in the coach to travel together, Adriana dreading the thought of sitting next to Maeve all journey. But when she arrives, Maeve has already made some excuse to be at the front on her own, saying she has started getting car sick. Adriana feels a bit embarrassed, walking past her, to go and sit next to Kira instead.

'So you guys hate the Swans?' says Kira, snacking on a huge bag of trail mix. If the Manchester Tigresses have a rival, it's the Liverpool Swans.

'Uh huh,' explains Elisa, leaning over from the nearby seats. 'They're so violent.'

'They could break your arm with their necks,' says Charlie.

'That's not a thing swans do,' says Elisa.

'But it's a thing the Liverpool Swans do,' says Charlie seriously. 'Remember when their captain Chloe fouled Maeve right off the bat last year? She slid in a two-footed lunge – late. Nearly broke Maeve's ankle.'

Kira whistles through her teeth. 'Ouch. And Maeve's already prone to ankle injuries.'

Adriana glances at Kira curiously.

'Wasn't the captain dating Maeve's ex?' chimes in Nat, from behind them.

Adriana feels Kira sit up. 'Is that so?' she asks, casually.

Adriana nods. 'Yeah, Hannah. Hannah's type is captains of rival teams, I guess…'

Kira's jaw clenches.

'Yeah, Maeve was such a trooper about it,' Nat continues. 'Barely flinched, all calm while the rest of us were shouting for red cards. Maeve still shook Chloe's hand at the end of the match and everything.'

'I'd have spat in her face!' says Milo. 'But yeah, Maeve was cool.'

Milo hesitates, looks to the front, at where they can see the back of Maeve's head at the front of the coach, then mutters, 'Back when Maeve was cool.'

Adriana glances up at Maeve's blonde ponytail too, shifting uncomfortably. She wants to put an end to this kind of talk, but it's a fine balance, not wanting to set herself up as policing her teammates' behaviour.

'We've all got to look out for the Swan's nasty tactics today,' Adriana says, her voice measured. 'Don't let their beaks get too near us.'

She directs this at Milo and Nat, who she knows love puns. 'Let them honk and squawk while we just… swan past them.'

They reward her with generous laughs, and the tension in the coach eases a little.

But when they arrive in Liverpool and file out into the dressing room, Adriana and Maeve seem to keep bumping into each other as they get into their orange kit. They always used to know what each other was thinking, but now her friend's anxious face is closed off from her, silent. And when they're getting ready for Coach's speech, Adriana notices that Maeve isn't using the matching personalised water bottle she got her, instead sipping from a plain grey one.

Adriana doesn't know why, but this is what really spins her out. She and Maeve have been together through so much. They made a pinky promise, that day at the Tigresses' match, to always support each other. And now here they are, living their dream of playing for their beloved team, together – but without their friendship. If little Adriana could see them now, she'd be so disappointed.

Adriana feels breathless, clutches at her chest like she truly might not be able to breathe properly. She knows she can't keep hiding Jacob from her friend – Maeve deserves to know, she *wants* her to know, so that they can have a chance to be united again, the way they used to be.

She needs to text Jacob, and tell him she's going to tell Maeve about them. Surely he will understand that her friendship is too precious to hang in the balance.

So before Coach comes in to give them their pre-game talk, Adriana slips out her phone and sees Jacob has already texted her.

```
Break a leg out there, Tiger.
Wait, not literally, please.
```

I mean good luck and have fun out there x (just from me and not in an official capacity)

Adriana's stomach flutters. She stares at the kiss at the end, which Jacob has never put before. She feels so happy and yet terrified at the same time.

Coach Hoffman enters the changing room, and Adriana only has a few seconds before she'll be expected to give the team meeting her full attention.

Thank you, truly x she types. Then she sighs, and before she can change her mind, she hastily types out and sends,

Can we find time to talk after the game? There's got to be another way. I can't stand lying to Maeve. Please can I tell her about us? xxx

Coach is standing before them, already looking more tired than when she joined a mere few weeks ago.

'Team, I want to start today's talk by saying that I know that the last few weeks haven't been easy for many of you. You were in a position of a lot of stability, and then there was a lot of sudden and dramatic change. New ownership, new coach, new leadership. I'm proud of how you've responded so far with two wins out of two. Congratulations.'

Kira leads a ripple of applause, acknowledging their perfect start to the season at home.

'Today, it's our first away game and we play the most competitive team in the league,' Coach continues. 'Swans are the top of the table on goal difference. This is when we need to pull the stops out and raise our level.'

'Maeve was our captain in pre-season, Kira for the first two games but I'm going to rotate again while I'm still getting to know you. My choices seem to have caused some confusion, so I have also made some consultations this time.'

Adriana frowns, looking round the room confused at where this is going and who exactly has been consulted. Not her, that's for sure.

Hoffman turns to Maeve who is standing to attention and Kira, whose arms are folded just as tightly.

'Maeve,' says Coach. 'I've heard that your conduct helped you to win that competitive match last season when you played the Swans. Your calming presence is valued on the pitch. But I'm still unsure it's what the team need for this season more broadly. This is why, I have decided to name you as our vice-captain.'

Adriana watches her old friend's face go pale. Maeve bows her head. Adriana hopes she can find a way to be proud – it shows she's proved something to Coach in the way she's trained this week, since Coach took her aside. Although Adriana is dreading how the team will cope with Kira as captain again, especially working with Maeve as vice, when as far as Adriana has seen, the two still avoid speaking to each other entirely.

Adriana is so busy watching Kira and Maeve trying to understand what their concerned frowns mean, that she barely hears Coach's next words.

'I am therefore very pleased to announce that my choice for our team's captain, for today at least … is Adriana Summers.'

A ripple goes round the room. Charlie and Elisa, standing next to Adriana, clap her on the back.

'Hey! Congratulations!' they say quickly in unison, their smiles broad.

But instead of happiness, Adriana's body just floods with cold, frozen, terror.

Maeve's eyes are on her, betrayed. Maeve must think that this is why Adriana has been off with her – that Adriana has been waiting for a chance to come up and steal the captaincy from her all along. Kira is frowning, looking at both her then Maeve, fury building.

All Adriana can think is, 'I didn't ask for this!'

Okay, sure, if someone had ever asked her if she wanted to be captain – like Jacob had a few days ago, funnily enough – she would have said, in theory, sure. But being club captain is *Maeve's* dream. Had always been her dream. And it was more important for Adriana to help her friends than to be too big for her own boots. She was there to be a team player.

She remembered how Jacob had replied that's probably exactly what would make her a good captain.

Adriana's stomach does a strange somersault.

Could Jacob have had something to do with this?

'I– I–'

Adriana knows she should be thanking Hoffman, or formally accepting the position. But it's all so strange, so unexpected, not something she's ever lobbied for, that Adriana can barely force a confused smile, while her other teammates clap her on the back.

Before she can even really understand what's happening, the referee knocks on the dressing room door. It's time to get out on the pitch.

In the tunnel, as the team line up, stretching and jogging on the spot, Adriana takes her usual place in line, only for Nat to nudge her affectionately.

'Addy,' Nat beams. 'You're not with us in the middle anymore – Captain goes up front!'

Adriana thinks her team are trying to be kind, pushing her up to the front, but she feels like their hands are buffeting her, pushing her up to where she believes Maeve should be standing.

Adriana can barely meet her friend's eye. When she glances at her, Maeve is staring at Adriana's captain armband, loose in Adriana's hand. The one she was wearing herself so recently. Her face is impassive.

Adriana can't thank her, her stomach churning so much she worries she might throw up.

'Is this what you wanted?' Maeve whispers. 'You and Jacob?'

Adriana opens her mouth to reply, but her throat is tight, her breathing shallow. Maeve walks away, to the back of the line. Kira watches her pass, then looks back to where Adriana is now stood, reluctantly sliding the captain armband on. Adriana is used to being in the spotlight as the team's joker, not its leader.

She worries that despite their congratulations, everyone in the team probably hates her or is jealous. Jacob might have been lying to her, or going against her wishes – what if she really has just slept her way to a captain position she doesn't even want. Does she?

Adriana picks at her skin, bites her lip, feeling suddenly self-conscious in her kit. She shouldn't be here, everything just feels wrong.

'It's time,' says Hoffman. Adriana has to lead the team out onto the pitch.

Adriana turns to face the light of the pitch, hearing the roar of the crowd waiting for them.

Adriana takes a deep breath and starts to run.

⚽

Adriana is so in her head that she doesn't do any of the captain things she is supposed to.

It takes her a few seconds of watching Chloe, the Swan's captain in the centre of the pitch by the referee, glaring round for the Tigresses' captain for the coin toss, for Adriana to realise it should be her.

As she runs over, her heart is pounding like a scared rabbit. If she can't calm herself down, she doesn't know how she's going to cope in the match.

Chloe grips her hand tightly, unsmiling. Instinctively, Adriana mentally runs through Chloe's social media pages, confirming that Chloe is still dating Hannah, and wonders whether Chloe is still jealous of Maeve, whether there might be any issues with her striking out at her in defense. Then Adriana shakes her head – surely as captain she should be thinking about tactics, not gossip!

Adriana loses the coin toss. It is the first bad omen in what she can already feel is a downwards spiral.

From the first whistle, the Tigresses are all over the place.

At the first chance, Kira dribbles with the ball, sprinting halfway up the pitch on pure determination. When the Swan's defense quickly surround her, Zuri breaks free out on the wing and shouts for the ball to be passed to her, but Kira tries to cling onto the ball instead, trying to dummy with the defense. Kira's risk doesn't pay off. The Swan's defence steamroller through her fancy footwork, winning the ball back and moving it quickly to their midfielders who start the counter attack.

It takes Adriana and Charlie each pressing them – and getting lucky with a mistake from their opponents – to regain possession. At a moment when they are getting their first momentum, and it looks possible that they might be getting close to breaking through, Adriana finds Kira. But then it happens again. Instead of passing to a teammate, Kira sprints off, and makes a desperate kick for the goal that flies over the bar with the Swan's goalie not even forced into making a save. The goalie grins smugly at Kira through her mouthguard and takes her time collecting the ball and taking her kick to restart play.

The goalie's condescension clearly riles Kira up even further. Maeve shouts instruction down the pitch, it being second nature to her as former captain, trying to help the team get it together.

'Hold your shape!' Maeve yells. 'Stop pressing so high!'

But Kira has gone rogue, trying so hard to get a goal at any cost and it's leaving them vulnerable to the counter attack. From then, Maeve's usually assured and tactical calls don't sound sure even of herself, because the team aren't responding. It feels like they're all playing their own individual games. The team is disintegrating.

The Swans, in their sleek kits, see their obvious weaknesses and barge right through the Tigress's midfield. They score.

With the Tigresses out of shape and trying to figure out how they conceded, a swift series of slick passes from the Swans slice through their defence again.

Adriana, normally a creative link in the middle of the team, feels stuck in a tug-of-war. She can tell the team are struggling so she wants to dig in and help them tighten up defensively, but she's supposed to be the spark starting the attack. It's clear to her that this is about the players each being in their heads, not knowing who they should be listening to, and not knowing who they should trust. But as Kira and Maeve both shout literally opposite instructions at her, she finds herself unable to do her usual mid-pitch mediation. If she were to shout too, it would just be yet another thing in the mix to confuse everyone. She finds herself longing for half-time so that Hoffman can give them all a stern talking to.

In her worst moments, she can't help looking towards the stands, trying to pick out her family's shining sun sign. Secretly, she hopes Jacob has surprised her by coming even though he hadn't planned to join for this away game. But she can't see them. And in even the seconds that she's looking for their motivating faces, the Swans are back up in her face, pushing through the disconnected Tigresses to score another goal. 2-0.

COUPLE GOALS

Each Swan celebration is a crush for the Tigresses. Chloe screaming proudly at the crowd, her teammates lifting her up, causes even more rupture between the Tigresses. Kira and Maeve are shouting at each other there on the pitch, and Adriana can't say anything, not trusting herself to choose between them. It's the worst the team have played since the season started. An abysmal start to Adriana's first game as captain.

By the thirty-fifth minute, there have been multiple near misses on the Tigresses' goal, only narrowly saved by Maeve making increasingly gritty tackles with Chloe. The Swan's striker seems blood-hungry, always wanting another goal, but also another opportunity to tackle with Maeve. But where last season, Maeve's response had been to be solid like a rock, not giving Chloe the chance through, now, Maeve's playing Chloe at her own agressive game. Those one-on-ones with Kira have been paying off, Adriana thinks, as she watches Maeve fight back – Maeve would never have used to be able to take someone's relentless tackles like this. Even if there's no love lost between Kira and Maeve, training together has clearly been good for Maeve's game.

It's the forty-second minute when it happens.

Chloe's broken through midfield, and trying to steamroller her way past Maeve to get another shot away at goal.

Maeve gets a good block on it, kicking the ball out of play but Chloe stamps down on Maeve's ankle.

Adriana almost imagines she hears a crunch.

There's a roar from the Tigress fans who have travelled to watch the game. 'Red card! Red card!'

Chloe is indeed sent off. But that's not what Adriana is worried about. She rushes to her friend, whose colour has drained from her face, doubled over and clutching her ankle, which is at an awkward angle. Yet she's not even crying or grimacing at the pain. She's clearly in shock.

Kira and Adriana are the first to arrive at Maeve's side. Kira must have run as fast as a rocket to make it from the other team's half. She's reaching automatically to help grasp Maeve's hand as she tries to stand.

'I'm okay,' Maeve winces, trying to lean away from them. 'I'm okay.'

'If you're actually okay, that's probably even worse, because the pain's numbing it,' says Adriana sternly.

Someone from the Tigress's backroom team is running towards them and quickly examining Maeve's ankle.

Maeve gasps at the pain. 'Okay. Maybe not okay.'

'You knew Chloe was out to get you!' shouts Kira. 'You could have got seriously hurt! You should have just left it!'

Kira reaches out like she wants to take over from the medics to check Maeve is okay and do something to help. Maeve lifts a hand up to her and they share a look that Adriana can't read. Kira kicks the air frustrated, and storms away.

The medics are helping Maeve onto a stretcher. Maeve is biting her lip so hard from the pain that it's bleeding along with the grazes on her legs.

Adriana tries to reach for Maeve's hand, but even as she's stretchered off, Maeve pulls it away, and grimacing, says, 'Don't worry about me. You better get back to the game, *Captain*.'

Chapter 24

Maeve

Maeve sits in the changing room, being checked out by the physios and a doctor. She wasn't around to hear what was said by Hoffman in half-time, what guidance was given to try to unite the Tigresses, though it doesn't currently feel like there's any way they can recover from their disastrous first half.

When she had just been injured, Maeve had looked up at her mum in the stands. She can't get her reaction out of her mind. Where Adriana's family had all been on their feet shouting for Chloe's red card, her mum had merely sat with her arms folded. Is getting injured really just another failure to her? In her eyes, if Maeve isn't the best, she isn't anything.

Sitting in pain, the medics discussing her to each other, Maeve holds back tears. She feels another sting of jealousy for Adriana, that her charming, beautiful, beloved best friend, seems to have everything going for her while it feels like everything is crumbling around Maeve. And now, she's Captain too – the *one* thing Maeve has always wanted. The one thing Maeve had that her friend didn't.

But fortunately, the ice pack to take the swelling down is cooling more than just Maeve's ankle. She closes her eyes, taking deep breaths, and, knowing she won't be returning to the field today, she has time to actually just… sit. With her feelings, with everything she knows, alone in the changing room waiting for her teammates to return.

She realises she completely lost her cool back there when Adriana was trying to check on her. She was in pain, shocked, and angry when she snapped at Adriana, frustrated by the Tigress's terrible play on the field, especially against the Swans, who have always been able to rile her up with their nasty tactics. But she hates that she took it out on Adriana.

Maeve has always been known for her strength at keeping a cool head in a crisis. That couldn't be further from her behaviour recently. She doesn't recognise herself anymore.

She scratches her arm, where the captain band is noticeable in its absence. She looks at her arm, the subtle row of pink eczema, tenderness formed from sweat under it being worn on the same place for so many past games. She looks at her bare arm. How obsessed she had been with having the armband there.

But now she doesn't have it anymore, and the world hasn't ended.

She's still here, in her orange away kit. She's still here, in a professional football team. She's still here, trying and actually improving on the pitch. Before the injury, she could match the domineering Chloe in her physicality today, which is definitely down to the extra training with Kira pushing her.

Maeve watches the TV of the match up on the screens, easily able to make out Adriana from her fiery hair. It reminds her of their times watching football games together as children. If little Maeve could see her now, would she be proud of her?

The music blasts and the crowd cheer and whoop as the teams run back onto the pitch for the second half.

Maeve watches, feeling the ghosts of past matches she and Adriana had been in. There's Adriana at the front of the team, in her captain armband, her bright red hair in her bun on the top of her head, her hand clutched to her chest, looking serious and powerful and… like she's in exactly the right place.

The whistle goes for the start of the match, and it looks like they might have had some kind of half-time miracle. They are on the defensive, and managing to hold their shape in the middle. Kira is reigned in, joining up with her fellow attackers rather than striking out alone. It's as if she isn't trying to prove that she is the star player anymore, but trying to listen to the needs of the team.

It hits Maeve finally. Adriana is *perfect* for Captain. Of course she is. Not only is Adriana a fantastically talented player, she has always, always prioritised the wellbeing of the collective team, always being so considerate, upbeat, and kind with them as individuals, on and off the field. She thinks back to Coach Hoffman's words of what she wanted in that role. A captain is there to set the tone of the team – and what a brilliant team the Tigresses would be if they were all a bit more Adriana.

Even though things have been strained between them, she also knows her friend, and Maeve firmly believes, in her heart of hearts, that if Adriana was made Captain, it was because of her own talent and nothing else. Whatever her relationship with Jacob, Maeve trusts that she didn't knowingly recieve any favouritism because of it.

Adriana deserves to be Captain. Maeve would be honoured to be in her team. She just hopes she can apologise enough to her, after this match. She'll come clean about Kira, and about seeing Adriana in the park with Jacob, and do everything she can to get them to how they used to be.

She watches the game for another moment. The Swans continue to be on the wrong side of aggressive with another player teetering with a yellow card. The crowd are lively, riled up too. The rival match has brought in a full crowd to the Liverpool stadium. The Tigresses' reputation is on the line with this match and she worries what the club owners might think if they take a real hammering today.

Maeve squints – she thinks she can see Jacob in the background of one of the screens, in the technical box. She notices him because he's out of his seat, gripping the railings, leaning towards the pitch, and now looking round shouting for help.

Maeve looks back round onto the pitch screens to see what he's looking at.

Adriana had seemed fine a moment ago – hadn't she? – but she is now frozen in the middle of the pitch while the ball is at the other end, the players around it not noticing what's happening behind them. Adriana is clutching at her chest, gripping her kit like it's suddenly too tight. She's clearly struggling to breathe, and her hands and legs are visibly trembling. She holds a hand out to the air, as if trying to hold onto something for balance, but nothing is there. She's looking around, her eyes wide with panic. As Maeve sees Adriana's expression, it sends a horrible electric shock through her. Adriana looks to be having some kind of fit.

'Shit!' Maeve says in the changing room. She gets to her feet, unthinkingly putting her weight on her injured ankle.

'Shit!' she says again, this time from the pain. The medical staff around her frown and reach out to make her sit down again.

'Addy!' Maeve says to them, pointing to the screens desperately. 'She- she needs your help!'

The medics glance up, as their devices start beeping – they run out onto the pitch, one calling back to Maeve to keep her ankle elevated and ice it every ten minutes. Maeve is left alone to stare uselessly up at the screens.

'Sunny,' she whispers.

She sees the medics get straight to her, and her being stretchered off just like she had been so recently, but through a different exit, perhaps to a more intense facility.

She sees Jacob on the screen now, hesitating by the exit in the stand, staring towards where Adriana has disappeared and looking like a loyal dog tethered outside, that desperately wants to follow her out, but knows he can't.

Maeve understands from his reaction something that makes her feel even worse – that he sensed the signals of Adriana's symptoms more than she did. Maeve feels numb. In being so caught up in her own obsession with Kira and stripped of being captain, she can't believe she has let her oldest friend down this badly.

What would the Tigresses do without Adriana? And what on earth would Maeve possibly do if she no longer had her friend by her side?

Chapter 25

Adriana

Adriana's phone keeps buzzing. Text after text, then another call. She lets it go through to voicemail like she did with all the others. She reaches a hand out from under her duvet to turn it onto silent, then buries deeper underneath.

She's hiding in her family home on the outskirts of Manchester. She's in her childhood bedroom, which is covered in football posters and memorabilia from games, alongside fashion magazine rip-outs and gig posters, polaroid photos of parties and friends and postcards from all around the world. The sheets she's buried in, soft from decades of use, are decorated with cartoon footballs, and overflowing with stuffed toys, one of whom – Teddy the teddy, who her dad gave her when she was one hour old – she is clutching now.

She starts feeling breathless under the blanket, reminding her of yesterday on the pitch. The way her chest had pounded and tightened so she couldn't get the air in. She'd thought she was dying. She'd really thought she was dying.

But now, she feels fine, and embarrassed that she's just made a big fuss about nothing. She feels like she lost the Tigresses the match against the Swans. In her first match with the responsibility of Captain, she didn't lead the team with pride to victory, but crashed them like the *Titanic*.

All Adriana's ever wanted was to be loved, to be adored by her friends and her family and her team, and maybe, in a secret part she didn't even want to admit, by a nice guy like she's found in Jacob. Now she's let everyone down, everyone must think she's so selfish – either making some big drama to be the centre of attention faking this ridiculous 'panic attack', or someone who's callously schemed their way to taking the armband.

She keeps seeing betrayed hurt in Maeve's eyes when it was announced she was going to be captain for the game. Maeve's loyalty is one of her most wonderful features, but it can turn into a grudge when she feels that trust is lost – you only had to look at how she was with her 'rival' Kira. She thinks of Maeve confessing to her about the pressure from her mum to always be the best, how Maeve had never trusted anyone else with that. And now, she'll be seeing Adriana as just another selfish bully, someone who's taken the thing she was proudest of.

Adriana throws the blanket off her and gasps for air. She tries to steady her breath counting the glow-in-the-dark stars on her ceiling.

'Twenty-two, twenty-three, twenty-four...'

She sighs and remembers doing the same thing when she was a teenager, not realising she was soothing herself with this counting, just intuitively needing a distraction from the heaviness in her heart.

She feels the ghosts of herself, lying here when she went through her first heartbreaks and disappointments. The times she messed up in games, and it felt like the world had ended and she would never recover. But her friends had always reassured her, had been in on it with her. She had always had Maeve by her side. But since lying to Maeve about her relationship with Jacob, she truly feels she will never be able to regain her precious friend's trust. And Maeve's right to hate her. She's a selfish liar, and a hypocrite, for continuing to see Jacob…

She really thought they could make something work, but now… It goes against her conscience in every way, especially because she's not sure if she got made captain because she deserved it or if it was something he had a hand in. She needs to call it off, but the pain at not being able to see him just feels too awful.

Did it always feel this bad when she was heartbroken? Was it always like her whole body was being crushed by a metal compressor?

When she was lying here as a tween, staring at the stars, her eyes puffy with crying over those boys who seemed not to care at all. James Ochoa in Year 7. Harry Adkins in Year 9. Kyle McDowell in Year 10. Yes, there had been a few she had thought were the end of the world at the time. But none had been as terrible as her heartbreak when she was sixteen, from Dylan Barr. Dylan, captain of the basketball team at the local school, and friends with her older brother Felix. Dylan had never even been her 'official' boyfriend, at his insistence, but he had been her first real love. He had loved how fun she was. Or at least, that's what he had said. He had said she was so different from the other girls, who were all so obsessed with being girlfriends, like they expected a man to want to marry them just because they had kissed. She had pretended to agree. She had been so proud that she could be casual, wearing it like a badge of honour that she could be fun, she could do anything she wanted, and not mind that he was doing it with other girls too. She could lose her virginity to him and not mind that he slept with someone else at a party the very next day. As soon as he slept with her, he lost interest. She could see that now. He was all about the thrill of the chase, about winning someone, and then having the power to say no to ever seeing them again. Well, she had learnt to beat Dylan at his own game. She was the only person he'd come crawling back to, and she had, with a broad smile, shrugged and said she only really did casual things, only slept with people once, it was easier that way. It was how that rule had formed.

She had really believed that was what she wanted. Until she met Jacob.

She should never have broken her no repeats rule. It had kept her safe. It had allowed her to just have fun, to be the good-time girl everyone liked, without ever having the risk of feeling this way or having to trust another person with her heart.

Adriana sits up suddenly in bed, and reaches for her phone, having made her decision. She tries to ignore the screen full of notifications, concerned messages from her teammates, including missed calls from Kira and Maeve. Neither of them left her a message though, so she doesn't know what they're calling to say and can't help but feel anxious about what it might be. Perhaps they want to tell her that they never want to be friends with her unless she resigns the captain position that's rightfully theirs.

Jacob called and texted her yesterday to try to meet with her, then must have taken her silence as meaning she was with people he was a secret from. Still, he has messaged her regularly today checking in. There's a new message since the last time, which feels self-destructive to read in her current mindset, but she can't help herself.

Addy, I'm so sorry that this is happening to you. I wish I had done more. I understand if you want time apart from me while you're recovering, but please know that if there's anything more I can do for you, please, please let me know. Anything x

Do *more* for her? What has he already done? Is this proof that he really had got her this captaincy without her asking for it?

She does not want or need a man pulling strings for her, especially when it pits her against her friends. She never wanted to be in a competition with anyone but on the playing field taking down the opposition alongside her teammates.

She scrolls back through the messages he sent while she was at training, in between their nights together. Pictures of his coconut mocha coffees. Asking her advice on crossword clues he thinks she might know the answers to. Or just the line, I'm thinking of you. I miss you.

COUPLE GOALS

Adriana finds it far too comforting, too wonderful, she knows she'll be tempted right back to him. But she can't be with him. Keeping him a secret has caused her so much stress that she's taken ill during a match. It's inarguable.

`I can't do this anymore,` types Adriana. `It's too hard. Please stop messaging me.`

She sends it and stares at her screen. Then she starts crying into her pillow and doesn't stop. She wails silently for what could be minutes or hours, her stomach feeling like someone keeps punching and punching her.

Adriana is only jilted out of her crying when she hears someone coming up the stairs. She recognises the sound of all her family's steps, and knows this is her mum.

Her mum waits outside the door, and Adriana holds her tear-filled breath.

Then there's a tentative knock.

'Addy?' she calls. 'I've got some tea and crumpets for you, love. Can I come in?'

Adriana crumples lower into the bed, like when she was a kid.

'I'm not hungry, mum,' she calls out. 'Please leave me alone.'

'You haven't come out for *hours*,' her mum says through the door, worried. 'Do you not even need a wee or anything?'

Adriana groans. She has of course snuck out to use the loo when she could hear her family were all in the kitchen.

'I'm fine!'

'Now, what did I tell you about using the f word?'

Adriana buries her face into tear-stained Teddy.

'It's okay to not be fine, darling,' her mum says again. 'Please just talk to us.'

Adriana is so tired. 'I don't have anything to say,' she mumbles.

'What was that?' her mum shouts. 'Please can I come in?'

'No!' Adriana calls out loudly, her voice cracking. 'Just leave me alone, *please* mum. I appreciate you being here but I just—' her throat chokes up again. 'I don't want to talk.'

There's more sets of steps up the stairs. God, the whole brigade is coming, and here's Adriana, trying to muffle her tears from them all.

'How is she?' her dad asks, 'whispering' so loudly next door can probably hear too.

'She doesn't want to talk,' says her mum.

'Addy? Our daughter? Queen of the yap? Doesn't want to talk?' her dad scoffs. 'Things must be bad.'

'Felix, pet, you try. Talk to her about all your funny Ticking Tocks.'

'It's called TikTok, mum. Look, if she doesn't want to talk to you she won't want to talk to me either,' he reasons. 'Let's just give her the space she's asked for and hope that if she wants any of us she knows we're all here.'

He says this last bit with his voice raised.

'And we have a lot of snacks,' he adds, even louder. 'Including some cakes from Emily. That I'm going to eat without her if she isn't here to claim them.'

Adriana's lucky, she knows, to have a family who want to look after her like this. But right now, it just feels like another set of people she's letting down because she's kept things from them. She hadn't even really understood what was happening to her, didn't have the words for the dizziness and cramps, the restlessness and pervading sense of insecurity. She'd thought it was normal, especially in this time of change and stress, so she didn't want to bother anyone. And it's the same now. She feels silly for not recognising the signs of anxiety.

She feels like she has been doing nothing but sneaking around, letting people down, pretending to be this kind, fun person, when really she's been crippled with fear and she never wants to feel like this again.

Through tears, she drafts an email.

'Coach Hoffman,

I would like to apologise again for my behaviour yesterday. I let the team down and I will never forgive myself. I do not mean to be disrespectful to your authority, but clearly I can't handle the additional pressure so I am not the right choice for Captain. Respectfully, I decline the position.

I know that you're thinking of freshening up the squad, so I'd understand if after yesterday I don't figure as part of your future plans. Being part of the Tigresses has been a huge part of my life, and I just want to do what's best for the team, even if that's moving on from the club.

It's been a pleasure,

Adriana Summers'

She sends it and turns her phone off.

For the rest of the day, Adriana pretends she can't hear her family inviting her to join them, and they pretend they can't hear her cry.

Chapter 26

Maeve

Maeve doesn't sleep, checking her phone constantly to see if Adriana has messaged her. Maeve's calls, which Adriana never picked up, stopped going through at all yesterday afternoon. She checked Adriana's location on Find my Friends to see if she is still at her family home, but it's not updating. Adriana's phone must be off. Maeve lies back, feeling hopeless.

Maeve had not been allowed to see Adriana when she was taken off the pitch, had had to watch to the end of their match from the dressing room screens, the Tigresses playing in a complete state of apathy, distraction and disarray after Adriana's dramatic exit and Maeve's earlier injury. They'd lost by a chastening 4-0 margin.

As soon as she had been able to she had messaged Adriana's family, who she has been on group chats with for years, and they at least replied yesterday confirming that Adriana is with them and they're looking after her. But since then, they had not replied to any other parts of Maeve's message, where she had asked if there's anything she can do, if Adriana is well enough for her to visit and that she can be there anytime, if she would only let her. She doesn't know if they're not replying because Adriana asked them not to, or if they've just been caught up in the unexpected turn of events. Should Maeve go there, to her family's place? Or if she isn't wanted, is it better to leave well alone? She just wants to speak to her, to know her friend is okay but if Adriana is feeling overwhelmed, the last thing Maeve wants to do is risk agitating her fragile health further.

She feels terrible, responsible even, for her friend's panic attack. She should have known, she should have been able to be a better friend to her. But now, her apologies feel feeble.

She messages around the Tigresses, but none of them have heard from her. So she tries something in desperation, and finds Jacob Astor's work email address. She sends him a quick email, apologising for the method, and asking if he knows if Adriana is okay – not saying anything about why she would be asking him and not caring about the consequences. He doesn't reply either.

But the next morning, she wakes to a text from an unknown number.

She opens it frowning, expecting spam – but it's a screenshot of an email, an email from Adriana to Coach Hoffman. An email where Adriana is not only turning down the captain appointment, but offering to move on from the club if everyone thinks it would be best.

Despite her injured ankle, Maeve leaps out of bed.

She doesn't know who the message is from, and doesn't think to ask, all she cares about is her friend, who is clearly not in a fit state of mind to be making these life-changing decisions. She needs to be there for her.

But after wolfing down a coffee, Maeve doesn't know what to do. Then she asks herself what she has asked herself in her wisest moments.

What would Addy do?

Addy would know that the best ideas don't come from being alone. They come from working together.

Maeve is finally going to follow the advice her friend gave her. She needs to apologise to Kira. She needs to put their overblown rivalry aside, for the good of her friend. And, she knows, for her own good too.

Maeve is going to have to be brave.

She forwards the message from the unknown number to Kira.

```
If you see this, please could we meet this
morning before training? Need to talk to
you, about everything.
```

She gnaws at her lip, wondering if she should be more upfront. But the reply is mercifully quick. Maybe Kira couldn't sleep either.

```
Usual place, usual time.
```

Kira's name on her screen sends a mixture of emotions running through her — a jolt of nerves and anticipation mixed with shame. But Maeve just sends a thank you.

Then she showers quickly and efficiently, ties her ponytail up into her confidence-giving hairstyle, and looks at herself in the mirror. It's going to take all her steadfast resolve not to just run away. But she doesn't feel like running away anymore. She needs to tackle her fears head on.

Kira and the rest of the team will be expected at training today, and Maeve is going in to be assessed by the medical team, but they should have a bit of time before the others arrive.

She arrives at the training ground when the early light is fresh and crisp, the pink glow of dawn still in the sky.

She heads to the pitch, her pulse racing. As she approaches, she hears the repeated thump and swoosh of a ball hitting the back of a net.

She sees Kira, in her Tigresses training kit, practicing alone.

It's a strange déjà vu, Maeve watching Kira from the doorway as she runs, fierce as if she is in the throws of a competition, yet all by herself.

Maeve watches her for a moment, Kira's lithe powerful body darting around, the way she pulls her messy hair back from her eyes, kicking the air, testing out her limits. She remembers the first day she met Kira. How drawn she was to this mysterious and intimidating woman. She still is.

But this time Maeve doesn't stay on the side in the dark corridor. She closes her eyes, takes a deep breath, and walks out to meet her.

Kira stops immediately, breathlessly watching Maeve coming towards her.

'Choksi,' she says quietly.

'Murphy.'

They hold each other's gaze for a moment. Kira hugs the ball to her chest.

Maeve shakes her head, looking down at her feet.

'Choksi, I'm so sorry. I'm so sorry for everything. I have been an absolute...' she shakes her head, searching for a word bad enough to do it justice. 'Fuckwit. I have been a hypocrite, messed you around and hurt your feelings. All the things I used to pride myself on like being level-headed, honest and a good friend, I have completely failed to be with you. And at my worst I have been not only unprofessional but actively mean, trying to turn teammates against you. I'm so sorry. There isn't a good enough excuse. I can only try to explain what I think was happening. I... You...'

She glances up at Kira whose expression is hard to read. She swallows, wipes her sweaty palms on her shorts.

'God, I'm so nervous. You make me so nervous. That's part of it! I– I– I'm a complete mess around you. I'm used to feeling in control, trying to feel in control at least. And then here you are, so powerful and confident and gorgeous and talented and whenever you look at me I–'

Maeve glances at her and, proving her own point, flushes bright red immediately. Kira bites her lip, smiling to herself which Maeve hopes might mean she's softening towards her but her arms are still folded.

'Can we... Can we–' she gestures at the ball Kira's holding. 'I think it would... help me be able to talk to you.'

Kira raises an eyebrow, but after a moment nods, and expertly bounces the ball between them, kicking to Maeve.

And so they kick between the two of them, in silence. And at first it feels silly, and Maeve feels embarrassed all over again, for asking for such a silly request, for not being able to just express how she feels like a normal person, especially as her ankle is still recovering, so she is taking it comically gently.

But then her body relaxes a little, the soothing motion of this action so innate in her.

Maeve starts speaking, her words falling between the rhythmic soft tap of their shoes on the ball passed between them.

'We got off on the wrong foot,' says Maeve. 'I realised we never really got to… know each other. It was so intense so immediately. This overwhelming… well, attraction to you–' Maeve flushes again, and Kira's face flashes with a smirk. She's not as good as Maeve at hiding her reactions.

'And then it was this, right off the bat, we were these rival enemies, you were fighting to steal everything I cared about, being team captain, Coach's approval, even Adriana's friendship.'

Maeve sighs.

'And at first I really thought we were both just matching each other, you know, giving as good as we got, and because we were hooking up at the same time I–'

She glances at Kira who is still infuriatingly silent, just gesturing for her to continue. 'Well, it was confusing. And hot! Confusing and hot.'

Kira smirks again but then at least does nod, gently tapping the ball back to her.

'I took our rivalry way too far,' Maeve owns up. 'I'm sorry. I completely lost my sense of perspective. I never should have resorted to nasty tactics, never. I don't know how I persuaded myself it was the right thing to do. I think I was so scared. I felt under so much pressure. My mum–'

Maeve fumbles the ball a little, then shakes her head, really not wanting to make excuses or drag Kira into her family.

'I don't mean to dump everything on you or anything. All I'll say is my whole life, the only thing I've been aiming for is to be the best I can be. It's been one step on the ladder after another. Training to improve, trying to be the best player in each team I'm in until I get promoted to the next one whether that was through the age groups when I was younger or now a club in a higher division coming in for me, and then the next one, and… It's one thing to aspire to be great, to fulfill your own potential, but… It took all this mess with you and me and Adriana to realise that I– I haven't even been happy.'

Kira hesitates on the ball, watching Maeve, but she doesn't seem to notice the ball anymore, lost in what she's saying to her.

'I haven't been happy for a long time,' Maeve's voice cracks at the admission. 'It's too much pressure, and I'm not letting myself enjoy it anymore. Football used to be my escape, the place I felt most alive. Now it's just another exam I feel I'm failing at, like I'm on a constant treadmill. I've been so focused, so blinkered on this one thing, being Captain!' She scuffs at the turf with her boot. 'I feel like such a failure so much of the time, it felt like the only thing I could do, the last thing I had left, was to at least be Captain of the Tigresses.'

Maeve wipes a quick hand over her eyes and wipes the tears off on her shorts. She takes a breath.

'And meeting you…'

Maeve looks at Kira now, through her lightly blurred vision, passing the ball only after she's looked back.

'When I met you I suddenly had something else I cared about. Something else I was scared of messing up. I hadn't felt like that about someone before. I… haven't, felt like this about someone before.'

She laughs to herself, kicking the ball faster now, trying to seem more casual as if she's not expecting Kira to respond to the feelings she's admitting to having.

'I know we hardly even know each other, not really. I don't want this to sound cheesy but when I'm around you… I feel like I'm lit up. And not just because I fancy you. Though I think that's obvious by now.' She swallows. 'But when we kissed, I… it felt like more than just a kiss to me. And whenever we were together, in the locker room, or in the shower, or in the—'

Kira's eyebrow raises as she puts her foot on the ball before passing it back, as if to force Maeve to continue along this line.

'*Hey*,' Maeve blushes again, gesturing for Kira to continue. Kira smiles a little before passing it back, but Maeve still doesn't know what the hell she's thinking. Is she just embarrassing herself by confessing all this to someone who literally doesn't care about her?

Oh well. If she's going to be able to be on the same team as Kira, and maybe even hopefully friends at some point in the future, she needs to be honest and take Adriana's advice to make amends.

'I'm sure you're way more experienced than me and probably hook up with people in every team you're in or whatever,' Maeve shrugs, 'but for me, that was a big deal, not just because it felt good but because I liked— I— I like you as a person. Not that it wasn't also good, you know, umm, physically,

I— well, it— it *obviously* was. It was the best sex of my life.' She blurts out.

Maeve is far more sweaty and breathless than she should be from a gentle kickabout. But when the ball doesn't come back to her she glances at Kira, who is close now, Maeve can feel the heat from her body.

'It was a big deal for me too, Murphy,' Kira tells her.

'Really?' Maeve asks, helplessly.

Kira nods, picking up the ball and tucking it under her arm to study Maeve.

'Murphy, I think you are not a very good judge of how you come across yourself. *I* am a mess around *you*. *I* want to impress *you*. *I* was intimidated by *you*!' She laughs, shaking her head.

'W-what? But you're like… unintimidateable.'

'I put on a pretty strong front, I know,' Kira admits, holding her hands up. 'And I'm not saying it's *all* an act. But the times I am the most like – "unintimidateable" are when I'm trying hard to prove myself, right? It's not a very helpful personality trait of mine, it must be said. The more I want someone to like me, the more unlikeable I become. I go too hard.'

'You're not unlikeable, Choksi. Not in the slightest.' Maeve swallows. 'In fact, I think it's quite the opposite. You're hard to stay away from.'

They stand looking at each other. Kira drops the ball gently, and steps instead towards Maeve, winding her hand slowly to the softness of Maeve's side. Heart in her mouth, Maeve gently mirrors the gesture, her hand around Kira's waist, until they're stood so close Maeve can feel Kira's rapid breath against her own body.

Kira strokes Maeve's side and they stand like that for a moment, Maeve aching to kiss her, but not daring to yet.

Noticing Maeve's ankle is tired, Kira guides Maeve towards the bench at the side, and they sit, side-by-side, looking at the empty pitch. They still hold hands, like they can't bear to not be touching any longer.

'On that first day, I met you, here like this, I was… immediately intimidated by you,' Kira confides, looking down at the pitch to avoid meeting her eye. 'I saw you play in training, and you were like this, conscientious, dependable, strong player. Everyone clearly respected you. It was like whenever a decision was made, yours was the voice they'd listen to. You and Addy. You two were so clearly like the heart of the team. I was jealous, I think. Jealous of your closeness, and the way everyone admired you both. And clearly adored you both. And then of course I was watching your form–'

Maeve blushes a little again at the thought of Kira checking her out. Kira laughs, nudging against her. 'In a professional capacity, of course! And… I think you'll laugh at this, because it's going to make me sound very arrogant, but it's rare for me to meet a player I really think I can learn from.'

Maeve snorts, a sound she's sure is very unattractive but she can't help it. Kira grins broadly, pulling her into her.

'It's not that other people aren't really great, legit,' she pauses, 'it's not just about talent or skill. It's just sometimes you meet someone and – bam.' Kira makes an explosion with her hands. 'Some kind of chemistry happens. And you think oh shit, this person is about to change my life. I have a lesson I need to learn here. That's what I thought when I met you.'

Maeve's heart swells. She knows what she means, because she felt that too. But it's wonderful – crazy and wonderful – to hear it was mutual.

'Well, I thought that,' says Kira, and winks, 'and, shit, she's hot.'

Maeve buries her face in her hands, then moves across to lean on Kira's shoulder. Kira puts a hand gently on her head, stroking her hair. The sensation seems to soothe them both.

'I've had to be completely independent, my whole life. Self-sufficient,' Kira explains. 'My family were moving around all the time, and so was I, back and forth between them. I'd be staying in bedrooms I never felt were mine, often sharing with my step-siblings who never liked me 'cos I was just this random kid suddenly stealing their hand me downs and second-best toys.' She sighs. 'Football was the only place I felt like a normal kid, 'cos everyone used to just kickabout with random people, so it didn't matter that I was a stranger. And I was lucky, I was good quite naturally, so I started getting attention from it early, and that was pretty addictive.'

'I know what you mean,' Maeve reassures her. 'It opened up a whole new world for me, being good at football. I never fitted in apart from on the pitch.'

Kira nods. 'I got used to chasing the high of like, arriving in a new place, finding a pitch, and running in and just like – wow, amazing everyone. Everyone being like who the hell is this incredible kid? Arrive, score, disappear again. That was my life.

'Then I got scouted, when I was at this school in Germany which meant moving again when I finally felt like I was settling. Now I'm working with Serena, I never know how long I'm going to be somewhere, never have a chance to put down roots, or make friends, or do anything really except focus on my own skill on the pitch. When you said it feels like football is the only constant you've had in your life. I get that. Honestly, I really feel that too. And I thought for a long time that was a strength of mine. Single-minded. Go-getting. Just know that all I'm chasing is the next goal.'

'What about your family now?' Maeve asks gently.

'My parents have never once come to visit me,' says Kira, shaking her head. 'Or see me play or anything. I guess they're used to prioritising their new families. We text every now and again but I feel like they don't really make any effort, they don't care about football or... well, about me, either.'

'I'm so sorry,' Maeve squeezes her hand. 'It sounds so useless for me to say, but I am.'

Kira looks at her, sidelong. 'Well, Adriana kinda let slip that you might know what that feels like. To have your parent move to be with another family.'

Maeve swallows hard and nods. It still hurts, every time she is reminded of the dad she's not spoken to in nearly ten years.

'I'm sorry too,' Kira says softly.

Instinctively, Maeve turns her head to kiss Kira's shoulder, then leans away, worried she pushed it too far.

'I've had Adriana though,' Maeve tells her. 'And my mum. I can't imagine how difficult it must be to not have anyone around me like that.'

Kira leans back, adjusting without Maeve's head there. 'It gets lonely. It does. And I try to ignore that feeling, and just distract myself with the next adrenaline hit or the next match. I've got used to it. Every team I've been in has always hated me. I've got used to that too. I know I don't exactly make a good first impression, especially because this time I'd followed Serena from our last team.'

She laughs, touching the back of her neck, but there's a real sadness in her expression too.

'I think now I've got so used to it that I kind of... lean into it. You know, make myself unlikeable so that it feels like it's on my terms, not being rejected.' She shakes her head. 'I know that probably sounds crazy.'

'I get it,' Maeve assures her. 'That actually makes a lot of sense to me. I was so scared the girls in school would ignore me that I avoided them first, made myself invisible so that they couldn't make me feel that way instead.' Maeve's chest stabs with guilt and she hangs her head. 'God, I am so sorry for then utilising that tactic, trying to get the team against you. I'm so sorry.'

'Murphy, it's okay. Honestly. I forgive you. I hope you can forgive me too. I've been chaotic too. I know I was goading you. I guess I wanted to get under your skin. Get your attention somehow.'

'Can we... Can we start over?'

Maeve nods, gripping Kira's hand tightly in a shake that lingers and now they're just holding hands. Kira holds her eyes, and brings Maeve's hand up to her mouth. She kisses her knuckles. Then her wrist. Maeve's body dances to life, electricity pulsing through her arms, down to her legs, her chest, her neck, as Kira presses her lips to Maeve's skin.

'It's like you said. We never got to just hang out,' says Kira. 'We have never really had a normal conversation. As two people who are getting to know each other. And there's so much I want to know about you.'

'There's so much I want to know about you too,' Maeve smiles.

That's what she finds most incredible about being around Kira, she realises. It's how she normally only feels when she's playing, or maybe laughing with Adriana: Maeve feels fully *alive* with her. Like she doesn't know what's going to happen next, but that, for once, that's okay. It's going to be okay.

'I don't know where to start!' says Maeve.

Kira's expression softens. She moves closer towards her. Slowly, deliberately, she reaches a hand out, and traces her thumb along Maeve's cheek, her jaw, tipping her chin towards her own.

'Well, you could start by calling me Kira.'

They hold each other's eyes.

'Kira,' Maeve says, softly.

Their faces are close now, so close that Maeve can't stop her lips from reaching for Kira's, but Kira smiles, holding her just far enough away.

'Maeve,' she whispers, and kisses her.

Maeve feels like she's floating. Kira pulls her in closer, and then their hands are under the other's kit, stroking along each other's sides, Kira's thumb skimming the lines of Maeve's sports bra, Maeve tracing the edge of her nails along her shoulder blades until Kira's back arches. She pulls Maeve onto her lap, straddling her, and as they kiss, harder, hungrier, Maeve barely even realises she's grinding into her, their bones creating waves of pleasure through her, still wanting more. Acting on pure impulse, Maeve starts tugging at the shorts between them, not knowing quite if they're her own or Kira's, just needing them off so there aren't this many layers between them –

And then Kira stops her.

'Believe me,' Kira pants. 'I could very happily carry on, and for a very long time. But firstly, we're very much in a public space, and secondly – you wanted to meet with me for a reason that wasn't just apologising and hooking up.'

'Right, right,' Maeve flushes, nodding. 'Yes. You're right.'

She looks down at Kira from atop her.

Maeve unstraddles Kira a little clumsily, and then they sit, panting, and then look at each other, and laugh.

'Let's pick that up again later, please,' Kira grins, and Maeve laughs.

'In a bed. When we won't be disturbed and have time.'

'Plenty of time,' agrees Kira. 'Which I intend to take.'

Kira grips Maeve's hand, and Maeve's crotch throbs and for a moment she really struggles to bring herself back. They kiss, gently, coming back to earth.

Then they both sigh, more serious now.

'To business,' Maeve tries to focus. 'Adriana.'

'Adriana,' Kira repeats. 'Serena told me about it too. Said she knew it was unconventional but asked if I knew what was going on, as it felt like it was coming from a personal rather than professional place.'

Maeve's expression crumples, but she feels ever more grateful for Kira's hand in hers, keeping her grounded, not losing herself to guilt instead trying to focus on finding a way through.

'Adriana and I have drifted apart recently. I let her down, I've been so caught up in myself, I wasn't there to see she was struggling. I can see looking back there were these signs I should have picked up on. I should have helped her earlier. But the least I can do is try to help her now. The Tigresses need her, but I think she needs the Tigresses too. Whether she wants to be captain or not is her choice, but *I* think she'd be brilliant.'

'Me too. I was actually someone Coach ran the idea by,' Kira admits, rubbing the back of her neck.

'That was really nice of you to back her,' Maeve smiles.

'Well, Serena said how she felt the team had fallen apart and said that to bring it together she thought the best appointment for captain would be Adriana, which I could totally see because she's so selfless in always putting the team first. Apparently the only reason Hoffman didn't offer it to Adriana before that match was because Jacob Astor had some hesitation?'

Maeve frowns. 'Jacob Astor?'

'Yeah, apparently he'd been like, concerned that she hadn't volunteered herself for the position, and that it should have been her choice. Whereas, well, you know Serena, she acts fast and can be single-minded in her way,' Kira laughs, self-deprecatingly pointing to herself. 'Like someone else I know. Serena was sure Adriana would be honoured, so just ploughed straight in. Now she's regretting it, obviously, in case it was the extra stress that made Adriana unwell.'

Their hands are tightly clasped in each other's. Maeve can only hope that this is the start of a more positive dynamic between them. But that's not what they need to be focusing on right now.

'I think I have a plan,' Maeve tells her. 'But I need your help.'

Chapter 27

Adriana

'But do you not *want* to be Captain, darling?' her mum asks.

Adriana has heard back from Coach Hoffman, an email inviting her to meet for a conversation to address her concerns whenever it suits her, but also saying that she should take all the time she needs away from training to recover. Adriana had shown her family the emails, and is now regretting it.

'It doesn't matter what I want,' Adriana says simply, like it's obvious — it is to her.

Her family exchange a look.

'Uhh,' says Felix. 'Yes it does, you weirdo?'

She just shakes her head. Her family know and love Maeve — how can they not understand it's like she's stealing from her? And then there is the whole gross possibility of Jacob getting the position for her, which she is too ashamed to tell them about. Her paranoia of being proven to be unworthy of the promotion has taken all the joy of playing away from her. If she thinks about it too long, the breathlessness in her chest starts to return.

She knows her family means well, but she can't bear how nice they're being to her at the moment and it's only making her feel worse for not telling everything that's been going on for her.

'I think it's time for me to go back to my own flat,' she says.

After trying to persuade her to stay for a while longer, they insist on at least calling her a taxi rather than her getting public transport back to her flat.

'If you change your mind, we'll drive over and bring you right back to ours if you ever want,' her mum offers, when the taxi arrives. 'Any second, we'll be there, okay?'

'Make sure you eat,' says her dad, tapping the pile of tupperware food they've packed for her, all the family favourites they've been trying to coax her with: generous rectangles of lasagne, way too spicy chilli, the ginger noodle soup that Adriana's dad always makes when she's sick.

Adriana mumbles more thank yous and feels guilty they're having to run around after her like this.

Felix just wraps her in a big, tight hug, giving her a noogie, and she pulls away, laughing in surprise, and notes her family all look relieved to hear that brightness coming back.

'Thank you, I'm fine, honestly. I'm just going to be resting.'

Now finally alone in the taxi, Adriana sighs deeply. She even feels glad that she doesn't know this taxi driver, and for a rare time in her life, Adriana doesn't try to make conversation or set him at his ease. She just allows herself to sit quietly, the wind from the window in her face, the sounds from the radio washing over her.

She checks her messages from Jacob. He had sent a reply to her break-up message.

`I'm sorry it's so hard, Addy, and I'm sorry if I shouldn't be replying here, but I also personally feel it would be good for us to talk more once you're feeling better. But it's up to you. Please could you at least let me know how you're doing? X`

She can't resist texting him now. Maybe she's a fool, but she tries to think if their roles were reversed, she would definitely want to know that Jacob wasn't in hospital or anything.

`I'm ok. Family were looking after me and now going back to mine, going to rest some more before returning to training.`

He replies immediately: `Thank you, Addy xx`

Adriana closes her eyes and sits there for the rest of the journey. Arriving at her flat is a relief, especially as it's particularly quiet and restful today, in the September sun. She takes it in, trying to breathe deeply, trying to let go of the tension in her. So much so that she doesn't notice that there is someone else there in the courtyard with her.

There he is on her doorstep holding a huge bouquet of sunflowers.

'Jacob,' she whispers, stunned.

Jacob leaves the flowers on the step, and walks over to her.

'Addy,' he says, seeming unsure of how to greet her. 'God, it's so good to see you. How are you feeling?'

She shrugs, teary. 'I'm— I'm okay.'

'I know I'm being cheeky with making a loophole from your message asking me not to text you… if you want me to leave, please tell me, and I will.' He speaks as if this is something he's practiced saying to her.

She finds his loveliness hard to bear. She feels herself welling up, and looks away, wiping desperately at her eyes to try to stop it.

'No, it's… you know it's wonderful to see you. I love seeing you, I just… it's hard. Hard seeing something I want and can't have.' She admits.

'Could I come in?' he asks gently. 'I'll leave whenever you want, I promise. But I have some things I would really like to talk to you about, and I…'

He gestures to the doorstep where, Adriana hadn't noticed, there is a large takeaway bag from Honey, with a drink in a holder.

'Your mocha might be a touch cold, but the brownies should still be good.'

Adriana's eyes well again in pleasure and gratitude. And then she laughs, thinking of how much of Emily's baking she's been consuming recently.

'You and my family have the same tactics,' Adriana says, wiping her eyes as she lifts the Tupperwares she's carrying. 'You better come in.'

Her body still feels heavy as she heads up the stairs to her flat, Jacob in tow. In her kitchen she gets them two glasses of water, feeling embarrassed at how much of a state of chaos her open plan studio is in the first time he's seeing it.

'May I?' Jacob asks, and lightly takes over setting up their teatime plates of brownies and pastries, and pouring her mocha over star-shaped ice from her freezer, into one of her chunky pink bubble glasses, with a metal straw.

'Iced mocha for Adriana?' he calls, like he's her barista.

Adriana raises her hand playing along. 'That's me!'

He hands it over and sits on the armchair opposite her on the sofa, bringing the smiling cloud shaped pillow from his back onto his lap, seemingly unconsciously stroking it softly. For a moment Adriana has a vision of the two of them, just being able to be silly like this, having these gentle, mundane moments together, sharing tea and cake. She wants it so much she starts tearing up again and the thought it can't be like this.

Jacob sits leaning forwards, arms on his knees and she wonders if this is how he looks when he is preparing for one of his big pitch meetings.

'Can I tell you something, Addy?'

She nods.

'When I got your text saying you didn't want to see me anymore, I was in the middle of having a big conversation with my dad.'

Adriana's head jolts up, watching him. Jacob's face is serious but calm.

'I had asked him to meet with me a while ago, and he had finally, begrudgingly I might add, found the time to fly over from – I can't even keep track of where in the world he was–' he shakes his head, makes a gesture of trying to get himself back on topic. 'It doesn't matter. What matters is, I had wanted to talk to him to formally step back from my position as club director.'

Adriana's stomach flips, and she blinks her big eyes at him.

'You're resigning? But… But why?'

'Getting to know you has made me believe for the first time that I really am not like my father.'

Adriana's heart swells. She can't stop herself from reaching out and squeezing his hand in support.

'It made me realise that in order for me to be proud of myself,' he continues, 'and to have any chance at happiness at work, or indeed outside of it, I needed to stop working for him. I told him I wasn't the right fit for the job.'

'But I thought you were… I thought you found it satisfying? Being so good at it?'

He shrugs, lines crinkling at the side of his eyes. 'My heart wasn't in it.' He hesitates for a moment, then meets her eyes. 'My heart was elsewhere.'

'Oh,' she's nervous to hear what this means. 'Go on.'

'I don't want you to think that I resigned just because of you, because of us. I want to be clear that I also have been feeling this way about working with my father for a very long time, you just helped me realise it was untenable.'

He sighs, unclenching his jaw.

'But it would be a lie to say that it wasn't a big factor for me. You. Us. And I don't mean this in any kind of pressurised way, I honestly don't believe I've given up a job for you so it has to work. I just want to be honest that I haven't felt this excited about someone before. I haven't felt that it's so *right*. In the end it was the easiest decision I could make. If the job was getting in the way of us developing our relationship even further and causing us to have to keep it a secret when I want to tell everyone how mad I am about you. I want to give this a proper shot.'

Adriana launches herself onto his lap, and snuggles up to him. She tucks her head onto his broad chest, and his long arms clasp round her giving her that feeling of safety and home. He strokes her hair, kissing the top of her head, and for a moment, she feels completely blissfully happy.

But then she remembers about her side of things. About her doubt of whether Jacob had a role in getting her the captaincy.

'I emailed Coach,' Adriana whispers, scared to break their happy bubble. 'Turning down the opportunity to be captain.'

She feels Jacob nod slowly above her.

'Ms Hoffman did inform me of your email,' he says. 'I think her exact words were "what the hell has gotten into you quitters this week?"'

They both chuckle a little.

'She was very concerned about you,' Jacob says, Adriana hearing his low rumble from his chest. 'She really did feel terribly responsible, and I know how much she wants to learn from this and improve the experience for players now. Before I resigned, I've signed off on new mental health guidelines and free therapy for any player who wishes it with budget ring-fenced for it.'

Jacob strokes Adriana's hair. She is breathing easily, finds it almost hard now in this state of peace to remember, the crushing tension in her chest that had been coming and going with terrifying unpredictability these last weeks.

She breathes in Jacob's smell, the light clean fragrance of his shaving foam and fresh laundry, and the light cedarwood cologne he wears on his neck deliciously close to her nose, the earthy saltiness of his skin underneath.

'So we find ourselves in a position where both of us have resigned from the job that hindered us from being together,' Jacob notes.

Adriana nods into his chest.

'There is one thing I wanted to clear up and that is that I did not have anything to do with Ms Hoffman choosing you as captain. Well–' he clarifies. 'Apart from agreeing with everything she said about her reasoning. If anything, I fear I might have nearly stopped her.'

Adriana sits up to look at him, frowning.

'Because when she came to me with her recommendation,' he says, 'my first question for her was have you asked Adriana what she wants?'

Jacob smiles sheepishly, removing his glasses and cleaning them on his grey sweater. 'Apparently she had not considered that. I said that if you wanted to accept the position, it would have my every blessing, but I think it's important for you to know it was on your own merit.'

Adriana feels her cheeks flushing. She had got so worried that Jacob had pulled strings for her but the only part he had played was making sure it was what she wanted.

'You are always bringing the team together,' Jacob observes. 'On and off the pitch. You are always motivating and boosting morale, trying to make peace between players who have any personal friction. You're always there for your teammates. And that's wonderful. It's inspiring. It's appreciated. And in my opinion, it's about time it was rewarded. You would be an excellent captain on a permanent basis, if you wanted to reconsider stepping aside from the team.'

Adriana blushes, looking down at her hands, taking a sip of water, not knowing what to say.

'You're always there for everyone else, Adriana. Now it's time for you to be there for yourself. And if you'll let me, I want to be there to support you too while you figure out what you want.'

He strokes her back lightly.

Adriana's thoughts feel overwhelming again as she tries to think. What does she want? Well, him, of course. But does she want to be Captain of the Tigresses?

She gets up from his lap, reaching for her mocha, her hands shaking a little.

'I don't know if this will sound absolutely ridiculous,' she paces around, watching the melting ice cubes as she swirls them gently round her glass. 'But I had never even thought about wanting to be captain, so I never thought I might be considered for it either. I was really worried when Coach told me that you might have had something to do with it. Plus, it's always been Maeve's dream, so I had never dared to think about it. And I still truly don't want to take it from her, I hate the way it makes it feel like I'm somehow *stealing* from someone I love.'

'What if you were to allow yourself to believe that you are good at what you do, and that it is a good thing for everyone — yourself, your friends, your teammates — for you to do it?' Jacob suggests.

'Well, yeah. Yeah, that does feel...' she laughs. 'Really fucking good, actually.'

'I know you're worried about Maeve, and Kira, and probably everyone else too,' says Jacob. 'And that's understandable, given how much you care about them. I think if you talk to them about it, they might surprise you by caring about you getting what you want too and if they're really your friends, they should be proud of you for getting something that's deserved.'

She blushes and then flops back onto the sofa to sit beside him.

'The irony is, it was always Maeve who encouraged me to take myself more seriously as a player,' sighs Adriana. 'I used to help her lighten up and make friends with the team, and she used to help me train and believe in myself as a player. It's part of why we work so well together. Well, *used* to work so well together, at least... I've been avoiding her calls because I'm scared she's going to say I've been such a traitor with the captaincy that she doesn't want to be friends with me anymore. It feels now like I'm choosing between being the captaincy or her friendship, and I don't even know if she would want that anymore anyway.'

'Well,' Jacob starts, sounding awkward. 'I am *pretty* sure she does want to still be friends with you.'

Adriana looks at him suspiciously.

He coughs, looking sheepish. 'She actually messaged me.'

'What?'

'Yeah, she contacted me at my work email address to ask if I knew if you were okay. She was awfully polite about it. Like she didn't want me to feel awkward about her knowing something had happened between us, but just wanting to know if I had information because she hadn't heard and was really worried.'

Adriana flushes with pleasure and worry. 'Oh Maeve…'

'She asked a favour of me, actually.'

'A favour?'

Jacob nods. 'She asked that if I saw you, could I ask if you'd be free to meet her tonight after training. At…' he checks his phone. '"The Old Pig?"'

Adriana smiles, but her stomach twists uncertainly. She still doesn't know how a conversation with her old friend will go right now, but she owes it to her to try, and for them to both have the opportunity to clear the air. Jacob has helped her realise, she should put herself first instead of other people all the time. Now, she knows she *does* want to be Captain of the Tigresses.

'So what do you think, Addy?' asks Jacob, softly. 'Do you know what it is that you want?'

Adriana goes to him then. She reaches her hand to him, strokes his cheek, his head tilting back to take her in. She leans her lips close to his.

'This,' she says simply, and kisses him.

Chapter 28

Maeve

Maeve sits alone at a large table in the back corner of The Old Pig.

It's quieter than usual in the pub, whose eclectic pink decor consists of hundreds of decorations celebrating cartoon pigs. There are a few regulars sat on barstools, chatting to each other over their pints, a few young people with laptops who seem to be chasing essay deadlines, and a couple of other groups of friends laughing together.

Seeing the groups reminds Maeve it's a place where she has so many memories made with Adriana here. It was where they came to celebrate Adriana joining her at the Tigresses. Over the years Adriana had charmed the bar staff so much that they added an orange liqueur cocktail named after the team. It was where Adriana had brought Maeve for Champagne to celebrate Maeve getting named Captain.

Her stomach twists at the thought, and she shakes her head, as if to try to dislodge her own worry. A bartender gives her a conspiratorial thumbs up, and Maeve gives them a grateful smile back. Maeve checks her phone and glances towards the door again, losing hope until she sees Adriana come through it.

They are a little nervous at first, Maeve gesturing for a tentative hug, Adriana accepting. But as soon as they're in each other's arms, their bodies cling tightly to each other, and they hug like that for a long time.

When they pull away they're both teary and laughing.

'God, I've missed you so much,' Adriana sniffles.

'I've missed you too,' says Maeve. 'I'm so sorry. For everything.'

'I'm sorry too,' Adriana says sincerely. 'But come on, we have so much to catch up on.'

Maeve nods. 'What a relief. I got us Tigresses,' Maeve, gestures to the lurid orange mocktails melting lightly on the table between them.

'Thanks, Moo.'

They smile at each other and sit down close together in the corner, Adriana flopping onto the soft bench.

'So, I'm dating Jacob,' announces Adriana.

Maeve lets out a rare squeal.

'I mean, you already knew,' Adriana looks sheepish. 'And I'm really sorry I didn't say anything earlier, it really wasn't something I wanted to keep from you.'

'I did already know, but it's still good to hear that you'd like to share. Tell me *everything*.'

So Adriana fills her in. Maeve follows the whole story with her usual devoted attention, gasping and laughing in all the right places, but she does hold a respectful hand up when

Adriana starts going into a little *too* much detail about how brilliant their sex is.

'I approve,' Maeve grins. 'I don't know him well yet, obviously, but what I've seen so far, I really like him. Obviously he got you here for me.'

'Yeah, did you guys like, email or something?' asks Adriana, and Maeve nods.

'I'm really, really glad you're happy with him,' says Maeve. Adriana's face broadens into her fullest sunbeam smile. 'I am,' she says realising how much she means it. 'Utterly and deliciously happy with him.'

Maeve sighs contentedly. Then she glances away, hesitating with her cocktail, before taking a big gulp.

'On the subject of being honest, there's something I want to tell you too,' Maeve says, blushing. 'Umm… You were right.'

'Of course I was!' Adriana pauses. 'Right about what?'

Maeve laughs. 'Me and Kira. We've been… umm… having a thing. Not just rivals but umm… you know… in our one-to-one training sessions we would just… you know… in the locker room…'

Maeve's cheeks heat a brighter pink than all the pigs around them. Adriana's jaw literally drops.

'Okay,' Adriana says, and downs the rest of her drink. 'I think we're going to need some alcohol in these cocktails now!'

Maeve tells her everything, and Adriana squeals and gasps, until finally she sighs with relief and delight at Maeve telling her where they left it last time they saw each other – that they're going to start dating openly.

'I can't believe it,' says Adriana. 'I mean, I *can* believe it, because obviously you guys were gagging over each other the second you saw each other. I totally called it! My flirtation radar is never wrong! Oh my God…'

'Addy, I really like her,' Maeve whispers as if she's still a little bit scared to admit it. 'Like, really really. We're actually going on our first official date this weekend and I'm already getting in a state about what to wear.'

Adriana knows what a big deal it is for her friend to say that. She clasps hard at her friend's hand, and they smile at each other tenderly for a moment.

'I can't believe how quickly everything is changing for us.'

Maeve nods and smiles, hugging her friend.

'I'm really sorry I've been a bad friend and not a nice person to be around but I love you so much,' says Maeve.

'I'm sorry I didn't tell you about Jacob and if it felt like I was abandoning you for Kira,' she says. 'I love you too.'

They toast and finish their Tigresses, and Adriana sighs to herself.

'Wait, Maeve, how *is* your ankle?' asks Adriana, realising they haven't even touched on that.

'Oh, they think it'll be okay,' says Maeve, glancing down at her bandage. 'Thankfully it's not fractured, but I'm going to have to do some rehab. I'll be out until Christmas. But… maybe it's a silver lining for me to have a bit of a break from pushing myself.'

Adriana smiles at her, nodding. It feels like a natural moment for them both to talk about the reason for Adriana leaving the pitch now, but Maeve doesn't want to be insensitive. She studies her friend's face. It feels strange, after laughing about their dating lives, to remember her friend collapsing on the pitch just a few days ago. But she knows all too well that someone can be suffering and put on a brave face. She hopes that now their friendship has thawed again, they can talk more openly.

'And... Sunny, how are you?' The question hangs in the air.

Adriana takes a deep breath. 'I'm doing better now, but... yeah, it was a panic attack.'

Maeve puts one hand to her mouth, then with the other reaches for her friend's hand over the table. She stays quiet, letting Adriana continue.

'I haven't had one like that before,' Adriana shakes her head, 'but, when I was talking to the club doctor more, I realised I have been having symptoms on and off for a long time now. And in the last few weeks it's really gone—' she points dramatically upwards. 'Through the roof.'

Maeve nods, adding gently, 'Is that when you get breathless sometimes?'

Adriana nods, squeezing her friend's hand. 'Yeah, it seems to me like it's all connected to feeling upset, out of control, often if I... if I feel like people are angry with me.'

Maeve flinches, feeling guilty if she contributed to that in any way.

'I didn't know it would lead to something like that, obviously,' Adriana confides. 'I didn't even realise really that it was all connected to stress, I just thought... Oh, I don't know, that I was being too sensitive, or too dramatic? That I should just try to distract myself, or that if I just ignored it all it would go away...'

Adriana pauses then laughs weakly. 'Turns out that isn't the most effective treatment.'

'I'm going to see a therapist, to have someone to talk things through with and hopefully get better at managing the symptoms or warning signs so I don't give anyone or myself another scare anytime soon.'

'So… you're going to stay on the team?' Maeve checks.

Adriana takes a deep breath and pulls her shoulders back. She meets Maeve's eye, her expression honest and open and knows she has to be the same back.

'Maeve, I know being Captain has always been important to you, and it's been horrible having that taken away. But since the surprise of Coach appointing me, I've done a lot of thinking, and realised that I do want to accept. You have always encouraged me to take myself more seriously as a player, and I realise that this role would really feel like a positive step for me, to feel like I'm channelling my strengths into the team.'

Maeve feels a shadow of her mother, as if she's sat with them, frowning at Maeve, telling her to sit up straighter to stand up for herself and fight. Her voice has been so loud in Maeve's mind for so long that it's overshadowed her own. Adriana's success isn't Maeve's failure – quite the contrary. Maeve doesn't have to be 'captain' of the team to be a valuable part of it.

'Maybe for a time I was the right fit for Captain,' says Maeve, thoughtfully. 'Having someone solid and dependable when we were just,' she shrugs a little, bashfully, 'chugging along on our routines under Pappi.'

'Moo, you were more than that – the team all respect you so much, and it did a lot to have you as such a reliable and cool-headed captain.'

'Thank you for saying that,' Maeve says softly. 'I'm glad. But what we've learnt is, I'm no good at being the captain at the front of the ship when we're on stormier seas. Coach Hoffman wants to put her own stamp on things. On a personal level, I actually think it's going to be good for me. I can focus on the rehab for my ankle, and not have to feel like I've always got to be striving relentlessly, for some imagined perfection that doesn't even exist. It's like you've always said, always encouraged me to loosen up or I'll break. I think that I broke. But now, I get to put myself back together in a way I can be more proud of.'

Adriana puts a warm hand on Maeve's arm.

'*I'm* proud of you,' Adriana tells her friend. 'I know it's so hard for you to be able to be gentle with yourself like that. Have you… talked to your mum about it at all?'

Maeve sighs, shakes her head a little. 'While you've been at your family's recovering, I think it really showed for me how fucked up my relationship with mum is. There I was, with *this* injury, and all she could do was text me to remind me whatever the medical advice was, it was just a guideline and I should try to make it back quicker to show I was diligent.'

Adriana clucks her tongue with repressed anger.

Maeve shakes her head. 'I have a lot of talking and letting go to do and the stuff with my mum is definitely going to be a process for sure. But I think it's also showing me how deeply these worries go for my mum, of *her* feeling like she was so easily replaced, she wants me to always be the best so that I don't have to go through what she did. And... I want to talk to her about getting back in touch with my dad. I want to finally be able to talk to him. To even have him come to one of my matches one day.'

Adriana grips Maeve's hand across the table, her blue eyes shining.

'But suffice to say,' Maeve says, as if coming back from her imagination. 'I think it will be nothing but good for me, for the team, for everyone, to accept that I am not the best fit for captain any longer. You are. Not only do I truly believe you are, and have always been, a brilliant choice for Captain, you are exactly the captain the Tigresses need right now. We need you! *I* definitely need you.'

Adriana reaches her hands out to Maeve's cheeks, clasping her affectionately, and Maeve holds them there with her own hands.

'Sunny, you're the best person to be on a team with, whether that's on the pitch or off it.'

Adriana throws her arms around Maeve, and they hug tightly, Adriana nodding into her shoulder.

When she pulls back, Adriana's wiping her eyes.

'God, I thought I'd run out of tears by now,' she laughs. 'But I'm glad these are happy ones.'

'So... you're going to be staying with the team and becoming our captain permanently?' Maeve flashes her an encouraging smile.

'I mean, first I need to check if the rest of the team want me. I know Hoffman apparently consulted some people, but

I want to be sure that there is a consensus now that people have had a chance to think.'

Maeve bites her lip, smiling mysteriously. 'Would you… want to hear from them right now?'

Adriana tilts her head, frowning. 'What? You think I should like, video call them or something like that?'

'Well something like that…' Maeve says cryptically before giving the signal in the group chat.

And within moments, the door of The Old Pig oinks open, and a rowdy crowd descend upon their corner of the pub. There's the whole Tigresses team, all in their bright orange kit, led up by Kira. And there's Adriana's family, holding their handmade signs with golden suns on. And bringing up the back, closing the pub door carefully behind them, there's Jacob.

He's not in one of his suits anymore, but in the simple white t-shirt and jeans he wore on their first not-date to Honey, his tortoiseshell glasses fogging a little in the heat from all their bodies. Over the crowd, he smiles and nods at Maeve, and she mirrors it back. She looks forward to getting to know him better as Adriana's date. Maybe they could double date with Kira… Maeve has a rush of giddy pleasure at the thought.

Then the Tigresses are gathering into a huddle in front of Adriana.

'Right,' says Charlie, shuffling some sheets of paper, which seem to have lots of different handwritings on them. 'We all wanted to write you a speech, to try to say why we think you'd be such a great captain.'

'But really, Maeve's the best at speeches like this,' says Elisa, 'and she's probably already done hers to you.'

Adriana laughs and tells them that's true.

'So instead, we thought we could best communicate with that old football tradition – a chant!'

'We know you're a fan of Chappell Roan,' adds Milo. 'So we tried changing the lyrics of one of her songs to try to convince you to stay.'

Adriana gasps, lifting a hand to her mouth, laughing.

'And then I'm afraid we may have got a bit carried away,' says Nat.

They gesture to the bar. 'Hit it!'

A karaoke version of Chappell Roan's 'Pink Pony Club' starts playing.

Charlie and Elisa step forwards dramatically, producing karaoke microphones from nowhere.

'We want you to know,' they sing, batting their eyelids, 'we all want you to stay.'

Adriana still can't believe this is happening, but the team keep singing for her, not afraid to make idiots of themselves to show how much she means to them.

'We can't ignore the lovely visions of you in the FA.'

Adriana laughs, tears in her eyes.

'We heard that there's a perfect place, where football girls can all be queens every training day.'

They pass the microphone quickly to a bunched together Nat, Milo and Liv who join in laughing.

'You're having quitting dreams, of leaving the Tigresses-ee–, But hear us, we're calling Adrianaa-ee– Make your family proud, cause a scene, they see their little girl, they're gonna scream...'

They run and hand it quickly to Adriana's mum. Adriana starts fully crying now as she realises that they've been in on this together, watching her parents and Felix sing with complete tone deafness and out of time.

'Addy, what have you done? You're an orange Tigress girl, and you play at the women's club...'

Everyone joins in now, all loudly shouting the altered chorus, at all their levels of tone deafness.

'Tigress Football Club, please keep on playing at the *Tigress Football Club*, please keep on playing down at, Training Pitch Two.'

After another rousing chorus of Tigress Football Club where the team try and fail spectacularly to do some coordinated choreography, the music from the bar suddenly glitches and stops. In the sudden silence, Kira, improvising, steps forwards and does some jazz hands, singing, 'Please be our Captain!'

Adriana takes a deep breath looking at them all gathered, and then, the happiness visibly bursting from her, she says proudly, 'I would *love* to.'

The team all cheer and hug her, lifting her up in a celebration worthy of the end of winning a championship game.

The rest of the pub whoop too, clearly all having been invested in this, and the original 'Pink Pony Club' blasts from the bar. Maeve watches Adriana squealing with delight as Charlie and Elisa parade her round on their shoulders. She feels a light tap on her back, and it's Kira, interlinking and squeezing her hand, not trying to hide it from the celebrating team around them. They smile at each other, before Maeve lets go, to head over to the bar, where The Old Pig staff are bopping festively. Maeve orders, requesting for part of it to be delivered to their now hectic table, and taking one bottle over with her.

Adriana turns to her, and Maeve holds out the sweating cold bottle of Champagne.

'This was a tradition we had to keep. For you, my Captain.'

Adriana's eyes tear up as Maeve hands her the bottle, and she closes her eyes as if to savour the moment. Then Adriana expertly pops the cork, and joins in the whoops of her team around her. Maeve takes over pouring the rest of the glasses and handing them out, then leads raising a toast.

'To our Queen of the Tigresses, Adriana Summers!'

Everyone cheers and raises the glass, and sips along with Adriana, who takes a generous gulp, grinning.

As Maeve tastes the golden bubbles pop on her tongue, she meets her best friend's eye, and they beam at each other. Celebrating the brilliance of her best friend is going to be one of her new favourite memories.

Chapter 29

Adriana

Adriana, pink, tipsy, and bursting with happiness, a few hours later, stops Maeve from topping up her Champagne.

'I want to remember tonight,' Adriana smiles. 'But Kira has been staring at you hungrily for the past hour. Wanna go put her out her misery?'

Maeve grins and waves Kira over, not trying to hide their changed relationship dynamic from anyone else. Kira, taking this permission, slinks an arm around Maeve's waist, and Maeve leans happily into her.

'So the secret's out?' Kira smiles.

'All the cats are out of all the bags,' Adriana laughs. 'I don't want to say I told you so but... you guys are a ridiculously gorgeous couple!'

Maeve's ears go pink.

'Or—' Adriana corrects herself quickly. 'You know, whatever it is that you two decide— sorry, I didn't mean to give you a random label.'

'It feels good to just be seeing where it goes, right?' says Maeve, looking more laidback than Adriana would have expected from her friend. 'We're in no rush.

Kira grins back at her. 'You're right. No rush. Feels good to take things one step at a time. But... I would like to be able to show you off to the team.'

Even Maeve, trying to match Kira's cockiness, looks a little dazed at this. 'Do you really want to?'

'Are you kidding me?' says Kira. 'If you're cool with it, I don't want to keep hiding that I'm snogging the hottest woman in the world.'

Maeve's ears go red, but she tries to match Kira's energy. 'Sure,' she laughs. 'I'll be out of training for a few months anyway, so... I've always wanted to be a WAG.'

Kira kisses her – and then taps a fork enthusiastically on the side of her Champagne flute.

'Hey everyone! I have some more incredible news to announce! Me and Murphy are shagging! I'm super into her!'

Maeve goes crimson. Kira wraps her arm confidently round Maeve, kisses her cheek, and gazes at her with such obvious pride that there could be no question of whether this is real of not. Everyone exchanges significant looks – some look surprised, having only recently been on the receiving end of their animosity, but Adriana is sure she hears Charlie mutter to Elisa, 'Alright, I owe you a fiver.'

'Hooray!' Adriana leads in a cheer, and the whole team join in with her, clapping them both on the back. Maeve looks round in astonishment at her team taking this in their stride. Adriana knows that even as she's trying to keep up a confident front with Kira, this is a big moment for her.

Then, Maeve's eyes looking a little teary, she lets out a bashful laugh, and shrugs. She turns to Kira, and, with a single movement of her arms, dips Kira, Hollywood style, into an extravagant low kiss.

But then, across the room, Adriana sees a terrifying sight. Jacob, backing into a corner, being approached by... her parents.

'Shit,' she says, hurriedly handing her glass to a teammate and running over, just in time to hear her mother say, 'And what exactly are your intentions with our daughter?'

'Mum!' Adriana cringes. 'Sorry, Jacob, ignore her.'

'Ignore your own mother-in-law?' Adriana's dad huffs playfully. 'How dare you.'

Adriana groans. 'Jacob, they're messing with you, please don't worry, they just don't have a sense of *what it's okay to joke about!* I'll see you guys for Sunday roast, *okay*?'

'Bring your boyfriend along, why don't you? But only if he's already put a ring on it by then!'

She manoeuvres Jacob away from them, as he hurriedly says, 'Lovely to meet you Mr Summers, Mrs Summers.'

'Yes, yes,' Adriana mumbles, eager to avoid any more awkwardness.

When Jacob is safely away, Adriana looks up at him.

'Sooo,' she fiddles with his tie. 'Wanna go home with the captain of the Manchester Tigresses?'

Jacob blinks at her in surprise.

'Well of course,' he says. 'But the night's still young? Or at least—' He glances at his watch. 'Wow, it's definitely not young, but your friends are all still here to celebrate you.'

'I know,' smiles Adriana contentedly. 'But sometimes it's nice to have an early night. And I like having you to go home with.'

He kisses the tip of her nose.

'You really are full of surprises, Adriana Summers. Come on then, let's get you home.'

Jacob hums to himself as he slips his keys into his key bowl when they arrive at his flat.

'Are you humming Chappell Roan?' Adriana laughs. He surprises her by then singing it loud and proud, with the lyrics that her teammates had invented for her, his voice a smooth baritone.

Adriana automatically slips off her shoes and puts them in the same gap in his shoe rack that she suspects he has made for her. She hangs her jacket neatly next to his, on two brass hooks. She has a moment of wondering where all her hundreds of colourful coats and clothes would fit in his sleek apartment if she were to ever move in…

Adriana has never looked at a man's house for storage capacity before, normally it was just checking where the nearest exit was for her early morning dash.

Meanwhile, Jacob has flicked the kettle on. He starts clipping them some fresh mint from his windowsill herb garden. Adriana swings herself up onto his kitchen counter and kicks her feet.

'I'm so happy,' she sighs.

Jacob looks round at her, his smile soft and gentle. 'I'm glad to hear it. Me too.'

'Honestly, since all of this crazy wonderful party tonight, and being back in the team, and Captain, and having therapy lined up, the *only* thing worrying me anymore is what other changes might be happening to the squad and if any players come or go.'

Jacob nods seriously, pouring the water over the mint in a pot.

'And I don't have any insider info on that anymore, I'm afraid. But—'

'La la la—' Adriana sticks her fingers in her ears. 'I don't wanna know anything I shouldn't know anymore! No secrets, ever again!'

Jacob brings her a round sienna-glazed ceramic mug, one that he has noticed is her favourite.

'Hungry?' He asks.

She shakes her head smiling. 'You?'

'Food isn't on my mind right now.' He steps forward and she wraps her legs around him and pulls him towards her. Sat on the counter is the only way she is ever taller than him, and she likes the way he looks, as she is able to tilt her face down and study his serious expression.

'This is nice,' he kisses her neck. 'I like it here.'

'Would be even nicer if we didn't have any clothes on,' she whispers in his ear.

Adriana barely has time to catch her breath before Jacob is pressing her against the cool surface of his kitchen counter. Her back arches as his large hands grip her thighs, positioning her with confident ease.

He slowly undoes the buttons of her dress, tracing a path of kisses down her bare skin.

'Why did I wear a dress with so many goddamn buttons?' she tuts. 'I can just slide it off over my head.'

She gestures to do so, and Jacob puts one of his huge hands over hers, pinning her to the table.

'I'm in no rush at all,' he says, as he ever so slowly toys with the button over her bra. 'I want to take my time with you tonight.'

Then his fingers are tracing along the lace at the top of her bra, and Adriana gasps as his thumb brushes teasingly over her nipple.

'Please,' she whimpers.

He keeps playing with her chest, softly stroking, the sensation building and building in her until she needs more.

'*Please*,' she moans again.

'You know I can't say no to you.'

Suddenly he pinches her harder. She cries out in pleasure, and he seems to know exactly what works for her, slowly increasing the pressure. Adriana feels blissfully overwhelmed with sensation. She thinks it can't get better than this – and then his mouth is on her other nipple. His tongue circles, his teeth ever so carefully pinch her, and the sensation from them both at the same time lights up her whole body.

She whispers, 'I'm so wet for you.'

He kisses her neck, his fingers on her thighs gripping hard.

His fingers have undone her dress now, and he parts it, sliding its soft fabric along her legs, over her arms, and off over her shoulders. He throws the dress and her bra on the floor and now she's only wearing her pink lace pants. As if he can't resist, he steps back to take her in.

'God, Adriana,' he says, his voice low and amazed. 'You look… unbelievably hot like that.'

Adriana's too turned on to reply, too desperate for him to touch her to say anything. And then he's there, playing with the lace at her hipbones, and she's lifting her hips to be closer to his touch, not afraid to tell him what she wants him to do next.

'You want this?' he asks.

She nods, gasping, grinding her fingers against him, trying to take her pants off for him, but he gently keeps her hands down, clasping both her hands against the counter with his broad left hand, while his right roams along the soft of her stomach and downwards.

'Like this?' he asks, tracing a long slow finger down inside the lace, moving the obstacle aside. She's so turned on that the material is completely wet. 'Or like this?' He presses a thumb to her clit, firm, then circling her.

'God, yes,' she cries out. 'Right *there*.'

Adriana grinds into him.

'Is this how you want it?' And he carries on what he's doing, stroking harder and faster.

'Oh God, I'm going to come,' she gasps. 'Yes, there– th–'

She throws her head back, holding his head to her chest, gripping his hair as she feels the tension burst into release, and his thumb still on her, keeping his hold on the waves of her pleasure, extending it even longer, harder.

'Jesus Christ,' she pants, still clutching onto him. 'I'm still–'

He responds to her cries with a groan, and she reaches desperately out, unclasping his thick belt, tugging at his zip, feeling how hard he is for her.

She looks at him. 'I need you to fuck me.'

He grabs his wallet from his trousers, and, because he doesn't seem to be fast enough for how much she wants this right now, she grabs it from him, pulling out the condom she knows is there because she teasingly replaced the last one. Jacob watches her as she rips open the packet, pinching the tip and then, meeting Jacob's eyes, rolls the condom down over his long shaft.

He closes his eyes in the pleasure of feeling her hands on him. And then he's kissing her, and lifting her from the counter, carrying her to his bedroom. She's still seeing stars when she finds herself on his bed, pulling him to her, lying back as she guides his cock into her. She wants him all, but he holds back, still teasing her even now to not give her everything she wants straight away, starting with just the tip, until even he seems unable to resist more, and more, and more, until he's gripping the headboard to thrust deep inside her and they're both crying out.

'Oh fuck—' he gasps. 'That feels so— that's too— shit you're so fucking good, I'm not going to be able to keep doing that for much longer—'

'I want you to,' she commands. She grips his shoulders, pulling him into her, feeling him fill her up. 'Please, come for me.'

With a shuddering gasp, he obeys.

His glistening body becomes heavy and she guides him, both panting, down onto the pillows. Their bodies entangle together, and she kisses his stubbled cheek as he wraps his arms around her, settling into her favourite position.

After, he gets up and gets them both water.

'Nice bum,' she calls after him. He salutes.

She raises an eyebrow on his return. 'Even better from the front,' she laughs. He shakes his head as she openly oogles him, then returns back into the bed to cuddle up to her.

'You've already had your wicked way with me,' he says. 'I thought you had some kind of "no repeats rule"?'

They chuckle together, and Adriana kisses him, then lies her head on his chest, nuzzling as close as she can.

'You know, about what your parents asked,' says Jacob, stroking her hair. 'About what my intentions are with you?'

'Oh God, please don't worry about that,' Adriana buries her cheeks into his chest. 'They just think they're funny.'

'Well…' says Jacob. 'I just wanted to say… I don't know where your set of dating rules stand on having a boyfriend…'

Adriana looks up at him.

'You know I have never been very good at seeing dating you as something casual,' he tells her. 'But I just wanted to be explicit. I'm in no rush, but whenever – or, *if*-ever you want I'd love to be your boyfriend.'

'Jacob,' Adriana sits up. 'I would love to officially throw all of my old rules out the window for you. I would *love* to be your girlfriend.'

They kiss, softly and tenderly, and Adriana decides that she rather likes being serious after all. Then she giggles suddenly.

'I can't believe I just kissed my *boyfriend*,' she pokes his chest.

'What has happened to you?' Jacob teases.

She leans in to kiss him again and again.

Chapter 30

Maeve

On Thurday, when Maeve's doorbell goes, she instinctively wants to skip down the stairs to see Kira, but instead she has to manoeuvre herself down to avoid putting weight on her ankle.

There is Kira, changed out of her training kit, looking impossibly hot in a white vest under a brown leather jacket, sunglasses resting on her hair. She's holding a delicate bouquet of irises, tied in paper.

Maeve breathes in their scent. 'But what's the occasion?'

'Just excited to spend the evening with you,' shrugs Kira.

Maeve closes the door, and kisses Kira against it.

Up in her flat, Maeve has kept all the overhead lights off (obviously), but has lit plenty of tall and sweet-smelling candles carefully in pastel-coloured holders. She's also moved *some* of the cow themed items from the living room to her bedroom cupboard. Adriana would understand it's not the vibe right now.

Maeve puts the flowers into a vase, humming, and places them at the centre of the small table she's already set, with olives and bread with oil.

'Sit! Sit!'

'Mmm, it smells *delicious*,' Kira swings off her jacket, putting it over a chair. 'What's this secret dinner you're cooking me?'

'Well, I wanted to make something special,' says Maeve, flustered, tucking her hair behind her ears. 'I made Adriana this apology galette the other day, and it didn't... er, end so well, so I wanted to rewrite that memory.'

Kira sniffs contentedly again. 'Wait, is that miso? And aubergine? I *love* miso and aubergine! How did you know?'

Maeve laughs. 'You said the other night on the phone when you called after training, when you were talking about that restaurant, remember? So I started there...'

Kira kisses her. 'You're so thoughtful, thank you. I wanted to bring wine, but I know neither of us are big drinkers, so I got us a couple of non-alcoholic wines to try. A white and a red. Shall I pour you some?'

Maeve takes both bottles laughing.

'I love that we keep trying to outdo each other, even when it's about thoughtful gestures.'

'*There's* a rivalry I can get on board with,' Kira chuckles.

She pours them each a glass of cold white wine, and they toast. Maeve holds Kira's beautiful golden eyes, feeling at peace.

Then Kira takes a breath, and Maeve's hand over the table.

'Before we eat, there's something I need to tell you.'

Maeve's stomach flips with anxiety that it has all been too good to be true. Just as she feared.

Kira touches her cheek affectionately. 'Hear me out,' she says gently. 'So another team have come in with an offer for me.'

Maeve's eyes widen.

'Already? Kira, that's incredible.'

'I had other offers in the summer before I signed for the Tigresses, because I was prioritising staying with Serena as my coach. But this is an offer which would mean me stepping up a league. For the Leeds Ravens. Their striker has just been injured, and I've made a pretty big entrance scoring for the Tigresses in the games so far so…'

Kira might be playing it cool, but she's grinning proudly, running a hand through her hair.

Maeve's chest is a rollercoaster of emotions. She's glad that she doesn't feel jealous – all the processing around the Adriana getting the captaincy has helped with her concentrating on her own career not on comparing to others. In fact, the overwhelming feeling is of sheer pride. It's amazing a WSL club have come in for Kira. Maeve has no doubt she'll continue to rocket up the tables. But the bittersweetness is that she's disappointed at Kira moving to another city when they *just* started dating and put their stupid rivalry aside.

'I'm really pleased for you. You absolutely deserve it. The Ravens will be lucky to have you,' says Maeve, trying to show she means it.

'It's also a good thing for the Tigresses,' says Kira. 'Because, well, it's a big fee, which will go to help improving the squad. And I feel really excited about it, as an opportunity. I think it's the best thing I could do for my career. Serena has been so incredible for me. I mean, she's basically been like a parent to me for years with my own family not living here. But I've realised that maybe that's going to stop me from growing and learning new things under a different coach.'

Maeve smiles and nods again, but her hands are shaking a little. This dinner now feels a bit more like a big check-in conversation than a date. Is Kira preparing to end things all over again?

'Plus, there's someone in the Tigresses team who keeps distracting me in training…'

Maeve glances up at her. Kira meets her eyes steadily, and smiles, reaching out to take her hand.

'In fact, the only drawback to all of this is that I… right now, I kind of just want to spend all my time with you.'

Maeve feels her shoulders lighten. She bites her lip, smiling back at her.

'But you know…' Kira continues. 'The train from Leeds to Manchester is only fifty-six minutes.'

Maeve laughs properly then, and leans across the table to kiss her. That had been exactly what she was about to look up. She's so relieved that Kira still wants to make time to see her, enough so that she's looked it all up already. That Kira is already thinking about how Maeve will fit into her future is enough for her to feel at ease again.

'I want to see you as often as we can,' says Kira. 'We can alternate visiting each other, maybe? I know you'll be recovering until Christmas, but then— I know our careers are a priority for both of us, and it's early days for us dating but I… I really think we can make it work. You're already so important to me.'

Maeve takes a second to close her eyes, to actually let herself process this information, to let the sensations move through her body. Kira's eyes flick over Maeve's face. 'But I just said a whole lot at about a hundred miles an hour, I'm sorry. I should let you talk. What do you think?'

Maeve puts her hand on Kira's knee, and clinks her glass smiling to hers.

'Congratulations, Choski. I am so proud of you.'

Kira's face lights up in surprise, then out of nowhere crumples a little.

'God,' she laughs, self-deprecatingly, wiping at her tearing eyes. 'That really hit hard.'

Maeve gets up to hug her, and Kira pulls her onto her lap for them to hug more tightly.

'We'll make it work, of course we will,' Maeve says. 'And while I'm sidelined with this injury, maybe I'll even get to come and watch you make your debut.'

Kira laughs, stroking her back. 'Every time I score a goal, I'll blow you a kiss from the pitch.'

They kiss then. Kira's mouth tastes moreish, like wine and olives.

Maeve doesn't know how long they've been doing this, but she could do it forever.

'Wait,' says Kira, pulling apart, her cheeks warm. 'Can you smell burn—'

The fire alarm goes off. Maeve leaps off her, limping to open the kitchen door which spills out steam and smoke. The alarm is easily stopped by Kira hurriedly fanning a teatowel vigorously underneath, but as Maeve opens the oven and pulls out the painstakingly twisted galette she finds that... it's completely ruined.

'I swear this pastry is cursed,' she shakes her head. 'Urgh!' She flops onto the kitchen floor completely given up. 'I'm so sorry.'

'Babe! It's just pastry!'

'It's not just pastry,' Maeve wails. 'I'm such an idiot, I've ruined everything.'

Kira puts her hands on her hips, sighs affectionately, and then gets right down onto the kitchen floor with her.

Maeve looks over at her, face flushed. Kira's composed and teasing, and puts an arm around her.

'Maeve, you didn't do anything wrong. I cruelly distracted you with my fantastic kissing.'

Maeve sniffs, laughing.

'It's not always your fault when something goes wrong,' Kira says gently. 'Sometimes shit just happens, okay?'

Maeve feels her shoulders release their tension and she sniffs, nodding into Kira's shoulder.

'Thank you,' she mumbles.

'You don't need to thank me for anything,' Kira says, kissing her cheek. 'Except *maybe* for the huge takeaway I'm about to buy us.'

Kira pulls her up from the kitchen floor and helping Maeve into the living room, places her on the sofa, and hands her a topped up glass of wine. Finally, they make their way through the options and place their order.

'Okay,' says Kira. 'Dim sum is going to be here in an hour.'

'An *hour*?' Maeve sighs dramatically. 'Oh God, I'm so sorry for being a terrible host, are you going to starve?'

Kira slowly, deliberately, places a kiss on Maeve's neck.

'Oh no, I don't think I'll get hungry,' she says, into Maeve's neck. 'In fact, I worry an hour isn't going to be enough time for what I've got planned.'

Maeve bites her lip, savouring the sensation of Kira's mouth on her skin.

They're kissing then, hungrily. Their tongues dance with each other, and Maeve bites Kira's bottom lip, knowing it will get the groan she wants to hear from her. Maeve hopes her delicate ankle won't make things too awkward, but actually, they can just laugh together about it. Maeve at one point wants to straddle Kira but can't — so Kira slides her legs over to straddle Maeve instead.

Kira grips Maeve's hip bones, then strokes the soft curves of her cheeks. Maeve tugs Kira's t-shirt off over her head, then her sports bra, and then Kira does the same for her, so that they can feel each other's soft chests pressed against each other, tracing their hands over each other's backs. Maeve loves when Kira's hair looks wonderfully messy like this, and runs her hands through it to rustle it even more, feeling the velvety sharpness of Kira's shaved undercut at the back of her neck. Kira copies her, tracing her hands over Maeve's face and neck to her hair, where she grasps Maeve's ponytail and tugs, so that Maeve's neck is pulled back and she gasps.

'God I love it when you do that,' Maeve whispers.

'Oh, I know,' says Kira, kissing her taut neck.

In retaliation, Maeve traces a nail down Kira's shoulder then, lightly at first, increasingly harder, scratches Kira's back. Kira arches in pleasure.

'Shit,' she says. 'Harder.'

'Even harder?' Maeve checks, tracing her nails down her back again.

'More,' groans Kira – and then in one smooth motion, too turned on not to move against her, Kira flips Maeve round so that Maeve is now on the sofa and Kira is on top of her, her leg between Maeve's. Kira's pressing her knee hard into her and grinds, Maeve gasping in pleasure and mirroring the motion with her own thigh against Kira's, the textures of their jeans between their legs adding to the layers of sensation. They keep moving hard against each other, Kira's hands on Maeve's chest, Maeve's hands on Kira's back, then grasping Kira's buckle, pulling her closer, wanting to touch her.

'Okay, wait, sorry,' says Kira. She seems to be furious at having to stop what they were doing for a single second. 'These *need* to come off now.'

Maeve enjoys hastily unbuckling Kira's buckle, and Kira doing the same back, unzipping. Kira kicks off her white boxers, and then groans fiddling with the lines of Maeve's black pants, which takes longer to get over Maeve's bandage. They laugh together for a moment, but then Kira kneels in front of Maeve and they become serious again. She's kissing and biting up Maeve's thighs, then presses her tongue into her. Maeve groans, her head falling back into the sofa cushions as Kira's tongue flicks, savouring how good it feels.

Maeve almost blacks out in pleasure for a moment, but then her hands, reaching into Kira's hair, pulling her up.

'Please,' Maeve stops her, a flush of pink in her cheeks. 'I want to touch you too.'

Kira groans, caught between two brilliant options, but returns to the sofa, kissing Maeve deeply.

Pressed against each other on the sofa, legs and arms entangled, mouths gasping together, they touch each other.

Kira says into Maeve's mouth, 'I want you to touch me like you touch yourself.'

Maeve closes her eyes, moaning as their fingers mirror the other's smooth motions, tracing their wetness. Their bodies melt into each other, not knowing where one begins and the other ends. Each gets as much pleasure from the other's as her own.

And then, sensing, their bodies shift as the waves of pleasure build, Kira moves the tip of her finger against Maeve and Maeve's against hers — until both of them in the same moment slide a finger into each other.

'Fuck,' Kira gasps. 'More. Harder.'

Maeve nods into her, using another finger now, then pins Kira's hands down behind her so that she can concentrate on fucking her harder. To Maeve's great satisfaction, it's only seconds later that Kira's face contorts.

'Oh fuck,' she cries, 'I'm gonna come if you keep doing that, stop— stop—'

Maeve grins, enjoying feeling powerful.

Kira breaks free from Maeve's grip, wrestling and jostling for a moment, until they finally agree in a position where they can fuck each other at the same time. Maeve readjusts so that she can oblige, her thumb against Kira's clit as she fucks her, and Kira in return is fucking her too, and the pleasure is so great that Maeve forgets everything else, left panting and desperate.

'Not so cocky now are we?' Kira whispers in her ear.

Maeve just groans, rocking against her.

'God, I love making you lose control like this,' says Kira. 'That's right, just like— fuck, yes, yes—'

And then they're just saying yes over and over as they fuck each other, and they build together, until rapidly they're both crying out, and feeling the other tense and pulse around them as they climax.

Then they fall back against the sofa, naked and breathing hard, spent by their exertions. They cuddle against each other, both shaking their heads and laughing gleefully, amazed.

'Ah,' says Kira, sighing happily. '*Now* I'm hungry.'

And as if on cue, there goes the doorbell.

Maeve leans back naked on the sofa, her hair loose around her, smiling as Kira leaps down the stairs to collect their takeaway. She sips on her wine. She can't believe she gets to spend her time off the pitch like this now. Relaxed, at ease, and laughing.

This weekend, her, Kira, Adriana and Jacob are going to go on a double date to crazy golf, and Maeve can't wait to see how ridiculously competitive they get. It feels like a good level of competitive to Maeve right now.

Soon, Kira will be playing for a bigger league, and Adriana will be Captain of the Tigresses while Maeve is vice. She's not 'the best' anymore. But she finally realises she doesn't need to be. She's never liked herself more.

Epilogue

6 months later

'Goal!'

The crowd roar.

'And Milo George makes an absolute stunner of a goal there! That takes us to 3-1 to the Tigresses!'

The orange-coloured home team fans are cheering wildly, while the white away team groan into their hands. On the pitch, the team all come and pile on top of a celebrating Milo, whooping.

'An elegant assist from Captain Adriana Summers! There's no coming back for the Swans now!'

When the final whistle blasts, the entire stadium filled with fans singing Survivor's 'Eye of the Tiger'.

The Tigresses whoop and cheer, running in towards each other to have a group hug, all united and lifting each other up – literally. Adriana is crying with happiness, highfiving and hugging her team, who then lift her up onto their shoulders as she shrieks in delight.

Maeve, laughing as she parades Adriana on her shoulder next to Elisa, who made some particularly impressive saves in the match, feels wonderfully, truly part of the team. Maeve recovered from her injury smoothly, and has been having a solid start to the season, her and Coach working together on finding an effective balance for her training. Maeve and Adriana have worked brilliantly together as Captain and vice, their old friendship flourishing in this new dynamic.

Adriana's fiery hair glints in the sunlight as she waves towards the VIP box. There, along with her family with their banners, is Jacob – proudly wearing a Summers Tigresses shirt with his tortoiseshell glasses and casual Levis, singing along as loud as anyone. He highfives Adriana's parents and her brother, who is filming the whole thing for the family group chat.

Grinning, Maeve turns out from the group to blow a kiss out towards the VIP box too. Kira grins and mimes catching it. She's screaming her support for her old team, waving her sign that just says 'MAEVE MURPHY FAN CLUB' covered in hearts. Her own team don't have a match today, so she's rarely been able to come and support Maeve – her recently official girlfriend. The women in the stalls near them, many of whom are holding hands with each other too, scream, whisper or cat-call Maeve and Kira's mimed kiss in the language of obsessed lesbians. Kira turns to Helena, animatedly gushing about the highlights of Maeve's defense this game, yet again, and Helena smiles back. Mirroring her daughter, Helena looks more at ease now too, her smile less forced, as she waves down at the pitch, finally letting her pride for her daughter show.

'Champagne,' says Jacob. 'We *must* all go and have Champagne.'

Down on the pitch, as the team start their happy return to the dressing room, laughing and clapping each other on the back, Maeve and Adriana come to a stop together. For a moment, it feels like it's just the two of them in the world again. Back to being teenagers at the Academy, two best friends with a big dream.

'We did it, Moo,' says Adriana. 'You and me.'

'Uh huh,' Maeve puts her hand around her friend's shoulder and kisses the top of her curls. 'I'm proud of us.'

'I wonder what we'll do next,' says Adriana.

'Whatever it is, it'll still be you and me, together.'

Maeve reaches out a ceremonial little finger to Adriana. She grins as wide as the sun, nods, and hooks her best friend in a pinky promise.

Acknowledgements

Thank you to Daisy Watt for pairing me with this project. I hope there are enough Chappell Roan references for you.

Thank you to everyone at HarperNorth who has worked on this book. It's a group effort to have anything published, and I am honoured to have that opportunity, especially for a story full of queer joy.

Most of all, thank you to the friends who shared their football love and knowledge with me through this process. You know who you are, not least because I named most of the Tigresses after you! Thank you so much for being on my team. I'm your biggest fan.

Oh, and lastly, to all the gays who look so very hot in sports kit – thank you for the inspiration x